FIRST LADY

Other Avon Books by
Susan Elizabeth Phillips

LADY BE GOOD
DREAM A LITTLE DREAM
NOBODY'S BABY BUT MINE
KISS AN ANGEL
HEAVEN, TEXAS
IT HAD TO BE YOU

Susan Elizabeth Phillips

First Lady

AVON BOOKS  NEW YORK

AVON BOOKS, INC.
An Imprint of HarperCollins*Publishers*
10 East 53rd Street
New York, New York 10022-5299

Copyright © 2000 by Susan Elizabeth Phillips
Back Jacket author photo by Sigrid Estrada
Published by arrangement with the author

ISBN: 0-7394-0688-4

www.harpercollins.com

To Cathie Linz, Lindsay Longford, and Suzette Vann—dear friends and three of the finest romance writers ever to set foot in DuPage County. Thanks for keeping the faith!

The following people, big and little, were especially helpful as I wrote this book and I thank them all: Jill Barnett, Marlene Cerny, Mary Kilchenstein, Ernie Locker, Susan Nicklos, Mary Jo Putney, Tillie Phillips, and John Roscich. Also Mommy Katie, Granny Lydia and my darling nephew Caleb; Nancy Heller and her beautiful granddaughter Natalie; Cathie and her adorable nephew Joshua. My continued appreciation to Steven Axelrod, Carrie Feron, and everyone at Avon Books.

You must do the thing you think you cannot do.

ELEANOR ROOSEVELT

1

CORNELIA LITCHFIELD CASE HAD AN ITCHY NOSE. OTHerwise, it was a very elegant nose. Perfectly shaped, discreet, polite. Her forehead was patrician, her cheekbones gracefully carved, but not so sharp as to be vulgar. The Mayflower-blue blood that rushed through her veins gave her a pedigree even finer than that of Jacqueline Kennedy, one of her most famous predecessors.

A French twist contained her long, fair hair, which she would have cut off years ago if her father hadn't forbidden it. Later her husband had suggested—oh-so-gently, because he was always gentle with her—that she leave it long. So there she was, an American aristocrat with a hairstyle she hated and an itchy nose that she couldn't scratch because hundreds of millions of people all over the world were watching her on their televisions.

Burying a husband sure could take the fun out of your day.

She shuddered and tried to swallow her hysteria as she crept another inch closer to falling apart. She forced herself to concentrate on the beauty of the October day and the way the sun gleamed on the rows of grave markers at Arlington National Cemetery, but the sky was too close, the sun too near. Even the ground felt as if it were pushing up to crush her.

The men on either side of her moved closer. The new President of the United States gripped her arm. Her fa-

ther clasped her elbow. Directly behind her, the grief of
Terry Ackerman, her husband's closest friend and advisor, rolled over her in a great, dark wave. They were
suffocating her, stealing the air she needed to breathe.

She beat back a scream by curling her toes in her neat
black leather pumps, biting the inside of her bottom lip,
and mentally launched into the chorus of "Goodbye Yellow Brick Road." The Elton John song reminded her that
he'd written another song, one for a dead princess.
Would he now write one for an assassinated President?

No! Don't think about that! She'd think about her
hair, her itchy nose. She'd think about the way she
hadn't been able to swallow food since her secretary had
broken the news that Dennis had been assassinated three
blocks from the White House by a gun fanatic who believed his right to bear arms included the right to use
the President of the United States for target practice. The
assassin had been killed on the spot by a Washington,
D.C., police officer, but that didn't change the fact that
her husband of three years, the man she'd once loved so
desperately, lay before her in a gleaming black casket.

She broke her father's grip to reach up and touch the
small enameled American flag she'd pinned to the lapel
of her black suit. It was the pin Dennis had worn so
frequently. She'd give it to Terry. She wished she could
turn around right now and hand it to him, perhaps ease
his grief.

She needed hope—something positive to cling to—
but that was tough even for a determined optimist. And
then she hit on it . . .

She was no longer the First Lady of the United States
of America.

A few hours later, that small bit of comfort was
snatched from her by Lester Vandervort, the newest
President of the United States, as he regarded her across

Dennis Case's old desk in the Oval Office. The box of Milky Way miniatures her husband had kept in Teddy Roosevelt's humidor had disappeared, along with his collection of photographs. Vandervort had added no personal touches of his own, not even a photograph of his deceased wife, an oversight she knew his staff would soon correct.

Vandervort was a thin man, ascetic in his appearance. He was fiercely intelligent, almost entirely humorless, and a confirmed workaholic. A sixty-four-year-old widower, he was now the world's most eligible bachelor. For the first time since the death of Edith Wilson eighteen months after Woodrow Wilson's inauguration, the United States had no First Lady.

The air inside the Oval Office was climate-controlled, the three-story windows that rose behind the desk bulletproof, and she felt as if she were suffocating. As she stood by the fireplace, staring blindly at Rembrandt Peale's portrait of Washington, the new President's voice seemed far away. ". . . don't want to appear insensitive to your grief by broaching this now, but I have no choice. I won't be remarrying, and none of my female relatives is remotely capable of handling the job of First Lady. I want you to continue in that role."

As she turned to him, her fingernails bit into her palms. "It's impossible. I can't do it." She wanted to scream at him that she was still wearing her funeral clothes, but excessive displays of emotion had been leached out of her long before she'd come to the White House.

Her distinguished father rose from one of a pair of couches covered in cream damask and assumed his Prince Philip posture—hands clasped behind his back, weight toward his heels. "This has been a difficult day for you, Cornelia. You'll be seeing things more clearly tomorrow."

Cornelia. Everyone who mattered in her life called

her Nealy except her father. "I'm not going to change my mind."

"Of course you will," he countered. "This administration has to have a competent First Lady. The President and I have considered it from every angle, and both of us agree this is the ideal solution."

She was an assertive woman, except when it came to her father, and she had to steel herself to challenge him. "Ideal for whom? Not for me."

James Litchfield gave her the patronizing look he'd been using to control people for as long as she could remember. Ironically, he had more power now as chairman of the party than he'd had during his eight years as Vice President of the United States. Her father was the one who'd first spotted the presidential potential of Dennis Case, the handsome bachelor governor of Virginia. Four years ago, he'd capped off his reputation as a kingmaker by escorting his daughter down the aisle to marry that very same man.

"I know better than anyone how traumatic this has been," he continued, "but you're the most visible link between the Case and Vandervort administrations. The country needs you."

"Don't you mean the party needs me?" They all knew that Lester's lack of personal charisma would make it difficult for him to be elected President on his own. Although he was an able politician, he lacked even a kilowatt of President Dennis Case's star power.

"We're not just thinking of reelection," her father lied as smoothly as new cream. "We're thinking of the American people. You're an important symbol of stability and continuity."

Vandervort spoke briskly. "As First Lady, you'll keep your old office and the same staff. I'll make sure you have everything you need. Take a month to recuperate at your father's place on Nantucket, and then we'll ease you back into the schedule, beginning with the white-tie

reception for the diplomatic corps. Keep mid-January
blocked out for the G-8 summit, and the South American
trip is a necessity. All of this is already on your schedule,
so it shouldn't be a problem."

He finally seemed to remember these events were on
her schedule because she'd been planning to do them at
the side of her charismatic, golden-haired husband.
Dropping his voice, he added belatedly, "I know this is
a difficult time for you, Cornelia, but the President
would have wanted you to go on, and keeping busy
should help ease your grief."

Bastard. She wanted to shout the word at him, but
she was her father's daughter, schooled from birth to
hide her emotions, so she didn't. Instead, she regarded
both men steadily. "It's impossible. I want my life back.
I've earned it."

Her father came closer, crossing the oval rug with the
presidential seal, stealing even more of the oxygen she
needed to breathe. She felt imprisoned, and she remembered that Bill Clinton had once called the White House
the crown jewel in the federal correctional system.

"You have no children to raise, no profession to pur-
sue," her father said. "You're not a selfish person, Cornelia, and you've been raised to do your duty. After you
spend some time on the island, you'll feel more like
yourself. The American people are counting on you."

And how had that happened? she wondered. How had
she managed to become such a popular First Lady? Her
father said it was because the country had watched her
grow up, but she thought it was because she'd been
trained from childhood to be in the public eye without
making serious missteps.

"I don't have the popular touch." Vandervort spoke
with the bluntness she'd frequently admired about him,
even though it cost him votes. "You can give it to me."

She vaguely wondered what Jacqueline Kennedy
would have done if LBJ had suggested something like

this. But LBJ hadn't needed a surrogate First Lady. He'd been married to the best.

Nealy had thought she'd married the best, too, but it hadn't worked out that way. "I don't want to do this. I've earned a private life."

"You gave up your right to a private life when you married Dennis."

Her father was wrong. She'd given it up the day she was born James Litchfield's daughter.

When she was seven, long before her father had become Vice President, the nation's newspapers had run a story telling how she'd turned over the Easter eggs she'd found on the White House lawn to a disabled child. The story didn't say that it was her father, a United States senator at the time, who'd whispered to her that she must give up those eggs and that she'd cried afterward because she hadn't wanted to.

At twelve, her mouth gleaming with braces, she'd been photographed ladling up creamed corn in a Washington, D.C., soup kitchen. At thirteen, green paint smeared her nose while she helped repair a home for seniors. But her popularity had been sealed forever when she'd been photographed in Ethiopia at the age of sixteen holding a starving infant in her arms as tears of rage ran down her cheeks. The picture had run on the cover of *Time* and established her as a symbol of America's compassion.

The pale blue walls were closing in on her. "I buried my husband less than eight hours ago. I won't discuss this now."

"Of course, my dear. We can finish making arrangements tomorrow."

In the end, she managed to buy herself six weeks of solitude, but then she was put back to work again, doing what she'd been raised to do, what America expected of her. Being the First Lady.

2

OVER THE NEXT SIX AND A HALF MONTHS, NEALY GREW
so thin that the tabloids began printing stories that she
was anorexic. Mealtimes became torture. She couldn't
sleep at night, and her sense of suffocation never went
away. Despite that, she served the country well as Lester
Vandervort's First Lady...until one small event
brought it all crashing down.

On a June afternoon, she stood in the pediatric reha-
bilitation facility of a Phoenix hospital and watched a
little girl with curly red hair struggling with a new set
of leg braces.

"Watch me!" The chubby little redhead gave Nealy a
bright smile, leaned on her crutches, and began the la-
borious process of taking a single step.

All that courage.

Nealy hadn't often felt shame, but now it over-
whelmed her. This child was putting up a gallant fight
to regain her life, while Nealy was watching her own
pass by.

She wasn't a cowardly person, nor was she incapable
of standing up for herself, yet she had allowed this to
happen simply because she hadn't been able to give either her father or the President a good reason why she
shouldn't continue to do the job she'd been born to per-
form.

Right then, she made up her mind. She didn't know

7

how or when, but she was going to set herself free. Even if her freedom lasted only for a day—an hour!—she would at least make the attempt.

She knew exactly what she wanted. She wanted to live the life of an ordinary person. She wanted to shop in a grocery store without everyone staring at her, to walk down a small-town street eating an ice-cream cone and smiling, just because she felt like it, not because she had to. She wanted the freedom to speak her mind, to make mistakes. She wanted to see the world as it really was, not polished up for an official visit. Maybe then she would finally be able to figure out how to live the rest of her life.

Nealy Case, what do you want to be when you grow up? When she was very little, she'd told everyone she wanted to be President. Now she had no idea.

But how could the most famous woman in America suddenly become an ordinary person?

One obstacle after another sprang up in front of her. It was impossible. The First Lady couldn't simply disappear. Could she?

Being guarded required cooperation, and contrary to what people thought, it was possible to get away from the Secret Service. Bill and Hillary Clinton had stolen away in the early days of his administration, only to be reminded that they had given up that kind of freedom. JFK had driven the Secret Service crazy with his disappearances. Yes, slipping away was possible, but there would be no point if she couldn't move freely. Now all she had to do was find a way.

A month later, she had her plan in place.

At ten o'clock on a July morning, an elderly woman slipped into a White House tour group that was making its way through the rooms on the State floor. She had snowy white hair in tightly curled corkscrews, a green and yellow patterned dress, and a large plastic purse. Her bony shoulders were bowed, her thin legs encased in elastic stockings, and her feet encompassed in a pair of lace-up brown shoes. She peered at a guidebook through a large pair of glasses with pearly gray frames and a bit of swirled goldwork at the stems. Her forehead was patrician, her nose aristocratic, her eyes as blue as an American sky.

Nealy's throat worked as she swallowed, and she had to resist the urge to tug on the wig she'd ordered through a catalogue. Another catalogue had supplied the polyester dress, shoes, and stockings. To preserve her privacy, she'd always relied on catalogue shopping, using the name and address of her chief of staff, Maureen Watts, plus the phony middle initial *C*, so Maureen would know it was Nealy's order. Maureen had no inkling of the contents of the packages she'd recently delivered to the White House.

Nealy stayed with the crowd as it crawled from the Red Room with its American Empire furnishings into the State Dining Room. Video cameras were recording everything, and her fingers felt cold and numb. She tried to steady herself by gazing at the portrait of Lincoln that hung over the fireplace. The mantelpiece beneath was inscribed with the words of John Adams that she'd read so often. *I pray heaven to bestow the best of blessings on this house and all that shall hereafter inhabit it. May none but honest and wise men ever rule under its roof.*

A female tour guide stood near the fireplace politely answering a question. Nealy might be the only person in the room who knew that all the White House guides were members of the Secret Service. She waited for the woman to spot her and sound the alert, but the agent barely glanced in her direction.

How many Secret Service agents had she gotten to know over the years? They'd accompanied her to high school and then college. They'd been with her on her first date and the first time she'd had too much to drink.

The Secret Service had taught her how to drive and witnessed her tears when she'd been rejected by the first boy she'd ever liked. A female agent had even helped her pick out a prom dress when her stepmother had caught the flu.

The group headed into the Cross Hall and from there, out through the north portico. It was muggy and hot, a typical July day in Washington. Nealy blinked at the bright sunlight and wondered how many more steps she could take before the guards realized she wasn't an elderly tourist, but the First Lady.

Her heart rate kicked higher. Next to her, a mother snapped at her young son. Nealy walked on, growing tenser with each step. During the dark days of Watergate, a tortured Pat Nixon had disguised herself in a scarf and sunglasses. Accompanied only by a single Secret Service agent, she'd escaped the White House to wander the streets of Washington window-shopping and dreaming of the day it would all be over. But, as the world had grown angrier, the time when First Ladies were permitted that kind of solace had disappeared.

She struggled for another breath as she reached the exit. The Secret Service code name for the White House was Crown, but it should have been Fortress. Most of the tourists passing by didn't know there were microphones located along the fence so that the security detail inside could monitor whatever was said around the perimeter. A SWAT team appeared on the roof with machine guns whenever the President entered or left the building. The grounds were armed with video cameras, motion detectors, pressure sensors, and infrared equipment.

If only there were a less complicated way to do this. She'd thought about holding a press conference and simply announcing that she was retiring from public life, but the press would have dogged her every step, and she'd have been no better off than she was now. This was the only way.

She reached Pennsylvania Avenue. Her hand trembled as she slipped the guidebook into her plastic purse, where it bumped against an envelope that held thousands of dollars in cash. Looking straight ahead, she began walking along Lafayette Park toward the Metro.

She spotted a policeman crossing toward her, and a trickle of perspiration slid between her breasts. What if he recognized her? Her heart nearly stopped as he nodded to her, then turned away. He had no idea that he'd just nodded to the First Lady of the United States.

Her breathing slowed. All members of the first family wore tracking devices. Hers, as slim as a credit card, rested under her pillow in the bedroom of the private apartment she kept on the fourth floor of the White House. If she were very lucky, she'd have two hours before her disappearance was discovered. Although Nealy had told Maureen Watts, her chief of staff, that she wasn't feeling well and needed to lie down for a few hours, she knew Maureen wouldn't hesitate to wake her if she thought a matter was urgent. Then she would find the letter Nealy had left along with the tracking device, and all hell would break loose.

Nealy forced herself not to hurry as she walked into the Metro. She headed toward one of the fare card machines she hadn't even known existed until she'd overheard a conversation between two of her secretaries. She needed to change trains, and she calculated the fare. After she'd slipped in her money, she pushed the correct buttons and received her fare card.

She managed to make it through the turnstile to the platform. Then, with her nose tucked into her guidebook and her heart pounding, she waited for the train that would begin her journey into the Maryland suburbs. When she got to Rockville, she intended to pick up a taxi and head for one of the used car dealerships along

Route 355. There she hoped to find a salesman greedy enough to sell an old lady a car without seeing her driver's license.

Three hours later, she was behind the wheel of a nondescript four-year-old blue Chevy Corsica heading toward Frederick, Maryland, on I-270. She'd done it! She'd made it out of Washington. The car had cost more than it should have, but she didn't care because nobody could link it with Cornelia Case.

She tried to relax her cramped fingers, but she couldn't. The alarm would have been raised at the White House by now, and it was time to make her call. As she got off at the next ramp, she couldn't remember how long it had been since she'd driven on a freeway. Sometimes she took the wheel when she was on Nantucket or at Camp David, but seldom otherwise.

She spotted a convenience store on her left, pulled in, then got out of the car and made her way to a pay phone mounted on the side. She was accustomed to the efficiency of the White House operators, and she had to read the directions carefully. Finally, she punched in the number of the most private of the Oval Office telephone lines, the one she knew couldn't be intercepted.

The President himself answered on the second ring. "Yes?"

"It's Nealy."

"For God's sake, where are you? Are you all right?"

The urgency in his voice told her she'd made the right decision by not delaying this call. Her letter had obviously been found, but no one at the White House could be certain she hadn't written it under duress, and she didn't want to raise more of an alarm than she had to.

"I'm fine. Never been better. And the letter's genuine, Mr. President. Nobody was holding a gun to my head."

"John is frantic. How could you do this to him?"

She'd been expecting this. Every member of the President's family was given a code to use in the event they were being coerced in any way. If she uttered a sentence with the name *John North* in it, the President would know she'd been taken against her will.

"This has nothing to do with him," she replied.

"Who?" He was giving her another chance.

"I'm not being coerced," she said.

He finally seemed to realize she had done this of her own free will, and his anger crackled over the line. "Your letter is filled with rubbish. Your father's frantic."

"Just tell him I'm taking some time to myself. I'll call in occasionally so you know I'm all right."

"You can't do this! You can't just disappear. Listen to me, Cornelia. You have responsibilities, and you need Secret Service. You're the First Lady."

It was useless to argue with him. For months she'd been telling both him and her father that she needed a break and had to get away from the White House, but neither would listen. "You should be able to hold the press off for a while by having Maureen announce that I've got the flu. I'll call again in a few days."

"Wait! This is dangerous! You have to have Secret Service. You can't possibly—"

"Good-bye, Mr. President."

She hung up on the most powerful man in the free world.

As she walked back to the car, she had to force herself not to run. Her polyester dress seemed to be permanently glued to her skin, and the legs beneath her elastic stockings no longer felt as if they belonged to her. *Breathe*, she told herself. *Just breathe*. She had too much to do to fall apart.

Her scalp itched as she turned back onto the highway. She wished she could take off the wig, but that had to wait until she'd purchased her new disguise.

It didn't take her long to find the Wal-Mart she'd located last week through the Internet yellow pages. She'd only been able to escape with what fit into her purse, and now it was time to do some serious shopping.

Her face was so familiar that, even as a child, she'd never been able to go into a store without people watching her every move, but she was too tense to appreciate the novelty of shopping anonymously. She finished up quickly, stood in line to pay, and headed back to her car. With her purchases tucked safely in the trunk, she returned to the freeway.

By nightfall, she planned to be well into Pennsylvania, and sometime tomorrow, she'd get off the freeway permanently. Then she'd begin roaming the country that she knew both so much and so little about. She was going to travel until her cash ran out or she was caught, whichever came first.

The reality of what she'd done sank in. She had no one looking over her shoulder, no schedule to stick to. For the first time in her life, she was free.

3

As Mat Jorik shifted in the chair, he bumped his elbow against the edge of the attorney's desk. Mat frequently bumped into things. Not because he was ungraceful, but because most of the indoor world had been built too small to accommodate a man of his size.

At six feet six inches tall and two hundred and ten pounds, Mat dwarfed the small wooden chair that sat across from the desk of the Harrisburg, Pennsylvania, attorney. Still, Mat was accustomed to chairs that didn't fit and bathroom sinks that hit him just above the knees. He automatically ducked when he walked down a set of basement steps, and the coach section of an airplane was his idea of hell. As for sitting in the back seat of nearly every car on the road—fuhgetaboutit.

"You're listed on the birth certificate as the children's father, Mr. Jorik. That makes you responsible for them."

The attorney was a humorless tight ass, the kind of person Mat Jorik most disliked, so he uncoiled a couple vertebrae and extended one long leg—more than happy to use his size to intimidate the little worm. "Let me spell it out. They're not mine."

The attorney flinched. "So you say. But the mother also appointed you their guardian."

Mat glared at him. "I respectfully decline."

Although Mat had lived in Chicago and L.A., the blue-collar Pittsburgh neighborhood where he'd grown up still clung to him like factory smoke. He was thirty-four years old, a steeltown roughneck with big fists, a booming voice, and a gift for words. One old girlfriend said he was the last of America's Real Men, but since she was throwing a copy of *Bride* magazine at his head at the time, he hadn't taken it as a compliment.

The attorney pulled himself back together. "You say they aren't yours, but you were married to their mother."

"When I was twenty-one." An act of youthful panic that Mat had never repeated.

Their conversation was interrupted by the arrival of a secretary with a manila folder. She was the no-nonsense type, but her eyes started crawling all over him the moment she entered the room. He knew women liked the way he looked, but, despite having seven younger sisters, he'd never figured out exactly why. In his eyes he looked like a guy.

The secretary, however, saw things a bit differently. When he'd walked into the office and announced himself as Mathias Jorik, she'd noticed that he was both lean and muscular, with broad shoulders, big hands, and narrow hips. Now she took in a slightly crooked nose, a killer mouth, and bluntly aggressive cheekbones. He wore his thick brown hair in a short, serviceable cut that couldn't quite subdue a tendency to curl, and his tough, square jaw had *just-try-and-punch-me* written all over it. Since she generally found outrageously masculine men more annoying than appealing, it wasn't until she'd given her boss the folder he'd requested and returned to her desk that she figured out what was so compelling about this one. Those flint-gray eyes reflected a sharp, unsettling degree of intelligence.

The attorney glanced at the folder, then looked back up at Mat. "You admit your ex-wife was pregnant with the older girl when you married her."

"Let me run it by you one more time. Sandy told me the kid was mine, and I believed her until a few weeks after the ceremony, when one of her girlfriends told me the truth. I confronted Sandy, and she admitted she'd lied. I saw a lawyer, and that was it." He still remembered the relief he'd felt at being able to leave behind everything he didn't want.

Once again, the worm glanced down at the folder. "You sent her money for a number of years."

No matter how hard Mat tried to hide it, sooner or later people figured out that he was a soft touch, but he didn't believe a kid should have to suffer for her mother's bad judgment. "Sentiment. Sandy had a good heart; she just wasn't too discriminating about who she slept with."

"And you contend you haven't seen her since the divorce?"

"There's no contention about it. I haven't seen her in nearly fifteen years, which makes it really tricky for me to be the father of that second baby she had last year." Naturally it was another girl. His entire life had been haunted by female children.

"Then why is your name on both children's birth certificates?"

"You'd have to ask Sandy that." Except no one was going to ask Sandy anything. She'd died six weeks ago driving drunk with her boyfriend. Since Mat had been on the road, he hadn't learned about it until three days ago when he'd finally gotten around to checking his voice mail.

There'd been other messages as well. One from a former girlfriend, another from a casual acquaintance who wanted to borrow money. A Chicago buddy needed to know if Mat was moving back to the Windy City so he could sign him up for their old ice hockey league. Four of his seven younger sisters wanted to talk to him, which was nothing new, since Mat had been in charge of them from the time he was a kid growing up in that tough Slovak neighborhood.

Mat had been the only male left after his father had walked away. His grandmother had kept house while his mother had worked fifty hours a week as a bookkeeper. This arrangement had left nine-year-old Mat in charge of his seven younger sisters, two of whom were twins. He'd struggled through his childhood hating his father for being able to do what Mat couldn't—walk away from a house that held too many females.

The final few years before his escape from the Hell House of Women had been especially bad. His father had died by then, putting an end to the fantasy Mat had entertained that he'd come back and take charge. The girls were growing older and more temperamental. Somebody was always getting ready to have her period, going through her period, getting over her period, or sneaking into his room late at night in quiet hysterics because her period was late, and he was supposed to figure out what to do about it. He loved his sisters, but being responsible for them had suffocated him. He'd promised himself when he finally got away that he'd turn his back on family life forever, and except for the short, stupid time with Sandy, that's exactly what he'd done.

The last call on his voice mail had come from Sid Giles, the producer of *Byline*. It was another plea for Mat to come back to the L.A. tabloid television show he'd left last month, but Mat Jorik had sold out his credibility as a journalist once, and he'd never do it again.

". . . first step is to bring me a copy of your Judgment for Dissolution of Marriage. I need proof that you were divorced."

He returned his attention to the attorney. "I've got proof, but it'll take me a while to get my hands on it." He'd left L.A. so fast that he'd forgotten to empty out his safe-deposit box. "It'll be quicker if I get a blood test. I'll do it this afternoon."

"DNA test results take several weeks. Besides, there'll

have to be proper authorization before the children can be tested."

Forget that. Mat wasn't going to have those birth certificates come back to bite him in the ass. Even though it wouldn't be hard to prove he was divorced, he wanted the blood tests to back him up. "I authorize it."

"You can't have it both ways, Mr. Jorik. The girls are either yours or they're not."

Mat decided it was time to go on the offensive. "Maybe you'd better explain why this is such a mess. Sandy's been dead for six weeks, so why did you just get around to letting me know about it?"

"Because I didn't find out myself until a few days ago. I took some diplomas into the frame shop where she'd been working and heard what had happened. Although I'm her attorney, I hadn't been informed."

Mat considered it something of a miracle that Sandy'd had an attorney, let alone that she'd bothered to make out a will.

"I went to the house right away and spoke to the older girl. She said a neighbor had been watching them, but there was no neighbor in sight. I've been back twice and still haven't seen any sign of adult supervision." He tapped his yellow pad and seemed to be thinking aloud. "If you're not going to take responsibility, I'll have to call Child and Youth Services so the girls can be picked up and put into foster care."

Old memories sifted over Mat like steeltown soot. He reminded himself that there were lots of wonderful foster parents, and the chances of Sandy's kids ending up with a family like the Havlovs were slim. The Havlovs had lived next door when Mat was growing up. The father was chronically unemployed, and the family survived by taking in foster kids, then neglected them so badly that Mat's grandmother and her friends had ended up feeding and bandaging them.

He realized he needed to concentrate on his own legal

entanglement instead of past history. If he didn't get this paternity issue straightened out right now, it could hang over his head for months, maybe longer. "Hold off on that phone call for a couple of hours until I check things out."

The attorney looked relieved, but all Mat intended to do was grab both kids and take them to a lab before they got turned over to social services and he had to deal with red tape.

Only as he followed the directions the attorney gave him to Sandy's house did he remember his ex-wife's mother. She'd been relatively young, as he recalled, and a widow. He'd just met her once, but she'd been impressive—a college professor out in Missouri or someplace who seemed to have little in common with her wild daughter.

He picked up his cell phone to call the attorney back, then caught sight of the street he was looking for and set it back down. A few minutes later he was parking the Mercedes SL 600 two-passenger sport convertible he'd bought with his sell-out money in front of a dingy bungalow in a run-down neighborhood. The car was too small for him, but he'd been deluding himself about a lot of things at the time, so he'd written the check and squeezed inside. Getting rid of it was the next item on his agenda.

As he approached the house, he took in the peeling paint, crumbling sidewalk, and well-used yellow Winnebago parked next to the overgrown lawn. Leave it to Sandy to spend her money on a motor home when her house was crumbling around her.

He stalked up the sidewalk, climbed one crooked step to the porch, then banged his fist against the front door. A sullen-faced, very young version of Winona Ryder appeared. "Yeah?"

"I'm Mat Jorik."

She crossed her arms and leaned against the door-jamb. "Hey there, Pop."

So that's the way it was going to be.

She was small-boned and delicate beneath the makeup she'd applied with too heavy a hand. Brown urban-decay lipstick smudged her young mouth. Her lashes were coated with so much mascara, they looked as though black centipedes had landed on them, and her short dark hair had been sprayed maroon at the top. Tattered jeans hung low on her thin body, revealing more than he wanted to see of her ribs and stomach, and her small, fourteen-year-old breasts didn't need the black bra that showed above the low neckline of her tightly cropped top.

"We need to talk."

"We got nothing to talk about."

He gazed into her small, defiant face. Winona didn't know there wasn't anything she could dish out that he hadn't already heard from his sisters. He shot her the same look he'd used on Ann Elizabeth, the toughest of his siblings. "Open the door."

He could see her trying to work up the courage to defy him, but she couldn't quite manage it, and she stepped aside. He brushed past her into the living room. It was shabby, but neat. He saw a tattered copy of a baby-care book lying open on a table. "I hear you've been by yourself for a while."

"I haven't been by myself. Connie just left to go to the grocery store. She's the neighbor who's been taking care of us."

"Tell me another one."

"You calling me a liar?"

"Yeah."

She didn't like that at all, but there wasn't much she could do about it.

"Where's the baby?"

"Taking a nap."

He couldn't see much resemblance between the girl
and Sandy, except maybe around the eyes. Sandy had
been big and bawdy, a gorgeous handful with a good
heart and a decent brain she must have inherited from
her mother, but never bothered to use.

"What about your grandmother? Why isn't she taking
care of you?"

The kid began nibbling on what little was left of a
thumbnail. "She's been in Australia studying the aborig-
ines in the Outback. She's a college professor."

"She went off to Australia knowing her granddaugh-
ters didn't have anybody to take care of them?" He
didn't try to hide his skepticism.

"Connie's been—"

"Cut the crap. There isn't any Connie, and unless you
shoot straight with me, Child and Youth Services will
be here to pick you up in an hour."

Her features contorted. "We don't need anybody taking care of us! We're doing great by ourselves. Why
don't you mind your own damn business?"

As he gazed into her defiant face, he remembered all
those tough foster kids who'd appeared and disappeared
next door to him when he was growing up. A few of
them had been determined to spit in the world's eye,
only to be swatted down for their efforts. He softened
his voice. "Tell me about your grandmother."

She shrugged. "Her and Sandy didn't get along. Because of Sandy's drinking and everything. She didn't
know about the car crash."

Somehow he wasn't surprised to hear her call Sandy
by her first name. It was exactly what he would have
expected from his ex-wife, who seemed to have fulfilled
her early promise of turning into an alcoholic. "Are you
telling me your grandmother doesn't know what happened to Sandy?"

"She does now. I didn't have a phone number so I
could call her, but a couple of weeks ago I got this letter
from her with a picture of the Outback and everything.

So I wrote back and told her about Sandy and the car accident and Trent."

"Who's Trent?"

"My baby sister's dad. He's a jerk. Anyway, he died in the accident, too, and I'm not sorry."

He'd known Sandy's current boyfriend had been with her, but not that he was the baby's father. Sandy must have had a lot of doubts about him or his name would have been on that birth certificate instead of Mat's. "Did this Trent have any family?"

"No. He was from California, and he was raised in foster homes." She thrust her small chin forward. "He told me all about them, and me and my sister aren't going to any, so you can just forget it! Anyway, we don't have to because I just got this note from my grandmother and she'll be back soon."

He regarded her suspiciously. "Let me see the note."

"Don't you believe me?"

"Let's just say I'd like some proof."

She regarded him sullenly, then disappeared into the kitchen. He'd been certain she was lying, and he was surprised when she returned a few moments later with a small piece of stationery imprinted with the seal of Laurents College, in Willow Grove, Iowa. He gazed down at the neat script.

I just got your letter, sweetheart. I'm so sorry. Am flying home to Iowa July 15 or 16, depending on airlines. Will call as soon as I get in and make arrangements for you girls. Don't worry. Everything will be fine.

Love, Granny Joanne

He frowned. Today was Tuesday the eleventh. Why hadn't Granny Joanne packed up her notebooks right then and caught the first plane back?

He reminded himself this wasn't his problem. All he cared about was getting those blood tests without having to jump through hoops for some bureaucratic busybody. "Tell you what. Go get your sister. I'll buy you both some ice cream after we stop at a lab."

A pair of streetwise brown eyes stared back at him. "What lab?"

He made it real casual. "We're all having some blood drawn. No big deal."

"With needles?"

"I don't know how they do it," he lied. "Go get the kid."

"Fuck that. I'm not letting anybody stick a needle in me."

"Watch your mouth."

She gave him a look that managed to be both condescending and contemptuous, as if he were the stupidest man on earth for objecting to her language. "You're not my boss."

"Get the baby."

"Forget it."

Some battles weren't worth fighting, so he headed down a hallway with a worn gray carpet and a bedroom opening off each side. One had obviously been Sandy's. The other had an unmade twin bed and a crib. A whimper came from behind the bumper pads.

Although the crib was old, it was clean. The carpet around it was vacuumed, and some toys were tossed in a blue laundry basket. A rickety changing table held a small stack of neatly folded clothes, along with an open box of disposable diapers.

The whimpering turned into a full-fledged yowl. He moved closer and saw a pink-clad bottom wiggling in the air. Then a head covered with a few inches of straight blond hair popped up. He took in a furious, rosy-cheeked face and a wet, down-turned mouth that was open and yowling. It was his childhood all over again.

"Quiet down, kid."

The baby's cries stopped, and a set of gumball-blue eyes regarded him suspiciously. At the same time he grew aware of an unpleasant smell and realized his day had taken one more turn for the worse.

He sensed movement behind him and saw the Winona lookalike standing in the doorway chewing on another fingernail and watching every move he made. There was something distinctly protective about the glances she kept shooting at the crib. The kid wasn't nearly the hard ass she pretended to be.

He jerked his head toward the baby. "She needs her diaper changed. I'll meet you in the living room when you're done."

"Like, get real. I don't change shitty diapers."

Since she'd been taking care of the baby for weeks, that was obviously a lie, but if she expected him to do it, she could think again. When he'd finally escaped from the Hell House of Women, he'd promised himself that he'd never change another diaper, look at another Barbie, or tie another frigging hair bow. Still, the kid had guts, so he decided to make it easy on her. "I'll give you five bucks."

"Ten. In advance."

If he hadn't been in such a foul mood, he might have laughed. At least she had street smarts to go along with all that bravado. He pulled his wallet from his pocket and handed over the money. "Meet me by my car as soon as you're done. And bring her along."

Her forehead creased, and for a moment she looked more like a soccer mom than a sullen teenager. "You got a car seat?"

"Do I look like somebody who's got a car seat?"

"You got to put a kid in a car seat. It's the law."

"You a cop?"

She cocked her head. "Her seat's in Mabel. The Winnebago. Sandy called it Mabel."

"Didn't your mother have a car?"

"The dealer took it back a couple of months before she died, so she drove Mabel."

"Swell." He wasn't going to ask how she'd come into possession of a battered motor home. Instead, he tried to figure out how he was supposed to get a teenager, a baby, and a car seat in his two-passenger Mercedes. Only one answer. He wasn't.

"Give me the keys."

He could see her trying to figure out if she could get away with mouthing off again, then wisely concluding she couldn't.

Keys in hand, he went outside to get acquainted with Mabel. On the way, he picked up the cell phone from his Mercedes, along with the newspaper he hadn't found a chance to read.

He needed to duck to get into the motor home, which was roomy, but not roomy enough for six feet six. He settled behind the wheel and put in a call to a doctor pal of his in Pittsburgh for the name of a nearby lab and the necessary authorization. While he was on hold, he picked up the newspaper.

Like most journalists, he was a news junkie, but nothing unusual caught his attention. There'd been an earthquake in China, a car bombing in the Middle East, budget squabbles in Congress, more trouble in the Balkans. Toward the bottom of the page was a picture of Cornelia Case with another sick baby in her arms.

Although he'd never been much of a Cornelia watcher, she seemed thinner in every recent photograph. The First Lady had terrific blue eyes, but they'd started to appear too big for her face, and nice eyes couldn't make up for the fact that there didn't seem to be a real woman behind them, just an extremely smart politician programmed by her father.

When he'd been at *Byline*, they'd done a couple of puff pieces on Cornelia—her hairdresser, her taste in

fashion, how she honored her husband's memory—
bullshit stuff. Still, he felt sorry for her. Having a husband assassinated would put a crimp in anybody's happy
face.

He frowned at the memory of his year in tabloid television. Before then, he'd been a print journalist, one of
the most highly regarded reporters in Chicago, but he'd
thrown away his reputation to make a pile of money he'd
soon discovered he had little interest in spending. Now
all he wanted out of life was to wipe the tarnish off his
name.

Mat's idols weren't Ivy League journalists, but guys
who'd used two fingers to punch out hard-hitting stories
on old Remington typewriters. Men as rough around the
edges as he was. There had been nothing flashy about
his work when he was writing for the *Chicago Standard*.
He'd used short words and simple sentences to describe
the people he met and what they cared about. Readers
had known they could count on him to shoot straight.
Now he was on a quest to prove that was true again.

Quest. The word had an archaic quality to it. A quest
was the province of a holy knight, not a steeltown roughneck who'd let himself forget what was important in life.

His old boss at the *Standard* had said Mat could return
to his former job, but the offer had been begrudging,
and Mat refused to go back with his hat in his hands.
Now he was driving around the country searching for
something to take with him. Wherever he stopped—big
town or small—he picked up a paper, talked to people,
and nosed around. Even though he hadn't found it, he
knew exactly what he was looking for—the seeds of a
story big enough to give him back his reputation.

He'd just finished his calls when the door swung open
and Winona climbed into the motor home with the baby,
who was barefoot and dressed in a yellow romper with
lambs on it. She had a peace sign tattooed on one
chubby ankle.

"Sandy had her baby tattooed?"

Winona gave him a look that said he was too dumb to live. "It's a rub-on. Don't you know anything?"

His sisters were grown up by the time the tattoo craze had started, thank God. "I knew it was a rub-on," he lied. "I just don't think you should put something like that on a baby."

"She likes it. She thinks it makes her look cool." Winona carefully placed the baby in the car seat, fastened the straps, then plopped down in the seat next to him.

After a couple of tries, the engine sputtered to life. He shook his head in disgust. "This thing is a piece of crap."

"No shit." She propped her feet, which were clad in thick-soled sandals, onto the dash.

He glanced into Mabel's side mirror and backed out. "You know, don't you, that I'm not really your father."

"Like I'd want you."

So much for the worry he'd been harboring that she might have built up some kind of sentimental fantasy about him. As he made his way down the street, he realized he didn't know either her real name or the baby's. He'd seen copies of their birth certificates but hadn't looked any farther than the lines that had his own name written on them. She probably wouldn't appreciate it if he called her Winona. "What's your name?"

There was a long pause while she thought about it. "Natasha."

He almost laughed. For three months his sister Sharon had tried to make everybody call her Silver. "Yeah, right."

"That's what I want to be called," she snapped.

"I didn't ask what you wanted to be called. I asked what your name is."

"It's Lucy, all right? And I hate it."

"Nothing wrong with Lucy." He consulted the directions he'd gotten from the receptionist at the lab and made his way back to the highway. "Exactly how old are you?"

"Eighteen."

He shot her his street fighter look.

"Okay, sixteen."

"You're fourteen, and you talk like you're thirty."

"If you know, why'd you ask? And I lived with Sandy. What did you expect?"

He felt a pang of sympathy at the husky note in her voice. "Yeah, well, I'm sorry about that. Your mother was . . ." Sandy had been fun, sexy, smart without having any sense, and completely irresponsible. "She was unique," he finished lamely.

Lucy snorted. "She was a drunk."

In the back the baby started to whimper.

"She has to eat soon, and we've run out of stuff."

Great. This was just what he needed. "What's she eating now?"

"Formula and crap in jars."

"We'll stop for something after we're done at the lab." The sounds coming from the back were growing increasingly unhappy. "What's her name?"

Another pause. "Butt."

"You're a real comedian, aren't you?"

"I'm not the one who named her."

He glanced back at the blond-haired, rosy-cheek baby with gumdrop eyes and an angel-wing mouth, then looked over at Lucy. "You expect me to believe Sandy named that baby Butt?"

"I don't care what you believe." She pulled her feet from the dash. "I'm not letting some jerkoff stick a needle in me, so you can forget about that blood crap right now."

"You'll do what I tell you."

"Bullshit."

"Here are the facts, smart mouth. Your mother put my name on both your birth certificates, so we need to straighten that out, and the only way we can do it is with three blood tests." He started to explain that Child Services would be taking care of them until her grandmother showed up, but didn't have the heart. The lawyer could do it.

They drove the rest of the way to the lab in silence, except for the Demon Baby, who'd started to scream again. He pulled up in front of a two-story medical building and looked over at Lucy. She was staring rigidly at the doors as if she were looking at the gates of hell.

"I'll give you twenty bucks to take the test," he said quickly.

She shook her head. "No needles. I hate needles. Even thinking about them makes me sick."

He was just beginning to contemplate how he could carry two screaming children into the lab when he had his first piece of luck all day.

Lucy got out of the Winnebago before she threw up.

4

NEALY WAS GLORIOUSLY INVISIBLE. SHE TILTED BACK her head and laughed, then flipped up the radio to join in with Billy Joel on the chorus of "Uptown Girl." The new day was exquisite. Puffs of blue clouds floated in a Georgia O'Keeffe sky, and her stomach rumbled with hunger, despite the scrambled eggs and toast she'd wolfed down for breakfast in a small restaurant not far from the motel where she'd spent the night. The greasy eggs, soggy toast, and murky coffee had been the most blissful meal she'd eaten in months. Every bite of food had slid easily down her throat, and not a single person had spared her a second glance.

She felt smart, smug, completely happy with herself. She had outwitted the President of the United States, the Secret Service, and her father. Hail to the Chieftess!

She laughed, delighted with her own cockiness because it had been so long since she'd felt that way. She rummaged on the seat next to her for the Snickers bar she'd bought, then remembered she'd already devoured it. Her hunger made her laugh again. All her life she'd fantasized about having a curvy body. Maybe she was finally going to get it.

She glanced at herself in the rearview mirror. Even though the old lady's wig was gone, not one person had recognized her. She had transformed herself into someone blissfully, sublimely ordinary.

A commercial came on the radio. She turned the volume down and began to hum. All morning she'd allowed herself to dawdle along the two-lane highway west of York, Pennsylvania, which happened to be the nation's first capital and the place where the Articles of Confederation were written. She'd detoured through the small towns that lay along the route whenever she'd wanted. Once she'd pulled off the road to admire a field of soybeans, although she couldn't help but ponder the complexities of farm subsidies as she leaned against the fence. Then she'd stopped in a ramshackle farmhouse with a sign outside that read ANTIQUES and browsed through the dust and junk for a wonderful hour. As a result, she hadn't traveled far. But she had nowhere specific to go, and it was glorious being absolutely aimless.

It might be foolish to feel so happy when the President was undoubtedly using all the power and might of the United States government to track her down, but she couldn't help herself. She wasn't naive enough to believe she could outwit them forever, but that made each moment more precious.

The commercial ended and Tom Petty began to sing. Nealy laughed again, then joined in. She was free-falling.

Mat was the world's biggest chump. Instead of being behind the wheel of his Mercedes convertible with only the radio to keep him company, he was driving west in a ten-year-old Winnebago named Mabel on a Pennsylvania back road with two kids who were as bad as all seven of his sisters combined had been.

Yesterday afternoon, he'd called Sandy's attorney to tell him about Joanne Pressman, but instead of guaranteeing that the girls would be turned over to her as soon as she got back in the country, the attorney had equivocated.

"Child and Youth Services will have to make sure she

can provide a satisfactory home for them."

"That's ridiculous," Mat had countered. "She's a college professor. And anything's better than what they have now."

"She still has to be investigated."

"How long will that take?"

"It's hard to say. It shouldn't be more than six weeks. Two months at the outside."

Mat had been furious. Even a month in the foster care system could chomp up a kid like Lucy and spit out her bones. He'd found himself promising to stay with the girls that night so Child Services wouldn't have to get them until morning.

As he tried to fall asleep on Sandy's lumpy couch after his aborted attempt to get the blood tests done, he'd reminded himself how much better the foster care system was now than it used to be. The background checks were more thorough, home visits more common. But the image of all the kids the Havlovs had abused kept coming back to him.

Toward morning, he'd realized his conscience wouldn't let him out of this one. Too much early influence from nuns. He couldn't let either the Teenage Terrorist or the Demon Baby spend months stuck in foster care when all he had to do was baby-sit them for a couple of days, then turn them over to their grandmother on the weekend.

Joanne Pressman's Iowa address had been in Sandy's date book. He needed to get the girls out of the house early, so he decided they'd catch a morning flight to Burlington. When he got there, he'd rent a car and drive to Willow Grove. And while he was waiting for Joanne Pressman to get home, he'd have the blood tests done, even if he had to carry Lucy into the lab.

Unfortunately, his plan had fallen apart when he'd discovered needles weren't Lucy's only phobia.

"I'm not getting on a plane, Jorik! I hate flying! And

if you try to make me, I'll start screaming to everybody in the airport that you're kidnapping me."

Another kid might have been bluffing, but he'd suspected Lucy would do exactly as she said, and since he was already skating on the thinnest edge of the law by dodging Child Services, not to mention taking the kids out of state, he'd decided not to risk it. Instead, he'd grabbed a pile of their clothes, some food he'd bought last night, and shoved them into the motor home. He had four or five days to kill anyway, so what did it matter if he spent it on the road?

He wasn't certain how aggressively the authorities would be looking for him, especially since Sandy's attorney would surely figure out where he was heading. Still, there was no point in taking chances, so he was staying off the interstate for a while where tollbooth operators and the state police might already have the Winnebago's license plate number. Unfortunately, between the Demon Baby's screams and Lucy's complaints, he couldn't enjoy the scenery.

"I think I'm going to hurl."

She was sitting in the motor home's small banquette. He jerked his head toward the rear and spoke over the sounds of the baby's howls. "The toilet's back there."

"If you don't start being nicer to me and Butt, you're going to be sorry."

"Will you stop calling her that?"

"It's her name."

Even Sandy wasn't that crazy, but he still hadn't been able to pry the baby's real name out of Lucy.

The howls subsided. Maybe the baby was going to sleep. He glanced over toward the couch, where she was strapped in her car seat, but she looked wide awake and grumpy. All wet blue eyes and cherub's mouth. The world's crankiest angel.

"We're hungry."

"I thought you said you were feeling sick."

The howls started again, louder than before. Why hadn't he brought somebody along to take care of these little monsters? Some kindhearted, stone-deaf old lady.

"I feel sick when I get hungry. And Butt needs to eat."

"Feed her. We brought bags of baby food and formula with us, so don't try to tell me there isn't anything for her to eat."

"If I feed her while Mabel's moving, she'll hurl."

"I don't want to hear another word about anybody hurling! Feed the damn kid!"

She glared at him, then flounced out of her seat and made her way to the sacks of baby food and diapers.

He drove for another fifteen miles in blessed silence before he heard it. First a baby's cough, then a gag, then a small eruption.

"I told you so."

Nealy backed out of the driveway from her first garage sale and pulled onto the highway. A huge green ceramic frog perched on the seat next to her. The lady who'd sold it to her for ten dollars said it was a garden ornament her mother-in-law had made in a craft class.

It was supremely ugly, with an iridescent green glaze, protruding eyes that were slightly crossed, and dull brown spots the size of silver dollars across its back. For nearly three years, Nealy had lived in a national shrine decorated with the very best American antiques. Maybe that was why she'd known instantly that she had to have it.

Even after she'd made her purchase and tucked the heavy frog under her arm, she'd stood talking to the garage sale lady. And she hadn't needed a gray old lady's wig or elastic stockings to do it. Her wonderful new disguise was working.

Nealy spotted a sign ahead for a truck stop. There'd

be hamburgers and french fries, thick chocolate shakes and slabs of pie. *Bliss!*

The smell of diesel fuel and fried food hit Mat as he stepped out of Mabel into the truck stop parking lot. He also caught a whiff of manure from a nearby field, but it beat the smell of baby puke.

A blue Chevy Corsica with a woman driving whipped into the parking place next to him. Lucky lady. Alone in her car with nothing but her own thoughts to keep her company.

Just beyond the gas pumps, a hitchhiker held a battered cardboard sign that read, ST. LOUIS. The guy looked like a felon, and Mat doubted he'd have too much luck getting a ride, but he still felt a pang of envy for the man's freedom. The whole day had been a bad dream.

Lucy climbed out behind him with another ten-dollar bribe in her back pocket. She'd tied a flannel shirt around her hips and had the smelly baby under the armpits so she could hold her as far away as possible. Lucy was small, and he doubted that she could carry the Demon very far that way, but he didn't offer to take her himself. He'd carried around too many screaming babies when he was a kid to be sentimental about them. The only good thing about babies was getting them drunk on their twenty-first birthdays.

He smiled at the memories, then pushed another ten-dollar bill into the back pocket of Lucy's cutoffs. "Buy yourself some lunch after you get her cleaned up. I'll meet you here in half an hour."

She gave him a long, searching look that hinted at disappointment. He wondered if she'd expected them all to cuddle up together to eat. Not a chance.

The woman he'd been envying got out of the blue Corsica. She had short light brown hair styled in one of those uneven cuts that was fashionable. The rest of her, however, wasn't so fashionable: cheap white sneakers, navy shorts, and an oversized yellow top with a row of ducks marching across it. She wasn't wearing any makeup. And she was heavily pregnant.

A Grand Am slowed down on the highway for the hitchhiker, only to shoot off as soon as the driver got a closer look. The hitchhiker flipped him the bird.

Mat glanced at the woman again as she walked past him. Something about her seemed familiar. She had fragile, finely carved features, a long, slender neck, and striking blue eyes. There was almost a patrician quality about the way she carried herself that was at odds with her bargain-basement clothes. She reached the door of the restaurant just ahead of Lucy and held it open for her. Lucy didn't acknowledge the courtesy. She was too busy tossing him a dirty look.

Something caught his eye on the seat of the Corsica. He leaned down and saw an ugly ceramic frog. He'd always wondered what kind of people bought things like that. Then he noticed the set of keys dangling from the ignition. He thought about going after her to say something, but figured anybody stupid enough to buy that frog deserved what she got.

The interior of the truck stop was arranged in a large L. He selected a small table in the back corner where he had room to stretch his legs and ordered coffee. As he waited for it to arrive, he considered the fact that it was going to take him at least two days to reach Iowa. Maybe longer, if that ominous pinging coming from the engine got any worse. How was he going to tolerate those girls for another two days? The irony of letting himself be saddled with exactly what he'd worked his whole life to get away from didn't escape him.

He should have left them both to foster care.

Nealy swabbed a thick, greasy french fry in catsup and watched the three people seated on the other side of the truck stop dining room. At first the man had been there by himself. She'd noticed him right away—his physical size would have made it hard not to. But it wasn't just his size that had caught her attention. It was everything about him.

He had that hard-muscled look of a working man, and it didn't take much imagination to picture him suntanned and shirtless, nailing shingles to a roof or wearing a battered hard hat over that crisp dark hair as he wielded a jackhammer in the middle of a city street. He was also drop-dead handsome, although not in that too-pretty way of a male model. Instead, his face looked lived in.

Unfortunately, he was glowering at the young girl who'd wedged herself in next to him, the baby propped in her lap. Nealy pegged him as one of those fathers who regarded his children as inconveniences, her least favorite kind of man.

His daughter was the girl she'd held the door open for earlier. Although she was overly made-up and had a maroon stripe in her hair, her delicate features gave her the potential of great beauty. The baby was adorable. One of those healthy, blond-haired, mischievous cherubs that Nealy avoided as much as she could.

The people-watching had been enjoyable, but she was anxious to get back on the road, so she forced her eyes away from the man and gathered up her trash as she'd seen others do. A middle-aged couple at an adjoining table smiled at her and she smiled back. People smiled a lot, she'd noticed, at a pregnant woman.

Her smile changed into a self-satisfied grin. Last night, before she'd gone to bed at the motel, she'd cut the long blond hair her father and husband had cherished and dyed it light brown, which was really her natural color, although it was so long since she'd seen it that she'd had to guess at the exact shade. She loved the shorter, tousled style. Not only did it make her look younger, but it was much too casual for an elegant First Lady.

Although maintaining her disguise as an elderly lady had been her first idea, she hadn't wanted the encumbrance of a wig and all that clothing. The fake pregnancy padding had been the perfect solution. Even if people noticed a pregnant woman's resemblance to Cornelia Case, they'd regard it as nothing more than a coincidence.

Last night she'd modified a small Wal-Mart pillow by reshaping its corners and adding some ties. With her short brown hair, discount store clothes, ring-free hands, and minimal cosmetics, she looked like a pregnant woman who was down on her luck. When she spoke, she completed her change of identity by reshaping her upper-crust vowels with the trace of a Southern accent.

As she left the truck stop restaurant, she fumbled for her car keys in the purse she'd left the White House with. She felt a packet of tissues, some mints, her new wallet, but no keys. Had she left them in the car?

She needed to be more careful. She'd grown accustomed to having a cadre of aides carrying things for her. This morning, she'd left her purse behind when she'd stopped at a diner for breakfast, and she'd had to run back to get it. Now it was her keys.

She stepped out into the parking lot and looked around for the Chevy, but she didn't see it. Odd. She thought she'd parked next to that trail-worn yellow Winnebago. She was sure she had.

She hurried forward, but the car wasn't there.

She stared at the empty parking place, then at the motor home next to it. Maybe she was mistaken. Maybe she'd parked somewhere else. Her heart raced, and her gaze swept across the parking lot. Even then she didn't want to believe it. The car was gone. She'd left her keys inside and someone had stolen it.

Her throat constricted. One day of freedom. Was that all she would get?

She struggled against the despair that threatened to

choke her. She could still salvage this. She'd brought thousands of dollars in cash with her. She could buy another car. She'd hitch a ride into the nearest town and find a dealer—

Her knees gave out beneath her, and she sagged down on a wooden bench. Her money had been locked in the trunk for safekeeping. All she had in her wallet was a twenty-dollar bill.

She buried her face in her hands. She'd have to call the White House, and within the hour the Secret Service would swoop down on this peaceful, ordinary place. She'd be whisked onto a helicopter and returned to Washington before dinner.

She saw exactly how it would unfold. Castigation from her father. Reminders from the President of her duty to the country. Suffocating guilt. By tomorrow evening, she'd be standing in a receiving line, her fingers aching from shaking another few hundred hands. And she had no one to blame but herself. What use was all her education, all her experience, if she couldn't remember a simple thing like taking car keys out of an ignition?

Her throat closed tight. She wheezed as she tried to draw a breath.

"She's heavy, and I'm not carrying her anymore!"

Nealy lifted her head and saw the young girl she'd been watching earlier set the baby she'd been carrying down on the sidewalk and yell at the Father of the Year, who was heading toward the yellow Winnebago.

"Suit yourself." Although he wasn't speaking loudly, he had a deep, carrying voice.

The girl didn't move from the baby's side, but neither did she pick her back up. The baby plopped forward on her knees as if to crawl, only to rebel at the midday heat coming from the sidewalk. She was a smart little critter, though, and she pushed herself up until only the minimal parts of her were in contact with the hot concrete—the palms of her hands and the soles of her feet. With her bottom shoved high in the air, she began to move forward in a spider crawl.

The girl spun toward her father. "I mean it, Jorik! You're acting like an asshole!" Nealy blinked at the girl's crude language. "She's not poison, you know. You could at least touch her."

"You're in charge of the baby, and I'm in charge of driving. Let's go." The man named Jorik might be a lousy father, but he was smart enough to have taken his keys with him, and now he shoved one of them in the lock on the door of the motor home.

The girl slammed her hands on her small hips. "This is bullshit."

"Yeah, well, so is ninety percent of life."

They were so involved in their argument that neither of them noticed the baby, who was slowly and fastidiously spider-crawling down off the curb into the parking lot.

Nealy rose automatically. A baby in danger. The one thing in life she hadn't been able to escape since she was sixteen.

"Quit complaining and get inside," the man growled.

"I'm not your slave! You've been bossing me around ever since yesterday, and I'm sick of it!"

An elderly couple in a Cadillac began to back out of a space much too near the crawling baby. Nealy shot forward, bent down, and snatched her up.

The kind of anger she couldn't ever express in her real life erupted. "What kind of father are you?"

Mr. Macho turned slowly and regarded Nealy with flint-gray eyes. She stormed toward him, the baby in her arms. The fact that holding babies terrified her made her even angrier.

She jabbed her finger toward the Cadillac as it drove away. "Your daughter was crawling right in the path of that car. She could have been hit."

He stared at her.

The closer she got, the taller he seemed. She belatedly remembered that she was supposed to be speaking with a Southern accent. "How could you be so irresponsible?"

"He doesn't care," the girl said. "He hates us."

Nealy glared at him. "Children need somebody watching out for them, especially babies."

He tilted his head toward the empty parking space next to him. "What happened to your car?"

She was taken aback. "How do you know about my car?"

"I saw you get out of it."

She refused to let him throw her off track. "Never mind about my car. What about your child?" She thrust the baby toward him, but he didn't take her. Instead, he stared down at the little one as if he weren't sure what she was. Finally he turned toward the teenager. "Lucy, take her and get in."

"You got a broken arm or something?" the girl shot back.

"Do what I say. And feed her before we start moving again."

His tone had grown so intimidating that Nealy wasn't surprised when the girl took the baby from her arms. Still, Lucy had enough defiance left to shoot him a lethal glare before she jerked open the door of the motor home and hauled the baby inside.

The man named Jorik gazed down at Nealy. Although she was tall, he loomed over her, and he looked even tougher close up than he had been from a distance. His nose had a small bump at the bridge, as if he'd broken it falling off an I-beam he was welding.

"She's not my kid," he said. "Neither of them are."

"Then what are you doing with them?"

"I was a friend of their mother's. So tell me about your car."

A yellow caution light flashed in her brain. "There's nothing to tell."

"It was stolen, wasn't it?"

He was regarding her so intently, she was afraid he'd recognize her, so she tilted her head a bit to keep him from looking at her full on. "Why do you say that?"

"Because I saw you park it there, and now it's gone. Besides, you left your keys inside."

Her head shot back up. "You saw them?"

"Yeah."

"You saw them, but you didn't do anything?"

"Well . . . I thought about stealing your car myself, but I was afraid of your frog."

If she hadn't been so upset, she might have laughed. His speech marked him as an educated man, which was disconcerting considering his tough-guy appearance. His eyes had dropped to her bulging stomach, and she had to resist the urge to look down and make certain the padding hadn't shifted.

"You'd better go inside and call the state police," he said. "There was a hitchhiker out here earlier. I wouldn't be surprised if he got tired of waiting for someone to pick him up and decided to take advantage of that free transportation you were offering. I'll stay around long enough to give them a description."

She had no intention of calling the police. "That's all right. You don't have to wait."

"I don't mind."

He seemed to be trying to place her face. She began to feel nervous. "I don't want to hold you up. Thanks anyway." She turned to leave.

"Stop right where you are."

5

WHERE HAD HE SEEN HER? MAT STUDIED THE WOMAN more closely as she looked warily back at him. There was something about her bearing that reminded him of royalty, but her thinness, along with that long, fragile neck, and hands that bore no sign of a wedding ring, spoke of hard times. Her arms and legs were almost comically slender in contrast to her heavy pregnancy, and there was a world-weary quality in her blue eyes that made him suspect she'd seen more of life than she wanted to.

Those bright blue eyes . . . they were so familiar. He knew he'd never met her, but he felt as if he had. Her reluctance to call the police piqued his journalist's curiosity. "You're not going to report the theft, are you?"

He watched a small pulse pound on the side of her neck, but she remained cool. "Why do you say that?"

She had something to hide, and he had a good idea what it might be. "Oh, I don't know. Maybe you can't report it because the car didn't belong to you."

Wariness flickered in her eyes, but not fear. The lady was down on her luck, but she still had a backbone. "None of this is your concern."

He was definitely on to something, and he took a wild stab. "You're afraid that if you call the police, they'll figure out that you stole the car from your boyfriend."

44

She narrowed her eyes. "Why do you think I have a boyfriend?"

He glanced down at her bulging abdomen. "I'm guessing it wasn't a girlfriend who did that to you."

She looked at her stomach as if she'd forgotten it was there. "Oh."

"You're not wearing a wedding ring, and you're driving a stolen car. It all fits." He wasn't exactly sure why he was giving her such a hard time. Habit, he guessed, born out of his professional curiosity about people who tried to hide the truth. Or maybe he was stalling because he didn't want to get back into the Winnebago.

"I never said the car was stolen. You're the one who decided that."

"So why don't you want to call the police?"

She gazed at him as if she were the Queen of Egypt and he was a stone-hauling slave building her a pyramid. Something about her attitude got his goat.

"You could just go back to him," he said.

"You don't give up, do you?"

He noted the combination of intelligence and aloofness in her expression. This lady had developed the knack for keeping people at a distance. Too bad she hadn't used it on her boyfriend.

Who did she look like? The answer was right there, but he couldn't quite grab hold of it. He wondered how old she was. Late twenties, early thirties? Everything about her manner and bearing screamed class, but her situation was too precarious for a member of the upper crust.

"I can't go back," she finally said.

"Why not?"

She paused for only a moment. "Because he beat me."

Was it his imagination, or did he detect a certain amount of relish in her words? What was that all about? "Do you have any money?"

"A little."

"How little?"

She still had her pride, and he admired her gutsiness. "Thank you for your help, but this really isn't your concern."

She turned to walk away, but his curiosity wasn't satisfied. Acting on the instincts that had made his reputation, he snagged the strap of her ugly plastic purse and pulled her to a stop.

"Hey!"

Ignoring her outrage, he lifted it from her shoulder and pulled out her wallet. As he looked inside, he saw no credit cards, no driver's license, only a twenty-dollar bill and some change. "You're not going far on this."

"You have no right!" She snatched her wallet and purse back and started to walk away.

He had more than enough problems of his own, and he should have just let her go, but his instincts were on full alert. "So what are you going to do now?" he called after her.

She didn't answer him.

A crazy idea hit him. He mulled it over for all of five seconds before making up his mind. "Do you want to hitch a ride?"

She stopped walking and turned. "With you?"

"Me and the kids from hell." He moved toward her. "We're heading west to Grandma's house. Iowa. We can drop you off if you're going that way."

She regarded him incredulously. "You're inviting me along?"

"Why not? But the ride's not free."

Her expression grew wary, and he knew exactly what she was thinking. But pregnant women weren't high on his list of turn-ons. "You have to keep Lucy off my back and take care of the baby. That's all."

He'd expected her to be relieved, but the moment he mentioned the baby, she seemed to stiffen. "I don't know anything about babies."

"Don't you think it's time you learned?"

It took her a moment to remember she was pregnant. He was getting the idea that she wasn't exactly over-joyed about her little bundle of joy. She only thought it over for a few seconds before her eyes began to sparkle with something that looked like excitement. "Yes. All right. Yes, I'd like that."

Her reaction surprised him. There was more to this lady than met the eye. He reminded himself that he didn't know anything about her, and he wondered if too much contact with Sandy's kids had shorted out his brain. But driving one more mile with Lucy's sullenness and a screaming baby was more than he could tolerate. Besides, if it didn't work out, he could give her some money and dump her at the next truck stop. He turned back toward the Winnebago. "One warning."

"What's that?"

"They both have delicate stomachs."

"What does that mean?"

"You'll find out." He opened the door for her. "What's your name?"

"N-Nell. Nell Kelly."

Her hesitation made him wonder if she was telling the truth. Her boyfriend must be a real loser. "I'm Mat Jorik."

She gave a nod of acknowledgment that looked al-most regal, and right then it hit him. *Cornelia Case.* That's who she looked like.

He must have celebrities on the brain. First he'd de-cided Lucy looked like Winona Ryder, and now this lady reminded him of a pregnant version of Cornelia Case. Even their voices were similar, but he couldn't imagine the nation's aristocratic First Lady ending up broke, pregnant, and abandoned at a roadside truck stop in rural Pennsylvania. "Anybody ever mention that you look like Cornelia Case?"

She blinked. "All the time."

"You even sound alike, but you've got an accent. I

can't quite place it. Where are you from?"

"The Carolinas. Alabama. Michigan for a while, then California. My folks moved around a lot. It affected my speech."

"Yeah, I guess it did." The sunlight hit the top of her head, and he saw a small brown stain on the skin near her temple, as if she'd recently colored her hair and hadn't gotten off all the dye. He automatically filed the detail away. Nell Kelly might be down on her luck, but she still had enough vanity left to take the time to color her hair. It was the kind of observation that used to set his newspaper stories apart.

She smelled good, and, as he moved aside to let her into the motor home, he felt something odd. If she hadn't been pregnant, he would have chalked it up to desire. It had been a while since he was in a relationship—he thought of the flying copy of *Bride* magazine—and his sex life had suffered. But it hadn't suffered enough to make him respond to a skinny pregnant lady. Still, there was something about her . . .

"After you, princess." He dipped his head.

"Princess?" Nealy's own head shot up, and she was met with a lady-killer grin that made her wonder if she'd lost her mind. Not only had she just hitched a ride with a stranger, but the stranger was a foot taller and a lot stronger than she was. And that smile . . . Although it wasn't lecherous, it had a challenging quality that she found unnerving.

"Somehow it seems to fit," he said.

She had no idea how to reply to that, so she slipped past him—not that easy to do—and stepped inside. Her decision had been impulsive, but not completely foolish, she decided, as she gazed around the interior of the motor home. Although there was definitely something dangerous about him, it wasn't a naked-female-left-dismembered-in-a-ditch kind of danger. He'd offered to stay and talk to the police, hadn't he? And, best of all, her excellent adventure wasn't over.

She hoped he'd bought her explanation about her accent, and she reminded herself to be more careful so it didn't keep fading in and out. She also reminded herself that she was now Nell Kelly, the first name that had popped into her head.

The baby was perched in a car seat sitting on a couch with worn blue and green plaid upholstery. Across from the couch and immediately to Nealy's right was a small banquette. The table held an open bag of potato chips, the remnants of a donut, a hairbrush, and a Walkman. A small refrigerator stood to her left, and beside it, a peeling veneer door led to either a closet or a bathroom. There was also a tiny kitchen with a three-burner stove, a microwave, and a sink littered with some Styrofoam cups and a Dunkin' Donuts box. At the very rear of the motor home, a sliding door that was only partially closed revealed a double bed piled with clothes and some towels. There were two bucket seats at the front, one for the driver and one for a passenger.

A challenging voice interrupted. "What are you doing here?"

Reluctantly, she turned toward the surly teenager named Lucy, who was sitting on the couch feeding the baby green peas from a jar. The girl definitely wasn't pleased to see her.

Nealy remembered seeing something needy in her eyes when she'd been arguing with Mat. Maybe she didn't like the idea of another woman horning in on her territory.

"I'm hitching a ride," Nealy replied.

Lucy stared at her resentfully, then looked toward the driver's seat. "What's the matter, Jorik? You couldn't go without sex so you had to bring her along?"

Definitely proprietary.

"Ignore her." Mat picked up a road map and began to

study it. "Lucy thinks if she talks dirty she'll make me cry."

Nealy gazed at Lucy and thought about the dazzling group of teenagers she'd hosted at the White House just last week. They were all National Merit Scholarship winners, and their contrast with this girl couldn't have been more pronounced. Well, she'd wanted a glimpse of ordinary life, and she'd found it.

Lucy set the jar of baby food down on the couch. The baby, whose mouth was rimmed in green, immediately let out a demanding shriek. The teenager rose and went to the banquette, where she slouched down. "She's not done eating, but I'm done feeding her." She reached for her Walkman, slipped the headset over her ears, and leaned back into the corner.

Mat glanced over his shoulder at Nealy and shot her a pointed smile. "Time to earn your keep, Nell."

For a moment Nealy couldn't think whom he was addressing.

"Finish feeding the baby so we can take off," he said.

Lucy was shaking her head to the music coming from the Walkman, but the watchful eye she kept on the baby indicated she was listening to every word. Nealy had the distinct impression she was being put to some kind of test.

She turned to the baby and felt the familiar dread. Although she related well to children, being around babies was torturous. It was one of her most closely guarded secrets, especially ironic in light of the disguise she'd adopted.

She didn't need a shrink to figure out why she had a problem. The famous *Time* magazine cover photo taken when she was sixteen didn't show that the starving Ethiopian baby she'd been holding had died in her arms moments after the photographer had walked away. The memory had never left her.

Although she picked up a lot of healthy, smiling babies for photo ops, those contacts were always brief. Instead, it was the desperately ill babies her job so frequently required her to spend time with. She'd gazed at dozens of crack babies in isolettes, cuddled a hundred HIV babies, cooed to babies suffering from unspeakable diseases, and brushed flies from the empty eyes of those who were starving. In her mind, babies and suffering had become inexorably linked.

"You have to distance yourself," Dennis had said before their marriage when she'd tried to explain it to him. "If you want to be of any use to those children, you have to detach."

But how could anyone detach from the tragedy of watching innocents die? Images of their swollen bellies and crippled limbs haunted her dreams. These babies had become both her cross and her crusade, and she'd ordered her staff to look for as many opportunities as possible to showcase their plight. It was the only way she could honor the memory of the Ethiopian baby she hadn't been able to help.

First Ladies traditionally had a cause. Lady Bird had her wildflowers, Betty Ford fought substance addiction, Nancy Reagan Just Said No, and Barbara Bush wanted everyone to read. Although Cornelia hadn't planned it that way, she became the guardian angel of the world's most vulnerable victims.

Now, as Nealy gazed down at this healthy, screaming, golden-haired little girl with bright blue eyes and peas smeared all over her face, she felt only dread. The dark side of her crusade was her panic when she saw a healthy one. What if her touch brought this beautiful child harm? The notion was illogical, but she'd felt like the Angel of Baby Death for so long that she couldn't help it.

She realized Mat was watching her, and she managed a shrug. "I'm—I'm not good with babies. Maybe you'd better do it."

"Afraid to get your hands dirty? In case you forgot, helping out is your ticket to ride."

He had her over a barrel, and he knew it. She took in the messy motor home, the surly teenager, and the fussing infant. Then she gazed at the big, roughneck of a man with his broad shoulders and devil's smile. Did she want to stay on the run badly enough to put up with all this?

Yes, she did.

With grim determination, she picked up the gooey spoon, dipped it into the jar, and brought it to the baby's mouth. The baby devoured the peas, then opened up for more, her eyes glued to Nealy's face. As Nealy brought the next spoonful to her mouth, the baby grabbed her fingers.

Nealy flinched, barely able to resist the urge to shake off her touch. "What's her name?" she managed.

"You don't want to know."

Lucy lifted one earphone. "Her name's Butt."

"Butt?" Nealy gazed down at the adorable pea-smeared face with its soft features and healthy skin. Her straight blond hair rose like dandelion fluff around her head. The baby smiled, exhibiting four small teeth, then blew a green-flecked spit bubble.

"I didn't name her," Lucy said, "so don't look at me."

Nealy looked at Mat instead.

"I didn't name her, either."

She quickly fed the baby the last spoonful of peas. "What's her real name?"

"Got me." He began folding the map.

"I thought you were a friend of her mother. Why don't you know her name?" And how had he come to be on the road with two children who weren't his?

Instead of responding, he turned the key in the ignition.

"I wouldn't take off yet, Jorik," Lucy said. "Butt

needs a good half hour for her food to settle or she'll hurl again."

"Damn it, we're never going to get out of here."

Nealy didn't think he should be using that kind of language in front of a teenager, no matter how foul-mouthed she might be herself. Still, it wasn't her concern.

Lucy yanked off her headset. "Turn on the air-conditioning. It's hot."

"Have you ever heard the word *please*?"

"Have you ever heard the words *I'm hot as hell*?"

Lucy had pushed him too far. Instead of turning on the air-conditioning, he shut off the engine, got up from the driver's seat, and calmly pocketed the keys. "I'll see you ladies in half an hour." He let himself out of the Winnebago.

It *was* warm inside, and Nealy lifted an eyebrow at the teenager. "Nice going."

"He's an ass."

"He's an ass who just left us without air-conditioning."

"Who cares?"

When Nealy had been Lucy's age, she'd been expected to dress neatly and carry on polite conversation with world leaders. Discourtesy would never have occurred to her. The teenager was beginning to fascinate her.

The baby had begun to smear her gooey fists into her blond fuzz. Nealy looked around for some paper towels, but didn't see any. "How am I supposed to clean her up?"

"I don't know. With a washcloth or something."

"Where are they?"

"Someplace. Maybe in that drawer."

Nealy found a dish towel, wet it at the sink, and, under Lucy's watchful eyes, began wiping up the baby's hair, only to discover that she should have started with her hands. As she worked, she tried not to notice the drooly smiles coming her way. Finally, the child was reasonably clean.

"Take her out of her seat and let her crawl around for a while." Lucy sounded thoroughly bored. "She needs some exercise."

The rug didn't look very clean. Thoughts of typhoid, dysentery, hepatitis, and a dozen other diseases ran through her mind, and she glanced around for something to set her on. She finally found a machine-made quilt in one of the overhead bins at the back of the Winnebago, and she spread it on the floor, between the couch and the table. Her hands fumbled with the straps on the baby seat before she got them to release.

She braced herself, just as she always did when she had to pick up an infant. *Don't die. Please, don't die.*

The child kicked and let out a happy squeal as Nealy lifted her from the car seat. She felt warm and solid beneath her hands, blissfully healthy. Nealy quickly set her on the floor. The baby craned her neck to look up at her.

Lucy had stopped making even a pretense of listening to her Walkman. "You shouldn't have bothered with the blanket. She won't stay on it."

Sure enough, the baby shot forward on her hands and knees. In seconds she was off the blanket heading for the front of the motor home.

"If you know so much, why don't you take care of her?" Nealy enjoyed the novelty of being rude. Wouldn't it be wonderful to snap at everyone who offended her?

The baby pulled herself to her feet, using the driver's seat for support, and began cruising on two wobbly feet balanced by one small hand smeared with dried green peas.

"What do you think I've been doing since my mother died?"

Nealy felt terrible. "I didn't know about your mother. I'm sorry."

Lucy shrugged. "No big deal. Leave that alone, Butt."

Nealy saw the baby had edged forward and was standing on her toes to reach for the gearshift. The infant turned toward her big sister, grinned, and plopped her fist into her mouth.

"I'm not calling her Butt," Nealy said.

"Then how's she going to know you're talking to her?"

Nealy refused to get drawn into an argument. "I have an idea. Let's give her another name. A nickname."

"What kind of nickname?"

"I don't know. Marigold."

"That's so lame."

"It may be lame, but it's better than Butt."

"She's doing it again. Move her."

Nealy was getting tired of taking orders from a teenager. "Since you know her behavior patterns so well, it would probably be better if you watched her."

"Yeah, right," Lucy scoffed.

"I think it would be best. You're obviously good with her."

Lucy's face reddened beneath her makeup. "I am not! I can't stand the little brat."

Nealy regarded the teenager closely. If she disliked the baby so much, why did she keep such a watchful eye out for her?

Baby Butt—Baby *Marigold*—reached for the gearshift again. Nealy dashed forward, slipped her hands under the child's arms, and carried her over to stand by the couch. The baby steadied herself with one hand and craned her neck toward her big sister, who was determinedly ignoring her. She let out a demanding squeal for attention.

Lucy bent her head and began picking at the blue nail polish on her big toe.

The baby shrieked again, even louder.

Lucy continued to ignore her.

Another shriek. Louder still.

"Stop it! Just stop it!"

The little one's face crumpled at her sister's anger. Tears pooled in her eyes. Her bottom lip quivered.

"Shit!" Lucy jumped up and stalked from the motor home, leaving Nealy alone with a heartbroken baby.

"Tell me it's my imagination and that pinging coming from the engine isn't getting worse." Mat glanced over at Nealy, who was sitting in the passenger seat. They'd been on the road for about an hour, but he'd seemed occupied with his own thoughts, and it was the first time he'd spoken to her.

"I haven't been paying attention." She'd been too busy enjoying the rural scenery.

"Let's stop," Lucy said. "I want to go to a mall."

"I don't think there's a mall near here," Nealy replied.

"Like how would you know? And let me drive. I know how to drive this thing."

"Quiet," Mat said, "or you'll wake up Butt."

To Nealy's relief, the baby had finally fallen asleep in her car seat. "Her name is Marigold."

"That's stupid." He reached for the can of root beer he'd taken from the small refrigerator. She'd already noticed that he was something of a root beer addict.

"Butt doesn't like it, either," Lucy said, "but *She* doesn't care."

Nealy had been relegated to *She* twenty miles ago. "Well, that's just too bad because it's what I'm calling her." *She* felt another surge of pleasure at her glorious rudeness. Imagine being able to talk to members of Congress like this. *Sir, the only thing that smells more than your breath is your politics.*

Quiet settled over the motor home, which Lucy had informed her was named Mabel. Even this broken-down

Winnebago had a better name than that baby.

Mat glared at the road, his head cocked to the side as he continued to listen for engine noises. Nealy realized she was enjoying herself, despite the less-than-desirable company. A beautiful summer day with no receptions or formal dinners ahead of her. Tonight, she wouldn't have to put ice packs on her hands to recover from another receiving line.

Soreness from too many handshakes was the bane of political life. Some Presidents had even developed their own systems for protection. Woodrow Wilson put his middle finger down, then crossed his ring and index finger above it so no one could get a good grip. Harry Truman grabbed the other person's hand first and slid his thumb between their thumb and index finger to control the pressure. Ida McKinley, wife of President William McKinley, held a bouquet so she didn't have to shake hands at all. But Elizabeth Monroe, the beautiful but snobbish wife of the nation's fifth president, had an even better system. She simply stayed away from the White House.

Public figures developed lots of little tricks to make formal occasions more tolerable. One of Nealy's favorites came from Her Majesty, Queen Elizabeth. When she wanted her aides to rescue her from a boring conversation, she simply switched her handbag from right arm to left.

"I want to go to a mall."

Where was that handbag when you needed it? "Why don't you listen to your Walkman?"

Lucy tossed down the bag of chips. "I'm sick of that. I want to do something fun."

"Do you have a book to read?"

"I'm not in school. Why would I read a book?"

Mat smiled. "Yeah, Nell. Why would she want to do that?"

Books had been Nealy's most faithful companions as

a child, and she couldn't imagine anyone not enjoying
reading. She wondered how parents entertained children
when they traveled. Although she was the First Lady of
the United States—the symbolic mother of the country—
she had no idea.

"Would you like to draw?" she asked.

"Draw?" It was as if Nealy had suggested she entertain herself by playing with a dead rat.

"Do you have some crayons? Colored pencils?"

She snorted and continued picking at her toenail polish.

Mat shot Nealy an amused glance. "It's the millennium, Nell. Crayons and colored pencils are old-
fashioned. Ask her if she wants drugs and a handgun."

"That's not funny."

"It's funny." Lucy looked up from her toe. "The first
funny thing I've heard you say, Jorik."

"Yeah, I'm a regular Jim Carrey."

Lucy got up off the couch. "We have to stop. I've got
to pee."

"We have a toilet. Use it."

"Forget it. It's gross in there."

"Then clean it."

Lucy's lip curled with disdain. "As if."

Mat looked over at Nealy. "Clean it."

Nealy looked back at him. "As if."

Lucy giggled and Nealy smiled at the sound.

"Sit down," he ordered Lucy. "And buckle up. There
are belts on that couch. Use 'em."

She grabbed her Walkman and carried it to the rear
of the motor home, where she flopped down on the double bed, shoved the headset back on, and banged her
fists against the wall to the rhythm of the music.

"Nice kid," Nealy said. "I'm sure she'll do well for
herself in prison."

"If she wakes up the Demon, I'm going to kill her
before she can get there."

Nealy studied him. "I've never traveled with kids, but I think you're supposed to plan frequent stops to keep them from getting bored. Scenic areas, playgrounds, zoos."

"If you see a sign for a snake farm, tell me right away so I can drop off all three of you."

"You're a very cranky man."

"And you're awfully cheerful for a woman who only has twenty dollars in her wallet and just had her stolen car stolen."

"It wasn't stolen, and earthly possessions are nothing but obstacles standing in the way of our spiritual enlightenment."

"Is that so?"

"Lucy said her mother died. When was that?"

"About six weeks ago. The woman never had any sense. She was driving drunk."

"What about the girls' father?"

"Fathers. Lucy's father was a one-night stand. The Demon's father was Sandy's last boyfriend. He died with her."

"That must be why Lucy's so hostile. She's trying to cope with her mother's death."

"I don't think so. My bet is that Sandy died for Lucy a long time ago. I think she's mainly scared, but doesn't want anybody to see it."

"It's nice of you to watch out for them, especially since you don't seem too fond of children."

"Nothing wrong with those little girls that some good concrete blocks and a real deep lake won't fix."

She smiled. People always put on their best faces for her. It was nice to be around someone so cheerfully perverse. "What do you do for a living? When you're not driving around children who don't belong to you, that is."

He took another sip from his root beer and set the can back down before he answered. "I work in a steel mill."

"Where?"

"Pittsburgh."

She settled back into the seat, thoroughly enjoying the novelty of chatting like an ordinary person. "Is it interesting? Working in the steel industry?"

"Oh, yeah. Real interesting." He yawned.

"What do you do?"

"This and that."

"It's incredible the way the industry is reviving despite competition with the Japanese. It's strange, though, to realize Indiana is our leading steel producer now instead of Pennsylvania. And Pennsylvania isn't even in second place."

He was staring at her, and she realized she'd revealed too much. "I read about it in the *National Enquirer,*" she said quickly.

"The *National Enquirer*?"

"Maybe it was the *Philadelphia Inquirer.*"

"Maybe."

A stab of resentment shot through her. She'd spent too many years watching every word she said, and she didn't want to have to do it now. "I have a photographic memory," she lied. "I know all kinds of trivia."

"Too bad you couldn't remember your car keys." He took another swig of root beer. "So Pennsylvania's number three?"

"Number four, actually, after Ohio and Illinois."

"Fascinating." He yawned again.

"Would you like me to drive so you can nap?"

"You ever drive one of these things?"

She'd driven tanks, both American- and Russian-made. "Something similar."

"Maybe I will. I had a lousy night's sleep." He slowed and pulled off onto the shoulder.

"What's going on?" Lucy called out from the back.

"I'm taking a nap. Come up here and torture Nell for

a while so I can have the bed. You can teach her all the dirty words you know."

"Quiet, both of you. You'll wake up B—Marigold."

Lucy came forward as Mat vacated the driver's seat, and before long, they were back on the road. The miles slipped by, but instead of enjoying the scenery, Nealy found herself wondering exactly what was happening at the White House.

The late afternoon sunlight slanting through the tall windows of the Oval Office fell across the polished shoes of Secret Service Director Frank Wolinski. He took a seat in one of the Duncan Phyfe chairs that sat near a nineteenth century landscape. The President's chief advisor stood near one of the inner office doors, all of which had shell-shaped niches above them, while James Litchfield had taken a chair by a pediment-topped outer door.

Wolinski's counterparts at the FBI and CIA sat next to each other on one of the couches. Their direct superiors, the Attorney General and the Secretary of the Treasury, had positioned themselves at the edge of the seating group as if they wanted to distance themselves from the proceedings.

Harry Leeds, the FBI director, and Clement Stone, Director of the CIA, already knew what was in Wolinski's report. The three men had been in constant contact for the past twenty-eight hours, ever since Cornelia Case's chief of staff had discovered she was missing. It was the President who had called this meeting.

As Lester Vandervort walked across the presidential seal that covered the rug in front of his desk, Wolinski shifted in his seat. The tension in the room was almost unbearable. He'd only been appointed Secret Service director six months ago, part of the sweep that had taken place at the agency following the Case assassination, but now his job was in jeopardy. He didn't like to think about going down in history as the first agency director to have lost a First Lady.

"Let's hear it," the President snapped.

"Yes, sir."

Everyone in the room knew Wolinski was sweating, and they were all waiting to see how he'd handle it. "Two hours ago we picked up a report that the Pennsylvania State Police pulled over a felon named Jimmy Briggs. There's a warrant out for his arrest for armed robbery. At the time of the arrest, Briggs was driving a blue Chevy Corsica registered to a Della Timms. The Chevy had temporary plates from a used car dealer in Rockville."

At the mention of the Washington, D.C., suburb, the men in the room who weren't yet familiar with Wolinski's information grew even more alert.

"As far as we can determine, Della Timms doesn't exist," he said.

"But you don't know for certain."

Clement Stone, the CIA director, knew damn well they needed more time before they could be sure, and this was his way of insulating himself from any blame. Wolinski hid his irritation. "We're still checking. The dealership has a reputation for playing fast and loose with the law, and the salesman didn't see a driver's license. We've questioned him, and he's described Timms as a thin, elderly woman with curly gray hair and unusually smooth skin."

He paused for a moment, giving them time to draw their own conclusions before he went on. "We know Mrs. Case used some kind of disguise to get out of the White House, and the timing's right."

"You *think* she used a disguise," Litchfield snapped. "We still have no way of being certain my daughter wasn't coerced."

Wolinski had never liked James Litchfield, but now he felt a pang of sympathy for him. Everyone in Washington knew how close the former Vice President was to his daughter. "All the evidence points to the fact that she left voluntarily."

The President gave Wolinski a hard stare. "You think she may have disguised herself as an old lady, sneaked out of the White House, somehow made it to Maryland, and bought a car. You'd better have more than that."

"I do, sir. The Pennsylvania State Police found an envelope in the trunk of the Chevy with fifteen thousand dollars in it." Wolinski dreaded the next part of his report. "They also found a sack of women's clothes and some toiletries. One sack had a gray wig in it."

"Jesus." Litchfield shot to his feet, his expression agonized.

"There might not be any connection," Wolinski said hastily, "but we're going over the White House security tapes right now to get a closer look at all the older women who came through on the tours that morning. We should have the results in another hour."

The President swore, and Litchfield lost what little color was left in his face. Wolinski knew exactly what was on their minds, and he spoke quickly. "There were no signs of violence. Jimmy Briggs said the keys were in the ignition when he took it, and that he never saw the driver. The car's heading for the lab right now."

"What did you tell the locals?" The President's chief advisor, a man who was known to be paranoid about White House leaks, spoke up for the first time.

"We've said that we're doing a routine investigation. That we've gotten some crackpot mail threatening the President and we think it might have come from the car's former owner."

"Did they buy it?"

"They seemed to."

The President's advisor shook his head. "So far there haven't been any leaks, but we won't be able to keep this quiet for long."

Litchfield erupted. "We have to keep it quiet! If the press finds out that my daughter has disappeared . . ." He didn't finish his sentence. He didn't have to.

"I have agents heading for Pennsylvania right now," Wolinski said.

"Not good enough." The President's gaze took in both Wolinski and Harry Leeds, the Bureau director. "I want a task force of special teams put together for this, with Bureau agents and Secret Service agents assigned as partners. Your best people."

Wolinski didn't know who sounded more alarmed at the idea of pairing the agents this way, himself or Harry Leeds. "But sir—"

"Sir, if I might suggest—"

"You'll do as I say." The President's gaze took in the Attorney General and Secretary of the Treasury before he returned his attention to Wolinski and Leeds. "I know how you men work, and I won't let anybody build a private kingdom on Mrs. Case's disappearance. I insist on complete cooperation between agencies. Setting up the teams this way guarantees that I'll get it. Does everybody understand?"

"Yes, sir."

"Yes, sir."

"Good." The President's eyes narrowed. "Now I suggest you all get busy because, I promise you, if Cornelia Case isn't located quickly, some people in this room are going to be out of a job."

6

"MA-MA-*MA*!"

Mat dreamed he was cleaning out a latrine. As the dream progressed, a malevolent-looking kitten appeared and sank its sharp claws into his arm. Gradually, he worked one eyelid open and then the other. He blinked. No kitten. Instead, a pair of baby blue eyes peered angelically at him over the edge of the bed.

"Ma-ma-ma-ma-*Ma*!" She dug her fingers into his arm. Her wispy blond hair was matted to one side of her head, and her chubby cheek bore a crease. Otherwise, she was bright-eyed, smelly, and ready to party. *"Ma!"*

"Wrong person, kid." He extricated himself, rolled to his back, and stared up at the roof of the motor home. They weren't moving, which explained the fact that the Demon was roaming. "Nell! Lucy! Butt needs her diaper changed."

No response.

"Da—*Da*!"

That brought him up off the bed fast. He shuddered and ran his hand through his hair. Then he shoved one side of his T-shirt back in his jeans and made his way to the front of the Winnebago. His neck was getting a crimp from having to keep his head ducked.

Lucy was nowhere in sight, but Nell sat in the passenger seat with her feet propped up on the dashboard and an expression of pure contentment on her face. He found himself pausing, just to watch her. A shaft of late afternoon sunlight had turned her skin to porcelain, and there was something almost ethereally beautiful about her.

She turned and caught him staring at her. He glanced down at the dashboard clock and saw that he'd been asleep for quite a while. "The baby's on the loose."

"I know. She needed some exercise."

The door swung open and Lucy came back in. "That's the last time I'm peeing in the woods."

"Then clean the bathroom," Nell countered.

Mat felt something clutch his leg, caught a whiff, and looked down to see the Demon hanging on to his jeans. She looked up at him, all drooly grin. Then, using his leg to balance herself, she began to bounce.

"Da-da-*Da!*"

Maybe he'd died without realizing it and gone straight to hell.

"Don't say that." Lucy took her sister's arms and drew her away, then knelt down and caught her small face between her hands to get her attention. "Say *jerk*, Butt. *Jerk. Jerk. Jerk.*"

Nell didn't even have the decency to hide her amusement as she gingerly picked up the baby and carried her over to the couch for a diaper change. "You've got quite a fan club."

He needed some fresh air. "I'll be back in a few minutes, but don't hesitate to take off without me."

When he returned, the Demon was safely fastened in her car seat and Nell sat behind the wheel.

"I'll drive," he said.

She pulled back onto the road. "Soon. Right now I'm looking for a place to stop for dinner."

"It's not even six."

"Lucy's hungry."

He tilted his head toward the teenager. "Eat potato chips."

"I'm hungry, too," Nell said. "And Marigold needs a decent meal."

"Stop calling her that!" Lucy exclaimed. "She hates it! She really does."

"Pull over," he ordered.

"Right up ahead. The sign says one-point-five miles. Grannie Peg's Good Eats."

"I just bet that'll be four-star cuisine."

"What does a steelworker know about four-star cuisine?"

"Don't stereotype."

"I don't type at all. That's why I'm unemployed."

She looked awfully pleased with herself for someone who was supposed to be desperate. He wondered how she'd react if he told her the truth about what he did for a living. He used to love telling people he was a journalist, but during the past year, he'd grown evasive. That alone had been a good reason for quitting. A man should be proud of his work.

"Oh, look! They're having a picnic!" Nell slowed to gaze at a family of four that had stopped by the side of the road to eat sandwiches off the tailgate of an old station wagon. Her blue eyes danced with delight. "It looks like so much fun. That's what we can do for dinner! We can have a roadside picnic."

"No way. I've got my heart set on Grannie Peg's fine cuisine."

"Picnics blow," Lucy grumbled.

"Both of you could use a happy pill," Nell said firmly.

"I feel sorry for your kid if you're going to make it eat dirt sandwiches off the back of some shitty station wagon."

Nell fixed her gaze on the road. "I can't hear you. I can't hear anything but happy words."

Mat smiled. The pregnant lady sure was good for entertainment.

*   *   *

Grannie Peg's flamingo-pink T-shirt, black leggings, and gleaming silver earrings delighted Nealy. All that on a plump, brassy-haired woman just past forty. Her restaurant had fake pine paneling, plastic flowers in a wall divider that separated the restaurant entrance from the dining area, and a long Formica counter with black vinyl stools. Exactly the sort of place she never got to see.

She was glad she'd been able to maneuver Lucy into carrying the baby. Feeling that healthy, vigorous wiggling beneath her hands as she'd changed Marigold's diaper had been difficult enough. She'd been terrified she'd somehow bring harm to her.

Grannie Peg stepped out from behind the register and nodded at them as they entered. "Hey, there, folks. Smoking or non?"

"Smoking," Lucy said.

"Non," Mat said.

Lucy's look indicated how pathetic she thought he was.

Nealy watched Mat studying the restaurant's counter, a purposeful gleam in his eyes. "Don't even think about it," she said quickly. "You're sitting with us unless you want Marigold strapped on the stool next to you."

The baby squealed in delight. "Da da *Da!*"

"Will you make her stop doing that?" Mat growled.

"Jerk. Jerk. *Jerk!*" Lucy said to the top of the baby's head.

Mat sighed.

Nealy laughed. Considering how unpleasant her traveling companions were, she shouldn't be having such a good time, but being with them felt like being with a real American family. They were all so gloriously dysfunctional. Except for Marigold. She was gloriously functional.

Mat sniffed. "Didn't you just change her?"

"I guess she enjoyed it so much, she decided to do it again."

One look at Lucy's face told Nealy she didn't have a chance of convincing the teenager to handle this diaper change. Reluctantly, she carried the baby back to the motor home.

When she returned, she found Mat and Lucy in a booth, with Lucy glaring at him. She had no intention of asking what was wrong, but Lucy told her anyway.

"He won't let me order a beer."

"The depth of his cruelty leaves me speechless." Nealy frowned at the high chair that had been placed at the end of the table. Who knew how many children had sat in that chair and what diseases they might have had? She looked around for a waitress to ask for disinfectant.

"What's wrong?" Mat asked.

"The high chair doesn't look too clean."

"It's clean," he said. "Put her in."

Nealy hesitated, then forced herself to gently lower the squirming baby into the seat. *Don't get sick, sweetheart. Please don't get sick.*

Nealy fumbled around trying to fasten the tray in place until Lucy pushed her out of the way and did it herself. "You're so pathetic. I feel sorry for your kid. I really do."

"Shut up." Although she hadn't put much heat behind her words, Nealy still enjoyed them. "Just shut up," she repeated for good measure.

"You're *rude.*"

"Like you've got room to criticize," Nealy countered. Oh, this was too much fun.

Mat looked amused. Marigold slapped her hands on the high chair tray, demanding her sister's attention. "Ma ma *Ma!*"

Lucy's face crumpled. "I'm not your mother. She's dead!"

Nealy glanced over at Mat, but he'd begun studying the menu. "Lucy, I'm really sorry about your mother. I lost my mother, too, when I was very young. Anytime you want to talk about her—"

"Why would I want to talk to you?" Lucy scowled. "I don't even know you."

"She's got you there," Mat said.

A gray-haired waitress appeared, pencil and pad poised for action. "Are you folks ready to order? Hey, sweetie. What a cute baby. How old is she?"

Nealy had no idea.

"Forty-seven," Lucy retorted. "She's a dwarf."

"Ignore her," Mat said to the waitress. "She's annoyed because we're getting ready to lock her up in an institution for the criminally bad-mannered."

The waitress nodded knowingly. "Teenage years are hard on parents."

Mat began to correct her, then seemed to decide it wasn't worth the effort. "I'll have a cheeseburger and fries. And whatever you've got on draft."

"That's so not fair!" Lucy sputtered. "How's come you can have a beer and I can't?"

"Because you're too old to drink." He discarded his menu.

Nealy smiled, then turned her attention to her own order. She realized she was famished. "I'll have the fried chicken, mashed potatoes, and green beans. Blue cheese dressing on the salad."

"Bacon sandwich," Lucy said. "No lettuce. No tomato. No mayonnaise. And white bread. And red Jell-O."

"We only have lime."

"That blows."

The baby slapped the tray and let out a demanding shriek. Clearly liking the sound of her own voice, she did it again.

The waitress nodded indulgently. "What's the little angel going to have?"

Mat snorted.

Nealy didn't know what the baby ate other than jarred food, and she was once again forced to look to Lucy for help.

"You can mash up some of your green beans and chicken real small with a fork. Don't put butter on the beans," she told the waitress. "And bring her some crackers to keep her busy until the food gets here, then some applesauce."

"How about scrambled eggs or something easy to eat like that?" Nealy said, trying to be helpful.

"Babies can't have egg whites until they're a year old. Don't you know anything?"

The waitress stared at Nealy for a long time—obviously pegging her as the worst mother of the century—then she turned away.

"*Buh-buh-buh!*" the baby shouted at the top of her small lungs. "*Gah!*"

Mat looked longingly toward the counter with its row of stools.

"Don't even think about it," Nealy said.

"She's so loud," he grumbled. "Why does she have to be so loud?"

"Maybe she's imitating you." Mat's voice wasn't really loud, but it was big, just like the rest of him.

Lucy smiled slyly and handed the baby a spoon, which she immediately began whacking on the high chair. A young couple in a neighboring booth looked over and frowned at the noise. Nealy gently took the spoon away.

Big mistake.

Marigold screamed.

Mat groaned.

Lucy looked pleased with herself.

Nealy hurriedly returned the spoon to the baby.

"*Gah!*"

"Don't cuss, Butt," Lucy said. "It upsets Jorik."

"Would you hurry up with that beer?" Mat called out to the waitress.

It didn't take long for the food to arrive. Nealy dug in, refusing to let the children spoil her enjoyment of Grannie Peg's. She'd eaten at the most famous restaurants in the world, from Tour L'Argent to the Rainbow Room, but not a single one of them was as atmospheric as this. Only when the check arrived did she remember she had a problem.

"Mat, I'd appreciate it if you could lend me some money. Just for a little while. I want to pay for my own food, and I'm going to need some clothes, a few incidentals. I could probably manage with five hundred."

He stared at her. "You want me to lend you five hundred dollars?"

"I'll pay you back. I promise."

"Yeah, sure."

Imagine anyone doubting Cornelia Case's word. Except she wasn't Cornelia Case. She was a pregnant drifter named Nell Kelly, and she could see his point. "Really I will. I have the money. I just can't get my hands on it right now."

"Uh-huh."

This was going to present a problem. She had no credit cards with her, since she couldn't have used them without blowing her cover, but she needed to get her hands on some money.

"I can loan you fifty," Lucy said.

Nealy was surprised by Lucy's generosity. "Really? Thanks."

"No problem." Too late, she saw the calculating look in the teenager's eyes. "All you have to do is whatever I tell you."

So much for the fifty dollars.

"I'll lend you fifty," Mat said begrudgingly.

Lucy sneered. "You should borrow from me. I won't make you take off your clothes."

"Did anybody ever mention that you're boring?" Mat said.

"I saw the way you were watching her today when she didn't know you were looking," Lucy countered.

"I was watching her because she looks like Cornelia Case."

"She does not."

A devil prodded Nealy. "A lot of people think I do."

"You wish," Lucy said.

"I hate to put an end to the good time we're all having." Mat stood. "But we need to hit the road."

"Butt just ate," Lucy reminded him.

"We'll take our chances," he snapped.

Easy for him to say, Nealy thought less than half an hour later as she tried to clean up the mess from the baby's latest episode of motion sickness. For the first time since her escape, she yearned for the efficient White House staff that took care of every kind of domestic unpleasantness.

By the time the baby was bathed, her car seat was swabbed down, and they'd found a discount store where Nealy could buy a few clothes to replace those she'd lost, it was dark, Marigold was screaming again, and Nealy had begun to feel as frantic as the baby. "We need to find a doctor! There's something wrong with her."

Lucy gave up trying to distract her sister with a Beanie Baby walrus. "Butt doesn't need a doctor; she's scared of doctors. She's hungry and she's tired, and she wants out of her car seat, and she needs her bottle. That's all."

Marigold held out her arms toward her sister and sobbed with frustration.

Nealy sat down in the empty passenger seat. "I think we should stop at the campground we saw advertised on those billboards."

"I'm not stopping," Mat said. "We're driving through

the night. One of us can sleep while the other takes the wheel."

Although he sounded determined, she suspected he knew his plan wouldn't work but hadn't gotten around to accepting it. "We won't be able to sleep with the baby screaming," she said reasonably. "If we stop now, we'll get plenty of rest and we can make an early start."

His sigh was as long-suffering as Lucy's. "We should be halfway through Ohio by now. We've barely crossed the West Virginia border."

"But we're having such a good time."

The corner of that steelworker's mouth quirked. "All right, we'll stop. But we're pulling out at daybreak."

Hoolihan's Campgrounds was a small RV park, with not more than a dozen vehicles angled in among the trees. Mat backed into the spot they'd been directed to, turned off the ignition, then got up to retrieve another can of root beer from the refrigerator. Within seconds, he'd left her alone with the children. Even though she knew that was why he'd let her come along, she resented his hasty exit.

Lucy gave Nealy the frantic baby. Nealy waited for her to follow Mat outside, only to watch the teenager make her way to the sink and fix her sister's bottle. When she was done, she took the baby back.

"I'll give it to her. She doesn't like you. You'll make her get sick all over again."

And then she'll die. . . . The awful, illogical thought flew through Nealy's mind. "I'll—I'm just going to take a little walk."

Lucy was feeding the baby and she didn't respond.

The night air felt like velvet as Nealy stepped outside. She gazed around and saw that the campground was set in a small clearing beneath a rim of foothills faintly visible in the moonlight. She heard the muted sound of a radio coming from the next campsite, smelled an old charcoal fire. Dim yellow bug lights mounted on crude

poles threw spots of weak illumination over the gravel
road. She walked toward it, only to hesitate. Something
was wrong, and it left her feeling unbalanced and dis-
oriented.

Then she realized what it was. There were no soft
footsteps behind her, no quiet murmur of voices whis-
pering her whereabouts into a two-way radio. For the
first time in years, she was by herself. Contentment
seeped through her, right down to her bones.

She'd barely gone ten yards, however, before a familiar voice intruded on her solitude. "Already running
away from our happy home?"

She turned to see a dark figure sprawled at a picnic
table set into the trees. He was sitting backward on the
bench, leaning against the table with those long legs
stretched out and the root beer can in his hand.

Even as she felt herself drawn to him, she realized
she knew nothing about him other than the fact that he
disliked children and worked in a steel mill. There were
questions she needed to ask, ones she hadn't been able
to pose around Lucy.

"Am I likely to get myself arrested for being with
you?"

He rose and began to walk beside her.

With his height and muscular build, he might have
been Secret Service, but he didn't feel safe like the
agents she was used to. Instead, he felt like danger.

"What makes you ask that?"

"For a man who wants to travel quickly, you did a
good job of keeping us off the turnpike."

"I don't like turnpikes."

"You love them. You're a turnpike kind of guy. Be
honest, Mat. What's going on with you and those kids?"

"I'm not kidnapping them, if that's what you want to
know."

She'd been fairly certain of that. Lucy complained
about bumpy roads and warm Coke—she'd hardly keep

quiet about being kidnapped. "So what are you doing with them?"

He took a sip, looked off into the distance, shrugged. "A long time ago, I was married to their mother. Sandy put my name on both girls' birth certificates, even though neither one of them is mine."

"So you *are* the girls' father."

"Aren't you listening? It's only on paper. I didn't even know Butt existed until a few days ago."

"Please stop calling her that."

"Anybody who screams like she does deserves a crummy name."

"She may scream, but she looks like a cherub."

He was clearly unimpressed.

In the distance, an owl hooted. "I still don't understand. You obviously don't want them, so why do you have them? It shouldn't be hard to prove you're not their father."

"You try getting Lucy to a lab for a blood test." He slid one hand into the pocket of his jeans. "You're right, though. It won't be hard, and as soon as we get to Grandma's house, I'll take care of it."

"You still haven't explained why you dodged the turnpike."

"Sandy's mother isn't due back in the country till the end of the week, and child services was getting ready to take them. The baby'd probably be all right, but can you imagine Lucy in a foster home, even if it was only for a little while? She'd end up in a juvenile detention center before she ever made it to Iowa."

"I know she's awful, but there's something about her I like. And I'm sure she could have survived."

"Maybe, but . . . I don't know . . . it seemed safer to get them to their grandmother."

As he told her about Joanne Pressman, the letter she'd sent, the red tape involved in turning the girls over, Nealy realized there was a lot more to Mat Jorik than that crusty macho exterior. "So you decided to sidestep the local authorities."

"Not from any affection for the little brats," he said dryly. "But despite what Sandy did to me, I have some good memories of her, and I figured I owed her a favor. At the same time, I didn't think the local authorities would be too happy about having me take them out of state before this was cleared up."

"So you did kidnap the girls."

"Let's just say I didn't have the patience to wait around until somebody got the legalities figured out. Originally I'd planned to fly, but Lucy took strong exception to that."

"Underneath the crusty exterior, you're a real softie."

"You just keep right on thinking that."

She had to admit that he didn't look much like a softie. He looked more like a man who'd been seriously inconvenienced. Still, since his need to keep to the back roads coincided with her desire to see small towns, she wasn't going to protest.

His eyes skimmed over her, lingering for a moment on her mouth, then moving to her eyes. "Now it's your turn to answer a few questions."

She felt slightly breathless. "Me? I'm an open book." God was currently off duty because lightning didn't strike her.

"Then why are you using a phony Southern accent?"

"How do you know it's phony?"

"Because half the time you forget."

"Oh. That's because I lived in California."

"Give it up, Nell. You're obviously well educated, and I didn't see anybody else at that god-awful restaurant eating their drumstick with a knife and fork."

"I don't like greasy fingers."

"Save it for somebody stupid."

Nealy thought fast. "All kinds of women get caught up in bad relationships."

"How bad?"

"Bad enough that I don't want to talk about it."

"Do you think he might be following you?"

"Not now," she said carefully. "But he might have been."

"Don't you have any friends who can help you out? Any family?"

"Not right now."

"No job?"

"I had to quit."

"Have you gone to the police?"

She was getting herself in deeper by the minute. "Restraining orders aren't always effective."

"What's his name? The baby's father?"

"Why do you want to know?"

"If somebody's on our ass, I don't want to be taken by surprise."

Only one name sprang to her mind, maybe because she'd recently pulled out her old video of *Titanic*. "Leo." She swallowed. "Leo . . . Jack."

"Weird name."

"Probably an alias. That's the kind of guy Leo is."

"If he's so bad, why did you hook up with him?"

"I have codependency problems."

He stared at her.

She'd thought it was a good response, but he obviously wasn't satisfied, so she embellished. "He's quite good-looking. Light brown hair, great eyes, nice body. Bad swimmer. A little young for me, but . . ." For God's sake, what was she doing? "I didn't realize until too late that he was psychotic," she said hastily.

"How does he feel about the baby?"

She tried to imagine Leonardo Di Caprio's reaction if she told him she was carrying his baby. She imagined he'd be quite astonished.

"He doesn't know."

"So you haven't seen him for a while?"

This time she didn't forget she had a wad of padding sticking out in front of her. "Not for a while. He wasn't around when I borrowed his car. I'd really rather not talk about this. It's quite painful."

He gave her a long, searching look that made her wonder exactly how much of this he was buying. He seemed to have an extremely agile mind.

"It's hard for me to imagine you getting mixed up with a psychotic."

"That's because you don't know me."

"I know enough. I'd even hazard a guess that you're a blue blood. Episcopalian, I'll bet."

"Presbyterian."

"Same thing. You're obviously intelligent and well educated, even if you don't have a lot of street smarts."

That annoyed her. "Lots of people have their cars stolen. And my mammy and pappy sure would love hearing me described as a blue blood."

"Did you know that the corner of your mouth scrunches up when you tell a lie?"

She deliberately tightened the corner of her mouth. "You're a kind and sensitive human being."

He laughed. "All right. I'll back off. But remember, you've only got a ride for as long as you keep the girls out of my hair, and you did a lousy job of it today."

Blackmail could work two ways. "You'd better be nice to me, or I'll leave you on your own. Just you, Lucy, and little baby Butt. Isn't it cute the way she says *da da*?" With what she very much hoped was a saucy smile, she picked up her steps and left him behind.

Saucy. It was so un-Cornelia-like. She loved it.

He smiled as she walked away. The lady had attitude, he'd give her that. From the rear, it was impossible to tell that she was pregnant. He didn't want her pregnant, he realized. He wanted her in sexy lingerie.

It wasn't often he shocked himself, but this time he'd managed it. His smile faded. Pregnant women represented everything he didn't want in his life, yet he'd just mentally undressed one. The idea made him shudder.

His relationship with the female sex had always been complex. Growing up surrounded by so many women had made him crave the masculine. He loved smelly locker rooms, rough contact, and no-holds-barred political debates. He enjoyed gruff voices and a little blood at hockey games. He liked shampoo that only had shampoo in it—no flowers, vegetables, or fruit salad. He loved having a bathroom to himself. No pink barrettes on the basin, no underwire bras hanging from the shower head. A cupboard beneath the sink that held shaving cream instead of boxes of mini pads, maxi pads, tampons of every size and shape, products for light days, heavy days, bad hair days, and I'm-too-fat days. He was a guy! He wanted to be surrounded by guy things. Unfortunately, the best guy thing of all was having sex with a great woman.

It was a dilemma he'd solved in the only way he knew how, by being up-front. He let women know at the beginning that he'd served his time as a family man, and he didn't ever intend to do it again. Then he laid out the rules—great sex, mutual respect, lots of personal space, and no permanent commitments.

Still, there were always women who had a death wish that attracted them to a man who set hard boundaries. A few of them had convinced themselves they could get him to the altar, although he couldn't imagine why they'd want to drag a commitment out of someone with such a deep-seated aversion to family life. As bad a husband as he'd be, he'd make an even worse father.

He still winced when he remembered all those sucker punches he'd thrown at his sisters when he was a kid and he hadn't known any other way to keep them in line. It was a miracle he hadn't hurt them.

He pitched his root beer can into a trash barrel and stuffed his hands in his pockets. At least one good thing was coming out of this misadventure—he didn't have time to brood about the way he'd screwed up a professional life he'd worked so hard to build.

Not long after he'd put himself through college, his mother had died. With more financial responsibility for his family, he'd worked harder than ever to build his career, and it had paid off as he'd moved from a small-town paper to the Chicago News Bureau and finally to the *Standard.* He'd had everything he'd wanted: a high-profile job in a great city, money in the bank, good friends, and enough leisure to play some ice hockey. And if he sometimes thought a man who'd accomplished all his goals should be happier . . . well, nothing in life was perfect.

Then Sid Giles had come courting. Sid had been developing a television news program called *Byline*, and he wanted Mat as his head producer. Although Mat had no experience in television, his journalistic credentials were impeccable, and Sid needed him for the credibility he'd lend the show. In addition to offering Mat an astronomical amount of money, Sid promised that he'd be able to do quality work.

Mat initially turned him down, but he couldn't stop thinking about the offer. Maybe this was what was missing from his life, he'd thought. A chance to push himself in a new direction. He'd finally accepted the job and set off for L.A.

At first Sid had kept his promise, and Mat had been able to do some good work. But *Byline*'s ratings didn't grow fast enough, and before long he found himself producing stories on cheating husbands, lesbian wives, and clairvoyant pets. Still, he held on, fueled by pure stubbornness and the inability to admit he'd made a mistake. Finally, as the stories had grown sleazier and his old newspaper friends started ducking his calls, he'd known he couldn't do it any longer. He'd turned in his resignation, put his luxury condominium up for sale, and walked away.

Now he wanted to find a couple of great stories to redeem his pride before he went back to Chicago. He'd already stumbled on some good stuff—a group of street kids in Albuquerque that'd tear a reader's heart out, a small-town bank making a fortune off farm foreclosures. But neither story was enough. He wanted something bigger.

Until two days ago, finding that big story was all he'd been able to think about. Now, however, he'd been distracted by a pair of kids who weren't his, along with a pregnant lady who had skinny legs, a quirky sense of humor, and an allure he didn't understand. Even though he wasn't much of a drinker, he decided he deserved to find a little oblivion in that pint of Jim Beam he'd spotted in one of Mabel's overhead bins.

7

"I'M NOT SLEEPING WITH YOU!" LUCY DECLARED. "HOW do I know you don't have lice or something?"

"Fine," Nealy sighed, pulling down the spread on the bed. "Then sleep up front."

"You said Mat was going to sleep up there."

"He probably will."

"Make him sleep in the back."

"Think for a minute, will you? Marigold's sleeping on the floor by the double bed because it's the only place to keep her contained, so it's not hard to figure out that Mat will make sure he sleeps in the front. The banquette makes up into a small bed. The couch makes up into another bed. You can either sleep back here in the double bed with me or up there with him."

"That's so gross. How do you know he's not one of those kiddy porn creeps or something?"

"Instinct."

"Yeah, well, that's easy for you to say. You're not the one who might get overpowered."

Why did the idea of being overpowered by Mat Jorik not seem all that awful? But sex was one thing she absolutely never let herself think about, so she looked around the kitchen for some cleanser.

"Let him sleep with you," Lucy said. "He wants to."

Spray bottle in hand, Nealy turned back to the hostile teenager with the small, perfectly proportioned features.

83

"You have no idea what you're talking about. He only likes me marginally more than he likes you, which isn't saying much. Now I'm taking a shower. Sleep anywhere you want."

Nealy didn't have much experience cleaning, but she couldn't stand using the bathroom as it was. It took her a while, but when she was done, she felt reasonably satisfied with the result. Afterward she showered, then reluctantly fastened the padding back around her middle. It would be uncomfortable for sleeping, but in such close quarters, she didn't have much choice.

She'd picked up the inexpensive long blue cotton nightgown she'd bought at the discount store. She was accustomed to silk, and the fabric felt strange as she settled it over her head.

When she emerged from the bathroom, she was relieved to see that Lucy had fallen asleep. Still wearing her clothes, she lay sprawled across the double bed. The smeared makeup formed a mask over her delicately innocent face.

Marigold lay on the bed Nealy had made for her on the floor. She was curled on her side, her plump, baby lips parted, fragile lashes lying in dainty half-moons on her cheeks, the Beanie Baby walrus under one knee. For the first time Nealy noticed that all ten of her tiny toenails were painted iridescent blue.

She smiled down at Lucy, then opened one of the back windows. As the night breeze touched her skin, she instinctively gazed toward the shadows outside for the guards who were always there. But tonight she saw only the gentle sway of tree branches. She felt completely isolated from the rest of the world and absolutely safe. Cornelia Case had vanished.

Lucy felt something poke her, heard a soft noise. It was too early to get up, and she didn't want to open her eyes, especially when she knew exactly what she would see.

"Gah?"

The word was soft, almost whispered. Lucy forced open one eye and then the other. For a moment, she simply stared at her sister as she peeked over the edge of the mattress. Little blond tufts stuck out here and there, most of them stiff from yesterday's meals, and a big smile, full of love and trust, was spread like peanut butter over her face. It made Lucy's stomach hurt.

"Gah," she whispered back.

The smile beamed brighter. Lucy lifted her head and saw a purple stain on her pillow from the color she'd sprayed in her hair. She also noticed a wet spot where she'd drooled while she slept. Gross.

Nell was asleep, and Lucy felt a stab of jealousy as she saw how pretty she looked lying against her pillow. Now that Nell was here, Jorik was paying attention to her instead of Lucy.

She didn't like thinking about how much she wanted him to pay attention to her. It reminded her of all those years she hadn't been able to get Sandy's attention. The only things her mother had cared about were booze and her boyfriends.

As Lucy sat up, she caught sight of Jorik sprawled face down on the couch, legs hanging off the end, one arm dragging on the floor. Fourteen years worth of resentment against Sandy churned inside her. Why couldn't Jorik have been her dad instead of some drunk Carnegie Mellon fraternity guy Sandy'd never seen again?

"Gah?"

Sharp little fingernails dug into her legs. She gazed at those dirty blond curls and grubby knees. Nell and Jorik thought they were so smart, but neither one of them seemed to know that babies needed a bath before they went to bed.

Freeing herself from her sister's grip, she stood up and began pulling some clean clothes from the pile she'd tossed on the floor yesterday morning before they'd taken off. When she had everything, she leaned down and grabbed the baby, too.

The digital clock on Mabel's dashboard read 6:02. Just one time Lucy'd like to sleep in late like other kids her age, but she never got to.

Her sister was heavy, and Lucy banged into the table on her way to the door, but Jorik didn't move. Then she saw the half-empty whiskey bottle lying on the floor. Betrayal burned inside her. Was he going to turn out to be a drunk, too?

The only time in the past four years when Sandy hadn't gotten drunk was when she was pregnant. Lucy's eyes filled with tears. That had been a pretty good time. Even though Sandy'd been with Trent a lot, sometimes it had just been the two of them laughing and talking about stuff.

Sometimes Lucy felt guilty for not being more sad about Sandy dying, but in a lot of ways, she felt like Sandy had died right after her little sister was born, when she'd started drinking again. All she was interested in from then on was partying. Lucy had sort of started hating her.

Outside it smelled like bacon and fresh air. She'd been to a place like this once with Sandy and Trent, and she knew there was usually a rest room with a shower for people who didn't want to use the one in their motor homes. She had to set the baby down in the grass a couple of times so she could rest her arms. Finally, she spotted a wooden building painted green. She hoped it wasn't too crappy inside.

She picked the baby back up. "You'd better start walking soon. I mean it. You're getting too heavy for me to carry. And stop poking me in the eye, will you?"

Babies were always doing crap like that. Waking you

up real early in the morning when you wanted to sleep, poking you in the eye, scratching you with their finger-nails. They didn't mean to be jerks. They just couldn't help it.

Nobody was in the rest room when they got there, and Lucy was glad to see that it wasn't too scummy. Her arms felt like somebody was trying to pull them right out of her shoulders, and she barely made it into one of two big shower stalls before they gave out. She plopped her sister on the concrete floor and dumped all their stuff on the wooden bench.

That was when she remembered that she'd forgotten soap and shampoo. She looked into the shower stall and saw that somebody'd left a little piece there, but it was green, and she didn't like green soap because of the way it smelled. Still, she'd have to use it because she didn't have any choice, just like she didn't have a choice about anything that had happened to her.

Her stomach started hurting again. It had been hurting a lot lately, mainly when she got scared about things.

The baby babbled while Lucy undressed her, and those soft, happy sounds made up for having to get up so early. While the baby crawled around, Lucy pulled off her own clothes and carefully tested the water to make sure it wasn't too hot. She stepped inside, then knelt down and held out her arms, but her sister was scared of the running water and didn't want to come in.

"Come here."

"Nuh!" She puckered up her face and crawled back-ward.

Lucy tried not to get mad because she was just a little baby, and she didn't know water wouldn't hurt her. But it was hard not to be mad with her stomach hurting and everything.

"Get in here right now!"

Her bottom lip stuck out, but the baby didn't move.

"I mean it! Get in here!"

Oh, shit. The baby's face crumpled and her eyes filled
with tears. She didn't even make any noise, just started
to shake, with her lip all quivery, and Lucy couldn't
stand it. She stepped out of the stall and, naked and cold,
squatted down to hug her.

"I didn't mean to yell at you. I'm sorry, Button. I'm
really sorry."

Button buried her face in her neck, just like she always did, and hung on because Lucy was the only person she had left in the world.

That was when Lucy started to cry, too. With goose
bumps breaking out all over her skin, and Button hanging on, and her heart hammering. She started to cry until
she was shaking because she didn't know how she was
going to take care of Button, and she didn't know what
Jorik would do when he found out about her grandmother.

She told herself she wouldn't be so scared if she was
by herself. She was fourteen, and she was smart, the
smartest kid in her class, although she made sure none
of those losers she went to school with knew about that.
A few of the teachers had figured it out, and some of
them made Lucy come up to their desks after class to
talk about how she should apply herself and crap like
that. But with a mother like Sandy, and never having
any money, and moving from one ugly, run-down house
to another, Lucy already felt like a freak. She didn't need
everybody knowing she had a smart brain, too.

Except her smart brain hadn't figured out how she was
going to take care of Button. Right after Sandy'd died,
she'd cashed her mother's last paycheck and used it to
pay the rent and phone and stuff. Then she'd started
baby-sitting one of the little kids in the neighborhood
while his mom went to work. She'd been doing okay
until that lawyer had found her.

If it was just her, she'd run away to New York City
or someplace like Hollywood, and get a job and make

a whole lot of money. But she couldn't do that and take care of Button, too.

Right now, she only knew one thing. She had to be tough. That was about the only good thing Sandy had ever taught her. *When somebody gets in your face, just spit right in their eye. If you don't stand up for yourself, nobody else is going to do it.*

So that's what she was doing. Being tough, standing up for herself, and trying to slow down this trip while she figured out how to take care of her baby sister.

Button started sucking on Lucy's neck. She did that sometimes when Lucy hugged her, and it made Lucy's stomach hurt so bad she wanted to start crying again because she knew Button couldn't tell the difference between her sister and a grown-up. Even worse, she knew Button didn't understand that Lucy wasn't her mom.

It had come to this, Nealy thought. The First Lady of the United States was traveling toward the heartland with a drunk, a teenage hellion, a baby she was terrified to touch, and an unborn Wal-Mart pillow.

"Where the hell are we?" Mat's big, booming voice bounced off the walls of the Winnebago.

She glanced over her shoulder and saw him uncoiling from the couch like a bear coming out of hibernation. Except he looked more like a gorgeous, rumpled pirate with his unkempt hair, wrinkled black T-shirt, and jaw covered in dark stubble.

"West Virginia."

He levered himself up, winced, and rubbed the back of his hand over his mouth. "I know that. Where in West Virginia?"

"This is the most beautiful state. Mountains, rivers, bucolic woodlands, winding roads." She thought about singing a little "West Virginia, mountain mama," but decided that might be pushing a man with a nasty hangover too far.

"The tollbooths are behind us for now, and we're not supposed to be on a winding road. We're supposed to be on a four-lane highway." His voice sounded gravelly, as if he might have swallowed dirt.

"We're near it," she said. "That's all that's important. Please go back to sleep. You're only causing trouble awake."

Lucy smiled. She was sitting in the banquette putting on makeup. Her eyelashes were already so heavy with mascara, it was a wonder she could lift them. The remains of their McDonald's breakfasts were scattered around her, along with a newspaper Nealy had picked up at the campground before they'd pulled out. While they'd been waiting at the drive-in window for their Egg McMuffins, Nealy'd glanced through it and found what she was looking for, a short item on page three announcing that Cornelia Case had been stricken with the flu and forced to cancel her scheduled activities for the next week.

Nealy had wedged the car seat into the booth this morning, and the baby, wearing a pair of candy pink overalls and blue sneakers with worn toes, was strapped into it looking increasingly unhappy. Nealy was fairly certain they'd have to stop soon, and she didn't look forward to sharing that information with Mat. "I made some coffee. It's a little strong, but your taste buds are probably pickled anyway, so I doubt it'll make a difference. Oh, and I took some money from your wallet for breakfast. I'm keeping a record of everything I owe so I can pay you back."

She'd eaten two Egg McMuffins all by herself, along with an orange juice. It was wonderful having an appetite again, even more wonderful being able to swallow.

Mat grunted, rose, and headed for the coffeepot, only to change his mind at the last moment and disappear into the bathroom.

"Do you think he's going to hurl?"

"I doubt it. He strikes me as the cast-iron stomach type."

Lucy outlined her lips with brown lipstick. "When Sandy was choosing a father's name for our birth certificates, I don't know why she couldn't have picked somebody like Mel Gibson."

Nealy laughed. "You know, Lucy, for the world's most obnoxious teenager, you're fairly amusing."

"It's not funny. How'd you like it if you had a last name like Jorik, and it came from him?"

Despite Lucy's words, Nealy thought she heard a touch of yearning in her voice. "Really? Jorik is your last name?"

"Like duh. What did you think it was?"

"Your mother's name, I guess."

"Jorik was her name. She never changed it back after they got divorced. She always liked him."

Nealy heard the shower go on. She waited a minute, then deliberately jerked the wheel to the left, back to the right, then to the left again. A bang, then a muffled curse came from the bathroom.

Lucy laughed. It was a good sound.

Nealy smiled, then returned her attention to the subject at hand. "So Marigold's a Jorik, too?"

"Stop calling her that!"

"Then give me another name. And not you-know-what."

"Shit." A long, put-upon sigh. "Call her Button, then. That's what Sandy did. And I know it's stupid, but I'm not the one who named her."

"Button?" So that's where *Butt* had come from.

Lucy slapped the lipstick tube down on the table. "Call her whatever you want, okay?"

"I like Button. It's cute."

They crested a hill, and Nealy devoured the view. She'd seen so many vistas throughout her life: Mount

McKinley on a crystal-clear day, the Grand Canyon at sunset. She'd seen Paris from the steps of Sacre Coeur, gazed out over the Serengeti from the front seat of a Range Rover, and watched a school of whales in the North Atlantic from the deck of a naval destroyer. But none of those sights seemed quite as glorious as these green West Virginia hills. This might be a poor state, but it certainly was beautiful.

The shower shut off. A minute ticked by.

"He might be shaving now," Lucy said, a vaguely hopeful note in her voice.

Nealy smiled, but kept the wheel steady. "I'm not that mad at him."

"He got drunk last night, didn't he?"

"He must have."

"I hate drunks."

"I'm not too fond of them, either."

"They think they're funny and sexy when they're drunk, but they're just pathetic."

Nealy had the feeling she wasn't talking about Mat. She wanted to ask about her mother, but she knew Lucy would lash out if she did.

The sound of an electric shaver penetrated the thin wall, and then the baby started to fuss. It wasn't safe to take her out of the car seat, but Nealy couldn't imagine how they were going to keep such an active child confined for another day. Apparently Lucy couldn't, either, because she got up and made her way over to her sister. In the rearview mirror, Nealy saw her get ready to unfasten the straps. "Keep her in the seat. It's too dangerous while we're moving."

"Then you got to stop soon so she can play for a while."

Nealy could just imagine how that would go over with Mat. The bathroom door swung open. "Gross!" Lucy exclaimed.

Nealy looked into the mirror and nearly drove off the road as Mat ducked through the door wearing only a baby-blue towel. He was anything but gross. His hair was damp and straight, but she suspected the hint of curl would spring back as it dried, and the electric shaver had temporarily tamed his pirate's stubble. She took in that long expanse of tan, muscular male. He was so over-sized for their small space that he should have looked ridiculous. He didn't.

"I have to get my clothes," he grumbled. "If you don't like it, don't look."

"Mel Gibson's got a lot better body than you," Lucy said.

"And that's supposed to bother me, why?"

Not better at all, Nealy found herself thinking, and Mat was taller. She didn't have her mind on the road, and she had to swerve to avoid a pothole.

He grabbed the doorframe. "Will you watch where you're going?"

"Sorry."

"You're all over the road."

"The scenery is distracting me." All six feet six of it.

"Well, pay attention to what you're doing."

As Mat headed for the back, Button held out her arms toward him and shrieked. He winced. Her pick-me-up message was unmistakable, but he closed the sliding door. She let out a howl. Lucy managed to distract her with the Beanie Baby walrus.

Nealy decided to enjoy the scenery before Mat insisted they get back on a bigger road. Sure enough, as soon as he emerged, he grabbed a mug of coffee, then told Nealy to pull over so he could drive.

She took in his worn jeans and gray athletic T-shirt. "I want Lucy to see the covered bridge first."

"What are you talking about?"

"This part of West Virginia has one of the best collections of covered bridges in the state. The brochure I picked up at the campground said so. A lot of taxpayer money has gone into maintaining these bridges, and I think it's important to her education that she see at least one of them."

"I don't care about Lucy's education."

"That's exactly the kind of attitude that's put this country's public school systems into jeopardy."

He stared at her, and she found herself wishing she'd kept her mouth shut. Then he shook his head. "Will you just pull over?"

"Stop being such a grouch. Lucy needs to broaden her horizons."

"She's going to spend her life as a convicted felon. What difference does it make if she sees a covered bridge?" He slouched down in the passenger seat.

"You're not funny, Jorik," Lucy retorted. "And *She* promised me I could see the bridge."

"It's not far," Nealy said. "Why don't you settle back and enjoy the ride? Or at least enjoy it as much as someone with a colossal hangover can."

"You got something to say, just say it," he grumbled.

"All right. Lucy and I don't fancy traveling with someone who gets drunk."

"*Fancy? You don't fancy?*"

"She means you're gross and we hate it."

"Pull over," he snarled. The baby started to fuss again.

"Here's the turnoff for the covered bridge." As Nealy made a left onto a narrow country road, she decided it might be best to change the subject. "Do you know why these were built, Lucy?"

"No, and I don't care."

"Some people say it was to keep horses from being spooked by the water, but it was probably done to protect the bridges from the elements so they'd last longer. Nobody knows for sure."

"You're a regular walking encyclopedia," Mat drawled.

"I told you I have a photographic memory." The baby's howls of protest were getting louder.

"Then what did that sign we just passed say?"

"I wasn't paying attention."

" 'Jesus Saves,' " Lucy offered.

Mat ignored her. "What about the big sign at the campground office? Right next to the front door?"

"It didn't interest me, so I didn't bother to read it."

Once again, the teenager piped up. " 'No open fires.' "

Nealy shot her a glare. "Don't you have something better to do with your time?"

"No." Lucy handed her sister an empty paper cup, but Button threw it to the floor with a yowl.

They rounded a bend and an old bridge came into view spanning a narrow ribbon of water at the bottom of a gentle hill. Built of weathered brown wood, it had a faded tin roof that might once have been painted red, and a pockmarked metal sign warning away vehicles over ten feet high. Even though this was West Virginia instead of Madison County, Iowa, the bridge was so picturesque she expected to see Clint Eastwood and Meryl Streep emerge from the dark interior. It was Americana at its very best, and she sighed. "Isn't this wonderful?"

When neither of her traveling companions responded, she chose to believe the bucolic beauty had left them too moved to speak.

"Let's stretch our legs." She parked Mabel on the shoulder. "Lucy, you can get your sister."

"She's not poison, you know. The two of you could carry her once in a while."

Nealy pretended not to hear.

"We're not staying long," Mat declared. "Two minutes, and then we're heading for the highway."

"Two minutes it is." There was no way two minutes would do it.

Outside, everything was drowning in sunlight, and the warm, humid air carried the fragrance of dust, grass, and country road. The river was low, as if it hadn't rained for a while, and the sounds were pure music: water lapping over rock, birdsong, the chirp of crickets and buzz of bees. On each side of the bridge a grassy bank covered with wildflowers sloped down to the water. Lucy set the baby in the grass.

"Gah!" She chortled and clapped her hands.

"It's your turn to watch her." Lucy took off for the interior of the bridge before Nealy could protest.

"Gah!" The baby made an unsuccessful lunge for a bumblebee.

"Watch it, Button. Those things aren't friendly."

"I thought her name was Marigold." Coffee mug in hand, Mat emerged from the Winnebago.

"Lucy says her mother called her Button. Bring the quilt that's in the back, will you?" She probably wouldn't stay on it, but it might keep her from getting too dirty.

Nealy hadn't failed to notice that Lucy had bathed her early that morning. Sunlight glinted in her dandelion hair, and her worn clothes were clean. She found herself wondering if any of the National Merit Scholarship winners she'd hosted at the White House would have taken such good care of a pesky baby sister.

Mat reappeared with the quilt. Nealy took it from him and tossed it down on the slope. She set the baby on it, but Button immediately headed for the open range. Her overalls protected her from the prickly grass, and she grew entranced with a butterfly hovering over a clump of buttercups. She sped toward it, then settled back on her bottom to issue an indignant protest as it flew away.

Nealy sat on the quilt and was surprised when Mat sprawled down beside her. She sighed and breathed deeply, savoring every moment of this stolen summer day.

"I don't usually get drunk, you know."

She closed her eyes and tilted her face into the sun. "Uhm."

"I mean it. I'm not much of a drinker."

"Good, because I don't think the girls should be exposed to that sort of thing."

She opened her eyes and saw that he was watching her. Something in his gaze made her feel as if she were being bombarded with a shower of sparks. He took his time before he looked away.

"They were probably exposed to a lot more when Sandy was alive."

Nealy realized she didn't want to hear about Mat's ex-wife, and she stood up. "Watch the baby, will you? I want to walk through the bridge."

"Hey! You're the nanny here, not me."

"I'm taking a coffee break."

Just like that, she left him behind and headed for the covered bridge. Mat glared at her back as she disappeared inside. It would serve her right if he dropped her off at the next truck stop and let her fend for herself. But he knew he wouldn't do it. She might not be the devoted child-care provider of his dreams, but she was the best he had. She was also an enigma.

It was hard to reconcile that upper-crust, Presbyterian bearing with her abundant good nature and boundless, almost childlike enthusiasm. She certainly was entertaining. Or at least she'd entertained him yesterday. This morning's hangover had pretty much put a damper on fun.

A flicker of movement caught his attention. Something pink. He looked up in time to see the Demon crawling backward down the grassy bank, heading directly for the river. His coffee flew as he threw down his mug and shot to his feet.

The baby was moving with lightning speed and fierce determination. The soles of his shoes slipped in the grass as he scrambled after her.

Without warning, her arms flew out and she began to slide. Her sneakers hit the water, and, a heartbeat later, the rest of her followed.

The river wasn't high, but it was too deep for a baby, and he watched in horror as her blond head immediately disappeared. He lost his footing, righted himself, and waded in after her.

The water hit him just above the knees. It was muddy. Too muddy to see anything. Then he caught a flash of pink traveling in the current and grabbed for it.

She came up with open, startled eyes, arms and feet dangling. He'd caught her by the back straps of her overalls.

She blinked, gasped for air, then coughed. He set her in the crook of his arm while she got her breath back. As his own heartbeat tried to return to normal, he felt the muddy river bottom sucking at his shoes. He barely managed to pull them free as he made his way out of the water.

She finally stopped coughing. For a few seconds she was still, and then he felt her chest expand as she took a deep breath. He knew exactly what was coming and tried to forestall it.

"Don't cry!"

Nell and Lucy were still inside the bridge, but he'd never hear the end of it if they found out he'd almost let the Demon drown. He looked down at the baby. River water dripped from her hair into her eyes. Her mouth was opening, her forehead puckering in outrage. The first chord of what was guaranteed to be a symphony of outrage began to emerge.

"Stop right there!" Shifting his hands so they were beneath her arms, he drew her up so she could look right in his eyes and know he meant business. "You just took a little water. It's no big deal. You didn't even come close to drowning."

The fierce pucker between those two small eyebrows eased. Her eyes widened, and she released the breath she'd been holding.

"No big deal," he said more quietly. "Got it?"

She stared at him.

Her pink overalls would never be the same, and she'd lost one of her sneakers. He quickly slipped off the other and pitched it into the trees.

Bickering female voices were coming from the covered bridge. Now he was in for it. He thought fast. "We're going back in that water."

"Gah?"

He stepped out of his own sodden shoes, returned her to the crook of his arm, and walked back into the river.

She buried her face in his shirt.

"Don't be a pansy."

She looked up and gave him a four-tooth grin.

"That's more like it, you little she-devil."

But when he tried to lower her into the water, she stiffened and dug her fingers into his arm.

"Relax, will you? I'm not going to put your face in."

"Nuh-nuh-nuh!"

It didn't take a degree in child psychology to translate that one. He realized he was going to have to do this with her, just as he'd done it with all his sisters. With a sigh of resignation, he put her to his shoulder and sank down into the muddy river.

She drew back and beamed at him. Oh, man, she was going to be a killer someday, with those baby blues and melty smiles. "Yeah, yeah. Save it for somebody who cares."

She smacked his jaw with the flat of her hand, then turned and smacked the water. It splashed in his face. He blinked it away and lowered her into the current.

"What are you doing?" Nell came charging out of the bridge, a pregnant commando wearing khaki shorts, a blue maternity top trimmed with daisies, and small white sandals. Tendrils of hair as golden brown as summer wheat flew around her flushed cheeks, and those amazing blue eyes, exactly the same color as the sky, were blazing. "Get the baby out of that dirty water right now!"

She flew down the slope. "Children can get typhoid from river water!"

He glanced down at the Demon, who seemed to be having a pretty good time as long as he didn't let her sink too low. "I don't think typhoid is too common in West Virginia."

Lucy emerged from the bridge and stared down at them.

Nell stopped at the edge of the river, hand to chest, face pale. He realized she was genuinely upset and wondered how she'd react if she knew he'd almost let the baby drown. "Will you calm down, for pete's sake? She's fine."

"She's fully dressed!"

"Yeah, well, I'm a guy. Guys don't think about things like that."

"*You're* fully dressed!"

"The whole thing was sort of an impulse."

She looked down at his muddy shoes lying on the bank. "I'll say."

He went on the offensive. "I slipped and got my shoes wet. Then I figured, what the hell?"

"She's going to catch cold."

"It's got to be eighty." He pulled the baby from the water and stood.

"*Nuh!*" She gave a shriek of protest, then began to twist, trying to get back in the water.

"Distract her, or you're really in for it." Lucy called down from the top of the slope.

Her shrieks were building in volume. "How am I supposed to do that?" he asked.

"She likes animal sounds, especially cows. Moo."

He shot Lucy a disgusted look, then shoved the screaming baby toward Nell. "Here. Distract her."

Nell clasped her arms behind her back and stepped away. "I don't know how."

The Demon's fists were going everywhere and she'd started to kick. *Shit.* He turned around and carried her back into the water.

He'd be damned if he'd moo.

8

MAT GAZED DOWN AT THE NAKED BABY PLAYING WITH his toes in the bottom of the shower stall. How had this *happened*? *How had he ended up taking a shower with a baby?* Now, taking a shower with Nell, that would be different.

He belatedly remembered that big, pregnant belly and shook off the image. They were still parked by the covered bridge, and at this rate, they weren't going to make it to Iowa before the Demon hit puberty. He slicked the last of the soap from his chest and decided he'd been caught in one of those nightmares where he was trying to get somewhere, but no matter what he did, he couldn't make it.

A frightening thought struck him. First he'd acquired two kids. Now he'd picked up a woman. It was as if some satanic force were building a family around him.

"How are you doing in there?" Nell called through the door.

The Demon bent forward and sank all four of her teeth into the top of his foot. He yelped, wedged himself down to scoop her up. "You little—"

"We have no idea what kind of microorganisms were swimming in that river water," Nell said. "Are you using lots of soap on her?"

He shoved her under the spray. "A whole bar."

"You'd better not be trying any funny business with

her in there, Jorik!" Lucy exclaimed. "I mean it!"

"Hush, Lucy," Nell said. "Don't make him any madder than he already is."

The Demon was starting to sputter, so he pulled her out from under the water, then tucked her against his bare chest. She went after one of his nipples with her fingernails.

"Ouch!"

"You're hurting her!" Lucy shouted. "I know you are!"

"I'm not hurting her!"

The Demon didn't like anybody yelling but herself, and she started that lip-quiver stuff.

"I'm immune," he growled down at her.

The quiver disappeared and a beamy smile took its place. He could swear he saw adoration glimmering in those blue eyes, and every bit of it was directed at him. "Forget it. I can't be bought."

She gave a delighted baby vampire squeal, turned her head into his chest, and bit.

"Damn it!"

Just then the shower spray faded to a trickle. He'd been in such a hurry to get away from Sandy's place that he hadn't bothered to fill the water tank all the way, and last night at the campground he'd been too preoccupied with his bottle of Jim Beam to finish the job.

"None of this would be happening if you hadn't taken the baby swimming in that dirty river," Nell felt dutybound to remind him, sounding just like a nagging wife.

He spun the Demon so her teeth were facing outward and squeezed himself through the tiny shower door and out into the minuscule bathroom. As he reached for a towel, he banged his elbow into the wall. *"Damn it!"*

"Two *damn its* already," Nell said from the other side. "It doesn't seem to be going very well."

"If you don't want to see a naked man, you'd better get back from that door." He wrapped the towel around the Demon, opened the door, and set her on the floor outside. "She's all yours."

He shut the door in the face of Nell's amusement. The baby immediately began to howl.

"She wants you," Nell said.

"Tell her to take a number."

He heard something that sounded like a laugh and he smiled—his first of this miserable day. As soon as he had the towel anchored around his hips, he opened the door and stepped out.

"Gah!" The baby reached up for him, her own towel still draped over her head. She yelped as he moved past her to the back and pushed the sliding door shut.

He heard a scurrying sound and knew she was crawling after him.

"Come here!" Lucy exclaimed. "You don't like him. He's a jerk."

Apparently the Demon didn't agree because a small head butted into the door he had just closed. There was a blessed moment of silence, and then all hell broke loose.

The eruption wasn't the pathetic whimpering of an upset baby. Instead, it was the outraged howl of a female who'd been denied her man. He whipped off his towel in frustration. Why couldn't Sandy have given birth to a *boy* baby?

Nell began to moo.

Once Button had been cleaned up, she needed to be fed, then they had to wait for her stomach to settle. Nealy watched from Mabel's window as Mat paced along the road, the soles of his shoes attacking the pavement, a deep frown of displeasure creasing his forehead. Every once in a while, he'd pick up a stone and hurl it into the river. Once he actually dropped down on the side of the road and performed a long series of pushups. His impatience annoyed her. Why couldn't he just enjoy the day?

As Lucy settled Button back into her car seat, Nealy opened the door and stepped out. "I think we can give it a try now."

"It's about time."

"There's no reason to be so grouchy."

He pushed past her—pushed past the First Lady of the United States!—and ducked into the motor home.

"Da!" Button squealed from her car seat.

He looked so ill-tempered that Nealy hurried forward. "Maybe I should drive. You've got road rage written all over you."

"Maybe you should sit down and watch for signs so we can get back on a decent highway." He squeezed behind the wheel.

"I'm bored," Lucy said. "I want to go to a mall."

"If I hear another word, I swear I'll tie up all three of you, throw you in the back, and lock the door."

Nealy looked at Lucy. Lucy looked at her. They had a moment of silent communication. Only Button was happy. She finally had her man back in sight.

They rode in silence for twenty miles, past tobacco fields, hardscrabble farms, and several tiny hamlets. They were passing through a slightly larger town not far from the interstate when Nealy heard an ominous thud coming from Mabel's front end. Mat immediately slowed, applied the brakes, and turned the wheel to the right, only to have it fail to respond. He cursed.

"What's wrong?"

"I've lost steering."

"I told you this thing was a pile of junk," Lucy offered unnecessarily from the back.

Mat maneuvered the vehicle off onto the shoulder at the very edge of the parking lot for an ancient drive-in restaurant called Hush Pups.

"Cool. Can I get a Slurpee?"

"Hush, Lucy. What do you think is wrong, Mat?"

"You know that engine pinging that was bothering me?"

"Yes."

"I don't think this is it."

"Oh."

He didn't move, just stared through the windshield. "Busted tie rod. Something like that."

He looked so forlorn that she reached over and gave his arm an impulsive squeeze. He turned his head and studied her. Their eyes met, and something hot leaped between them. Embarrassed, she slowly removed her hand. Her palm felt warm where she'd touched him.

She rose and turned to Lucy. "Let's go spend Mat's money on junk food while he figures out what's wrong with Mabel."

Hush Pups didn't offer the luxury of indoor seating, and Nealy camped out with the girls at one of three metal tables just beyond the parking lot, where they watched the tow truck haul both Mat and Mabel away. While Lucy ate, Nealy chased after Button. Eventually, however, the baby grew tired and curled up for a nap on the quilt.

"I'm totally bored."

"Why don't you go explore? Just check back."

Lucy gazed at her little sister, then studied Nealy suspiciously.

Nealy smiled and spoke quietly. "I'll watch her every minute."

Lucy's brown-painted lips did their best to sneer. "Like I'd care."

"Oh, you'd care, all right. Give it up, Lucy. The day Button got you for a big sister was the luckiest day of her life."

Lucy blinked and turned away, but not before Nealy caught a glimpse of the vulnerable fourteen-year-old who lived beneath that tough facade.

After she left, Nealy stretched out her legs on the

quilt, propped her back against one leg of the metal table, and contented herself watching the life of the small West Virginia town pass by.

She'd just started to doze when an ancient red Oldsmobile pulled into the parking lot and Mat climbed out of the driver's side, looking even more ominous than he had earlier. "I was right. It's a busted tie rod, and it won't be ready until tomorrow morning." He stopped next to her. "Mabel's parked at the garage, which seems to be part of the county junkyard. There's some kind of landfill next to it, and the whole place smells like a Mafia burial ground."

"So we can't spend the night there."

He slumped down into the chair across from her. "There's a Holiday Inn about five miles away."

He looked like a man in desperate need of a drink, and she pushed what was left of her watery Coke at him. "I'll get you a hamburger."

"See if you can find one with some nice *E. coli* tucked inside."

"I believe it comes with the order."

He smiled, then fastened his lips around her straw and took a sip. She'd expected him to drink from the rim, and she stared at him for a moment. He set down the paper cup. Something crackled between them, an awareness that made her edgy and self-conscious.

She'd never met anyone who emanated so much male sexual energy. She saw it in his eyes, the set of his shoulders, the curl of his fingers. She heard it in that blast-furnace voice. It was almost as if he'd managed to escape female influence. He belonged on the back of a bucking horse, behind the wheel of a ship, building roads, or leading a military charge.

She shook off her fanciful thoughts and headed for the drive-in window. She knew nothing about men like Mat Jorik, and furthermore, she didn't intend to learn.

Lucy returned just as Mat finished eating. She

watched Button try to crawl up his leg into his lap, then looked over at the ancient Oldsmobile. "Couldn't you get a Camero or something?"

"They were fresh out."

Button spent the ride to the garage attempting to catch Mat's attention by alternately gurgling at him and shrieking. He determinedly ignored her. When they reached the garage, Nealy discovered the adjoining junk-yard was just as smelly as he'd indicated. She was re-lieved when they'd finished loading everything they needed into the car and set off for the Holiday Inn.

The desk clerk regarded Mat uncertainly when he asked for two rooms as far away from each other as possible. Nealy had no intention of taking sole respon-sibility for the girls, and she quickly stepped forward. "Don't pay any attention to him. He's a big kidder."

They ended up with adjoining rooms.

As Nealy set her satchel on the bed, she tried to figure out what was missing. And then she realized it was the smell of fresh paint. Every hotel in the world wanted to put its best foot forward when the President or First Lady stayed there, and this nearly always meant redec-orating the largest suite. Nealy had fallen asleep with a headache from paint fumes more times than she cared to remember.

She saw Lucy standing at the window, gazing at the pool below. "Why don't you go swim?" She checked the floor for hazards, then set Button down on it.

"I don't have a suit."

"Wear what you have on. You can wash it out when you come in."

"Maybe."

Nealy realized Button had disappeared, and she rushed through the open door into the adjoining room, then stopped as she saw Mat standing on the other side of the king-sized bed with his head buried in the T-shirt he was pulling off. Why couldn't he keep his clothes on?

He had exactly the sort of chest that she'd always found most attractive. Broad at the shoulder, narrow at the waist. A little dark hair. Muscles that were well defined but not bulky. She was very much enjoying the sight until she realized he was watching her.

The corner of his mouth kicked up. "See anything you like?"

She searched her mind to find a plausible excuse for staring at him. "Didn't you just put that shirt on after your shower?"

"It got greasy when I was checking out Mabel. And why do you care?"

"Because . . . we all seem to be running out of clothes."

"You can do our laundry tomorrow."

"Me?" She'd never done laundry in her life. "Not part of my job description. I'm the nanny. Remember?"

"Da!"

He winced, then frowned down at the baby, who had a death grip on his jeans.

"She's too young to know what that word means," Nealy said. "Why don't you just pick her up? I'm sure if you showed her a little attention, she'd be content to go off and play."

"Forget it."

"Try playing hard to get, Button. Men don't like it when you're too obvious. At least that's what I've heard."

"No personal experience?"

She made a noncommittal murmur, braced herself, then leaned down to pick Button up. But the baby wanted Mat, and as Nealy rose, she lunged toward him and grabbed his shirt, throwing Nealy off balance. "Oops. Sorry."

He caught her automatically, and his chest felt warm

against her side. She'd spent so many years suppressing her sexual feelings that denial had become automatic, but this contact was a shock treatment, reminding her she was still a woman.

He didn't move away. Instead, a slow smile caught the edges of his mouth and traveled right up into those gray eyes. "I thought you didn't believe in being obvious."

Was he coming on to her? No one ever came on to Cornelia Case. When she'd been in college, she'd had to ask boys out herself because they were too intimidated to approach the daughter of the Vice President. And they were definitely too intimidated by all the Secret Service hovering around to try to get her into bed. Even so, she was certain she could have managed a few sexual encounters here and there, but she hadn't done it.

From her earliest years, she'd been raised with the constant reminder that the smallest misstep on her part would bring disgrace to her father. Eventually, her caution had become so ingrained that she lived a shadow life, suppressing her natural curiosity, her sense of adventure, her sexuality, suppressing so much that would have helped her figure out who she was. When she'd met Dennis, she'd been a virgin.

For once, the memory of Dennis didn't bring her pain. Maybe time was finally starting to do its healing job, or maybe she was simply too distracted by the man standing before her.

The baby lunged again. Mat shifted his weight against Nealy, then looked at her oddly.

"I—I'll take her down to the pool," she said.

His reply was slow in coming. "You do that."

Button howled as Nealy carried her from the room.

Nealy spent the next few hours sitting at the side of the baby pool worrying about Button getting a sunburn or drowning. Since the pool sat in the shade and the

only time the baby was more than a few feet away occurred when Lucy took her in the big pool, she knew
she was being foolish. Some of her fretting might be a
defense to keep from thinking too much about Mat.

Maybe the freedom of not being herself was affecting
her in more ways than she'd imagined. Who was this
Nell Kelly person? In addition to having an active libido,
she didn't seem to care much about offending people.
Nealy smiled. She liked everything about Nell except
her fascination with Mat Jorik's body.

She told herself it wasn't unreasonable to be thinking
about sex. She might be repressed, but she was still human, and Mat was so different from the men she knew.
Too assertive in his dealings with women to be politi-
cally correct. All hard muscle and square jaw, broad
hands and blunt-tipped fingers. She loved the way he
smelled of soap, shaving cream, and skin. He was big
and brawny, and she liked his teeth.

His teeth? Oh, God, she was losing her mind. With a
groan, she turned her attention to helping Button pour
water into Styrofoam cups without drinking it.

Lucy eventually got bored and decided to go up to
the room to watch TV. Before she left, she told Nealy
she was a moron for not knowing that Button needed a
bottle, and she took her little sister with her.

Nealy sighed and settled back on the lounge, determined not to think about Lucy, Button, or Mat Jorik, but
that only led to worrying about money. Steelworkers
made good salaries, but this was proving to be an expensive trip. Could Mat handle the repairs for Mabel on
top of the other trip expenses? And did she really want
to spend the rest of her grand adventure in two pairs of
shorts, a couple of tops, and a change of underwear?

She had to have money, and Terry Ackerman was the
only person she could trust to get it for her without turning her in. She made her way to a pay phone and called
him.

*   *   *

FBI Special Agent Antonia "Toni" DeLucca pulled out of the parking lot of the truck stop near McConnellsburg, Pennsylvania, where Jimmy Briggs had stolen the Chevy Corsica. She and her partner had questioned employees and truckers, but no one had seen anything. In a few hours, they'd come back to talk to the workers on the next shift.

She gazed across the seat of the government-issued Taurus at her new partner and wondered how she'd ended up with someone named Jason. Secret Service Special Agent *Jason Williams*. Nobody over the age of thirty had the first name of Jason. And maybe that was what irritated her the most because Jason Williams wouldn't see thirty for another four years, while Toni had passed it more than a decade and a half ago.

When Toni had entered the Bureau in the late seventies, she had been one of only two hundred female agents. More than twenty years later, she'd managed to survive the gender wars by being tougher and smarter than everybody she'd started out with. She'd considered it her duty to rise through the ranks, only to discover that what she loved most was working as a field agent. Three years ago she'd gone back to doing just that, and she'd never been happier.

Late last night she'd been ordered to report to the resident agency in Harrisburg, which was too small to have a field office, and at the early morning briefing, she and the other agents who'd been called in had learned of Cornelia Case's disappearance. As concerned as she was about what had happened to the nation's First Lady, she was excited to be part of an elite task force of agents assigned to find her. Unfortunately, she'd been given a new partner—one who wasn't even with the Bureau. And, although she'd worked with the Service before, the agents had been seasoned veterans, not twenty-six-year-olds named Jason.

He had that scrubbed-up white bread look of a lot of Secret Service agents. Short light brown hair, symmetrical features, and what looked like a tiny zit on his chin. How could they have given her a partner who still got zits?

They'd also given her a partner who didn't have to battle his weight or worry about wrinkles. A partner with no gray in his hair. She didn't have to look in the rearview mirror to know how much of it threaded her own short dark hair. Still, her olive skin was relatively unlined, and even though her shape was curvier than she'd like, she was still fit.

So far, she and the kid hadn't said more to each other than they needed to, but now Toni decided it was time to put her new partner through his paces.

"So tell me something, kid. Whose butt did you have to kiss for this assignment?"

"Nobody's."

"Yeah, tell me another one."

He shrugged.

She was Italian, and she hated being put off with white bread shrugs. The kid sank another rung lower in her estimation. "Interesting. All you had to do was show up, and they decided to put you on an elite task force. Aren't you the lucky one? In the Bureau, we have to work for assignments like these."

He turned to her and smiled. "I was handed this assignment because I'm very good at what I do."

"They gave me a real live hotshot," she drawled. "Isn't this my lucky day?"

He frowned, so she knew that she'd scored. Her satisfaction faded, however, as she realized the frown wasn't a sign of irritation but deep thought.

"How bad do you want this?" he asked.

"What are you talking about?"

"How bad do you want to find Aurora?"

Aurora was the Service's code name for Cornelia

Case. The members of a president's family always had code names that started with the same letter. Dennis Case had been Arrow.

She took her time deciding how to answer. "I wouldn't mind having it on my record."

"Not good enough. And not honest, either. The word is, you're the one who's a hotshot."

"Is that so? What else have you heard?"

"That you're arrogant, hard to work with, and one of the best field agents in the Bureau."

"Snoopy little shit, aren't you?" She decided to turn the tables on him. "I don't like failure. And I don't like scrubbed-up kids who think just going through the motions means they've done their job."

"Then we've got something in common."

"I doubt it. Your career's so new it doesn't matter whether you're the one who finds Aurora."

"It matters to me. Setting aside the fact that it's hard to stomach the idea of losing the First Lady, I'm ambitious."

"Yeah? How ambitious?"

"Ambitious enough to know that finding Aurora gets me noticed by the director, the Secretary, even the President."

She gazed at his earnest, unlined face. "Lots of people are ambitious, hotshot. It's doing the work that's hard."

His eyes skimmed from her graying hair to her slightly overweight body. "Oh, I don't think I'll have too much trouble keeping up with you."

He'd thrown down the gauntlet, and she smiled. "Yeah? Well, we'll see about that, little boy. We'll see which one of us knows the most about how to find a missing First Lady."

Both girls were cranky, so Nealy ordered room service for them and pretended she wasn't annoyed with Mat for not returning. Lucy watched a movie, then fell asleep with Button curled beside her. Nealy showered, strapped the detestable padding around her middle, and slipped into her nightgown.

When she came out of the bathroom, she was startled to see Mat standing in the open doorway between their rooms. He was barefoot and his T-shirt hung out of the denim shorts he'd changed into earlier. His body seemed even larger silhouetted against the light, and despite the two girls sleeping on the bed, she felt as if they were very much alone.

She spoke softly, her tone light. "So you decided not to abandon us after all?"

"I want to talk to you."

His low, harsh tone made her uneasy. "I'm tired. Let's talk tomorrow."

"We're going to talk right now." He jerked his head toward his room. She thought about refusing, but something in his expression told her it would be a waste of breath.

He shut the door behind them, and his eyes were wintry. "I don't like being lied to."

Although he hadn't touched her, she realized she was backed against the wall. "What do you—"

Her words got lost as he caught the hem of her nightgown and pulled it up. She tried to jerk away, but he clasped her arm.

"Stop it!"

He stared down at her, taking in the pillow tied to her waist and the lavender lace panties just below.

She struggled, pushing against his chest, but he was too strong for her. "Let me go."

He'd seen what he wanted, and he slowly released her.

The fabric slid back down over her legs. She tried to push past him, but that big solid body was in the way.

His eyes bored through her. "You haven't told me the truth about anything."

He knew her pregnancy was phony, but did he know who she was? She tried to swallow her panic. "I—I told you I wasn't endangering you or the girls. That's all that counts."

"Not in my book."

"We can talk about this in the morning."

"You're not going anywhere." He caught her shoulder and pushed her into the chair.

In all her life, no one had ever manhandled her, and she was so astonished she sputtered. "That was uncalled for!"

He splayed one hand on each arm of the chair, caging her. A cold finger ran down her spine as she gazed up into those hard eyes. This man had rough edges that she couldn't even begin to comprehend.

"Play time's over, princess. Let's start with your real name."

Her *name*? He didn't know who she was! She gulped for air. "Don't call me that," she managed. "And Kelly *is* my real name. My maiden name." She'd been thinking on her feet all her life, and she struggled to put a story together. "There's no reason for you to know my married name."

"You're married?"

"I'm . . . divorced, but my ex-husband won't accept it. His family is very powerful, quite wealthy. I—I need some time to . . . to—" What? Her mind went blank. She regarded him haughtily. "My personal life is none of your business."

"You made it my business."

He straightened so she was no longer caged, but he didn't move away. She struggled to sound reasonable. "It's complicated. I needed to disappear for a while, that's all. There might be some . . . detectives chasing me, so I decided to disguise myself as a pregnant woman to throw them off." She couldn't let him push her around any longer, and she glared at him. "Stop looming over me. I don't like it."

"Good." He didn't move, and as she gazed at that tough, grim mouth she realized how fond she'd grown of his smile. He didn't use it a lot, but when he did, it melted her bones.

She knew scores of military men, so she understood the value of a retaliatory strike. "You're going to be nasty about this, aren't you? Even though it has nothing to do with you. You physically attacked me!"

"I didn't attack you." He scowled, but he backed off half a step.

"Why didn't you just ask me if I was really pregnant? And how did you know, by the way?"

"You fell against me, remember? Right after we got here when you were holding the Demon. Pregnant women's bellies don't feel like pillows."

"Oh." She remembered how strangely he'd looked at her. At the time, she'd thought he was reacting to the sexual chemistry she'd felt percolating between them, but apparently the percolation was only working one way. She rose. "Your behavior is inexcusable and boorish!"

"*Boorish*? You do have some vocabulary, princess. What comes next? Off with his head?" He rested the heel of one hand against the wall, about a foot from her head. "In case you haven't noticed, you're alone in a motel room with a man you don't know real well."

His words were an implied threat, but she wasn't afraid. Mat might be stubborn and crotchety. He might not have any soft edges, and he certainly wasn't in touch with his feminine side, but she couldn't imagine him physically hurting her.

She regarded him levelly. "Back off. You need me a lot more than I need you." That wasn't true, but he didn't know it. "Starting right now, I don't want any more questions about my past. I'm not involved in anything illegal, and I've said it doesn't concern you. You'll just have to accept that."

"Or what? You'll take away all my castles?"

"And marry you off to the ugliest lady in the kingdom."

She'd hoped to make him smile, but he looked as grouchy as a bear being poked with a stick. "Take off that damned pillow. It looks stupid."

"Go pound your chest and eat a banana." Oh, God, she was playing with fire, and she didn't even care.

He went completely still. "What did you say?"

"Uhmm . . . nothing. A slight case of Tourette's. It comes and goes."

He almost smiled. "You don't scare easily do you?"

"Well . . . you are acting a bit like an ape."

"As opposed to your civilized rich boy ex-husband who's hunting you down with a team of detectives?"

"On the positive side, he . . . uh . . . hates bananas."

"You're making this up. Every bit of it. There isn't any ex-husband."

She lifted her chin. "Then how did I get pregnant? Answer that one, wise guy."

The corner of his mouth quirked, and he shook his head. "All right. I give up. We'll play this your way for a while."

"Thank you."

"Except for one thing . . . I have to know the truth about whether or not you're still married."

This time it wasn't hard for her to meet his eyes. "No. I promise you. I'm not married."

He nodded, and she saw that he believed her. "All right. But I don't want to see that damned pillow around your waist ever again. I'm serious about this. Traveling with Sandy's kids and me is all the camouflage you're going to get. Understand?"

She realized she wasn't going to be able to fight him on this, but would the presence of two children be enough to hide her identity? "What am I going to say to Lucy?"

"Tell her you gave birth during the night, then sold the baby to a band of gypsies because it reminded you of her."

"I will not."

"Then tell her the truth. She can handle it."

She shrugged, something he could interpret any way he chose.

Silence fell between them. She heard a door thud across the hall, the clatter of a room service cart, and she suddenly felt awkward.

He smiled. "At least now I don't feel like such a pervert."

"What do you mean?"

"For getting turned on by a pregnant lady."

Her skin prickled. "Really?"

"Don't act like you're surprised."

"I don't think men usually get . . . turned on by me." A lot of men liked her, and even more were attracted to her power. But they weren't attracted to her sexually. She was too powerful. Her position, her *dignity,* had leached the sexuality out of her. "I really turn you on?"

"Isn't that what I just said?"

"Yes, but . . ."

"Want a demonstration?" The husky note in his voice felt like a caress.

"I— Oh, no . . . No, I don't think—"

He smiled and came toward her. His jeans brushed her nightgown, and as she gazed up at him, she had the unfamiliar sensation of feeling petite. And very female.

His big hands settled at her waist, and he drew her close. He was smiling a little bit, as if he knew a secret that she didn't. She realized he was going to kiss her, and she was going to let him.

Would she remember how? Surely it was one of those things a person wouldn't forget, like riding a—

Their mouths met. Her eyelids drifted shut, and she felt herself melt against him. Then she stopped thinking and simply gave in to the sensations.

Those big hands moved along her spine, around her sides. His lips parted. Demanded. She felt as if she were drowning.

And then panic set in because he didn't know he was kissing a national institution. He didn't understand he was kissing someone who knew all about how to be First Lady . . . but very little about what it took to be a woman.

9

Nealy took a deep breath as she broke the kiss.

Mat let her go, then gave her a slow smile. "You kiss like a little girl."

His smile took the sting out of his words, but they still hurt. Without knowing it, he'd touched on her most painful insecurity. Still, she managed to respond with the perfect composure of a woman who'd been born to rule. "How many little girls have you kissed?"

"More than you can imagine."

"Really? How bizarre."

"Not too bizarre. I have seven younger sisters."

"You're kidding."

"Believe me, it's not something I kid about." He walked over to the mini bar. "Would you like a drink?"

She knew she should leave while she had the chance, but she didn't want to. Instead, she wanted to be reckless and irresponsible, more like easygoing Nell Kelly than uptight Cornelia Case. "I don't suppose there's a nice merlot in there."

He bent down to look. "There's a merlot, but it's got a screw top, so I don't know how nice it is." He withdrew the bottle, then crossed his arms and lifted an eyebrow at her stomach. "No drinking while you're pregnant."

She smiled and self-consciously slipped her hands under her nightgown from the back to release the straps. The pillow fell.

He eyed her baggy nightgown as he unscrewed the lid. "Not much of an improvement."

She picked up the pillow and held it in her lap as she sat in the chair. "I had to leave all my sexy peignoirs behind."

"Too bad. And I mean that from the bottom of my heart." He poured the wine into a glass, handed it to her, then pulled a Coke out for himself. "How's come you're so skittish?"

"I'm not skittish," she said defensively. "Just because I didn't slobber all over you doesn't mean I'm skittish."

He threw a pillow against the headboard and stretched out on the bed with the Coke can propped on his chest. As he leaned back and crossed his bare ankles, he looked a lot more comfortable than she felt.

"So you're not attracted to me." There was a glint in his eye, a subtle male audacity that spoke of a wealth of sexual confidence.

She felt like a kid seeing how close she could get to the traffic before someone swatted her back. "I didn't say that."

"You *are* attracted to me."

"I didn't say that, either. And why should you care? After all, I kiss like a little girl." She wanted to bite her tongue. Why hadn't she just let it go?

"I didn't mean it as an insult."

"It's certainly not a compliment."

"I apologize."

"It's just not a nice thing to say."

"I'll never say it again."

The note of amusement in his voice made her snappish. "I supposed if I'd tried to remove your tonsils with my tongue, you'd have been happy."

"I've already apologized."

"I can't abide kisses like that. They're suffocating."

"Each to his own, I guess."

"*Her* own, and taking the plaque off someone's teeth is my idea of dental work, not a romantic kiss. People should keep their tongues in their own mouths."

"I guess this means I shouldn't ask you about oral sex."

"*What?*"

He threw back his head and let out a bellow of a laugh.

She flushed, but as she took a long sip of wine, she was surprised she wasn't more embarrassed.

"Come on, Nell. The night's long and we're all alone. Tell Father Mathias where this hang-up of yours comes from."

"Mathias? I thought your name was Matthew."

"Mathias is the Slovak version. It's Mat with one *t*. My sisters' doing. Unfortunately, it stuck. And don't change the subject on me. I take it your ex-husband isn't much of a kisser."

She sipped her wine, then found herself saying, "Not with me anyway."

"With someone else?"

She hesitated, then nodded slowly. He had no idea who she was, and she was so tired of pretending she and Dennis had been blissfully happy. At least Nell Kelly could tell some small part of the truth.

"A lot of someones?"

"No, only one. He was faithful. He just wasn't faithful to me." She toyed with the pillow in her lap. "He wasn't anything with me."

There was a long pause. "Are you trying to tell me you didn't have sex with your husband?"

She realized what she'd almost revealed. "Yes, of course I did. It just wasn't great sex."

That was a lie. There had been a few weeks of fumbling attempts that had left her with this humiliating uncertainty about whether or not she was still a virgin. She felt like a fool. All through high school and college, her healthy body had ached for a man's touch, but she'd been raised to be daddy's good girl, so she'd said no the few times a boy had gotten up the courage to ignore the Secret Service.

"The guy must have a problem."

A big one. He was buried six feet under at Arlington National Cemetery. She choked back a laugh that felt like a sob. "Are you sure I wasn't the one with the problem?"

He paused for a moment, and she realized he was really thinking it over. "Yeah, I'm sure."

She found herself smiling. "Thank you."

"Feeling a little insecure, are you?"

"A little."

"So he had great sex with his girlfriend, but not with you."

"I don't know what kind of sex he had with his ... his ... girlfriend."

He straightened, and his eyebrows shot together. "Crap."

"What?"

"It wasn't a girlfriend," he said slowly. "It was a guy."

Wine sloshed over the rim of her glass, and she sent the pillow tumbling as she jumped up from her chair. "That's ridiculous! Why would you say something like that? How could you even think it?"

"I don't know. It just popped into my head. And the corner of your mouth is tight again. Your ex-husband's gay. That's why you divorced him."

"No! That's absurd. It's ridiculous." She rubbed at the wine spill with her other hand. "If you'd ever met him ... He was—he is a very masculine man. Very good-looking. Athletic. The kind of man other men are comfortable around. You're completely wrong!"

He didn't say a word. He simply gazed at her, and his gray eyes were filled with pity.

She tried to curb her panic. Why had she been so reckless? It was a secret she'd kept for so long—the secret that would have brought down an administration and made the Clinton sex scandals look tame. The married President of the United States was a homosexual.

The only person who had known besides herself was Terry Ackerman, Dennis's oldest friend, deputy chief of staff, and lifelong lover. She stepped over the pillow she'd dropped and walked to the window carrying her wine. Through the sheers, she could see the lights of the swimming pool, and just beyond, a truck whizzing by on the highway.

Until Dennis and Terry had met during their junior year at Harvard, both had been in deep denial about their sexuality, but once they'd set eyes on each other, that was no longer possible. They had everything in common. They were from prominent families. Both were ambitious and popular with their peers, two young lions on the fast track to glory. They dated new girls every week and told themselves lies about the sexual fantasies they were having. But their attraction had been so strong that they were powerless against it.

She remembered the November night six weeks after she and Dennis were married when she'd finally forced her husband to confess the truth. They'd been campaigning in New York City and staying at the Waldorf-Astoria. She'd been miserable. Her marriage hadn't quite been consummated, and she'd finally realized it wasn't her fault.

Tears had clouded Dennis's eyes as he'd sat on the end of the bed and stared down at his hands, his voice so choked with guilt it had been hard to understand him.

"The moment Terry and I first looked at each other, we knew we'd found our only soul mate. Neither of us has ever looked at anyone else since." He'd gazed up at her, his golden brown eyes stricken. "Except for Terry, you're the best friend I've ever had. I do love you, Nealy."

"Like a sister," she said dully. "You love me like a sister."

"I'm sorry." His tears had glistened. "I'm so sorry."

His betrayal ran so deep, she wanted to die, and at that moment, she'd hated him.

"I had to have a wife if I wanted to be President," he said. "I'd always been so fond of you, and when your father started pushing us together, I—I—"

"You decided to use me," she'd murmured. "You knew I'd fallen in love with you, and you used me."

"I know," he whispered.

"How could you do it?"

"I want to be President," he said simply. "And there'd been some whispers."

She hadn't heard them. She'd never suspected a thing, not even before their marriage when he'd used the microscopic scrutiny they were receiving from the media as an excuse to postpone making love until they were married.

The morning after his confession she'd fled to Nantucket, where she'd sealed herself in the guest house of her father's estate and tried to come to terms with what had happened. She'd made up her mind to get a quick divorce. Dennis deserved nothing better.

But every time she picked up the phone to call her attorney, she set it back down. Dennis had betrayed her, but he wasn't evil. In every other way, he was the most decent man she knew. If she divorced him as he was launching his presidential campaign, she would ruin him. Was that what she wanted?

Part of her craved the revenge she deserved. But she'd never had an appetite for bloodlust, and her stomach rebelled each time she looked at the telephone.

It was Terry who'd finally talked her into continuing with the marriage. Terry, the funny, irreverent man she'd known as Dennis's oldest friend, had barged into the guest house, poured her a drink, and looked her straight in the eye.

"Don't divorce him, Nealy. Stick it out. You know there's not another man running who'll make as good a President." His expression had been filled with urgency as he took her hands and squeezed them. "Please, Nealy. He never meant to hurt you. I think he convinced himself he could pull it off and you'd never know."

"The lies people tell themselves." She'd walked out on Terry and wandered the beach for hours, but he was still waiting when she returned.

"I'll give him one term, and then I'm filing for divorce." Even as she spoke the words, she knew that something was dying inside her, all her romantic dreams.

Terry, who did deadly imitations of their political opponents and loved to laugh, had started to cry. She realized he'd made a devil's bargain of his own.

Afterward, Dennis did everything he could to show his gratitude. In all ways but the most essential, he was a wonderful husband. Although she could never entirely forgive him for his deceit, she didn't want to become a victim of her own bitterness, and she forced herself to accept his friendship.

Her relationship with Terry was more complex. She held the place that was rightfully his, and some part of him resented her for it. At the same time, he was an honorable man, and he tried to compensate by becoming her tireless defender. It had been he, rather than her hardworking husband, who protected her from her father's meddling. The night Dennis had died, she and Terry held each other, but even in the midst of her grief, she'd known his own ran deeper.

"How long did you stay married to him?"

"What?" She jumped as Mat's voice penetrated her thoughts.

"Your gay husband. How long were you married?"

"A—a few years. And he wasn't gay."

"Come on, Nell. Why are you still trying to protect him?"

Because now she had his legacy to guard, and in some ways that was an even bigger responsibility than being his First Lady.

Mat set his Coke on the nightstand. "There's a big hole in your story, you know. It's a little hard to imagine why he's trying so hard to find you."

"It's his family that wants to find me," she managed. "They're very conservative, and they're determined to protect their image."

He rose in a movement that was curiously graceful for such a large man. "Nell, I hope you've taken care of yourself. There are a lot bigger problems for women with gay husbands than a broken heart."

She didn't have to ask what he meant, and she wasn't going to explain that there was no need to worry. "My husband was never promiscuous; he just loved someone else . . . another *woman*," she repeated out of habit. "I'm not a fool, and I'm not a health risk to anyone. I was a blood donor less than a month ago. Can you say the same?"

"I'm not a fool, either," he said quietly.

There was only one reason to have a discussion like this, and she felt too raw at the moment to face it. She set down her wineglass and stood. "I'm tired."

"The night's young." He gazed over at her and smiled. "I'll bet I was wrong about that kissing thing because you sure don't look like a little girl, especially in that nightgown. Maybe we should try it again and see."

"Maybe we shouldn't." Oh, but she wanted to, which was why she made herself head for the door. "Thanks for the wine."

"I guess you don't have the courage of your convictions."

"I guess I wasn't born yesterday, either." She heard

him chuckle as she closed the door between their rooms.

Her skin felt hot. She couldn't believe how much she'd wanted to stay. But he was still only a step away from being a stranger, and she needed more time to think about this.

Button lay curled next to Lucy in the double bed. Nealy made a place for her on the floor, then gently picked her up. The baby snuggled against her breast. She brushed her lips against that warm, downy head, then gently laid her on the makeshift bed and crawled in next to her sister.

It was a long time before she fell asleep.

As soon as Nealy awakened the next morning, she crept into Mat's room to steal his keys so he couldn't take off in the Oldsmobile and leave her behind. Once she got inside, however, she simply stared.

He lay face down across the bed with the white sheet tangled at the base of his bare, tan back. His hair was dark against the pillow bunched so aggressively beneath his head, his hand curled in a fist. As she stood there watching, he stirred and shifted his weight so that one leg angled out from beneath the sheet. It was strong and muscular, lightly dusted with dark hair. The sight of him filled her with a deep, un-Cornelia-like hunger.

She remembered everything she'd told him in her reckless confession last night. It had been so tempting to hide inside another person's identity and spill her secrets. Tempting and foolish. She palmed the Olds keys, crept from the room, and made her way to the bathroom. This new day was a gift, and she refused to spoil it with old heartache.

An hour later and freshly showered, Mat poked his head into her room. He frowned as he saw the padding beneath her top. "I thought I told you I didn't want you wearing that again."

Button let out a squeal of delight as she caught sight

of him. She began to squirm to get away from Nealy, who was trying to dress her in her last clean outfit. "I believe you mentioned it."

"Well?"

"Are you under the illusion that I pay attention to you?"

"Da!"

"I want to go to the mall," Lucy said as she came out of the bathroom. Her hair was wet from her shower and, for once, it wasn't maroon.

"Nell's not pregnant," Mat announced. "That big stomach under her clothes is a pillow."

"No way."

He poked the padding before she could stop him. "It's bogus."

Lucy studied Nealy's stomach. "Why?"

"She robbed a bank, and she's on the run."

"Cool." For the first time Lucy regarded Nealy with respect. "So did you kill anybody or anything?"

Nealy spent a moment enjoying the fantasy of herself as Bonnie Parker. "I didn't rob a bank. Mat's just being cute. I'm . . . hiding from my ex-husband and his family."

"That's dumb." Lucy shoved her clothes into her bag.

"Yes, well, I'd appreciate it if you would keep this to yourself." She shot Mat a dark look. "Unlike *some* people who need to tell the world everything."

"Da!" The baby squealed as Nealy fastened the final snap on her romper and released her.

Mat winced.

"I'm going to the mall today whether anybody wants to or not," Lucy said.

Nealy saw trouble brewing, and to arrest it she imitated Mindy Collier, her perky social secretary. "I thought we might all go on a picnic."

"Picnics suck. I'm going to the mall."

Button scrambled to the end of the bed closest to Mat

and would have fallen if Nealy hadn't grabbed her by the ankle, then gently lowered her over the side. "I don't think there are too many malls around here."

"There's one in the next town," Lucy countered. "This girl at the pool told me."

Button pulled herself up on the side of the bed and shrieked at Mat, who was looking around the room for the keys that were tucked into the pocket of Nealy's shorts.

"Let's go to the mall and then go on a picnic," she said reasonably.

"What's this thing you've got with picnics?" Mat stopped just behind her. "And where are the keys to that old junker?"

"I think picnics are fun. *No!*"

But she'd grabbed for her stomach too late. He'd already reached under her top from the back and pulled open the ties. "First I'm going to burn this, then I'm heading down to the garage to hold all the mechanics hostage until Mabel's fixed."

She grabbed the padding from him and thrust it in her satchel. "We can stop at the garage on our way to the mall before the picnic."

"Ohmygod, look!" Lucy exclaimed.

Nealy turned just in time to see Button take three tottery steps across the open carpet toward Mat.

"She's walking!" Lucy's eyes danced. "I was getting so worried. She's a year old, and her dad was a moron, and—" She snapped her mouth shut, unwilling for them to see any emotion from her except disdain. Even so, she still couldn't quite hide her pride, and Nealy wanted to hug her.

Button made a lunge for Mat's leg, but he was too far away, and she began to tumble. He scooped her up like a linebacker retrieving a loose football.

"Daaaa . . ." She gazed at him worshipfully.

Mat frowned.

She cocked her head to the side and fluttered her lashes.

"I think I'm gonna hurl," Lucy said.

Nealy giggled.

He shot her a sour look, then tucked Button under his arm like a potato sack. "Nobody's going anywhere if I don't find the keys."

"I'm driving," Nealy said brightly. "You had a hard day yesterday."

"You've got them?"

She'd had years of practice avoiding answering direct questions. "I just hope it doesn't rain today. Grab the diaper bag, Lucy. We're off!"

She snatched up her own purse, along with the satchel that held her things, clutched them in front of her flat stomach, and charged into the hall. The doors of the elevator were starting to close, but she managed to slip inside, leaving the rest of them behind. When she reached the lobby, she didn't glance either right or left, just kept her stomach covered and headed for the parking lot.

As she settled into the antique Oldsmobile, she reached for her satchel, then had second thoughts about putting the padding back on. Mat clearly detested it, and he was perfectly capable of making a public scene. With her short hair and cheap clothes, she was a far cry from America's stylish First Lady. Would it be riskier to test Mat or go without and hope that she could pull it off?

As she debated, Mat came out of the lobby door with a scowl on his face, while Lucy trailed behind carrying Button.

Nealy stared at the Fed Ex envelope he was holding and realized she'd once again let the business of daily living get away from her. Three years of enjoying the efficiency of the White House mail room had made her lose touch. But this package had been too important for her to forget, and she needed to remember she no longer had an army of secretaries ready to hand over her private mail.

The system the White House used to separate personal correspondence from the thousands of pieces of public mail the first family received every day was simple and effective. Intimates of the President and his family were given a numerical code to include with the address— she and Dennis had chosen 1776—which shot private mail straight to their desks.

Mat braced one hand on the roof of the truck and stared through the open window at her. "The desk clerk stopped me. You didn't tell me you were expecting a package."

"And your point is?" She held out her hand, but he didn't pass over the envelope.

Lucy disengaged Button's fingers from her hair. "He's pissed because the desk clerk made this big deal about was he sure this was for his wife because her last name wasn't the same as his."

She eyed the envelope. "I guess I should have used your last name like everybody else."

His expression grew ominous. "What do you mean, *like everybody else*?"

This was the kind of slip she never made in Washington. "I didn't mean a thing. Stop glowering and get in, will you?"

Lucy snickered. He slowly turned to stare at her. Button melted into smiles and gurgles, but he ignored her. "What's Nell talking about?"

"You think I like having Jorik for a last name?" Lucy retorted. "You think Button does?"

"Are you telling me your last name is *Jorik*?"

"What did you think it was?"

Mat shoved his hand through his hair. "Shit."

"Sit!" Button crowed.

"That's it!" Nealy exclaimed. "No more foul language

from either one of you. Button's turning into the first R-rated toddler!"

"*Sit!*" Button shouted, clapping her hands and looking pleased with herself.

It was Nealy's turn to glower, and she made the most of it as she thrust her hand through the window. "I'll take that."

He looked down at the envelope. "From John Smith?"

Why couldn't Terry have used a little more imagination? The old Terry would have written Homer Simpson or Jerry Falwell or something like that. But Dennis's death had stolen Terry's laughter. "My cousin," she said.

Mat tested the weight of the package, then regarded her quizzically before he handed it over to her. She knew he expected her to tell him what was inside, but somehow she didn't think volunteering that her dead husband's lover had loaned her thousands of dollars in cash would put an end to his questions.

She tucked the edge of the package against her hip. "Time's a-wastin', cowpokes. Let's head out."

For all her insistence that they go to a mall, Lucy didn't seem too enthusiastic once they arrived. As the teenager wandered away, Nealy wondered if she might not be more interested in postponing their arrival in Iowa than in going shopping.

With Button in her arms for camouflage, Nealy slipped into the rest room to dispose of the Fed Ex envelope and put the money into her purse for safekeeping. When she came out, Mat was waiting for her, even though he'd said he was heading for Mexico as soon as they disappeared.

"Trouble with the border guard?" she asked.

"*Shaaaaa!*" Button screeched in delight.

"So what was in the envelope?"

"Money so I can go clothes shopping. You're welcome to come along."

"Somebody actually sent you money?"

"It's amazing what the Mafia pays for a kill these days."

"You've been hanging around Lucy too much." He fell into step next to her. "So how much do you have?"

"Enough to pay you back and buy something for myself that doesn't blow." Another sweet smile. "Enough to take off on my own if you irritate me in even the most minuscule way."

His expression turned distinctly cocky. "Why do I think you're happy right where you are?"

"It doesn't have anything to do with you."

"No? That kiss last night said something different."

"What kiss?"

"The one you fell asleep dreaming about."

She gave an honest-to-God snort.

He frowned. "I hate shopping. I especially hate shopping with a woman."

"Then don't come with me." She marched into the center of the mall, then came to a dead stop. She was in a real American shopping mall, and she didn't have to shake a single hand or solicit a vote. "This is wonderful!"

He looked at her as if she were crazy. "It's a third-rate mall in the middle of nowhere, and every store is part of a chain. For a blue blood, you sure are easy to please."

She was too busy making a beeline for the Gap to reply.

Despite Mat's grumbling, he'd been well trained by those seven sisters, and he turned out to be a first-rate shopping companion. He held Button with only minimal complaint while Nealy looked through piles of clothes, and he passed generally astute judgment on what she should and shouldn't buy. Since she'd been raised with a keen eye for fashion, she didn't need his opinion, but it was fun asking for it.

In addition to basics for herself, she picked out a couple of sundresses for Lucy, then made a quick detour through Baby Gap to buy some outfits for Button. Mat, however, spoiled her fun by refusing to let her pay for their clothes. While he was handling the transaction, she slipped to another register and purchased a jaunty little pink denim cap.

After she set it on Button's head, Mat studied it for a moment, then turned the bill backward. "This is the Demon we're talking about."

"Sorry."

She expected the baby to pull off the cap, but because her adored Mat had positioned it, she let it stay. "I bought you that hat, not him," Nealy grumbled.

Button tucked her head into his neck and sighed.

Nealy could hardly believe that no one was paying any attention to her. Between her altered appearance, the fact that no one expected to find Cornelia Case in a small West Virginia shopping mall, and the camouflage Mat and Button provided, she'd acquired a glorious invisibility.

They moved on to the mall's main department store. She loved the novelty of being able to look over the merchandise without a dozen people trying to help her. It was nearly as much fun as eavesdropping on everyone's conversations while she stood in line at the register.

When she located the lingerie department, she set about getting rid of Mat. "I'll carry Button now. Would you mind taking my packages out to the car?"

"You're trying to get rid of me."

"Of all the paranoid notions. You told me you didn't like to shop, and I was just being courteous."

"Tell me another one. You either want to buy Tampax or underwear."

All those sisters . . . "I need some lingerie," she conceded, "and I'd rather do it by myself."

"It's a lot more fun as a group activity." He charged toward the lingerie department. Button bounced happily in his arms, looking adorable in her pink cap with the bill turned backward.

Nealy was forced to trot to keep up with him. "You'll be the only man there. You'll embarrass yourself."

"Embarrassment is being the only man in the lingerie department when you're thirteen. At thirty-four, it doesn't bother me at all. Matter of fact, I'm looking forward to it." He headed straight for a lacy black nightie that was almost entirely transparent. "I think we should start with this."

"I don't."

"Okay, how about these?" He approached a display of black bikini panties.

"How about not."

He held up a black demi bra. "Let's negotiate with this."

She burst out laughing. "You like black underwear, do you?"

"There's just something about the way it looks on a fair-skinned woman."

That sent a sizzle right through her. She made a dash for the Jantzen cotton briefs.

"You're one cruel woman."

What was she going to do about him? Cornelia Case was so insecure about sex that she wouldn't do anything. But Nell Kelly . . . Nell just might have the guts to take a chance.

As she paid for her purchase, she realized she had enough money now to go off on her own again, but a solitary adventure had lost its appeal.

They were leaving the department store when she spotted Lucy charging toward them, her eyes alive with excitement. "I've been looking for you guys everywhere. Come on, Nell. Hurry!" She grabbed the packages from

Nealy's hands, shoved them at Mat, and began dragging her forward.

"Wait! What's going on?"

"You'll see."

Nealy looked back at Mat, but he was retrieving one of the packages she'd dropped. She let Lucy pull her, pleased by that fact that she was acting like a normal teenager instead of a hostile burnout.

"I already signed you up. But you've gotta tuck in your maternity top so you don't look pregnant. And, hurry! Ohmygod, they already started."

"Signed me up for what?"

"This is so cool." She dragged her toward the center of the mall. "First prize is a TV. It'll be great in Mabel."

"Lucy!"

"*Hurry!*"

A crowd had gathered in front of some kind of platform where music blared, and a group of people wearing numbers were lined up. "Wait a minute. I'm not going a step farther until—"

"Here she is." Lucy pushed Nealy toward a young woman with a long, dark ponytail. She was carrying a clipboard and wearing a plastic smiley pin.

"You just made it." The woman stuck a tag printed with the number eleven on Nealy's shirt. "You're our last entry. Who is it you think you look like?"

Dumbfounded, Nealy stared at her. "What . . ."

"She looks like Cornelia Case!" Lucy exclaimed. "Anybody can see that."

Only then did Nealy spot the banner hanging above the platform.

CELEBRITY LOOKALIKE CONTEST!

10

NEALY FELT ALL THE BLOOD DRAINING FROM HER head. "Lucy, I'm not doing this!"

"Too late. It cost me ten bucks. And I want that TV, so you'd better win!"

"We have one more contestant," the announcer exclaimed. "Step up, Number Eleven! Your name is . . ." He glanced down at the card the woman with the clipboard had handed him. "Brandy Butt?"

"I made that up so your ex-husband couldn't find you," Lucy whispered as she pushed Nealy toward the steps.

"Don't be shy. Come right on up."

Everybody in the crowd had turned to stare at her. Her limbs felt numb and her fingers icy. She thought about running, but that would only make her more conspicuous. Her legs were wooden as she found herself mounting the three steps.

Why had she let Mat take away her padding? The others were standing in a ragged line. She took a place at the end and willed herself to become invisible, but the crowd was regarding her curiously. She was going to murder Lucy.

"Brandy, tell us where you're from?"

Her voice quivered. "*¿Qué?*"

"Where you're from? Where you live?"

"No hablo inglés."

Lucy shot her a murderous glare.

The announcer gave the woman with the clipboard a helpless look. Lucy called up from the bottom of the steps, "She's from Hollywood, California. And you can't kick her out of the contest because I already paid ten dollars!"

"We won't kick her out, young lady," the announcer said in the unctuous voice of the microphone-infatuated. He turned back to Nealy. "Who is it you think you look like, Number Eleven?"

"¿Qué?"

"She looks like Cornelia Case!" Lucy exclaimed. "The First Lady!"

"How about it, ladies and gentlemen?"

Gooseflesh broke out all over her as the crowd applauded.

"We've got a real contest going here, folks. Who are you going to vote for? Because it's time to pick our finalists."

The other ten contestants were a mixed lot: male and female, child, adult, one teenager. None of them resembled any celebrity she knew, certainly not like she did.

The announcer asked everyone to form a line along the front of the platform. Nealy's feet felt as if they'd been dipped in concrete. He stepped behind the contestants. "Support your favorites with your applause, and don't forget that this contest is brought to you by the wild and woolly WGRB-FM 1490!"

He held his hand over the contestants one at a time. Dread made her heart hammer. The lady with the clipboard checked the applause each person received on a small meter sitting at the edge of the platform. As he came up behind Nealy, she dipped her chin and tried to look like someone who only spoke Spanish. The applause was much too enthusiastic.

Finally the voting was over, and the woman handed

a note with the results to the announcer. He glanced down at it.

"You've chosen our three finalists, and here they are!" He indicated a gaunt woman with bleached blond hair. "Miss Joan Rivers!" The crowd clapped. He moved to a potbellied elderly man with a full white beard. "Santa Claus!" More clapping. Inevitably, he stopped next to Nealy. "And First Lady Cornelia Case!" Big applause.

The announcer began a long-winded promotion of the radio station's "wild and woolly" programming. Nealy kept her eyes on her feet.

"And now it's time for our final round. It's up to you, ladies and gentlemen, to select WGRB's Celebrity Look-alike Champion!"

Nealy caught sight of Mat and Button off to the side. They seemed to be enjoying themselves.

"Let's hear it for Joan Rivers, Mrs. Janine Parks!" A scatter of applause for Janine, whose plastic flip flops dampened the Rivers illusion.

"How about Santa Claus here? Clifford Rays!" The applause was much louder.

"And our final entry. Brandy Butt, First Lady Cornelia Case!" She tried not to wince as someone actually whistled.

The woman with the clipboard checked the meter, then called the announcer over to whisper in his ear.

He returned to the center of the platform. "Ladies and gentlemen, we have a winner!" Dramatic pause to heighten the tension. "The champion of WGRB's Wild and Woolly Celebrity Lookalike Contest . . . and the owner of a brand-new nineteen-inch Zenith TV is . . . *Mr. Clifford Rays!*"

To her astonishment, the announcer began shaking hands with the potbellied, bearded man at her side.

She'd lost! Stunned, she stared out at the crowd. Mat gave her a go-figure shrug, and Button clapped, mimicking the applause she heard around her.

A chill shot through her as she spotted a photographer lifting his camera. She ducked. Then she began sidling toward the edge of the platform.

"Wait a minute, Brandy. You're our first runner-up. We have a prize for you."

She pretended she didn't understand and darted off the stage. People made way for her as she pushed through the crowd to Mat.

"Aren't you going to claim your prize?" he said when she reached him.

"I just want to get out of here," she whispered furiously.

His eyebrows arched in mock surprise. "Hey, I thought you only spoke Spanish."

"Don't be cute. I'll meet you at the car. *You* can find Lucy; I don't ever want to see her again! And let me have Button." If the photographer spotted her, she could duck behind the baby.

"Gladly."

As she took the baby from him, Button screwed up her face to protest. Nealy had already attracted far too much attention, and a screaming fit was the last thing she needed. "Don't cry, sweetie. Please."

Button screwed her face tighter. "Sit!"

Nealy turned toward the exit. "How does the piggy go? *Oink . . . oink . . .*" Just then Lucy came rushing toward them, a Black and Decker box in her hand, a scowl on her face. "What am I supposed to do with a freaking power drill? And Nell looks more like Cornelia Case than that old fart looked like Santa Claus. Why did you vote for him?"

Nealy stopped in her tracks. "You voted for him?"

He shrugged. "You've got to admit, he really looked like Santa. That beard was real."

Nealy stared at him. "I don't believe it. Two days ago you couldn't stop talking about how much I look like you-know-who, but you didn't even vote for me?"

"I had to vote my conscience."

She was surprised she could still laugh.

To Mat's relief, Mabel was ready to go when they reached the garage. "What about my picnic?" Nealy complained as they headed for the highway.

"Promise her she can have her picnic, Jorik, or she'll complain all day."

"You should talk, Miss Mall Rat," Nealy countered.

"Girls, girls . . ." Mat's sigh was long-suffering.

"I can't believe you only won a power drill," Lucy complained. "You should have tucked in your top like I told you so you didn't look so fat."

"I don't look fat."

"Trust me, Lucy," Mat said. "She doesn't look fat."

"And why did you have to start talking Spanish?" Lucy slapped the drill down on the table. "I want to find one of those places where you sell stuff and get money back."

"A pawnshop?" Nealy asked.

"That's it! I want to go to a pawnshop. Maybe I can even get an old TV there."

"You're not going to any pawnshop!" Mat's jaw was starting to twitch.

"Too much television rots your brain," Nealy said.

"It's not for me. It's for Button. Don't you know anything?"

"Apparently not. Why does Button need a television?"

Lucy gave another of her patented you're-a-moron looks. "So she can watch *Teletubbies* like all the other kids her age. I guess you don't care if she ends up flunking kindergarten or something."

"Buckle up," Mat growled. "And I don't want to hear another word about pawnshops or Tele-whatever or anything else. Does everybody understand me?"

They all did.

Mat chose to cross West Virginia into Ohio on Route

50, a divided highway, but not an interstate, so Nealy knew he was still worried that the police might be looking for the girls. As lunchtime approached, the sky clouded over and it began to rain, forcing Nealy to abandon her plans for a picnic. They ate hamburgers instead as they drove through the wet, picturesque hills of southeastern Ohio, home of eight presidents, although Warren Harding had done such an abysmal job, Nealy didn't know why any state would want to claim him.

Button remained relatively content just gazing at her beloved, but Lucy kept demanding that they stop at every strip mall, convenience store, and roadside rest area. Mat generally ignored her, which only made her more demanding. Nealy was beginning to suspect that Lucy didn't want to get to Iowa, and that worried her.

She forced Mat to stop at a highway K mart and emerged with a couple of handheld games, as well as some books and magazines to distract the teenager.

"*The Hobbit?*" Lucy tossed it aside seconds after Nealy handed it to her. "That's a kid's book."

"I'm sorry, honey," Nealy replied with fake sympathy, "but *Ulysses* was out of stock."

Since Lucy had no idea what Nealy was talking about, she could only shoot her a dirty look. A few minutes later, she flopped down on the double bed in the back with the offending book, and Nealy didn't hear another word from her for the rest of the afternoon. With Button sound asleep in her car seat and the teenager occupied in the rear, Nealy leaned back to enjoy the scenery.

"I'm real sorry you missed your picnic," Mat said.

"You're not sorry at all." She smiled. "And the weather looks like it's clearing, so we can have a dinner picnic."

"I can't wait."

"You're so cynical about everything. Why is that?"

"It goes with my job."

"I didn't know cynicism was an occupational hazard for steelworkers."

His eyes flickered oddly. "It comes and goes." And then he smiled. "I enjoyed last night."

She suddenly felt as awkward as a teenager. "I didn't. You were completely out of line with that pillow."

"You've got to admit you're happier not wearing it."

"You also leaped to all kinds of erroneous conclusions about my marriage. Not only that, you're—"

A great kisser?"

She repressed a smile. "You're all right, I suppose."

He sighed. "I guess our styles just don't match."

"That's true."

"I like big, aggressive, man-sized kisses . . . the kind that make your toes curl. You, on the other hand, like wimpy, girly kisses that wouldn't curl a hair ribbon."

"Girly kisses?"

"Yeah, the kind of kisses little girls give to uncles who smoke cigars."

"Trust me. I would never kiss an uncle the way I kissed you last night!"

"Prissy kisses."

"Prissy!" She was beginning to get annoyed. "I don't have a prissy bone in my body."

"You bought white underwear."

"Only because I wanted to irritate you. If you hadn't been there, I would have chosen something more exotic."

"Like what?"

"Like none of your business."

"No, I'm serious. This is an important question. The kind of underwear a woman buys reflects her character."

"I can't wait to hear this."

"That's why the idea of you wearing white panties bothers me."

"I seem to be having trouble keeping up."

"Isn't it obvious? That's the favorite underwear of female serial killers."

"Ah." She nodded wisely. "You know this for a fact?"

"I read it somewhere. Women who wear that type of underwear are the same women who put signs in the windows of their houses advertising rooms for rent. The next thing you know, the neighbors start complaining about a bad smell coming from under the back porch."

"A girl's gotta make a living."

He laughed.

Bantering about underwear wasn't her strong point, and she knew she should change the subject, but that little trollop Nell Kelly wouldn't let go. "I don't think this has anything to do with serial killers. I think you have a black underwear fetish."

"I like red, too. Although just about any color'd look good on you."

"You think so?"

"Yeah, I do." He smiled and let those gray eyes slide over her like molten metal. "So what are we going to do about this kissing problem?"

Cornelia Case didn't have a silly bone in her body, but Nell had lower standards, and she was enjoying their conversation. "Resign ourselves, I guess, that some things aren't meant to be."

"Or . . . and here's an idea . . . we could work on it."

Her skin tingled. "And how would we do that?"

"Wait until the little buggers fall asleep and practice."

"Ahh. That would be one way, I suppose."

"Come to think about it, the hotel last night was a lot more comfortable than sleeping in this thing. I think I'll find another hotel just like it for us to stay in tonight."

Cornelia chose that moment to raise her cautious head. "And I think you're moving too fast. We only met two days ago."

"And we'll be separating in another few days. That makes it even more important that we don't waste time."

"Just get right to it, is that it?"

"Sure. Haven't you ever fantasized about having sex with a stranger?"

A strong, gorgeous stranger who would sweep her off her feet, without knowing who she was, make delirious love to her, and then disappear in the morning. "Absolutely not."

"Liar." His grin was cocky and supremely confident.

"Would you be quiet so I can enjoy the scenery?"

From the rear of the motor home, Lucy set aside her book to watch the byplay between Jorik and Nell. They seemed to have forgotten she was around. She couldn't hear what they were saying, but she sure could see that they were hot for each other.

An idea began to form in her mind, and her stomach got all fluttery, but this time it was the good sort of fluttery. Neither of them was married. Jorik was bossy and thought he knew everything, but Button liked him. Nell was sort of a geek, and she didn't know much about babies, but she was always checking everything to make sure Button didn't hurt herself. She was also nice—buying Lucy those dresses and everything. And even though Jorik had gotten drunk once, he didn't show any signs of being an alcoholic. He'd also been driving a great car, so he had money, and he was pretty funny, although she wasn't going to tell him that.

What if she could get them together? The butterflies moved faster in her stomach. She trusted both of them to take care of her baby sister a lot more than she'd ever trusted Sandy. Maybe they'd fall in love, then get married, and adopt Button to be their own kid. Button was cute, not an obnoxious teenager like Lucy, and Nell and Jorik seemed to be starting to like her a little. Jorik had quit complaining about picking her up, and Nell didn't seem as nervous around her as she'd been that first day.

The more Lucy thought about it, the more she decided

they were her best hope. Somehow she had to get Jorik and Nell together, then convince them to adopt Button. Once her baby sister was settled, Lucy could take off on her own.

Some of Lucy's excitement vanished as she thought of saying good-bye to Button. She told herself not to be a jerk. This was what she wanted, wasn't it? To go off on her own. She'd do great. She was tough, she was smart, and she wouldn't take any crap from anybody.

Still, for the millionth time, she wished she could have a real family. All her life, she'd dreamed of having a dad who mowed the lawn and called her some kind of lame pet name, and a mom who didn't get drunk and keep losing jobs and having sex with everybody. All of them would live in a real house, not ones you rented and got evicted from. She'd be able to take advanced classes without everybody making fun of her and hang out with nice kids, not just burn-outs. She could be in some clubs, and sing in the choir, and boys who didn't do drugs would like her. That's what she wanted.

She stabbed angrily at the bedspread with the end of her finger. She wasn't going to get what she wanted, and there was no use pretending she would. Right now, she had to think about her sister, and that meant she needed to get Jorik and Nell together. It wouldn't be easy because they were both smart, but Lucy figured she was smarter. All she had to do was push them in the right direction.

And try to keep them from getting to Iowa too soon.

Button waited until they were in Indiana before she fell apart. This time Mat didn't have to be convinced to stop. They'd left West Virginia and Ohio behind them, Mabel hadn't broken down again, and he was feeling more optimistic about actually making it to Iowa.

He drove into the small campground they'd chosen for the night and smiled at the variety of barnyard noises coming from behind him as Nell tried to appease the baby. She was something, smart and funny. But it was her subtle sexiness that kept sending a whole filmstrip of X-rated images flashing through his mind.

All afternoon he'd been driving in a haze of lust. Every time she crossed those too-slender legs, let a sandal dangle from her toes, brushed her arm against him, he felt as if he were going to explode. The mystery lady might not have completely accepted it yet, but she was about to take herself a lover. And if he had anything to say about it—which he damn well did—she was going to take that lover tonight.

It would be tricky since they were sharing a small space with two kids, but the door at the back had a lock on it, and both girls seemed to be sound sleepers. It wasn't an ideal solution—he wanted to make her scream—but he couldn't wait any longer.

As they bumped along the gravel road to the campsite, he wondered how long those flawless upper-crust manners would last in bed. If only they could have some real privacy . . . The small part of his brain that was still functioning rationally warned him to wait, but some predatory instinct told him he needed to put his mark on her as soon as possible.

Put his mark on her? Where had that idea come from? If he weren't careful, he'd be dragging her into the trees by her hair. He smiled as he imagined how she'd react to that, then maneuvered Mabel into their campsite and turned off the ignition.

The Demon was starting to hiccup from screaming, and Nell rushed to unfasten her from the car seat. Her cheeks were flushed from all the animal noises, and as she leaned forward, he could see the outline of her breasts falling against the soft cotton top. He was in bad need of fresh air.

He stepped outside, even though he knew he'd have to come right back in to settle the baby down himself.

As he looked around, he congratulated himself on choosing a small campground instead of one of those big commercial ones. Here they'd have some privacy.

Just then, a chubby woman in a floral print top, bright blue shorts, and plaid sneakers came charging toward him, a pair of reading glasses bobbing on a multicolored chain around her neck. She was trailed by a thin man dapperly dressed in neatly pressed navy shorts, a plaid sports shirt, black socks, and brown leather sandals.

"Hi, there!" the woman trilled. "We're the Waynes from Fort Wayne. I'm Bertis, and this is my husband Charlie. We were hoping a nice young family would camp next to us."

Mat felt all his plans for solitude and quiet seduction crumbling around him.

"Your little one seems to be kicking up in there," Charlie said. "Our granddaughter used to scream like that, but Bertis here could always make her stop, isn't that right, Bertis? Bring that baby out here and let Grandma settle her down."

At that moment Nell emerged with Button twisting in her arms and screaming away at the top of her lungs. Her cheeks were wet, her rosy mouth crumpled in outrage.

"I thought maybe some fresh air would—" Nell broke off as she saw the Waynes.

"Hi, there, honey." Bertis went through the introductions again, then slipped on her glasses and reached for Button. "Let me have her. I'll calm her down."

No way was Mat letting a stranger get her hands on the Demon, and he whipped her out of Nell's arms before the other woman could touch her. "Pipe down, brat."

A 747 could have landed on her bottom lip, but she stopped howling.

"That's better."

Her bottom lip retracted. She hiccuped and gave him

an injured pout, the kind that suggested she expected a diamond bracelet or, at the very least, a fur jacket, as a make-up present.

"Will you look at that? You have a way with that little girl, now, don't you? It's just not fair." Bertis gave Nell a conspiratorial look. "We go to all the trouble of giving birth to them, then they turn to their daddies."

"I didn't give birth to her," Nell said. "I'm—"

"Mommy? Daddy? Thank you so much for that wonderful book you bought me. It was really educational."

He looked up to see Lucy step out of the motor home, her demure expression completely at odds with her hooker makeup. "Hi, I'm Lucy Jorik."

Mat winced. He still couldn't believe Sandy had given her kids his last name.

"This is my dad Mat and my mom Nell and our baby Button. Isn't she cute? They were going to get a divorce because my father was having an affair with my best friend, but then they got back together, and Button was their make-up present."

Mat looked at Nell. "I think I'm going to hurl."

Nell laughed and turned to Bertis. "Lucy's precocious. Don't pay any attention to her. Mat and I aren't married. I'm just his nanny."

Bertis's look said she didn't believe a word of it but, at the same time, had seen too much of life to judge. She regarded Lucy's many earrings. "I hope you don't have your tongue pierced, young lady. Our oldest granddaughter Megan had her tongue pierced, and she swallowed her earring. The doctor made her do her business in a bucket for a week and go through it with rubber gloves looking for the missing object."

Mat was happy to see that Lucy looked appalled, and his respect for Bertis rose.

"You folks come on over and have dinner with us as soon as you get settled. I brought along a Honey Baked Ham and my Ore-Ida potato casserole, and wait till you taste my Dole fruit cocktail cake. Everybody at church makes me bring it for potluck. Come on, Lucy, you can help Charlie move those picnic tables together. And you, little darlin', we'll find something special for you to eat."

Mat glanced at Nell, hoping she'd come up with a good excuse, but she seemed entranced by the Waynes.

"Thanks for the invitation," he said, "but—"

"We'd love to!" Nell exclaimed. "Just give us a few minutes to get settled."

The next thing he knew, Nell had shot back inside, Lucy was walking off with the Waynes, and he was left standing there with the Demon, who reached inside the open collar of his shirt and pulled his chest hair.

"Ow!"

Pleased with herself, the Demon clapped.

He followed Nell into the motor home and set the baby down to roam. "Damn it, Nell, why did you have to say we'd eat dinner with them?"

"Because I want to. But what are we going to take? We have to take something with us, don't we?"

"How the hell would I know?"

She started bustling around the motor home, her eyes shining with excitement. He forgot his annoyance long enough to enjoy the way her body formed a long, slender curve as she stood on her toes to look into a top cupboard.

He had a bad feeling about tonight. From the time they'd met, he'd noticed how much she appreciated the ordinary things in life: fast food, a pretty view, even pumping gas. This afternoon, she'd had a long wait in line at a convenience store because the girl behind the register was too busy talking on the phone to tend to the customers. Instead of getting annoyed, Nell acted as if being ignored were a privilege. Dinner with the Waynes was going to be right up her alley.

She turned to him, a small frown creasing that

smooth, upper-crust forehead. "Do you know how to make biscuits?"

"You've got to be kidding."

"Or cornbread? She said she was having ham. Cornbread would be nice."

"We've got an unopened package of tortilla chips, a couple of cans of pop, and some baby formula. I don't think cornbread's an option."

"We have more things than that."

"Yeah, but they all have Gerber on the label."

"Gah!" Button shoved a cheese curl she'd scavenged from the floor into her mouth. Luckily, Nell didn't see it.

"Cheerios!" She withdrew the box from the bottom cupboard as if she'd found buried treasure. "I knew we had something else. They're such nice people."

"Yeah, you could mix the Cheerios with that baby formula and throw some tortilla chips on top."

"You might be more helpful."

"I'm getting ready to eat dinner with the two worst dressers in Fort Wayne, Indiana. I guess it's affected my attitude."

She smiled at him, and for a moment he couldn't do anything but look at her. At first she held his gaze, but then his scrutiny seemed to make her nervous and she began studying his right ear. Some perversely male part of him was glad she was nervous. It showed that she understood everything was about to change between them.

Time to stake his claim.

As Nealy felt Mat's hand on her shoulder, her heart began to race. One moment everything had been easy and fun between them, but in the space of an instant something had shifted.

She felt his breath falling soft against her cheek, and the brush of his fingertips on her chin was feather light. He spread his big hand across her back, and as he drew her close, she realized he was aroused. This, she remembered, was the way a man was supposed to feel against a woman.

She had to do everything right. She couldn't bear having him say she kissed like a little girl. When she was younger, she'd known how. Surely she could do it now.

Self-control had been bred into her Litchfield bones, and as his mouth covered her own, she forced herself to concentrate. One thing was certain. Passionate women didn't kiss with their lips sealed.

She eased hers open and angled her head a bit more. She needed to relax! But what about her tongue? She was definitely going to use her tongue, but how much of it? And when?

Mat felt Nell's growing tension and started to draw away to see what was wrong, but some instinct made him hesitate. One moment she'd been soft and warm, but now she was stiff as a board. She seemed to be working at it instead of just enjoying what was happening.

He could almost hear the hinge on her jaw creak as she parted her lips. The tip of her tongue ventured forward, then stalled. He remembered that stupid comment he'd made last night about the way she kissed. For someone who knew a lot more than he wanted to about female psychology, he'd made an unbelievable blunder. Now he had to fix the harm he'd done.

Although it cost him, he drew back from that determined little hard-pointed tongue, grazed her earlobe with his mouth, and whispered, "Take it easy with me, sweetheart. A man can only handle so much."

Her eyelids flickered against his cheek, and he knew he'd given her something to think about. Her body relaxed. She cupped his head in her hands and sealed her mouth right across his. This was a lot more like it. He smiled to himself.

She jerked back, her eyes stricken as she looked up at him. "You're laughing!"

His stomach sank. He really was a jerk, even when he wasn't trying to be. "You bet I am. Kissing you makes me the luckiest man in the world right now, and I'm celebrating."

She didn't look quite so agitated, but she did look suspicious. "Go ahead and critique me," she said. "I know you want to."

"What I want to do is get back to kissing you." Screw it. He'd given sensitivity his best shot, and now he pulled her hard against him. Some men were better off just being jerks.

This time he didn't give her a chance to get those mental wheels turning. Instead, he staked his territory and let her keep up.

Their kiss was deep and so lusty she didn't have time to think about where her tongue was going because his was already there. He'd never been able to understand men who only wanted to get to the main event. He loved kissing. And kissing this innocent, classy woman was especially sweet.

Her fingers dug into his shoulders, and he slipped his hands under her top so he could do what he'd been wanting to all day.

Her skin was as soft as her mouth. He moved his palm up along her side, only to discover she wasn't wearing a bra. Just like that, he captured the sweet, small mound of her breast beneath his hand.

She quivered.

He brushed the nipple with his thumb. She made a small, throaty sound. He lost control. No more slow seduction. No waiting until tonight. He had to have her now.

"Gah?"

He curled his free hand around her bottom. Her breathy, helpless sounds were driving him wild.

"Da?"

All day he'd been imagining her breasts, and now he had to see them. He pushed up her top.

"*DA!*"

Nell stiffened. Sharp little fingernails dug into his leg. He whipped his hand out of her top.

She jerked away from him. Her lips were wet and swollen, her cheeks flushed, her expression appalled.

Both of them gazed down at their infant chaperone, who was regarding them with all the disapproval of a Pentecostal church organist. Mat wanted to throw back his head and howl.

"*Nah!*"

Nell pressed a hand to that sweet breast he'd only just begun to explore. "Oh, my God. She knows what we were doing."

"Damn," he growled. "Now we'll have to kill her." He glared at the baby.

Nell dropped down and swooped her up. "Oh, sweetie, I'm sorry. You should never have seen that." Her eyes flew to his. "Something like that could traumatize her."

"I sincerely doubt that." Right now he felt a lot more traumatized than that baby.

She regarded the Demon earnestly. "You shouldn't have seen what you did, Button. But you need to know there was nothing wrong with it. Well, almost nothing . . . I mean, we're adults and not teenagers. And when a mature woman is with an attractive man . . .".

"Yeah? You think I'm attractive?"

When was he going to learn to keep his big mouth shut? She cuddled Button to her breast and regarded him critically. "I'm sure you think it's silly to explain this to an infant, but no one really knows how much babies understand."

"Somehow I don't think that she's going to understand this for a few more years." He thought about throwing himself in the shower, clothes and all.

She returned her attention to the baby. "Mat and I are responsible adults, Button, and we know . . ." She paused just when he was starting to enjoy himself, and sniffed the Demon's breath.

"She smells like . . ." She whipped some orange slime from the corner of the baby's mouth and examined it. "She's been eating *cheese curls*! Oh, God! She ate them off the floor. Is there any ipecac in that first-aid kit?"

He rolled his eyes. "You're not giving that baby ipecac. Come here, Demon, before she threatens you with a stomach pump." He took the baby, even though he was feeling less than charitable with her.

"But—"

"Look at her, Nell. She's as healthy as they come, and a little floor dining's not going to hurt her one bit. When my sister Ann Elizabeth was a baby, she used to eat pieces of gum that had already been chewed. It wasn't so bad when she did it in the house, but she scavenged on the sidewalk, too."

Nell blanched.

"Let's go rescue the Waynes before Lucy can finish them off. And Nell . . ." He waited until she was looking at him fully, then he gave her his slowest, most dangerous smile. "As soon as the kids are asleep, we're going to pick up exactly where we left off."

11

LUCY LOVED THE WAYNES. THEY WERE DOPEY, AND Bertis had already lectured her on covering up a pretty face with all that makeup, but they were nice, too. The whole time Bertis had been lecturing, she'd been giving Lucy homemade cookies and patting her shoulder. Lucy especially loved the way Bertis kept touching her, since nobody but Button touched her anymore. Even Sandy had hardly touched her unless she was drunk and needed help getting to the bathroom.

Lucy liked Charlie, too, even though only a moron would wear socks with sandals. He'd called her Scout when she'd helped him move the picnic tables together. *A little more to the right there, Scout.*

She wished she could give Button to the Waynes, but they were too old, so she was still stuck with Jorik and Nell.

She looked up from the silverware she'd been putting on the table and saw them coming toward her with Button. They looked funny, and she studied them more closely. Nell had a red mark on the side of her neck and her mouth looked puffy. When she saw that Jorik's mouth looked that way, too, her spirits soared.

Nealy inwardly groaned as she spotted the knowing look on Lucy's face. The teenager was too smart for her own good. She concentrated on maintaining a pleasant expression while she tried to figure out what had just happened to her. Even more important, what was she going to do about it?

America's First Lady would have pulled out a yellow pad and come up with a plan, but Nell Kelly wasn't as well organized. Mat intended to pick up where they'd left off, which was exactly what she wanted, too, but it was too soon. Wasn't it?

She decided to worry about the food allergies Button might get from eating cheese curls instead of dwelling on the tall, gray-eyed man at her side who was turning her emotional world upside down.

"Why, look who's here! Now, Nell, why don't you sit there with the baby, and Mat, you go bring that cooler outside. Every time Charlie tries to lift anything heavy, his hernia kicks up."

"You make sure you lift with your knees," Charlie said. "Hernias aren't anything to mess around with."

Nealy smiled. No one ever talked about hernias in front of her.

"You look so familiar, Nell. She looks familiar, doesn't she, Charlie? Have you ever been to Fort Wayne?"

"She looks like Cornelia Case, even though not *everybody* thinks so." Lucy shot Mat a trenchant look just before he disappeared into the Waynes' motor home for the cooler. "Now I'm stuck with a lame power drill."

"Good gracious, you do! Look at her, Charlie. She looks just like Mrs. Case. Why, the two of you could be sisters."

Nealy definitely didn't want the conversation continuing in this direction. "I'm sorry I didn't have anything to bring with me for dinner. We're a little short on groceries."

"Now, don't you worry about that. We have more than enough."

As the meal progressed, Nealy found herself thinking of all the state dinners she'd helped plan, formal affairs where each place setting held as many as twenty-seven items. Not one of them could match the pleasure of this evening. She and Mat kept exchanging glances so full of wordless communication it was as if they'd known each other forever. Lucy giggled at Charlie's teasing. Button toddled around the table so she could visit everyone and, inevitably, found her way into Mat's lap.

Nealy was entranced with the Waynes. Bertis had been a homemaker all her life, and her conversation was filled with stories about her children and grandchildren, her church, and her neighbors. Charlie had owned a small insurance agency and recently passed the reins to his oldest son.

The Waynes weren't reluctant to share their views of Washington, and neither was Mat. Over the Dole fruit cocktail cake, she discovered that he was a political junkie who was very much disillusioned with the country's elected officials.

By the time darkness settled over the campsite, she knew the Waynes were staunch patriots, but not blind ones. They rebelled at the idea of giving handouts to everyone who asked, but were more than willing to share all they had with those who were truly in need. They wanted the federal government to stay out of their private lives, but at the same time find a way to put an end to drug traffic and violence. They worried about having enough health insurance and expected Social Security to work for them, but didn't want their children paying the economic price for it. Although Mat didn't agree with them about everything, they found common ground in their opinions of politicians as ineffective, blindly partisan, self-serving, and willing to sell out the country to protect their own interests.

That view always depressed Nealy, even though she was used to it. She knew elected officials who fit the description, but she knew many who didn't. And couples like the Waynes were America's bedrock. Was a nation of cynics the best that more than two hundred years of democratic government could produce?

Still, Washington had reaped what it had sown, and she and Dennis had shared dozens of conversations over the years about this very issue. Although Dennis thought she was naive for someone who'd breathed the air of politics since birth, she believed the country was ready for a new species of politician. Sometimes she found herself daydreaming about running for office herself. The first rule she'd follow would be honesty, and if that made her a pariah inside the Beltway, she'd take her cause straight to the people.

Mat moved a knife out of Button's reach. "You've been awfully quiet, Nell. For someone who has opinions about everything, I'm surprised you don't have any thoughts about politics."

Oh, she had a million of them, and she'd been biting her tongue ever since the discussion began. Still, she couldn't resist making one comment. "I do believe a political life can be an honorable one."

Charlie and Bertis shook their heads, and Mat gave a cynical laugh. "Maybe fifty years ago, but not now."

Words sprang to her lips, dozens of them. Thousands! An entire speech on patriotism and public duty, complete with quotations from Lincoln, Jefferson, and FDR. Politics could be an honorable profession, and once again the urge to prove that nagged at her.

"Even now," she said. "We just need a few more courageous politicians."

They regarded her skeptically, and she had to clamp her mouth shut to keep from saying more.

Everyone pitched in to help with the cleanup, except Button, who was growing cranky from being kept up too late. Nealy had just begun to excuse herself to put the baby to bed when Lucy came out of the Waynes' motor home. "*They* have a television," she reported loftily.

"We like to keep up with the news shows," Charlie said. "*Dateline*'s on tonight."

"*We* don't have a television."

"And you won't die from it, young lady." Bertis gave Lucy a hug. "You read a nice book tonight. Something educational."

"Mat, can I borrow one of your *Playboys*?"

"You're such a dickens, Lucy." Bertis regarded the teenager fondly. "Our Megan would love you."

Lucy gave a long-suffering sigh but made no effort to disengage herself from Bertis's grandmotherly arms.

"Now, remember, Nell, you're going to send over Button's romper so I can mend the seam while we're watching *Dateline*."

When Button had torn her outfit, Nealy'd had no idea Bertis would volunteer to fix it, and she was embarrassed. "You don't have to do that. Really."

"You'll be doing me a favor. If I don't keep my hands busy, I snack."

Nealy thanked her, then she and Lucy returned to the motor home with the baby. As she went inside, she thought how nice it was to receive a favor from someone who didn't have a single thing to gain by it.

The baby was dirty from crawling in the grass around the picnic table, something Nealy had tried desperately to prevent, only to have everyone else act as if she were being unreasonably overprotective. Since Charlie had asked Mat to help him with an awning bracket, it was up to Nealy and Lucy to coax the cranky baby through a quick bath in the sink. She was sobbing from fatigue by the time she was dressed in a clean pair of pajamas, and she refused to let Nealy comfort her.

Lucy took her in the back to give her a bottle. As the teenager slid the door shut, Nealy felt vaguely melancholy. She wasn't exactly jealous, but it hurt to know the baby so clearly preferred everyone else to her. Button probably sensed there was something wrong with her.

The Angel of Baby Death . . . She shook off the terrible image.

The door swung open, and she whirled around. Mat stepped in, looking even larger than normal and more gorgeous. Her mouth felt dry. She turned away and spotted Button's torn romper. "Would you mind taking this over to Bertis? I forgot." She thrust it toward him.

"No problem." He sounded unusually cheerful for someone who could be the world's biggest curmudgeon. "No problem at all." He smiled as he reached out to take the romper and his hand brushed hers. "Be back in a few minutes."

He was deliberately torturing her. And what was the point? He might think they were going to make love with two children only a few feet away, but she knew differently. Frustrated, she made her way to the bathroom and stripped off her clothes.

As the water poured over her, she remembered the way those big hands had cupped her breasts. She'd loved every moment of his urgent, single-minded seduction. It had felt so good to be desired.

She reminded herself that they barely knew each other. They had no common interests, no shared background. But then she'd had those things with Dennis and look what it had brought her.

Her eyes prickled with tears. Despite everything, she missed Dennis. More than anyone, he would have understood her confusion now, and he would have offered wise counsel. Whenever she let herself forget how he'd betrayed her, she also remembered that he'd been her best friend.

She took her time in the shower, so she was surprised to discover that Mat still wasn't back when she came out of the bathroom. Why did life have to be so complicated? There was only one thing she knew for certain.

She loved being Nell Kelly. Living in another woman's skin had been the best gift she'd ever given herself, and she wasn't nearly ready for it to end.

All day she'd blotted out images of the hoard of government agents who would be trying to track her down, and now she breathed a silent prayer. *Please. Just a few more days. That's all I ask. Just a few more days . . .*

Toni DeLucca was barely paying attention to *Dateline* as she sat in her hotel room not far from McConnellsburg, Pennsylvania. She and Jason had spent another fruitless morning at the truck stop and an equally fruitless afternoon questioning Jimmy Briggs. Now she was propped in bed munching an apple, instead of the salt and vinegar potato chips she really wanted, while she studied the preliminary lab report on the Chevy Corsica. Cornelia Case's fingerprints had been all over it, but there hadn't been any bloodstains or signs of violence. She set the report aside to read through the information they'd just received from Terry Ackerman.

Dennis Case's chief advisor had reported that he'd talked to Aurora the night before. According to Ackerman, she hadn't used the code phrase *John North* during the conversation, nor had she led him to believe her disappearance was other than voluntary. It was a relief to know that Jimmy Briggs hadn't harmed Mrs. Case, but she wished Ackerman had pressed harder to find out where she was.

"This is Ann Curry with a special report from NBC News . . ."

Her half-eaten apple rolled off the bed as she found the remote and turned up the volume. Thirty seconds later, she grabbed the phone and dialed Jason Williams's room.

"NBC just reported that Aurora's missing. CNN's coming on right now."

"Got it."

She heard the television go on in his room, and they both listened.

"Just where is Cornelia Case? Reliable sources in Washington are saying that the nation's First Lady, who was reported to be in bed with the flu, has, in fact, disappeared. No one has seen her at the White House since Tuesday morning, three days ago. She isn't at the home in Middleburg, Virginia, she and President Case shared or the Litchfield family estate on Nantucket. While there's been no official confirmation of her disappearance by the White House, unofficial sources are saying that Mrs. Case left of her own volition. Apparently she told no one of either her plans or her destination. Most alarming, she left without Secret Service protection."

The screen showed James Litchfield hurrying into a limousine.

"Her father, former Vice President James Litchfield, refused to answer questions today when . . ."

Toni turned down the volume as the report began to speculate about foul play. She propped the telephone receiver in the crook of her neck and frowned. "It was bound to come out."

"Does it make our job easier or harder?"

She'd been wondering the same thing. "It'll be harder for her to hide, so there's a better chance she'll be forced to surface. But it also raises the stakes. Now every crackpot in the world knows that she's vulnerable."

"Come down to my room, will you?"

"Why, babycakes, I didn't know you cared."

"Cut the crap. I've got something I want to show you."

"How big is it?"

"Sexual harassment can work two ways, DeLucca," he snapped. "And you just stepped way over the line."

"Well, excuuuze me." She hung up the phone and smiled. Jason might not have much of a sense of humor, but she had to respect his professionalism. She pulled

on a pair of baggy sweats that were held together at the
waist with a safety pin, picked up her room key, and
headed down the corridor.

When he opened the door, she flicked her fingers
against his chest. "Mommy's here. Did you want me to
fix your night-light so you won't get scared in the dark?"

He rolled his eyes in exactly the same way her twenty-
three-year-old daughter Callie did when Toni was annoying. Only young people could manage such an
extreme degree of eye rolling.

"Take a look at this." He gestured toward the laptop
computer sitting on the desk.

She'd forgotten her reading glasses and had to squint
at the screen to see that he'd pulled up the web site for
tomorrow morning's edition of a small West Virginia
newspaper.

"What am I supposed to be looking for?"

"Right there." He jabbed his finger at the screen.

" 'Santa Wins Celebrity Lookalike Contest'? Why
would I be interested— Whoa." She readjusted her distance from the computer and went back to the beginning
of the article to read more slowly. "How did you find
this?"

"Just surfing around. I've been checking the newspapers in a hundred-and-fifty-mile radius of Mc-
Connellsburg. It says the woman was Hispanic, so it's
probably not important. Besides, why would anyone
who was trying to hide enter a lookalike contest?"

"Still . . . Damn, I wish there was a photo. Get into
the telephone directories and see if you can find a . . ."
She squinted at the screen. "Brandy Butt. Doesn't sound
Hispanic to me. And most Hispanic women don't look
like Aurora."

"So far I've come up empty, but I have a few more
places to check."

"Let me see what I can dig up." Toni began to head
for the phone, then paused. Normal procedure would be

to hand this off to a West Virginia field office, but there was nothing normal about the task force assigned to find Aurora. She and Jason, for example reported directly to Ken Braddock, the assistant director in charge of the National Security Division, and they could either follow their own leads or pass them off.

She picked up the phone, cradled it in her neck, and regarded her partner. "I intend to head for West Virginia first thing tomorrow, Boy Howdy. How about you? Is seven o'clock too early?"

"I was planning to leave at six, but if you need a little more rest, I understand."

Oh, she was starting to like this kid.

The nape of Mat's neck was still prickling. It had been so weird, standing there in the middle of the Waynes' motor home with Button's yellow Bo Peep romper in his hand and listening to *Dateline* report Cornelia Case's disappearance. The whole thing was one of those weird coincidences, but as he walked back to Mabel, his neck still tingled. It was the same feeling he got when he was working on a big story.

He couldn't help but make a mental comparison between Nell Kelly and Cornelia Case. Despite their surface similarities, Mrs. Case was cool and sophisticated, almost ethereal, while Nell was funny, approachable, and very real. After the first impression, they didn't even look that much alike. Nell's hair was different, and even though she was thin, she didn't have that upper-class clothes-hanger look Mrs. Case had. Mrs. Case's forehead was higher, she was taller than Nell, and her eyes weren't as blue. And, most of all, Mrs. Case wouldn't have let Mathias Jorik kiss her.

He chuckled to himself. If Nell put on a wig, spruced herself up a little, and wore higher heels, she might be able to walk right to the doors of the White House and pass herself off as the First Lady. Then, when the real

Mrs. Case came back, no one would believe it was her. It'd be a chick version of *The Prince and the Pauper*. What a great story!

He opened the door and stepped inside the motor home all ready to tell her about it when he saw her sitting on the couch, and his smile faded. She was wearing her blue cotton nightgown with her feet tucked beneath her. All the lights were out except one small lamp. The light spilled across her face. She looked as delicate and ethereal as a fifteenth century Madonna, and he found it impossible to imagine her doing anything as silly as buying a ceramic frog, driving a motor home, or mooing to a cranky baby.

The skin at the back of his neck prickled. She looked very much like Cornelia Case.

She lifted her head and smiled. "You took a while. Did Bertis offer you another piece of her fruit cocktail cake?"

"Cake? No. No, we were just . . ." The wide cotton strap on her nightgown slipped on her shoulder, and the impression faded. She looked like Nell again, the woman he'd been thinking about all evening. "We were just talking."

As he sat on the edge of the banquette, the idea of making love with her passed from desire into a consuming need. "Are the girls asleep?"

"Out cold." She studied him for a moment. "Is something wrong?"

"No, why?"

"I don't know. You looked odd when you came in."

He started to tell her about Cornelia Case, but came to his senses just in time. He had seduction in mind, not a discussion of current events, and the news could definitely wait until later. "Must have been that fruit cocktail cake resettling in my stomach."

She stood, and the light provided a hazy silhouette of

her body through her nightgown. "Do you want something to drink? Another root beer?"

The most he could manage was to shake his head. He found himself rising, taking a step toward her.

She gazed up at him, and he saw wariness in her eyes, the last emotion he wanted her to feel.

"Mat, we need to talk about this. There are two children just behind that door."

"Yeah, I know." He had been thinking of little else. It was one thing to tell himself they were sound sleepers, but now he realized how thin that door really was. Time to improvise. "It's hot in here. Let's go for a walk."

"I'm in my nightgown."

"It's dark. Nobody'll be able to see a thing. Besides, that nightgown covers up more of you than the clothes you were wearing all day."

"Still . . ."

"There's a path right behind us that heads into the woods a little way. We can keep Mabel in sight."

Unexpectedly, her mouth curved, and he remembered her delight in simple pleasures. "I'll get my shoes."

A few minutes later they were walking down a path strewn with mulch chips. Just enough light penetrated the trees from the campsites to show the way. Nealy took a deep breath, inhaling the scents of woodsmoke and rich, damp vegetation, absorbing the idea that she was wandering around outside in her nightgown. "Isn't this wonderful?"

"Yeah, it's pretty nice. Give me your hand so you don't trip."

She didn't believe she was in danger of tripping, but she slipped her hand into his. It felt big, solid, and unfamiliar. Although she was the veteran of tens of thousands of handshakes, the only hands she held for long belonged to children. "I had a good time tonight."

"I hate to admit it, but I did, too."

"They were nice to Lucy. She didn't swear once while we were with them?"

"I noticed. And she had provocation with the way Bertis kept fussing over her."

"I think she liked it."

"Yeah, I think so, too." He slowed, and for a moment she wondered if he'd spotted something in their path. "Come here. Out of the light."

The husky note in his voice made her senses quicken. She felt a queer combination of excitement and misgiving as he drew her off the path into a thicket, then led her to the base of a large tree. Without letting go, he braced his back against the trunk and pulled her in front of him. Then he kissed her.

It was urgent and carnal, revealing decades of sexual experience, but this time she didn't let herself worry about whether she was doing things right. She simply wound her arms around his neck and gave in to it.

His hands skittered over her body, igniting fires wherever he touched. "I can't get enough of you."

He cupped her breast through her nightgown, ran his thumb over the crest. His head dipped, his lips found her nipple, and he suckled her through the thin cotton fabric.

She moaned. The sensation was exquisite—deeply arousing, magical . . . exactly right. She heard herself murmur, "I don't want—"

"Yes, you do."

She'd meant to say that she didn't want to be outside—she wanted privacy. But she couldn't be bothered to explain.

He reached under her nightgown. Found her panties. Gently cupped her through the nylon. "You're wet."

His blunt words made her shiver. Was this the way lovers talked to each other? He began stroking her. She arched her back and clung to him, her legs parting of their own volition.

"Take off your nightgown," he whispered.

His words jolted her back to reality. She could only handle so many new experiences at a time. "We're outside."

"That makes it even better." He gathered the gown in his hands.

She began to resist, then stopped herself. She was sick of caution, sick of following other people's rules. She relaxed her arms.

Cool air slid over her bare skin as he pulled it off and dropped it. "Now your panties," he whispered. "Hand them to me."

She hesitated.

"Do it."

His rough, sensual command thrilled her. At the same time, some primitive female instinct made her want to play a little, too, so she tried to sound put-upon. "Oh, all right."

She was rewarded with a dark chuckle that ran like warm honey through her blood. As she bent over, she was thrilled by the tawdriness of what she was doing. Even though no one in the campground seemed to be stirring, they were still in a public place.

He took her panties from her, and she thought he might be slipping them into his pocket. "Stand completely still," he whispered.

She couldn't have moved for the world.

He cupped her bare shoulders, kissed the nape of her neck. Then he touched her breasts, dallying there until she was breathless. Her foot arched, then wrapped around his calf. Sensation spiraled through her until she couldn't bear it any longer. She clasped his wrists to still his movement.

"It's your turn." Her voice was throaty, barely audible. "You take off your clothes."

Another of those low, rumbling chuckles. "Are you

crazy? We're outside. Only a rampant exhibitionist would get naked outside."

"You're a dead man," she managed.

"Humor me." His palms slipped along her spine and the teasing faded. "You feel so damn good."

His stroking felt even better.

He touched her bottom, the back of her thighs, pulled her more tightly against him. "Do you have any idea what I want to do with you right now?"

Yes, but she still wanted him to tell her. She wanted to hear words that weren't polite. Lovely sexual dirty talk that would stir her blood. "Tell me," she heard herself say. "Tell me exactly."

He squeezed her nipple. A deliciously sensuous threat. "You like playing with fire?"

"Yes."

"Then get ready to burn."

And burn she did . . . at the graphic descriptions. The lusty demands. The earthy language of sex and lust.

". . . stretch you out . . . open your legs . . . open you . . ."

He spoke into her mouth. Claimed her with his tongue. And his hands . . . oh, his hands . . . they were everywhere. Possessing her body as if he owned it.

". . . touch you here . . . press right here . . ."

Between her legs . . . fingers seeking . . .

". . . in here."

No reticence, no hesitation, no repulsion because she was female.

"And here . . ."

Reveling in her woman's scent and feel . . .

"A little deeper . . ."

Burning for her.

His touch quickened. She cried out and shattered.

He held her and kissed her through the tender earthquakes.

As the aftershocks faded, she grew aware of his strong

bare back beneath her palms, the skin hot and damp, muscles taut from self-control. She reached between their bodies and touched him.

He leaned into her hand. His breath rasped in her ear. And then he jerked away. "Damn those kids!"

She dragged air into her lungs.

"I want you to myself!" His voice was ragged with frustration. "I don't want to worry about how much noise we're making or whether somebody's going to wake up for a drink of water." He uttered a blistering obscenity, one he'd used in an entirely different way only moments before. And then he straightened. "Iowa!"

Her brain felt muzzy. "What?"

"No kids. And a bed . . ." His hands slicked over her. "Not just a pile of pine needles. As soon as we get to Iowa, we'll have real privacy, and then we can finish this."

"Iowa . . ." So far away.

He bent over, and she heard a rustle. He pressed her nightgown against her. "I'm not giving back the panties."

He sounded as cranky as an animal with a thorn in its paw, and she gave a shaky laugh. "Iowa?"

"That's right. Iowa. Mark it in ink on your calendar, sweetheart."

Just like that, the Hawkeye State became the Land of Lust.

12

MAT SPENT THE NIGHT ALTERNATING BETWEEN WAKE-fulness and fever-hot dreams. The next morning, he mainlined his first cup of coffee, then poured a second as Nell and Lucy left with Button to say good-bye to the Waynes. He slouched in the passenger seat with his mug and told himself that he was an adult, not a randy teenager, but the sight of Nell as she'd emerged from the bathroom less than an hour ago in that plain blue nightgown had been just about more than he could handle. He turned on the radio to distract himself.

"*. . . the disappearance of Cornelia Case continues to have the entire nation on edge . . .*"

He was slipping. He'd been so caught up in his sexual frustration that he'd forgotten all about the Case story. It was hard to believe she still hadn't surfaced. How many places were there where one of the most famous women in the world could have disappeared?

A funny tingling crept down his neck.

The door of the motor home flew open, and Lucy stormed in, glaring at him. "I don't know why we couldn't stay here another day like Bertis and Charlie! You have to have everything your way!"

"You're damn right," he growled. "Now buckle up. We're leaving."

Nell was coming in with Button, and she raised an eyebrow at his surly tone, but he pretended not to notice.

She knew better than anybody why he was so irritable.

He felt guilty about the way he'd snapped at Lucy, so he ignored the fact that his favorite Blackhawks cap was perched on her head. He couldn't begin to count how many items of his clothing had ended up in his sisters' closets.

After they'd finished filling the water tank and using the flushing station, they began heading west across Indiana. Nell seemed to be spending an unusual amount of time with Lucy, so he figured she was self-conscious about last night. The kids felt like even bigger millstones. If it weren't for them, Nell's self-consciousness would be a thing of the past.

He tuned in the radio again and listened to the news, keeping the volume just low enough so that no one else could hear. He wanted a little more time to think this over.

The story grew bigger as the morning progressed, and with each report, the pronouncements of the fatuous Washington pundits became more irresponsible.

"Although no one likes to think about it, Mrs. Case's life could be in danger . . .

". . . It's impossible not to speculate on the repercussions if the First Lady fell into unfriendly hands . . .

". . . domestic enemies to consider as well as foreign ones. Imagine if a militia group, for example . . ."

When a popular radio psychologist suggested that Cornelia Case might have experienced a nervous breakdown because of her sorrow over the President's death, Mat flipped off the radio. Idiots. It was a lot easier speculating about a story than it was doing the legwork to get at the truth.

But who was he to cast stones? Not long ago, he'd spent three days following a transvestite with a camera crew. He had too many of the same sins on his own conscience to criticize the way other journalists sensationalized the news.

The morning slipped by, and as the passenger seat next to him remained empty except for occasional visits from Lucy trying to talk him into making unnecessary stops, he realized Nell was deliberately avoiding him. Maybe it was better that way. He wouldn't be so distracted. Still, as they approached Indiana's western border, he realized how much he missed her cheerful running travelogue.

Those cloud formations remind me of a circus parade.
Who do you think is funding that recycling center?
What a pretty town! They have a blueberry festival. Let's go!
Wildflowers! We have to stop!

And at least every other hour . . . *Let's see where that road goes.*

Even though he missed her enthusiasm, he was still surprised when he heard himself say, "Anybody for a picnic?"

"Yes!" Nell exclaimed.

"I guess." Lucy tried to hide her enthusiasm but couldn't quite manage it, and half an hour later, he was parking in front of a Vincennes, Indiana, Kroger grocery store. He picked up Button and followed Nell and Lucy inside.

"William Henry Harrison lived right here in Vincennes," Nell said. "He was the ninth president of the United States, but he died in office a month after he was inaugurated."

He told himself it was information anyone could know. The fact that Vincennes was Harrison's home had been printed on one of the signs as they were coming into town.

Nell headed for the produce department, still chatting about William Henry Harrison and his successor, John Tyler. He watched her happily examining a display of blueberries, then admiring cartons of strawberries as if she'd never seen them before. This whole grocery store thing was way too domestic for him, and he started feeling claustrophobic. The feeling got worse when the Demon sighed and tucked her head under his chin. "Daaa . . ."

"Take her, Lucy. I've got to go buy some . . . some . . . guy stuff."

"*EEOOWWW!*"

"Never mind," he sighed. "I'll take her with me."

They left Vincennes and almost immediately crossed the border into Illinois. Nell hummed as she stood at the counter, swaying with the motion of the Winnebago while she made sandwiches. She looked so happy that he was glad he'd come up with the idea of having a picnic.

His hand crept back to the radio when he heard one of Mrs. Case's old college friends being interviewed.

"*. . . we knew we could count on Nealy to have the best class notes when it was time for an exam . . .*"

Nealy? He'd forgotten that was Mrs. Case's nickname. The press seldom used it. *Nealy. Nell.* Close.

Forget it. He was a journalist. He dealt in facts, not fancy. He'd always been proud of having no imagination, and only someone with a big imagination could believe that the First Lady of the United States would take off across the country in a Chevy Corsica, then hook up with a man hauling around two kids who didn't belong to him so she could change diapers, put up with a teenager's sass, and practice tongue kisses.

But the nape of his neck was still tingling.

Toni peered through a magnifier to study the proof sheet the photographer for the small West Virginia newspaper had given her. There wasn't a single clear shot of the Cornelia Case lookalike. A shoulder here, the top of her head, part of her back. That was it.

She handed them to Jason. "Does anything strike you as strange?"

While Jason took his time studying the photographs, she moved restlessly around the newspaper photographer's tiny office. Their interview with Laurie Reynolds, the promotion manager at WGRB radio and the person who'd been running the contest, hadn't given them much to go on.

According to Reynolds, the woman who'd called herself Brandy Butt had only spoken Spanish and seemed to have been forced into the contest by the teenage girl who was with her. Afterward, she'd run off the stage and Reynolds had seen her leave the mall with a good-looking dark-haired man, a baby girl in a pink cap, and the teenager.

Jason set down the magnifier. "It looks like she was deliberately dodging the camera."

"Hard to tell, but it does seem that way."

He shook his head. "I don't know. A husband, a baby, a teenager. Highly unlikely this woman is Aurora."

"I agree. But—this is a small town. Why doesn't anybody know who she is?"

"She was probably just traveling through with her family. The girl said she was from Hollywood."

"Nobody in Hollywood even knows where West Virginia is. And why did she dodge the camera, then disappear so fast afterward? Even more interesting—why did the teenager give a phony address when she picked up the prize?"

"Because Brandy Butt or somebody in her family doesn't want to be found."

She picked up the proofs again. "And she only won second place. Let's not forget that."

"Yeah. Pretty hard to forget." He pulled a tin of Altoids from his pocket and slipped one in his mouth. "So do we agree that we have exactly nothing?"

"I'd say that's about right. Still, this morning we had less than nothing, so we're working our way up."

*   *   *

Nealy vetoed two potential picnic spots before she found a location that pleased her. It was in a park on the edge of one of the small farming towns that lay just west of Vincennes across the Wabash River. She chose it for its duck pond, baby swings, and nice open space where they could throw a Frisbee around.

"We don't have a Frisbee," Lucy said when Nealy mentioned this.

"We do now." As Nealy pulled one from a grocery bag at her feet, she saw Mat's frown and knew he was about to announce that they didn't have time. "Lucy and I are throwing a Frisbee," she said firmly. "If you don't like it, you can go to Iowa without us."

Iowa. As he gazed at her, the word seemed to hang between them like a particularly alluring sex toy. She remembered the box of condoms she'd slipped back into the pharmacy to buy because she couldn't figure out how to ask Mat if he had any. Another new experience.

"Oh, goody . . ." Lucy muttered. "I get to throw around a freakin' Frisbee."

"Take these." Nealy shoved a bag of food at her.

"You are sooo rude."

"I know. And I like it."

Mat smiled, then banged his elbow into a cupboard as he retrieved some soft drinks from the refrigerator. The motor home was too small for him, but he didn't complain about it. She suspected he was accustomed to things being too small for him.

She swallowed hard, quickly handed over Button, and forced her one-track mind away from sex to contemplate her food choices. Would everyone like turkey sandwiches? She'd made them with Swiss cheese, but Lucy'd probably rather have American. The tortellini salad might be too exotic, and the precut baby carrots too plain. The chocolate cupcakes with panda faces had looked cute in the store, but both Mat and Lucy had stared at them when she'd taken them out of the sack.

At least Button should like her special surprises.

The irony of fretting over a simple meal like this in light of all the elaborate White House social functions she'd overseen didn't escape her. But this was so much more personal.

"Where do you want everything?" Mat asked as they stepped out into the midday sunshine beating down on the small park.

She pointed out a picnic table set in some shade not far from the playground, then smiled to herself as she thought about putting out Dixie plates instead of Lady Bird Johnson's wildflower china. Lucy gazed toward the far edge of the parking lot where three teenage boys were cutting back and forth on their skateboards.

"Go watch while I set out the food."

"Why should I watch a bunch of losers like that?"

"Because, if you're lucky, one of them will break his leg, and then you can laugh at him."

Lucy smiled. "You're such a loser, Nell."

"I know." Impulsively, Nealy reached out to hug her. Lucy's entire body went rigid, and Nealy immediately backed away. Lucy rubbed her arm and wandered off, not moving toward the boys, but not exactly moving away from them, either.

Mat set the baby in the grass, then popped a root beer. "What were the two of you talking about this morning?"

She frowned as Button started to prowl, but she knew if she mentioned anything about dirt, bugs, or dogs he'd ignore her. "Mainly whether or not Lucy should get her navel pierced."

"Over my dead body."

He sounded very much like a father. She began putting out the food. "I told her I definitely thought she should."

"Why'd you tell her that?"

"Because a navel's better than a nose or eyebrow. Besides, anything I'm in favor of she'll automatically reject. Then we discussed whether I should get my ears done."

"Your ears are already done." He touched the small hole in her left lobe, lingering longer than he had to.

She cleared her throat. "According to Lucy, one pierce doesn't count, and I should get another one in each ear."

"You're going to start wearing two earrings in each ear?"

"I'm thinking about it."

He got the strangest expression on his face. It almost seemed like relief. "Maybe you're not such a blue blood after all."

She put out the carrots, and he started to sit down on the bench, only to have Button pull herself back up on him. He glanced toward a sandbox sitting a few yards away. "Come on, Demon."

"The sand box? No, Mat. She's too young. She'll eat it."

"After a bite or two, she'll stop." He hoisted the baby in his arms, tossed her once into the air, and carried her toward the sandbox, where two little boys were already playing.

"She'll get dirty," Nealy called out. "And sunburned."

"It's in the shade, and she'll wash. You want to try out the sandbox, Demon?"

"Gah!"

"I thought so." He dropped her in, then glanced toward the other children playing there. "May God have mercy on your souls."

Keeping one eye on the baby, he moved back to the table to claim his root beer. "Panda-face cupcakes? Do we have little pointy hats to go with them? Hey, Demon, knock it off!" The baby was about to heave a plastic bucket at one of the other children.

"Go watch her while I finish putting the food out."

He looked as if she'd asked him to poke needles in his eyes.

"And don't call her Demon in front of the other kids," she added. "They'll tease her."

He managed a pained smile and trudged off to supervise the sandbox.

The boys with the skateboards had disappeared, and Lucy came drifting back to the table. She sat down on the bench and began picking at the wood. Nealy knew something was on her mind, but if she asked what it was, Lucy would shut her off, so she waited.

The teenager glanced toward the sandbox, where Mat's frown was intimidating all of the children except Button. "I guess Jorik's not as much of a jerk as I first thought."

"Well . . . he's hardheaded and domineering. And *loud*—I don't know how he has the nerve to complain about Button." She smiled. "But I know what you mean."

Lucy dug at the wood with her fingernail. "He's pretty hot. I mean, older women like you probably think so."

"He'll do, and I'm not an older woman."

"I think he likes you."

Nealy replied slowly, "We get along all right."

"No, I mean, I think he really likes you. You know."

Nealy did know, but she wasn't going to explain that the attraction was sexual.

"We're just friends. That's all." Until they got to Iowa. Then they'd be lovers. If the White House didn't find her first.

Lucy's expression grew belligerent. "You could do a lot worse, you know. He drives a Mercedes sports car. A convertible."

"He does?"

"Yeah. It's really cool. Dark blue. I'll bet he's got gobs of money."

"I don't think steelworkers make gobs of money." How could he afford a Mercedes? she wondered.

"Whatever. All I know is, you could probably have him if you wanted."

"Have him?"

"You know . . . go out." Lucy's voice dropped to a mutter. "Get him to marry you or something."

Nealy stared at her.

"Yeah . . . if you'd just, you know, fix yourself up or something. Wear a little more makeup. And get some clothes that aren't so lame. He'd probably be a good husband and everything. I mean, he wouldn't beat you up like that jerk you were married to."

Nealy felt something inside her melt in the face of Lucy's earnestness, and she sat down so she could look right at her. "There's a lot more to marriage than finding a husband who won't beat you up. Good marriages are based on companionship and mutual interests. You want to marry somebody who's a friend, not just a lover. Someone who . . ." Pain hit her in a dizzying wave. She'd done exactly that, and her marriage had been a mockery.

Lucy regarded her sulkily. "You two've got mutual interests. You both like talking, and good manners, and crap like that. And you both like Button." She picked at the wood sliver. "You might, you know . . ."—she drew a deep breath—"decide to adopt her or something."

Nealy finally understood what this conversation was about, and it broke her heart. She didn't care whether Lucy wanted to be touched or not. She reached across the table and cupped her hand. "Oh, Luce . . . Mat and I aren't going to get together, not the way you want. I'm sorry. We can't make a home for Button or for you."

Lucy shot up from the table as if Nealy had struck her. "Like I'd want to live with either one of you. You're so fucking pathetic!"

"Lucy!" Mat came storming toward them with Button tucked under his arm. His expression was angry, and he shot one hand toward Mabel. "Get in there."

"No, Mat . . . it's all right." Nealy rose, trying to stem his anger.

Button began to whimper.

"It's not all right." He gave Lucy a blistering look. "You're not going to talk to Nell like that. If you want to act like a brat, you can do it by yourself. Now get going."

"Fuck you, too!" Lucy stomped off through the grass toward Mabel.

Mat clenched his fist. "I want to hit her."

"Lucy can be maddening, but I think—"

"No, you don't understand. I really want to hit her."

Button looked up at him, eyes wide, lower lip beginning to tremble. He set her to his shoulder and patted her back. His expression was troubled. "It's what I used to do with my sisters when I was a kid."

"Did you?" She was torn between listening to him and going to Lucy. If only he'd been more patient with her instead of flying off like that.

"They used to enrage me, just like Lucy did, and when I couldn't stand it any longer, I'd haul off and slug them. A couple of times I left bruises on their arms. I'm no damned good at this. It's why I hate being around kids so much." He shifted Button to his other shoulder.

"You hit them?" She watched Button poke a wet finger into his ear canal. "How old were you?"

"Ten. Eleven. Old enough to know better, that's for sure."

Not all that old. But Nealy knew nothing about relationships between brothers and sisters. "Did you keep hitting them as you grew older?"

His eyebrows shot up. "Of course not. I started to play hockey instead and took out my anger on the ice. During the summer, I boxed a little. Looking back on it, I think sports saved my sisters' lives."

"So you didn't keep hitting them?"

"No, but I sure wanted to. Just like now. She's such a brat."

"She's having a hard time. And wanting to hit her isn't the same thing as doing it. I don't think you have to worry too much about being a batterer."

He looked as if he were going to argue, but at the moment she was too concerned about Lucy to listen. "I'd better go talk to her."

"No. She'll wrap you around her finger. I'll do it."

"Wait a minute! You need to know what—"

"Save it. There aren't any excuses for that kind of behavior." He passed Button over to her and set off for the motor home.

As Nealy watched him go, the baby twisted in her arms and started to cry. Nealy stared glumly at the table of uneaten food. So much for her wonderful picnic.

Lucy lay face down on the bed, with her fist crushing her heart. She hated him! She hated them both. She wished she'd gotten hit by a car and gone into a coma. Then they'd be sorry for the way they treated her.

She clenched her fist tighter and squeezed her eyes shut against her tears. She was being such a brat that she couldn't even stand herself. It was no wonder they hated her. Nell had just been trying to be nice. Why did she always have to screw everything up?

The door of the motor home banged and Mat charged in. Now she was really going to get it. She didn't want him to see her lying on the bed slobbering, so she got up real quick and sat on the edge.

She wondered if he'd hit her. Sandy'd never hit her, not even when she was drunk, but Trent had once.

Mat came stomping back to the bedroom. She sat up straighter and got ready to face him. "I'm sorry!" she yelled before he could yell at her. "That's what you want to hear, isn't it?"

He just looked at her, and the expression on his face

made her want to cry all over again. He looked really mad, but he looked disgusted, too, like she'd really disappointed him.

He looked like a dad.

She bit her lip so she didn't start crying and thought about all those years she'd dreamed about him. She used to write his name in her notebooks and whisper it as she fell asleep at night. Mathias Jorik. Her dad.

She'd grown up knowing he wasn't her real father. Sandy'd never lied to her about that. Her real dad had been a student at Carnegie Mellon Sandy had met in a bar one night and never seen again. Sandy didn't even remember his name. She'd always said that, in her heart, Mat was Lucy's dad.

She'd heard lots of stories about Mat while she was growing up. How he and Sandy had met. How cute and smart he'd been. How nice he'd treated her, even though he didn't have any money because he was only twenty-one and he'd just graduated from college.

Lucy'd always dreamed that he didn't care that Lucy wasn't his kid. She'd imagined him telling her mother, *That's okay, Sandy. It's not like it's the baby's fault that you got pregnant or anything, and I already love her just like she's mine.*

As if.

"You're not getting away with talking to Nell like that."

"She started it." That was such a lie that Lucy couldn't even believe she'd said it.

"What did she do?" He didn't say it like he believed her. He said it like he knew she was full of it, and he was just giving her a chance to dig a deeper hole for herself.

She thought about how bad she'd screwed up today. She was supposed to be getting them together, but all she'd done was cause trouble. If only Nell hadn't said how she and Mat weren't ever going to get married, and how they couldn't adopt Button. And then she'd said that part about not being able to adopt Lucy, either, and it had made Lucy go sort of nuts, even though she hadn't ever thought they'd adopt her.

But Nell was only part of this, Lucy remembered. Jorik was the other part, and maybe he saw things between him and Nell different. The only way Lucy could find out was to swallow her pride. But it was hard. It felt as if she were trying to swallow a whole mouthful of broken glass.

"Nell didn't do anything. It was me. I was being a bitch." Now that the words were out, she didn't feel so bad, and she was almost glad she'd made herself say them.

"Damn right you were."

"Nell said you're not supposed to swear around me."

"Then we won't tell her, will we? Just like we won't tell her that I'm thinking of keeping you locked up back here until I turn you over to your grandmother."

Lucy poked at the frayed hole in her denim shorts. "I don't care what you do."

"You ruined Nell's picnic. You know that, don't you? You saw the way she was fussing over those sandwiches like they were the most important thing in the world. She bought cupcakes with faces! Stuff like that means a lot to her, and now you've spoiled it."

Everything he was saying was true, and it made Lucy feel awful. But right now she had to think about Button, not her own feelings. "I said I was sorry. You like her a lot, don't you?"

"Nell?"

Who'd he think they were talking about? But Lucy held back her sarcasm. "She likes you a lot, too. She said you were hot."

"She did?"

"Uh-huh. And that you're smart and really, really sensitive." What did a few more lies mean when she'd already screwed up so bad?

"She said I was sensitive?"

"That means a lot to women. I think it's because you like Button so much." She didn't mean for it to come out like a question, but it did anyway.

She must have gone too far because he looked at her suspiciously. "What does Button have to do with this?"

"Nothing," she said quickly. "I was just using her as an example. And I wanted to tell you . . . if you want to be alone with Nell for a while for anything, me and Button can, you know, disappear. You just let me know." She'd gotten good at disappearing with Sandy and Trent.

"Thanks." Now he was the one who sounded sarcastic. He crossed his arms and looked at her in a way that made her want to squirm. "You've got an apology to make. And it had better sound so sincere that it puts a lump in her throat, understand?"

Even though she felt like her neck was breaking, she nodded.

"And you eat everything she puts in front of you, even if it tastes like crap."

She nodded again.

"One more thing . . . after we're done eating, you're going to look her straight in the eye and beg her to let you throw that stupid Frisbee around."

"Sure." Lucy was starting to feel lots better because he wouldn't care about all this if he didn't like Nell so much. Maybe Button was going to have a home after all.

Considering its disastrous start, Nealy's picnic turned out well. Lucy offered a quiet apology, which Nealy quickly accepted. Then she and Mat proceeded to eat everything Nealy put out, including the tortellini salad, although she noticed Lucy saved hers until last and

puffed out her cheeks while she was chewing. Button
enjoyed all her food, but especially her banana, which
she rubbed into her hair with glee.

They'd barely finished eating before Mat said,
"Where's that Frisbee? Let's see how good you are,
Nell."

"You two go ahead while I clean up Button. I'll be
there in a minute."

Lucy and Mat set off for a grassy space just beyond
the picnic tables. Nealy watched them as she changed
Button, but she hesitated just as she was about to join
them and decided to put Button in a baby swing instead.
Let Mat and Lucy have this time together.

She wasn't surprised by Mat's athleticism. He threw
the Frisbee behind his back, made graceful catches, and
in general enjoyed horsing around. Lucy was more of a
surprise. After the first few awkward minutes, a lively
young teenager surfaced. Lucy was a natural athlete,
quick and agile. Mat alternated between taunting and
praising her.

*You'll never catch it. I'm way too good for you.
Hey, not bad for a smart aleck . . . Whoa, you got some
spin on that one. Okay, ace, see what you can do with
this . . .*

Something inside Nealy ached as she watched them.
Lucy's brown eyes shone, her child's laughter floated on
every wisp of breeze. She looked young and happy, like
the girl she should have been rather than the one she'd
been forced to become. When Mat had to walk over to
the playground to rescue an errant throw, Lucy followed
him with her eyes, and her yearning was so intense it
could only have come from the loneliest of hearts.

She thought of her own difficult relationship with her
father. Because he was so manipulative, she saw herself
as his victim. Now she found herself wondering what
part she'd played in being victimized. It was pathetic to

be First Lady of the United States and still so concerned about pleasing Daddy.

Maybe if she hadn't been so young when she'd lost her mother, it would have been easier. Although she and her stepmother had a cordial relationship, it had never been an intimate one, which made her father even more important in her life. She'd frequently protested his manipulations but never completely defied him, not until she'd walked out of the White House four days ago. Had she been afraid that he wouldn't love her if she rebelled? She promised herself that, from now on, James Litchfield would have to accept her on her own terms or be moved to the fringes of her life.

"Come on, Nell," Mat called out. "Set the Demon in the grass over here and see if you can keep up with us young folks."

Feeling as if a burden had been lifted from her shoulders, Nealy joined them. Although her skills didn't match theirs, they tolerated her, and she had a wonderful time.

Eventually, Mat threw his arm around Lucy's shoulders and rubbed her head with his knuckles. "Time to get back on the road, ace. You did all right."

Lucy beamed as if he'd given her a priceless gift.

Button soon fell asleep in her car seat, and Lucy curled up in the back with her book. Nealy took her time putting away the last of the picnic food. Without the children as a barrier, she felt awkward around Mat. Just thinking about those hot words he'd uttered last night, the intimacy of his caresses, made it hard for her to meet his eyes. She didn't like herself for it. Thirty-one was too old to be insecure about sex.

She realized how accustomed she'd grown to keeping people at a distance, but it was an act of self-preservation for First Ladies who lived in an age of tabloid journalism and tell-all memoirs. In the past few years, even her friendships from childhood had suffered.

Maybe what she enjoyed most about being Nell Kelly was that Nell didn't have to worry about anyone's place in history. She could just be herself. Nell, she realized, wouldn't have a problem talking to Mat after last night's delicious escapade.

She moved to the front and sat in the passenger seat. "Do you want me to drive for a while?"

"Not on your life. You'll decide that Button can't enter kindergarten if she hasn't seen Lincoln's law office in Springfield or the riverboat in Peoria."

"There's a riverboat in Peoria?" She'd already seen Lincoln's law offices.

"It sank."

"You're lying. Let's do it, Mat. Let's go to Peoria. It's such a perfect symbol of middle America. It'll be like a pilgrimage."

"Iowa's just as good a symbol of middle America as Peoria, and that's the only pilgrimage we're going to make." He glanced over at her and those smoky gray eyes took a leisurely stroll from her chest to her toes. "Besides, we can't make love in Peoria."

Nell Kelly, the hussy, extended her legs just a little bit farther. "There is that."

"There sure is."

He'd definitely liked her legs. She smiled to herself. "Lucy loved throwing the Frisbee with you."

"Yeah. She's a pretty good athlete."

"I wonder what's going to happen to her. I asked about her grandmother today, but she wasn't very forthcoming."

"I met her once, and I don't think she's your typical gray-haired grandmother. Sandy was born when she was young, so she's probably only in her early fifties now."

"That's good for the girls. They need someone younger. I just hope she can handle Lucy without breaking her spirit."

"Nobody's going to break that kid's spirit. She's got a lot of guts."

She hesitated. "When you talked to her earlier, was she acting strangely?

"What do you mean?"

"Did she . . . say anything about the two of us?"

"Yeah. She said you thought I was hot and sensitive."

"I never said that."

"Extremely smart, too. But then I always knew you were a good judge of character. She also volunteered to disappear for a while if I wanted to put any moves on you." He paused. "Which I do."

She began to smile, but didn't quite make it. "Lucy's doing some matchmaking. I think she believes that if she can get the two of us together we'll adopt her and Button. That's why she blew up at me. I told her it wasn't going to happen."

His own expression sobered. "This is what I wanted to avoid. I swear if Sandy were still alive, I'd kill her for this."

"She also doesn't seem to be in any hurry to get to Iowa. The whole thing is starting to worry me. What are you going to do if things don't work out with the grandmother?"

Nealy didn't like the way his eyes narrowed. "The girls are Joanne Pressman's responsibility. She'll have to make them work out."

She glanced back at Button sleeping in her car seat, the Beanie Baby walrus curled over one chubby thigh, then gazed at Lucy sprawled across the bed with her head buried in a book. These little girls deserved a family and she could only pray that they'd find one.

Mat had hoped they'd be closer to the Iowa border by nightfall, but the picnic had held them up. Then Nell saw a sign for a county fair, and the next thing he knew, he was perched on the back of a merry-go-round horse with a wide-eyed baby on his lap. Now, as they hit a deserted stretch of highway in central Illinois, that same baby was falling apart. With the closest campground forty miles away and her screams getting louder, he pulled off the highway at a weather-beaten FOR SALE sign.

A narrow, rutted lane led to an abandoned farmhouse. He parked the Winnebago in a small clearing between the house and the skeleton of an old barn.

"I bet a chain-saw murderer or somebody lives here."

He heard apprehension behind the bravado in Lucy's voice, but he wasn't going to make her swallow her pride by mentioning it. "You chicken, ace?"

"No, I'm not chicken! But Nell looks nervous."

Nell, in fact, looked delighted. But then every new adventure seemed to delight her. "Do you think anyone will mind if we stay here?" she asked.

He opened the door and gazed around at the weedy drive and sagging house. "It doesn't look like anybody's been here for a while. I don't think we have to worry too much."

He was given Button-duty while Nell boiled some water for the spaghetti he'd bought for emergency rations, along with a jar of sauce. Lucy picked up the debris from their day and set out the dishes without being asked. Nell, who didn't seem to be able to enjoy a meal without ants, announced they were eating outside, and they dined on the old quilt spread on the ground in an overgrown apple orchard.

Afterward, Nell wanted to explore. Since there were too many hazards lurking around the ramshackle property for her to go off on her own, he propped Button on his shoulders, and he and Lucy went along. As an occasional spit bubble dripped into his hair, he let his female posse poke around the farm. Near the foundation of the old house, he spotted something pink. When he bent down to see what it was, he discovered an old, weed-strangled rosebush. He plucked off one of the buds that was just beginning to open and handed it to her.

"A perfect rose for a perfect lady."

He'd meant to tease, but it didn't come out that way. It sounded sincere, and Nell looked as if he'd given her the Hope diamond.

They wandered around until it was too dark to see. That was when Lucy seemed to remember her role as matchmaker.

"Give me Button, Jorik. Even a moron could figure out that it's way past her bedtime, and she still needs a bath."

Button, however, refused to separate, and while Nell stayed outside to enjoy the evening, his rose tucked behind her ear, he found himself on bath duty. He didn't have the patience to fuss around with putting her in the sink the way Lucy and Nell did, so he set her in the bottom of the shower stall and turned on the spray. Quick and effective.

Lucy put her into bed, then propped herself on the couch with her book and told him to get lost so she could concentrate on what she was reading. He thought about telling her that her matchmaking wouldn't work, but decided he'd be a fool to pass up a chance to be alone with Nell.

Outside, the moonlight in the old orchard made gnomes from the gnarled tree trunks. She stood in the long grass with her head tilted back, gazing at the stars that were just becoming visible. She was a million miles away.

He moved quietly, unwilling to disturb her. Light silvered her hair and fell softly on her skin. She looked beautiful and exotic, both at home in the old orchard and alien to it.

Once again, he felt that uncomfortable tingling at the back of his neck, along with an odd pitching in his stom-

ach. She was just Nell. Nell Kelly, an upper-crust runaway with a soft heart and a zest for life.

The night was too peaceful to spoil by talking, especially when all he wanted was to make love, so he was
surprised when he felt his lips move. Even more surprised by what he said.

"Mrs. Case?"

"Yes?" She turned automatically.

13

FOR ONE ETERNAL SECOND, NEALY STOOD THERE WITH an idiot smile on her face waiting to see what he wanted. And then, when she realized what she'd said, she felt as if the ground had fallen away beneath her.

A thousand thoughts raced through her head, a jumble of images—her hopes . . . her dreams . . . her lies . . .

Too late, she said, "You've . . . you've really got this fixation with . . . Cornelia Case, don't you?"

He didn't respond. Didn't move.

She tried to brazen it out. "W-what's wrong?"

Only his lips moved. "This is . . . this is crazy."

She began to push her hands into her pockets, but her arms were as stiff and creaky as the Tin Man's, and they wouldn't move. "Did you get Button settled?"

"Don't." The word was softly spoken, intense.

She tried to conjure up something to say that would make everything right again, but came up empty. She turned away and crossed her arms over her chest as if that would contain her secrets.

"It's true." There was no doubt in his voice.

"No. I don't know what you're talking about."

"It's been all over the news since last night."

"What?"

"The fact that Mrs. Case . . . that *you* disappeared from the White House."

She hadn't bought a paper this morning—hadn't even

glanced at them in the grocery. She didn't want to know. Now she remembered the way he'd been fiddling with the radio while he drove.

The mantle of the First Lady was enveloping Nell Kelly like a magician's cape. But she didn't want Nell to disappear. Nell was a new person being born inside her, the person she might have been if she hadn't allowed herself to become a tool of her father's ambition. Nell had Cornelia Case's strengths, but not her insecurities.

"I'm sure you're aware that everyone in the country is looking for you."

She heard formality in his voice. That awful formality people used when they addressed the First Lady. He'd never once sounded like that with Nell, and she knew right then that she'd lost him. Before they'd ever had a chance.

The secret fantasy she hadn't known she was weaving unraveled. The fantasy of Mat and Nell traveling around the country in a battered Winnebago with two kids. Fishing in the Great Lakes, visiting Disney World, seeing sunsets over the Rockies, making love in the Arizona desert. An endless road trip.

"The wind's picking up," she said in a creaky old woman's voice.

"I think you should call someone."

"Lucy's showers take forever. I hope there's enough water in the tank."

"We need to talk about how best to handle this."

"I'm glad we used paper plates for dinner. Less to wash up."

"Nell—*Mrs. Case*, we have to discuss this."

She whirled on him. "No! No, we don't need to at all. I'm going to check on Button."

He shot in front of her, blocking her path without touching her. His features were stony in the moonlight. "I'm sorry, but I'm going to have to insist."

She gazed at the mouth she'd kissed only last night. It looked grim and forbidding. They'd planned to make love when they got to Iowa, but now they wouldn't. Even men as confident as Mat Jorik didn't make love to icons.

She struggled against a wrenching sense of loss. "Insist? Insist on what?"

"I need to know what's happening. What you want." That awful formality.

"That's simple. I want you to forget about this."

She slipped past him, and he didn't try to stop her. He'd had no qualms about manhandling Nell, but he wouldn't touch the First Lady.

Mat stared at Nell's back as she disappeared inside the motor home. Nothing in his experience had prepared him for this. She hadn't admitted she was Mrs. Case, and for a moment he tried to convince himself he had it all wrong. But there was no sidestepping the truth. Despite that pink rose tucked behind her ear, the woman he knew as Nell Kelly was Cornelia Case, the widow of the President of the United States and the country's First Lady.

He felt as if he'd taken a sucker punch right to the gut as he moved blindly toward the old farmhouse and sagged down on the crumbling front step. He tried to sort it all out. For three days, they'd traveled together. They'd laughed, argued, taken care of Sandy's kids. They'd been friends. And they'd almost been lovers.

He remembered those blood-boiling kisses, the caresses. His skin grew hot, as much from embarrassment as arousal. The things he'd done . . . the suggestions he'd made. To the First Lady.

He was suddenly furious with her. From the very beginning, she'd lied. She'd toyed with him like Marie Antoinette amusing herself with a peasant she could enjoy and then discard. And he'd been sucked right in. She must have been laughing her ass off.

He swore and began to rise, only to feel as if he'd been hit again. He sagged back down onto the step. Drew a ragged breath.

He'd just been handed the story of a lifetime.

The First Lady was on the run, and he was the only reporter in America who knew where she was.

Through his daze, he realized he'd just been given back his professional pride.

He jumped to his feet, began to pace, tried to think, but anger kept getting in his way. She'd broken a trust—broken his trust—and he wouldn't forgive that.

The story, he told himself. Think about the story. He wouldn't tell her he was a reporter, that was for damn sure. She'd lied to him from the beginning, and he didn't owe her anything.

He forced himself to organize his jumbled thoughts. Why had she fled and how had she done it? He tried to figure out how much time had lapsed between her disappearance from the White House and the moment he'd picked her up at the truck stop. But nothing would come together. Instead he found himself thinking about the way they'd planned to make love when they got to Iowa. Another deception. She'd known it would never happen.

He remembered her silly story of a gay husband. It was laughable the way he'd actually believed her. But her lies had been so convincing, the way she'd manipulated him with those coy hesitations so that he'd drawn an entirely erroneous conclusion. He'd been used by a master.

He began to outline a plan. Sooner or later, she would have to tell him at least part of the truth—why she'd done it, how she'd managed to get away. The conspiracy nuts were already having a field day with this, but—

Every muscle in his body tightened, and for the third time that night he felt as if he'd been struck. Her gay husband . . . What if she hadn't been lying? What if she'd been telling the truth?

For a moment he was actually dizzy. Dennis Case, America's squeaky-clean young President, had been the perfect antidote to years of Clinton's womanizing. What if the reason Case hadn't looked at other women was more complicated than strong moral character?

A thousand caveats blasted through his head. He needed facts, not speculation. This was too big a story to ruin with even a single mistake. *Truth. Accuracy. Fairness.* What he wrote would go down in the history books with his name attached to it, and he couldn't let anything screw that up.

At least an hour passed before he let himself inside the Winnebago. The door at the back was shut, even though it was too early for her to have gone to bed. She couldn't have made it clearer that she didn't want to talk.

He kicked off his shoes, pulled a root beer from the refrigerator, and began to plan. But even as he sorted and organized, he felt a bone-searing anger. There was nothing he hated more than being played for a chump.

Nealy woke at dawn. For a few seconds she simply lay there, content to the tips of her toes, and then it all came crashing in. Mat knew who she was.

She wanted to curl up next to Lucy and stay there forever, but she forced herself to get out of bed. Button was still asleep on the floor. She stepped around her and let herself in the bathroom to shower and dress. So far he'd kept the news to himself. If he hadn't, the Secret Service would already have pounded on the door this morning. She tried to feel grateful for these past four days instead of bitter because they were being snatched away, but she couldn't quite manage it.

Lucy was still asleep when she came out, and Mat was holding Button while he made baby cereal. Although the baby still wore her sleeper, he'd added her pink cap. This morning the bill was turned to the side, giving her a Little Rascals look. For a tough guy, he had a big soft spot. But not for her. That had ended last night.

Her throat tightened. They'd all grown so precious to her. How was she going to leave them behind?

"Gah!" The baby pumped her legs and regarded Nealy happily from her perch in his arms.

Nealy smiled back. "*Gah* yourself." She reached for the box of baby cereal. "I'll fix it."

"I'll take care of it."

His formality hadn't faded. If anything, it seemed to have settled in deeper. Now, however, she heard the angry edge behind it. Mat was stiff-necked and proud. In his eyes, she'd made a fool of him.

She gazed at his messy hair and the wrinkled T-shirt he'd thrown on with a pair of shorts. His jaw was unshaven, his feet bare. He looked disheveled and gorgeous, so thoroughly at home in his oversized body that the act of making baby cereal seemed as masculine as growing a beard.

"I've made coffee if you want some." He usually made the coffee, but this was the first time he'd felt the need to announce it. She'd become a houseguest.

"Thank you."

"There's not much for breakfast."

"I know. We went shopping together, remember?"

"If you need anything—"

"I'm fine."

"There's some cereal left, a little milk, but I don't think there's any—"

"Stop it! Just stop it!"

His expression stiffened. "Excuse me?"

"I'm exactly the same person today that I was yesterday, and I don't need you tiptoeing around me."

"I didn't mean to offend you," he said stiffly.

She turned away and went outside.

Mat cursed himself for letting anger get in his way. The story was the only thing that counted now, and he had to put his own feelings aside so he could do his job. He grabbed a teething biscuit from a box on the counter, shoved it in Button's hand, and carried her outside with him.

The day was gloomy, humid, and overcast. Weeds, wet with morning dew, brushed his bare feet as he walked toward the orchard where she stood with her arms wrapped around herself. For a moment he felt himself weakening. She looked so damned vulnerable. But the moment passed.

"Mrs. Case."

"I'm Nell!" Wisps of light brown hair fluttered as she whirled around. "Just Nell."

"With all due respect, you're not. And that's a problem."

Her hands slammed on her hips. "I'll tell you where you can put your *due respect*!"

"I need to know what's going on."

"No, you don't!" And then her arms fell. "I'm sorry. I didn't mean to sound imperious."

"You owe me the truth," he said stonily.

He was right, but she'd lost the habit of confiding in anyone. First Ladies couldn't afford to tell their secrets. Still, she owed him something.

"I had to get away. I just—I just wanted to be ordinary for a while."

"Isn't this a little extreme?"

"I'm sure it seems that way to you, but—"

"Hey, where is everybody?" They both turned as Lucy stuck her head out the door. The T-shirt she'd slept in came to her knees, and her hair must have been wet when she'd fallen asleep because it stuck up in a rooster tail. Just the sight of her lifted Nealy's spirits. At least there was one person who thought of her only as Nell.

"We're out here," she replied unnecessarily.

"Are you arguing?"

"Not exactly."

Mat seemed as glad of the interruption as she was. "Where'd you get that T-shirt?"

Lucy scowled. "I found it somewhere."

"Yeah, in a stack of my clothes."

Nealy had no desire to continue her conversation with Mat, so she made her way back to the motor home. She was living on borrowed time, and she intended to use every second.

Lucy stepped aside to let her in. "So do we have anything to eat for breakfast that doesn't blow?"

Nealy restrained herself from hugging her. "Next time let's just ask if there's anything edible, okay?"

Lucy glowered. "I'm sick of cereal."

"Make some toast."

"Toast blows."

"Lucy, don't talk to . . . Nell like that," Mat said from the doorway.

Nealy rounded on him. "This is between Lucy and me."

"Yeah, Jorik, just butt out."

"That's enough, Lucy," she said. "You have a . . . a . . . time out for being disrespectful."

"A *time out*?" Lucy regarded her incredulously.

Nealy knew about time outs from her visits to nursery schools, and she pointed toward the back. "Fifteen minutes. And shut the door. That way you'll have some privacy so you can think about how to address adults properly."

"You've got to be shittin' me."

"That's another fifteen minutes for inappropriate language. Do you want to try for longer?"

Lucy looked toward Mat as if s..e expected him to rescue her from what was clearly Nell's latest insanity, but he jerked his head to the back. "You've got it coming."

"This sucks! I haven't even had *breakfast*!" She stomped away, then banged the door as hard as she could.

Mat set Button down. "I'm sorry. You shouldn't have to deal with that."

"Why not? I've been dealing with it since Wednesday."

"Yes, but—"

"Stop treating me like a guest," she snapped. "I'm going to fix Button's cereal. If you have something intelligent to say, then say it. Otherwise, just shut up."

As she stalked over to the sink, she decided that Nell Kelly might not be dead after all.

Mat smoldered. He was the one who'd been wronged, but she acted as if this were his fault.

The fact that his emotions were still getting in the way of his journalistic detachment only made it worse. The biggest story of his career was unfolding right in front of him, and all he wanted to do was grab his subject by her shoulders and shake her until those aristocratic little teeth rattled.

His self-control snapped a few hours later as he was paying for some groceries at a combination service station and convenience store in rural southern Illinois and realized that Nell—Mrs. Case—had disappeared. A chill shot through him. For the first time, it hit him that this woman should be protected by a cadre of Secret Service agents, and she only had him.

He grabbed the groceries and shot outside. She hadn't gone into the motor home. It was parked right by the door, and he would have seen her. He took in a collection of dusty vehicles, a gas pump, and a mean-looking German shepherd. Where in the hell was she?

The dire predictions of all the conspiracy nuts he'd heard on the radio came rushing back to him. He hurried to the side of the building and saw a weedy field and a scrap heap of old tires, but no runaway First Lady. He

raced for the other side and found her standing at the
pay phone that was mounted next to an air hose.

"*Damn it!*"

Her head shot up as he dropped the groceries and
charged toward her. She spoke quickly into the telephone, then hung up.

"Don't you ever do that to me again!" He knew he
was yelling, but he couldn't help himself.

"I hope there weren't any eggs in those sacks. And
what did I do?"

"Disappear like that! I thought you were— Damn it,
Nell, when we're not in that motor home, I want you
stuck to my side, do you hear me?"

"Won't that be a little uncomfortable for us both?"

First Lady or not, they were going to get a few things
straight. He lowered his voice to a hiss. "You may think
this is goddamn funny—playing the runaway princess,
amusing yourself with the hoi polloi—but it isn't a
game. Do you have any idea what could happen if some
kind of extremists got hold of you?"

"I have a better idea than you," she hissed back. "And
you're the only person who knows where I am. Granted,
your behavior can be a little extreme at times, but—"

"Don't you dare start making jokes!"

She smiled at him and whispered, "This is more like
it."

His blood hit the boiling point. "You think this is
funny?"

"Not funny. It's just nice to have you back to your
normal arrogant self again." Her smile faded. "And I'm
not amusing myself with the hoi polloi."

"What else would you call it?"

"Freedom!" Her eyes flashed. "It's the basic right of
every American citizen unless she happens to be First
Lady. You listen to me, Mat Jorik . . ." She stunned him
by jabbing his chest. "In the past year, I buried my husband and got maneuvered into keeping a job I didn't

want. I've lived in the spotlight since I was born, doing
the right thing, putting everybody's interests in front of
mine. If I'm being selfish now, well, that's tough! I've
earned it, and I'm going to enjoy every minute."

"Is that so?"

"You bet it is, buster!"

He was the one who should be yelling, and he
couldn't figure out how he'd managed to lose the upper
hand. "Who were you calling?" he snapped.

"Barbara Bush."

"Yeah, tell me another—" He broke off as he realized
it was entirely possible she had called Barbara Bush.

Her expression was annoyingly close to a smirk. "Do
you know what she said just before I hung up?"

He shook his head.

"She said, *'You go, girl.'* "

"Uh . . . did she?"

"And Hillary Clinton said words to the same effect
when I called her yesterday from that gas station."

"You called Hillary—"

"You may not understand why I'm doing this, but
they certainly do."

"Did you—did you call them for a reason?"

"I'm not irresponsible, despite what you think. I've
called someone nearly every day so the White House
knows I'm still alive. Now if you think you know more
about national security than I do, maybe you'd better tell
me about it."

He had a long list of questions he wanted to ask about
that very topic, starting with how she'd managed to escape the White House, but they'd have to wait until he'd
straightened her out. "I'm not saying that you're irresponsible. I'm just saying that I don't want you going
anywhere without me. That's the deal. Take it or leave
it."

"Maybe I'll leave it. Don't forget I have money, and
I can go off on my own anytime I want."

He gritted his teeth. "You're not going any-damn-where by yourself!"

She smiled again, which nearly drove him wild. He took a couple of deep breaths and tried to reconcile this bratty lady in the khaki shorts and buttercup-yellow top with the cool, sophisticated First Lady.

He tried to regain lost ground. "Who sent you the money?"

At first he didn't think she'd answer, but she shrugged. "Terry Ackerman."

Ackerman had been the President's chief advisor as well as Dennis Case's oldest friend. No time to examine *that* relationship at the moment, so he filed the information away. "How do you know he hasn't told the White House where he sent it?"

"Because I asked him not to."

"And you trust him?"

"As much as I trust anybody." He suspected that she meant her words to come off as flippant, but they sounded sad.

He could fight her when she was being haughty and unreasonable, but it was hard to fight sadness. His frustration boiled to the surface. "I don't even know what to call you!"

"You'd better keep calling me Nell. Or maybe you'd rather call me Mrs. Case, and tip off all those extremists lurking in that cornfield over there?"

"This isn't anything to joke about."

"Just worry about yourself, all right? I'll take care of me."

As she bent over to pick up the groceries, he heard the squeal of brakes, the blast of a radio, and what sounded like an explosion.

He didn't even think about it. He just threw himself at her.

They both flew through the air, away from the sidewalk, into the weeds. He heard a small "Oof" as the air rushed from her body.

"Don't move!" He wanted a gun. He needed a gun!

A long silence, followed by a croaky gasp for air . . . "Mat?"

His heart was pounding so hard he knew she had to feel it.

And then he got an uneasy prickling along his spine. That explosion he'd heard . . . now that he could think again he realized it hadn't sounded all that much like a gunshot.

It had sounded like a car backfiring.

14

RAIN PUMMELED THE WINNEBAGO AS THEY CRAWLED across the flat Illinois landscape toward the Iowa border. Nealy gazed out at the fields of corn and soybeans, gray and lonesome under the dreary afternoon sky, and smiled to herself. It really had been valiant of Mat to try to protect her from that vicious backfire, and with the exception of a scrape on her shin, she wasn't any the worse for wear.

A passing car tossed a rooster tail of water at the windshield. Mat flicked to another radio station for an update on her disappearance. Although he barely spoke to her, when he did, the awful formality had disappeared. And he hadn't made any move to turn her in. This morning she'd believed her adventure was over, but now she wondered.

"Why don't you let me drive for a while?" she asked.

"Because I don't have anything better to do."

"Except sulk."

"Sulk!"

"I know it was a bitter blow to you that the car had rowdy teenagers in it instead of a band of armed militia coming to take me hostage, but I'm sure you'll get over it." She grinned. "Thanks, Mat. I really do appreciate the gesture."

"Yeah, right."

Just then Lucy reappeared from the back of the motor

home. She'd been restless ever since they'd left the service station, alternating between entertaining Button and sealing herself in the back. "It's so weird," she said. "We kept talking about Cornelia Case, and now all they're saying on the radio is how she disappeared." She was wearing one of the sundresses Nealy had bought her and only half her customary makeup. She looked darling, but she'd shrugged it off when Nealy had told her so.

Now she retrieved the Beanie Baby walrus from the floor and handed it back to Button, who was fussing because Mat wasn't paying attention to her. "Wouldn't it be cool if somebody at that lookalike contest thought you were really her in disguise, and we had all these army guys chasing us?"

Mat shuddered.

"Very cool," Nealy managed.

"What's that noise?" Mat cocked his head to the side. "It's coming from the back now."

"I didn't hear anything," Lucy said.

A flying Beanie Baby walrus hit Mat in the shoulder. Nealy turned around to see that Button had stopped fussing. She looked smug.

Nealy regarded her suspiciously. "That had to be an accident."

"You just go on believing it." He glowered at the baby.

"Gah!" She glowered back, and her expression so perfectly matched his that it was hard to believe he wasn't her real father.

"How much farther?" Lucy asked.

"The Mississippi's just ahead. We're going to cross at Burlington, then go north along the river to Willow Grove. Probably another hour or so."

"Let me drive. I know how to drive."

"Forget it."

She began chewing her thumbnail. Nealy regarded her

with concern. "What's the matter, Luce? You've been acting nervous all afternoon."

"I have not!"

She decided the time had come to pry a little deeper. "You haven't said much about your grandmother. What's she like?"

Lucy abandoned her orange juice and sat down in the banquette. "She's like a grandmother. You know."

"No, I don't. There are all kinds of grandmothers. How do the two of you get along?"

Lucy got that familiar belligerent look. "We get along great! She's the best grandmother in the world. She's got tons of money, and she's this real nice college professor, and she loves me and Button so much."

If she loved them so much, why hadn't she flown back the moment she learned her daughter had died? And why was Lucy working so hard at matchmaking if they got along so well? "She sounds almost too good to be true."

"What do you mean by that?"

"I mean that Mat and I are going to meet her ourselves very soon, so you might as well be honest about it."

"This isn't any of your damn business!"

"Lucy." Mat's voice sounded a low warning note.

"I'm *going*." She flounced to the rear of the Winnebago and banged the door.

"I'm getting a really bad feeling about Grandma," Nealy said.

"She's a college professor. How bad can she be?"

"What are you going to do if she doesn't measure up?"

"She will. Don't worry about it."

She wondered who he was trying to convince.

Just then, a loud yip came from the back.

"That's not an engine noise!" Mat swore under his breath, braked, and pulled off onto the shoulder. "Lucy! Get out here!"

The door at the rear slowly opened. Her head was

down, shoulders slumped. She crept forward. "What'd I do now?"

Mat regarded her stonily. "You tell me."

A mournful howl echoed through the Winnebago.

He vaulted up from the seat and charged to the back. *"Son of a—"*

"I guess he found Squid," Lucy mumbled.

"Squid?" Nealy said weakly.

"That's what the guy at the service station called him. I'd like to give him another name, but I don't want to confuse him."

Another curse from the back, then Mat stalked forward, followed by a dirty, malnourished dog that appeared to be part beagle and part everything else. It had a mottled brown coat, long droopy ears, and a mournful expression.

"I didn't steal him!" Lucy pushed past Mat to kneel by the dog. "The guy at the service station said he was going to shoot him! Somebody dropped him off on the side of the road yesterday, and nobody wanted him."

"I can't imagine why." Mat glared down at the pathetic animal. "Shooting him would be a gift to humanity."

"I knew you'd say something crappy like that!" She hugged the dog to her thin chest. "He's mine! Mine and Button's."

"That's what you think."

While Mat and Lucy scowled at each other, the dog disengaged himself and hoisted his weak body up onto the couch next to the car seat. Nealy was just moving forward to get him away from the baby when he gave Button a doleful look, then covered her from chin to forehead with a long, slow lick.

"Oh, God! He's licking her face!" Nealy charged forward to push the dog away.

"Stop it!" Lucy cried. "You're hurting his feelings."

Button clapped and tried to grab the dog's ear.

Mat moaned.

"Get him away from her!" Nealy tried to wedge herself between Button and the dog, only to feel Mat slip his arm around her waist and pull her back.

"Where's that handy cyanide capsule when you need it?"

"Don't! Let me go! What if he has rabies?" Even as Nealy struggled to get away from Mat, one part of her was thinking about how good it felt being right where she was.

"Calm down, will you? He doesn't have rabies."

Mat drew her toward the front of the Winnebago, then let her go so suddenly she nearly fell. She knew he'd just remembered he was manhandling Cornelia Case and not Nell Kelly. She rounded on Lucy. "Get that dog off the couch."

"I'm going to keep him!"

"Put him in the back!" Mat jammed himself behind the wheel and pulled back onto the highway. "First it was just me. Exactly the way I wanted it! Then I got stuck with two kids. The next thing I know—"

A Greyhound flew past from the opposite direction and water thwacked the windshield. He made a disgusted sound, then flicked on the radio.

"... *reports from citizens across the country who believe they've seen First Lady Cornelia Case—*"

Nealy leaned over and snapped it off.

Every surface of the room was covered with knickknacks. Glass candy dishes sat next to figurines of animals with bows on their heads, which nestled next to ceramic plaques printed with Bible verses. Where was a good earthquake when you needed one? Toni wondered.

"You sure you don't want some coffee?" The woman that Toni and Jason had driven across two states to question regarded Jason apprehensively. She wore a short-sleeved blue knit pant suit with a rhinestone umbrella pin and white spiked heels.

Jason shook his head, anxious as usual to cut to the
chase, and gestured toward a blue velour couch that sat
underneath the window in the small second-floor apartment. "Do you mind if we sit down and ask you a few
questions?"

"Oh ... yes ... no. I mean ..." She twisted her
hands. She'd just returned from church when they'd arrived, and having members of the FBI and Secret Service in her home had clearly undone her. The woman
was in her early forties. She had a pudgy moon face,
overly permed brown hair, and exquisite porcelain skin.

Toni smiled at her. "I'd appreciate a glass of water,
Miss Shields, if it wouldn't be too much trouble. I get
a little carsick when I ride too long, and water settles
my stomach."

"Oh, no trouble at all." She scurried toward the
kitchen.

Jason shot Toni an irritated glance. "Since when do
you get carsick?"

"It comes and goes at my convenience. Listen, pal,
you and your steely-eyed stare are making her so nervous that she's starting to worry about rubber hoses and
bamboo slivers."

"I'm not doing anything."

"Witnesses who get too nervous either forget important details or make them up to please the person asking
the questions."

Jason frowned at a ceramic statue of a clown. "I want
to get this over with."

He wasn't the only one. Special teams all over the
country were tracking down tips that had been phoned
in from citizens who were sure they'd seen Cornelia
Case getting out of a limousine at an airport or lazing
on the beach at Malibu. But the tip from Barbara
Shields, a grocery store clerk in Vincennes, Indiana, was
the one that had caught Toni and Jason's attention.

Shields had reported seeing a woman who looked like

Cornelia Case shopping in the Kroger's where she worked. The woman had been traveling with a dark-haired man, a teenager, and a baby in a pink cap. The cursory description matched the description of the woman in the celebrity lookalike contest, right down to the short light brown hair.

Toni and Jason had discussed it. They both considered it unlikely that a woman traveling with three other people, two of whom were children, could be Cornelia Case. But they still wanted to talk with her in person, and their boss, Ken Braddock, had agreed.

Shields came out of the kitchen with a frosted blue water glass. Toni was ninety percent convinced they were on a fool's errand, but she managed a smile. "Do you mind if we sit down?"

"Mind? No, no. Go ahead." She rubbed her palms on her blue slacks, then perched on the edge of an armchair across from the couch. "I'm just a little nervous. I never met real government agents before."

"Perfectly understandable." Toni took a seat next to Jason. He opened his notebook, but Toni left hers in her purse. "Why don't you just tell us what you saw?"

More palm-rubbing. "Well, it was Friday, two days ago. It was my first day back at work since my surgery." She indicated her wrist. "I got carpal tunnel from scanning groceries. Repetitive stress injury, they call it. Everybody talks about helping office workers who get it from using computers, but nobody thinks about cashiers. I guess we're not important enough." Her expression indicated she was used to coming out on the short end of the checkout line.

"Anyway, this woman came through my line with a really good-looking man and these two kids, and I was so surprised when I saw her that I ran a can of baby food through the scanner twice."

"Why were you surprised?" Toni asked.

"Because she looked so much like the First Lady."

"A lot of women resemble the First Lady."

"Not like this. I've always admired Mrs. Case, ever since the campaign, so I started keeping a scrapbook of pictures and articles about her. I know her face nearly as good as I know mine."

Toni gave her an encouraging nod and tried to decide whether the fact that the woman was a Cornelia Case groupie made her testimony more or less valuable.

"She'd cut her hair. It's short and light brown, but her face was the same. And I don't know if you've ever seen any blown-up pictures of her, but—here, let me show you."

She hurried over to a bookcase and pulled out several fat scrapbooks. After rustling through the pages for a moment, she showed them a head shot of the First Lady taken last year for the cover of *Time*.

"Look. Right there. Next to her eyebrow. She's got this little freckle. I'll bet I stared at this picture a dozen times before I saw it. The woman in my checkout line. She had a freckle in the exact same place."

Toni gazed at the place where she was pointing, but the spot looked more like a blur on the negative than a freckle.

"Her voice was the same, too," Barbara Shields went on.

"You're familiar with Mrs. Case's voice?"

She nodded. "Every time I know she's going to be on television, I try to watch. This woman sounded just like her."

"What did she say to you?"

"She wasn't talking to me. She was talking to the man about what he liked on his sandwiches."

"She was speaking English?"

She seemed surprised by the question. "Sure she was."

"Did she have any kind of foreign accent?" Jason asked.

"No. She sounded just like Mrs. Case."

He and Toni exchanged a glance. Then he leaned forward. "Tell us as much as you remember of the conversation, right from the beginning."

"She asked the man what he wanted on his sandwich, and he said he liked mustard. And then the teenager said she wanted to buy this little paperback we had in the display with the astrology books. *Ten Secrets to a Better Sex Life*. The woman said no, and the teenager started to argue. The man didn't like that, and he said something about how the girl had better listen to Nell or she was going to be in trouble. Then the baby—"

"Nell?" Toni gripped the water glass tighter. "That's what he called the woman?"

Barbara Shields nodded. "I thought right away about how much Nell sounded like Nealy. That's what Mrs. Case's friends call her, you know."

A similar name. A freckle that might have been a negative blur. Not enough to build a case on, just enough to keep them interested.

They continued their questioning, and Shields provided them with more detailed descriptions of the man and the teenager, but it wasn't until they were ready to leave that she recalled her most useful piece of information.

"Oh, I almost forgot. They were driving a yellow Winnebago. I watched them leave through the window. I don't know much about motor homes, but it didn't look real new.

"A yellow Winnebago?"

"It was pretty dirty, like they'd been driving it for a while."

"You didn't happen to get the license plate, did you?"

"As a matter of fact, I did." Barbara Shields went for her purse.

Willow Grove, Iowa, sat on a bluff looking down over a branch of the Iowa River. It was a town of church steeples and antiques shops, a town where red brick houses alternated with white clapboard and where mature maples shaded the narrow streets. A small private college occupied several blocks near the center, and an old inn sat across from City Hall, which was topped with a copper cupola. The rain had ended, and the copper glinted in the frail streaks of late afternoon sunshine that managed to peak through the cloud cover.

Nealy told herself there couldn't be a more perfect place for children to grow up, and apparently Mat was thinking the same thing. "This is going to be great for the girls."

He'd stopped at a store on the outskirts to buy dog food and get directions to the street where the girls' grandmother lived. It was close to the downtown area and ran along the top of the bluff. In the spaces between houses, she caught occasional glimpses of the river below.

"Number one-eleven," he said. "There it is."

He pulled up in front of a red brick two-story with white trim. All the houses on the street seemed to have front porches and detached garages. This one was square and solid, the kind of house that generations of families all over the Midwest had grown up in.

It looked a bit more neglected than the others on the street because there were no summer flowers blooming by the shrubbery or growing from pots on the front porch. The grass needed mowing, and the white trim didn't look as fresh as its neighbors'. But it wasn't run-down. Instead, it simply appeared as if its inhabitant had other things she'd rather do.

"That mangy mut's staying locked up until Grandma's had time to get over the shock of the girls," Mat said.

She realized he was nervous. So was she. At least he'd stopped snapping at her.

Button had calmed down when they'd entered the town, almost as if she knew something monumental was about to happen to her life, and Lucy had sealed herself in the back with Squid. As Nealy began to unfasten the baby from the car seat, she noticed the old food stains on her romper, a small hole in the sleeve, and the fact that her hair could use a fluffing. "Maybe we should fix Button up a little before she meets her grandmother. For all we know, this might be the first time she's ever seen her."

"Good idea. I'll get her out of this. See if you can find something decent for her to wear." Then he remembered who he was talking to. "If you don't mind."

"I'm the one who suggested it," she snapped.

Lucy lay stretched out on the bed with the dog curled against her, dirt and all. She pretended to be reading her book, but Nealy wasn't fooled, and she squeezed her ankle. "It's going to be all right, Lucy. This is a great place."

Lucy pulled the book closer to her face and didn't answer.

Nealy chose the little peach denim jumper she'd bought at Baby Gap. It had a row of tiny blue flowers embroidered across the yoke and a matching knit top with puffy sleeves. As she emerged with it, she saw that Mat had stripped Button down to a diaper and was giving her a pregame pep talk.

"I want you on your best behavior, Demon. No b.s. And not too loud, okay? No yelling. No hurling. Just be a regular baby, for a change." He frowned at her as he fastened the tabs on a fresh diaper, and she cooed back at him. "Yeah, yeah . . . save the goo-goo eyes for Grannie."

Nealy handed him the outfit, and he had the baby dressed in less than a minute. "You're so good at that. It takes me forever to get her into her clothes."

"You're too tentative. With babies, you have to take charge or they'll walk all over you. Just like with women."

"Oh, yeah?" This was more like it, and she shot him a challenging grin, only to see the mischief fade from his eyes.

"You want to see if you can find her shoes?"

She turned away without a word. She wasn't going to beg for his affection. Not that she wanted his affection, exactly. She wanted his . . . well, she wanted his body, no need to lie to herself about that. But she also wanted his friendship, his irreverence, even his annoying male chauvinism.

The words to an old Sheryl Crow pop song skittered through her head. *Was he strong enough to be her man?* Had she really thought he might be?

She was skirting dangerously close to self-pity, and she pulled herself together. "Lucy doesn't seem to want to come out."

"She probably knows her grandmother's going to run a lot tighter ship than Sandy did."

"Maybe." She slipped the hairbrush through the baby's fluff. To her astonishment, she found herself the target of the megawatt smile Button normally reserved for Mat. Her heart ached. "No way," she muttered. "You're not going to start flirting with me right before I have to give you up."

Button gave a shriek of delight and held out her arms for Nealy to pick her up. Her throat constricted, and she turned away.

Mat lifted her from the couch. "Too little, too late, Demon. Some people can't be bought." He bent down, opened one of the built-in drawers underneath, and pulled out the Wal-Mart pillow. "As much as I hate to say it, you'll need to wear this." His expression showed his distaste. "Other than me, it's the best protection you have."

He was right. They were going to be in town for a while, and the whole world was looking for her. She located one of the old maternity tops and slipped into the bathroom. As she came out, she heard Mat talking to Lucy.

". . . the detectives Nell's ex-husband hired might be showing up. She needs to throw them off, so she's going to make herself look pregnant again. If anybody asks, I'm saying she's my wife, so back me up, okay?"

"Okay." Lucy sounded sad.

A few beats of silence ticked by. "I'm not going to just dump you and leave, you know. I'll stay around for a while to make sure you get settled. This is going to be great. You'll see."

Lucy moved toward the door as if she weighed a thousand pounds. Squid lumbered after her.

"I think we'd better leave the dog here for now." Mat pulled his shirt collar from Button's mouth.

It was a silent group that made its way up the steps to the front door. As Mat pressed the bell, Nealy glanced at Lucy. She was leaning against the porch rail looking miserable.

Nealy moved over to her and slipped an arm around her waist. She wanted to tell the teenager that everything was going to be all right, but she couldn't do that because it so obviously wasn't.

Lucy looked up at her, and Nealy saw a whole world of anxiety in her eyes. "I'm not going anywhere, either," she whispered. "Not until I know you're all right." She just hoped she could live up to her promise.

"Nobody's answering," Mat said. "I'll look around back." He passed Button over to her.

Lucy stared at the front door.

"Do you want to tell me about your grandmother now?" Nealy asked.

Lucy shook her head.

Mat was muttering under his breath as he came back around. "The windows are open, and there's music playing. She probably can't hear the bell." He banged on the front door. "More good news, Lucy. Your grandmother likes Smashing Pumpkins."

"Cool," Lucy murmured.

The door swung open. A young man in his mid- to late twenties stood on the other side. Everything about him screamed that he was a charter member of the slacker generation: close-cropped hair, goatee, earrings. He wore a T-shirt with a pair of cargo shorts and Teva sandals. "Yeah?"

Out of the corner of her eye, Nealy saw Lucy swallow and step forward.

"Hi, Grandpa."

15

MAT CHOKED—NOT EASY TO DO WITH A MOUTH AS DRY as dust. He spun toward Lucy. *"Grandpa?"*

Her hands were clasped in front of her, she was biting her lip, and she looked like she was going to cry. Then he turned back to the slacker, who was scratching his chest and looking confused.

"I don't know who you think . . ." He paused and studied her more closely. "Hey, are you—Laurie?"

"Lucy."

"Oh, yeah." He gave her an apologetic smile. "You don't look too much like your pictures anymore. How you doin'?"

"Not too good. My mom died."

"Man, that's a drag." He looked back at Mat and seemed to realize this was more than a social call. "You want to come in?"

"Oh, yes," Mat said through tight lips. "We definitely want to come in." He gripped Lucy by the arm and pushed her ahead of him. Out of the corner of his eye, he saw that Nell looked as dismayed as he felt. Only the Demon seemed to be unaffected. She was patting Nell's cheek trying to get her attention.

They followed the slacker into a living room that held a hodgepodge of comfortable furniture upholstered in dark green and brown velvets, along with a few dusty arts and crafts style tables. There were bookcases on each side of the fireplace, with contents that appeared to be well-read. He spotted some primitive wooden figures, a few pieces of pottery, and a couple of etchings. The sound system that was playing the Smashing Pumpkins sat on a library table cluttered with stacks of CDs. There were magazines lying around, a guitar, a pile of free weights in the corner, and a duffel bag open on the coffee table.

The slacker turned down the music. "You want a beer or something?"

"Yes, please," said Lucy, darting Mat a nervous glance as she broke away.

Mat shot her a hell-to-pay glare and tried to figure out where to start. "No, thanks. We're here to see Mrs. Pressman."

"Joanne?"

"Yes."

"She's dead, man."

"Dead?"

Nell reached for Lucy, as if she could somehow cushion her from the shock. But Lucy didn't look shocked. Instead she looked as though she knew she was in big trouble.

Mat stared at the slacker, forced out the words. "Lucy didn't tell us her grandmother had passed away."

"Joanne died almost a year ago. It's rough, man."

"A year?" Mat was so furious he could barely contain himself. "I was told that Mrs. Pressman had been out of the country for a few months."

"Yeah, man. Way out." His pitch rose. "She took my bike one day and wrecked it on County Line Road."

Nell absentmindedly patted Button's leg. "She was riding a bike?"

"I think he means a motorcycle," Mat said tightly.

Lucy tried to slide behind the couch, apparently under the mistaken notion furniture would protect her.

"My new Kawasaki 1500. I was really bummed."

"About the bike or Mrs. Pressman?"

The slacker regarded him with steady eyes. "C'mon, man, that's low. I loved her."

Mat wondered why nothing in life was ever simple. He'd never thought to question the authenticity of the note Lucy'd shown him because the stationery had been embossed with the college seal. Also, the handwriting hadn't looked like the work of a teenager. Fool. He knew how smart she was. Why hadn't he done some digging?

He asked the question he'd been avoiding ever since Lucy had called the slacker Grandpa. "Who are you?"

"Nico Glass. Joanne and I'd only been married a couple of months when she died."

Nell seemed to be having as much trouble as he was taking it in. "The two of you were married?"

Nico's eyes held a hint of challenge. "Yeah. We loved each other."

Nell made the understatement of the day. "There seems to be quite an age difference."

"In a lot of people's eyes, maybe, but not in ours. She was only fifty-three. She was my anthropology professor at Laurents. They tried to fire her after we got involved, but because I was over twenty-one, they couldn't do it."

"Laurents?" Nell said. "That's the college in town?"

"Yeah, I changed my major a couple of times, so it was taking me a while to graduate."

Mat finally confronted Lucy. He decided it was a good thing there was a couch between them after all because he wanted to do serious harm. "Who forged the letter?"

Her thumbnail came to her mouth, and she took a step away from him, misery etched in every line of her body. He didn't feel one bit sympathetic.

"This lady I was baby-sitting for," she mumbled. "And it wasn't for you! It was for Sandy's lawyer! I knew he was getting suspicious, so I was going to show it to him next time he showed up, only you came instead."

He clenched his teeth. "You knew your grandmother was dead. You lied about everything."

She regarded him mulishly. "I might have known she died, but I didn't know about the Kawasaki."

Nell must have realized he was losing it because she put her hand on his arm and gave a light squeeze.

"Look, man. Am I supposed to know you?"

He struggled for composure. "I'm Mat Jorik. I used to be married to Sandy, Joanne's daughter. This is . . . my wife Nell."

He nodded at Nell. Button started batting her baby blues at him, and he smiled back. "Cute kid. Joanne was worried when Sandy got pregnant because of her drinking. They didn't get along too good."

"Sandy didn't drink when she was pregnant." Lucy started working on the other thumbnail.

Button wanted down, and Nell lowered her to the floor. The toddler immediately began waddling around the coffee table, toes pointed outward like a drunken ballerina. Mat needed to get himself under control, so he headed for the framed snapshots sitting on the dusty wooden mantel in the feeble hope that they might tell him something.

The pictures in the front were all of Joanne and Nico. They could have been mother and son, except for the hungry way they looked at each other. Joanne had been an attractive woman, slim and well proportioned, with long salt and pepper hair parted in the center and held away from her face with barrettes. Her gauzy skirts, loose-fitting tops, and silver jewelry bore the indelible stamp of an aging flower child. The proprietary way she leaned against Nico's bare chest in one photo after another made it obvious that she'd been sexually smitten by him. As far as his attraction to a woman thirty-some years older—that was probably best sorted out on a psychiatrist's couch.

The row of pictures in the back showed both Sandy

and Lucy at various ages. He lingered over the pictures of Lucy. In the early ones she was too young to have figured out how to put on her tough act, and her bright eyes and wide smile showed a little girl in love with life. The hospital picture of Button with a misshapen head and mashed-in face bore no resemblance to the baby beauty queen who was currently trying to stuff a finger up her nose.

He was about to turn away when he caught sight of the photograph at the end of the row. It was a picture of Sandy and himself that had been taken at a friend's party. Both of them were holding drinks, something they'd done a lot of in those days. She was beaming and beautiful with her dark hair and full mouth. He wondered if the tall, gangly kid sitting next to her trying too hard to look older could actually have been him. The photograph was depressing, and he turned away to see Nico staring at Nell.

"Don't I, you know, know you from somewhere?"

Before Nell could respond, Lucy said, "She looks like Cornelia Case, the First Lady."

Nell tensed, but Nico only smiled. "Yeah, man, you really look like her." He turned to Mat. "So, are you on vacation or what?"

"Not exactly. Lucy, get lost."

Normally she would have mouthed off, but now she didn't dare. Instead, she snatched up Button and headed out the front door. Through the window, he watched her take a seat on the glider, where she'd be near enough to the door to eavesdrop.

He turned to study the kid who was the closest thing the girls had to a relative and began to dig in. "Here's the way it is, Nico . . ."

Nealy eventually went outside to check on Lucy. The teenager had retrieved Squid from the motor home, and the dog lay next to her on the porch like a pile of smelly rags. Button was watching a robin hop on the ground while she gripped a spindle of the railing with one hand and sucked the other. Nealy refused to let herself think about lead poisoning from old paint. This time with Button had been good for her, she realized. She no longer felt quite so much like the Angel of Baby Death.

She sat on the top step across from Lucy and gazed out at the shady street. At one end, an elementary school with a small playground sat beneath the maples; at the other end, two boys dodged puddles with their bikes. Across the street, a man in a business suit was studying his lawn. Nealy heard the tinkle of an ice-cream truck and the sound of a mother calling a child inside. These everyday sights were as exotic to her as foreign lands were to most people.

Lucy toyed with one of Squid's ears. "What do you think Mat'll do to me?"

"I don't know. He's definitely upset. You shouldn't have lied to him."

"What else was I supposed to do? They'd have put us in foster homes!"

And that's where they were still going. Not for a moment did Nealy believe Mat would leave the girls with Nico Glass, despite the fact that he'd been going to great lengths inside to point out that Nico was the girls' only relative.

Of course, Nico wasn't having any of it. When he'd announced he had a rock-climbing trip to Colorado planned, Mat told him to forget about it, but Nico kept throwing his things in a duffel bag.

She glanced over at Button, whose peach denim jumper was already dirty from crawling around on the porch, and then at Lucy, who looked miserable. What was going to happen to these girls? Mat was a decent man, and he was trying hard to do the right thing, but he'd made it clear that his life didn't include raising children. That left foster care or adoption. Families would jump at the opportunity to adopt Button, but nobody was going to adopt Lucy. She'd be separated from the little sister she was trying so fiercely to protect.

Lucy had moved from thumbnail to forefinger. "He's going to kill me when he comes out."

Nealy tried to clear the knot of emotion from her throat. "You should have told him about your grandmother right away. And you shouldn't have forged that letter."

"Yeah, right. Then Button wouldn't have had any chance at all. They'd have taken her away from me that same day."

It occurred to Nealy that this teenager already knew more about courage than most people learned in a lifetime. She spoke as gently as she could. "What did you hope to accomplish by making Mat believe your grandmother was still alive?"

"When something bad happened, Sandy used to say, 'It ain't over till it's over.' And I thought that, if the trip took long enough, something good might happen on the way."

"Mat might decide to keep you."

Lucy didn't answer. She didn't have to.

"I'm sorry, Luce. You know there are lots of great foster homes. And Mat will check up on you." Mat had never said anything of the kind, but Nealy knew he would. "I will, too."

"There won't be any reason to check up on me because I can take care of myself," Lucy said stubbornly, "and I won't go to a foster home." Her bravado faded. "You guys both like Button a lot, I know you do. She's really a great baby. She's cute and smart, and she's hardly any trouble. Well, maybe a little, but she'll grow out of it real soon, probably next month or something." Lucy gave up on subtlety. "I don't see why you and Mat can't get married and adopt her."

Nealy regarded her with dismay. "Lucy, we're not going to—"

"That's bullshit, man!" Nico's angry voice cut in. "Those kids don't have anything to do with me!" The door flew open and he shot out carrying his duffel and a guitar, with Mat following. "Look, I'm taking off. If you guys want to crash here for a while, that's fine with me. But that's it."

He tossed a set of house keys at Mat, then vaulted off the steps without looking at either Lucy or Button. A few moments later, he shot down the narrow drive on his motorcycle.

Grim-faced, Mat pointed a finger at Lucy. "You. Get in the Winnebago. The two of us are going to have a talk."

She wasn't stupid. She immediately snatched up Button as a human shield.

"Alone!" Mat boomed.

She set Button down, narrowed her eyes, lifted her chin, and marched toward the motor home.

Nealy watched her go and shook her head in admiration. "Are you sure she's not your daughter?"

Mat ignored her and set out after the teenager, his lips compressed in a taut line. Worried, Nealy grabbed Button and began to follow him, only to stop herself. He looked like he was going to commit violence, but she knew better. Mat had some bite behind his bark, but she didn't believe it was lethal.

And bark he did, until she expected the walls of the Winnebago to bulge. When she couldn't stand it any longer, she carried Button inside to explore. They would be spending at least one night here, and she wanted to see the house.

In the back, a roomy, light-filled kitchen opened onto a wonderful sunporch. Cozy brown wicker furniture clustered around a worn Oriental rug, and a collection of mismatched tables held scholarly journals, back issues of *Rolling Stone*, and junk food refuse. Clay saucers that looked as if they'd once contained houseplants sat here and there, along with some pottery lamps. Through the windows, she caught sight of a small backyard defined by shrubs and a little grape arbor. The weedy flower bed contained several old rosebushes full of blossoms.

The upstairs held a bath and three bedrooms, the smallest of which had been converted into a storage room. A portable CD player, some scattered clothes, and an open book on Zen indicated that Nico occupied the master bedroom. In the guest room, an India cotton throw printed in blues and lavenders was tossed over the double bed, and simple woven curtains hung at the window. The bathroom was old-fashioned, charming, and in need of a good cleaning. Tiled in gray and white, the room held a clawfoot tub with a spray attachment, a wicker basket overflowing with out-of-date magazines, and an open window of honeycombed glass that looked out over the backyard and, in the distance, a sliver of the Iowa River.

She heard the side door slam and went downstairs to see that Mat had sealed himself behind the French doors of Joanne Pressman's abandoned office, which looked as if it had once been the dining room. Through the glass, she saw him pick up the phone. Her spirits sank. He was beginning the process of divesting himself of the children.

"He didn't hit me or anything."

Lucy's soft voice came from behind her, and Nealy turned to see her standing in the kitchen. Her cheeks were flushed, her eyes sad. She looked defeated, but determined not to show it.

"I didn't think he would."

"He was really mad, though." Her voice cracked. "Because I disappointed him and everything."

Nealy wanted to hug her, but Lucy was working too hard at holding on to her pride. "Let's see if we can find someplace to order pizza for dinner. And Button's out of clean clothes. Can you show me how to use the washer?"

"You don't know how to use a washer?"

"I had servants."

Lucy shook her head at Nealy's utter lameness, then patiently demonstrated the basics of doing laundry.

By the time the pizza arrived, Mat had disappeared. She found him outside with his head under Mabel's hood. He grunted that he would eat later. She suspected he needed some time alone, and she was more than happy to give it to him.

After dinner, Nealy scrubbed the tub, undressed the baby, and set her in the water. She gave a gleeful shriek, then began splashing with the plastic measuring cups Nealy'd brought up from the kitchen. "You certainly do know how to have a good time," she said with a laugh.

"Da!"

She turned and saw Mat standing in the door. His arms were crossed and one shoulder pressed against the jamb. "I'll take over," he said wearily. "I didn't mean to stick you with her."

"I don't feel stuck." Her words sounded sharper than she'd intended, but she was angry with him. Angry with him for not being the man she wanted him to be—a homebody who would hold on to these girls.

She knew she was being unfair. Mat hadn't asked for any of this to happen, and it said a lot for his character that he had gone to so much effort on their behalf. But she was still angry with him.

Button slapped both arms into the water and sent up a tidal wave to impress him.

"I just saw Lucy heading downstairs carrying a portable television," he said. "I hope I don't have to worry about pawnshops again."

"Where was she taking it?" She did her best to wash

one of Button's ears, but it was a catch-as-catch-can proposition.

"To the motor home. She said she and Button weren't going to stay in the guest room no matter what you said."

Nealy sighed. "There's a double bed with one side against the wall so Button couldn't roll out. I thought it would be a good place for them. Obviously Lucy didn't agree."

"Lucy's a brat."

The pizza must have revived the teenager's fighting spirit because Nealy would bet anything that she was matchmaking again—making certain Nealy and Mat were going to be alone in the house.

Squid followed Mat into the bathroom and plopped on the tile near the tub. Button shrieked and sent up a splash to welcome him. The dog regarded her balefully, then mustered the energy to crawl beneath the sink where the undertow wouldn't get him.

"That's the most pathetic excuse for a dog I've ever seen."

"On the positive side, I made Lucy take him outside and give him a bath, so at least he doesn't smell anymore. And he certainly has a healthy appetite."

"Three different neighbors came over to introduce themselves while I was moving the motor home into the driveway. It's a good thing you're keeping that damn padding on."

"People are naturally friendly in the Midwest."

"Too friendly." He picked up the rag Lucy'd used to scrub the tub and began swabbing the water Button had splashed on the floor. "I don't know about you, but I've had more than enough of driving around in that motor home, so I reserved a rental car. We can pick it up tomorrow morning."

She wanted to ask him what he was going to do about the girls, but Button had lost interest in her bath, and she wanted to get her settled first. "I'll finish up here."

While Mat got Button's bottle ready, Nealy dried her off and dressed her in a clean pair of cotton pajamas. Then she carried both Button and the bottle out to the motor home to turn over to Lucy.

When she returned, she found Mat sitting on the back step with a cup of coffee and Squid curled at his feet. She eased down next to him and gazed at the quiet backyard. Fireflies flickered above the peony bushes, and the sweet scent of honeysuckle drifted in the air. Through the back window of a neighbor's house, she caught the glow of a television set. She wanted to drink it all in so she'd never forget this perfect summer night in the heartland.

Mat took a sip of coffee. "I called Sandy's lawyer earlier. I told him where the girls were and what had happened. As you might expect, Pennsylvania Child Services isn't too happy with me."

"You're going to take the girls back." She'd meant to ask a question, but it came out as a statement.

"Of course. As soon as the bloodwork's taken care of."

"You're having the paternity tests done here?"

"There's a lab in Davenport. I don't want to deal with all the red tape waiting for me in Pennsylvania."

"So you'll have the tests done, and then you'll be able to wash your hands of them," she snapped.

"That's not fair."

She sighed. "I know. I'm sorry."

"This isn't what I want! I put in my time as a family man before I was twenty-one, and I hated it." He gazed around at the quiet yard. "I've worked my whole life to get away from all this."

It hurt knowing something that meant everything to her was repugnant to him. "Was your childhood so terrible?"

He set his coffee mug on the step. "Not terrible, but

you can't imagine what it was like growing up without any privacy and being responsible for so many females."

"What about your mother?"

"She'd work fifty, sixty hours a week as a bookkeeper. She had eight kids, and she couldn't afford to turn down overtime. The girls ran rings around my grandmother, so most of the time it was just me. I couldn't even leave after I graduated from high school. My grandmother was getting frail, and my mother still needed me, so I lived at home while I went to college."

"Surely some of your sisters were old enough by that time to take charge of things."

"They were old enough, but that didn't mean they were reliable."

Why should they have been, she thought, when their older brother had such a strong sense of responsibility?

The dog shifted closer to Mat's feet. Mat rested his arms on his splayed thighs and let his hands drop between them. The dog nuzzled his fingers, but Mat didn't seem to notice. "Look at me. In less than a week, I've acquired two kids, a pregnant woman I'm telling everyone is my wife, and a damned dog. If that isn't bad enough, now I'm living in a house in Iowa."

She smiled. "All you need is a station wagon and a mother-in-law."

He moaned and sagged forward. "When I was on the phone earlier . . . I rented a Ford Explorer. I wasn't thinking."

"Explorer?"

"An SUV, today's station wagon."

She laughed.

His innate sense of humor surfaced, and he managed a pained smile.

"What about your job?" she asked. "Don't you have to get back to work?"

"It'll hold."

There were some things that didn't add up here. "Lucy

tells me you drive a Mercedes. Nice car for a steel-worker."

It took a moment for him to respond. "I never said I was a steelworker. I told you I worked in a steel mill."

"The difference being?"

"I'm management."

"I see." She slipped her hands between her thighs. "How long before you go back?"

"It takes two weeks to get the results."

Hope flared inside her, only to fade as he went on. "I'll probably fly back with them tomorrow night, maybe the next day. I guess it depends on you."

"What do you mean?"

"I'm not leaving you alone."

"I don't need a bodyguard. That's why I left in the first place."

He reached down and absentmindedly scratched behind Squid's ears. "The President held a press conference this afternoon. You were the main topic of discussion."

She'd deliberately avoided listening to the news, and she didn't want to hear this.

The dog propped his muzzle on Mat's foot. "Vander-vort reassured everyone there was no reason to be alarmed about your safety, that you'd spoken with Mrs. Bush just this afternoon."

"Uhm."

"Apparently the special task force of agents looking for you has narrowed their search, and they expect to locate you soon."

She propped her elbows on her knees and sighed. "They probably will."

"I don't know. You seem to have covered your tracks pretty well."

"They're the best. Sooner or later, they'll find me."

"He blamed your disappearance on the nefarious villains that make up the opposition party." His mouth twisted in a cynical smile. "He said you'd become increasingly distressed watching your husband's political opponents put their own narrow interests above the best interests of the American people."

She gave a soft laugh. "He would say that."

"So which First Lady are you going to call tomorrow?"

She leaned back. "No more First Ladies. All of their phones will be monitored by now. I'll have to move on to the Supreme Court or the Cabinet."

He shook his head. "It's still hard for me to believe."

"Then don't think about it."

"It's tough not to." That flinty note had crept back into his voice. "You should have told me."

"Why?"

"How can you ask something like that?"

"What would you have done if you were me?"

"I guess I'd have taken control of my life before it got this far."

That made her angry. "Spoken by someone who knows absolutely nothing."

"You asked."

She jumped to her feet. "You're a jerk, you know that, Mat? Lucy's right."

He shot up, too. "You led me on!"

"Well, excuse me for not running up to you in that truck stop and announcing that I was Cornelia Case!"

"That's not what I'm talking about! You had plenty of time after that to tell me the truth."

"And end up having you either snarl at me or bow and scrape?"

Outrage flashed in his eyes. "I never bowed and scraped in my life!"

"This morning you told me you'd made *coffee*! As soon as you knew who I was, you treated me like some kind of houseguest!"

"I told you I made *coffee*? What the hell's that supposed to mean?" His eyes were turning the color of storm clouds, but she didn't care.

"That's not all, and you know it!"

"No, I don't know it! And I never bowed and scraped to anybody in my life!"

"Then tell me why we're sitting out here instead of finishing what we started two nights ago! This is Iowa, Mat! *Iowa!*"

The fact that she'd had to remind him—that it mattered who she was—hurt too much. "Forget it. Just forget it." She yanked open the door to the sunporch and hurried inside.

Mat watched the screen door slam and tried to figure out what had just happened. How had he become the bad guy? Was he supposed to throw the First Lady of the United States on her back and do everything to her he'd been thinking about all day? Damn her for not being Nell! And what was all that crap about bowing and scraping?

He jerked open the door. "Come back here!"

She didn't, of course, because when had she ever done anything he'd asked her to?

He heard the side door slam and realized she was running off. Out to the motor home where she could lock herself away from him. Out to the motor home after he'd ordered her to stick like glue to his side. Had she once stopped to consider the crackpots who might be looking for her? Of course not.

He didn't let the fact that he'd already made a fool of himself today with the backfiring incident keep him from charging through the house to the side door and out into the yard. On the way, he tried to calm himself down, and he'd almost succeeded when he found the door of the Winnebago *unlocked*. He nearly went catatonic. She was an idiot! And, First Lady or not, he intended to tell her so.

He stomped inside and found her throwing a sheet

down on that miserable miniature couch where he'd spent the past four nights. "Are you out of your *mind*?" he exclaimed.

She whirled around, every inch the Queen of Sheba. "What do you want?"

"You didn't even lock the damned door!"

"Quiet! You'll wake up the girls."

He glanced toward the closed door at the back, lowered his voice, and bore down on her. "As a taxpaying citizen of the United States, I resent like hell what you're doing."

"Then write your senator."

"You think that's cute? What if I were a terrorist? Exactly where do you think you'd be right now? And where do you think this country would be if some nut decided to take you hostage?"

"If the nut turned out to be as cracked as you, I'd be in big trouble!"

He thrust his hand toward the door. "Get back in that house where I can watch you!"

Those patrician nostrils flared, her aristocratic spine stiffened. "Excuuuse me?" She drew out the syllables like a long line he'd just stepped over. Her expression reminded him that, while his ancestors had been strapped to a plow in Eastern Europe, hers had been sipping martinis on country club verandas. He knew he'd gone too far, but he wanted her so damn bad that he couldn't seem to stop himself.

"Do you ever think about anybody but yourself?"

Her eyebrows shot right into that highborn forehead. "Get out!"

He was making a fool of himself, and if he stayed a moment longer, he'd only dig in deeper. But he'd never been good at backing away from a fight, so instead of acting like a reasonable adult, he leaned down and scooped her into his arms, blanket and all.

"Put me down! What do you think you're doing?"

"My patriotic duty!" He kicked the door open, then had to juggle both her wiggling body and the door so he could lock it behind him before he carried her to the house.

"You are out of your teeny-tiny mind!"

"Probably."

"Stop it right now! You're acting like a Neanderthal!"

"Yeah, well, live with it."

Inside Mabel, Lucy lay awake. The sound of the argument had brought her stomach pain back. She'd never expected them to fight like this. And she couldn't even figure out what they were fighting about, since nothing Jorik said made sense. At least she understood it when Sandy and Trent used to fight about money.

But Jorik and Nell were a lot smarter than Sandy and Trent had been, smart enough to know that people needed to talk over their problems instead of just yelling at each other. What if they decided to break up?

Her stomach cramped.

She glanced over at Button, and the soft baby snores reassured her that her sister was still sleeping soundly. Making up her mind, she slipped out of bed and, moving as quietly as she could, made her way into the house.

"Put me down!"

"When I'm good and ready."

She peeked around the corner and saw Mat carrying Nell up the stairs. Nell kept ordering him to let her go, and her voice sounded like she was shooting ice picks at him, but he wasn't paying any attention.

Lucy's stomach ache grew worse. Any minute now Jorik would go stomping off and get drunk, then Nell would start crying and get drunk, too. And then they wouldn't talk to each other for a long time.

Lucy couldn't stand it. She crept up the stairs in time to see Mat marching into the guest bedroom. There was a soft thumping sound as if he'd just set Nell down. Lucy reached the top step.

"Get out of here!"

"You bet I will!"

Lucy pressed her body against the wall and turned her head far enough to see inside. The only light in the room was coming from the hallway, but it was enough. And even though Mat had said he was leaving, he didn't seem to be moving.

"Don't think you're going anywhere!" he exclaimed. "I'll be sleeping right outside this door to make sure you stay where you are!"

"Stop telling me what to do!"

"Somebody has to!"

"Right! You never know when another car might backfire!"

They were so engrossed in their argument that they didn't notice her. Nell just looked pissed, but Jorik looked really upset—like something big was wrong— and Lucy wished Nell would calm down long enough to ask him why he was so bummed. Any minute now Mat would stomp off, just like Trent used to.

Lucy started to turn away when she spotted the old skeleton key in the lock. Right then, she knew what she was going to do. It would get her in even bigger trouble, but Mat was already so mad at her, what did it matter?

Nell saw her just as she pulled the key from the lock. "Lucy? What—"

Lucy slammed the door, shoved the old key in the outside of the lock, and gave it a hard twist.

"Lucy!" Nell shrieked at the same time Jorik let out a yell.

Lucy put her mouth to the door and yelled right back. "You two have a *time out*!"

16

MAT RUSHED TO THE DOOR AND TWISTED THE KNOB,
but it didn't budge. He banged his fist against it. "Lucy!
Open this door right now!"

Nothing but silence met his demand.

"Lucy, I'm warning you . . ."

With the door shut, the room's only illumination came
from the streetlight outside. Nealy hurried to the open
window and looked down at the motor home in time to
see the teenager run inside. She pressed her cheek
against the glass. "You're wasting your breath."

He came over to stand beside her and followed the
direction of her gaze. "This time she's gone too far."

Nealy wasn't ready for their argument to end. She'd
been ill-used, abused, and she had a whole litany of sins
that she still wanted to rain down on his head. At the
same time she wondered how he could look so good in
a worn white T-shirt and gym shorts.

Straightening, she let the curtain fall back in place,
turned on the small light that sat on top of the dresser,
and glared at him. "This is all your fault."

He pushed himself back from the window and sighed.
"I know."

That took the wind right out of her sails. Although
she wasn't proud to admit it, she'd been enjoying their
fight. Imagine having someone yell at her like that. And
imagine yelling right back without any need to censure

her words or stifle her emotions. Her Litchfield ancestors must be spinning in their well-tended graves.

Even though he'd manhandled her, she hadn't been the slightest bit afraid of him. He might believe he was capable of battering the females who upset him, but she knew differently.

She gave an injured sniff. "You frightened me to death."

"I'm sorry. I really am." He looked so dejected that she thought about taking pity on him, but then she thought not. First she wanted her pound of flesh.

Moving away from the window, she crossed her arms and stuck her nose in the air. "You stepped way over the line."

"I know. I—"

"You manhandled me! Terrified me!"

"I didn't mean . . . I'm sorry."

"Do you know that it's a high crime to harm a member of the first family? You could go to *prison*."

Unfortunately, she hadn't been able to keep the relish from her voice, and he gave her a sideways look. "For how long?"

"Oh, ages and ages."

"That long, huh?"

"I'm afraid so." She gave him a biting glare. "But look on the bright side. In prison, there won't be any *females* to clutter up your life."

He moved away from the window toward the bed. "That does put a different spin on it."

"Just tattooed men with names like Bruno. I'm sure a number of them will find you quite attractive."

He lifted an eyebrow at her.

She glanced toward the locked door. "I'm glad I went to the bathroom before we started arguing. It looks like it might be a while before I get there again."

He said nothing, but she still wasn't finished annoying him. "Did you?"

"What?"

"Go to the bathroom."

"For what?"

He was messing with her. "Forget I asked."

"I definitely will."

"When do you think she'll let us out?"

"When she's good and ready."

She caught the flicker of a smile. "Don't you dare condone what she did."

"I'm going to beat her within an inch of her life."

Now she was the one with the raised eyebrow. "Of course you are."

He smiled again. "You've got to admire her guts. She knows there's going to be hell to pay when I get out, but that didn't stop her."

Nealy's own smile faded. "She's desperate. I hate thinking about what she's feeling."

"Life's tough."

He wasn't nearly as coldhearted as he pretended to be. She watched as he began to pace the room, slowly at first but picking up steam.

"I'm going to break down the door."

"Spoken like a man."

"What do you mean by that?"

"Men like battering things. Bombing things."

"*Your* friends bomb things. My friends just cuss, kick the couch, then fall asleep in front of the TV." Once again he rattled the knob.

"Calm down. She'll open the door in the morning."

"I'm not spending the night closed up in here with you."

"If you're afraid I'll attack, don't worry," she snapped. "You're stronger than I am, so I'm sure you can defend yourself."

"Come on, Nell. We haven't been able to keep our hands off each other for days."

She gave him a snooty look. "I haven't had one bit of trouble keeping my hands off you."

"That's a bald-faced lie. You want me so bad you can't stand it!"

"I was dallying with you, that's all."

"Dallying?"

"Amusing myself. Really, Mat, you didn't believe I was serious, did you? The lies men tell themselves to protect their fragile egos."

"The only thing fragile about me right now is my self-control. You know exactly what's going to happen if we spend the night in here together!"

She congratulated herself on getting him riled again. "Of course I do. You'll scowl and insult me. Then you'll remember who you're insulting, and you'll back off."

"I don't know what you're talking about."

She bore in on him. "I'm Cornelia Case, the widow of the President of the United States. And you can't deal with it!"

"What the hell's that supposed to mean?"

He was starting to yell again, which gratified her because there was nothing she wanted more than to go back to that place of yelling and passion and raw, biting emotion. "Things were fine when you believed I was poor little abandoned Nell Kelly, weren't they?"

"Talk to me when you're ready to make sense."

"You could feel superior to poor Nell. But now that you know who I am, you aren't man enough to handle it!"

Oh, boy . . . she'd done it with that one. Nobody challenged Mathias Jorik's manhood and got away with it.

His gray eyes gleamed, he shot toward her, and the next thing she knew, she'd hit the mattress.

The bed frame shook as he sprawled next to her, triumph gleaming in those flint-gray eyes. She finally had him where she wanted him, but her victory wasn't satisfying because she'd used psychological warfare when what she really wanted was to be courted.

He looked down at her, a myriad of emotions going to war on that magnificent battlefield of a face. "I've tried to be a gentleman about this . . ."

"A wimp is more like it."

He reached beneath her top, whipped off the padding, and tossed it to the floor. "I've tried to be respectful . . ."

"You probably have rug burns on your knees from all that bowing and scraping."

His eyes narrowed. "I've tried to point out the obvious . . ."

"The fact that I threaten you?"

He paused, then he deliberately cupped one hand over her breast and thumbed the nipple. "You do like to live dangerously."

She turned her face away. "I want you to get off me and go away."

"Not a chance in the world."

"I've changed my mind."

"About five minutes too late."

She gazed back up at him. "You intend to force me?"

"Damn straight."

"Oh." She tried to look bored. "Get it over with, then."

He chuckled and drew a gentle spiral around her nipple with his thumb. "An army of Secret Service couldn't rescue you now."

It was getting harder and harder to remain indifferent. "You cad."

His tone softened, and the hand at her breast grew even more gentle. "Give it up, Nell. Just give it up, so we can make love the way we both want to."

"My name is Nealy." She needed to hear him say it. She needed to make certain he knew who he was making love to.

He took a deep breath. "Nealy."

"Not easy, is it?" She couldn't quite manage the breezy note she wanted.

"If you don't shut up," he said softly, "I'm going to gag you."

"I think I should get up now."

"Don't say you weren't warned." His lips brushed hers, then settled over her mouth, silencing any other protests she might have made. As his body pressed against hers, his kiss stripped away the last of her stubbornness. He was good at that.

Suddenly he jerked away and sank back on the mattress with a muffled curse. "I don't believe this."

Her eyes flew open. Once again he'd remembered who she was. Or maybe it was something more fundamental. "There wasn't anything wrong with that kiss!"

His smile looked forced. "The kiss was out of this world. It's what we're leading up to that's complicated." He caressed her cheekbone with the pad of his thumb. "Sweetheart, I've got a whole box of condoms. Unfortunately, they're on the other side of that wall."

She regarded him smugly "Lucky for us, I'm better organized. Look in my satchel." Thank goodness she'd left it here when she finished putting on Button's pajamas.

"The world can't be this good." He shot off the bed and returned a few moments later with the box. Then he took up right where he'd left off.

Their mouths met hungrily, and she didn't think she'd ever get enough of kissing him. He rolled her on top of him. She cradled his big, square jaw in her hands, angled her head, and reveled in taking control.

The kiss was subtly different with her in charge—clumsier, maybe, and not as well practiced, but eager . . . oh, so eager. She drew back and gazed down at those hot steel eyes, that tough mouth, softened now with desire. She shifted her position, hooked her foot around his calf, centered her breasts over his chest—romped on top of his great big body.

He groaned. "I hope you're having a good time because you're killing me."

"Good." She smiled down at him. "You're killing me, too."

"You have no idea how glad I am to hear that."

One of his hands slipped to the inside of her thigh. "You feel wonderful. For days, this is all I've been able to think about."

She smiled and toyed with his earlobe. "All I've been able to think about is seeing you naked. All of you."

"You want to see me naked?"

"Very much." Without waiting for permission, she slid off him and rose to her knees. "Stand up so I can enjoy the view."

"You sure you're ready for this?" He slowly uncoiled.

"I think I can handle it." She pulled off his T-shirt, then touched the elastic waistband of his shorts. He watched with half-closed lids as she drew them down an inch at a time. Her eyes widened. "Where's your underwear?"

"In the dryer." His drawl took on a delightfully menacing edge. "You got a problem with that?"

"I don't know. Let me see." She dallied with his navel for a moment, playing the part of a sexual tease, but really giving herself a little time to adjust. Finally she tugged the shorts away from the heaviness they weren't doing anything to conceal.

The sight was stupendous, but she hadn't nearly begun to look her fill when she was on her back again.

"Hey! I wasn't finished looking."

"Another time. We have all night."

"Then what's the rush?"

"Only a woman could ask a question like that. A very smart, sexy woman . . ." He nuzzled her neck, trifled with the corner of her mouth, drew her into another deep kiss. Then his hands moved to her clothes and, before she knew it, she was as naked as he.

He drew back far enough to gaze down at her too-thin body, and she began to wish she hadn't turned on the lamp. But she saw no criticism in his expression, only desire.

His mouth softened in a sensual smile; his hand covered her breast. He gave a ragged groan as her fingers closed around him. She rose to her knees and let her hands play where they wanted. Before long, their limbs were entwined, their mouths wild.

He pulled away with effort, knelt beside her, and cupped his hands over her knees. Their eyes met, and his look told her this would be slow. First, he intended to see her, and he expected her to submit to his wicked curiosity.

She relaxed her legs, but didn't part them. In an age of casual sex, her reticence might be old-fashioned, but she wanted this to be a gift to him. A gift that needed to be opened by the recipient.

Maybe he understood because his hands grew firmer around her knees. With gentle pressure he began to ease them apart.

She felt like a very young, very virginal bride. If she was no longer quite so young, it didn't matter, and if she was still almost virgin, that hadn't been her intention.

His hands slid onto her thighs, pushing them upward, opening them farther, making her increasingly vulnerable. A pulse throbbed at the base of his throat. He was fully aroused and very determined.

A ribbon of warm breeze curled from beneath the curtain and blew across that hot, moist place she was revealing to him. He gazed down at everything, and the look in his eyes grew fierce and territorial.

He shifted his position and brushed the light brown

curls with his thumb. She gave a hiss of pleasure as he parted her in the most intimate way.

His finger touched her, and she sucked in her breath. He was so gentle for such a strong man. As he explored her, she felt as if he were marking his territory. Then he dipped his head and marked it with his mouth.

His dark, crisp hair brushed her inner thighs. She felt the tug of his lips, the nip of his teeth. With her eyes open, she stared at the ceiling, fighting the ecstasy because she couldn't bear for it to end so quickly. But all the years of self-control hadn't made her strong enough to resist this.

"Don't," she moaned. "Not until . . . I don't want . . . Not until you're inside me."

He gazed up at her, his eyes dark with passion, his skin sleek with sweat. And then his powerful body settled over her smaller one. She felt sheltered, protected, and exquisitely threatened. Once she let this man inside her body, nothing would ever be the same again.

His entry was slow and determined, and although her body was slick with passion, she didn't accept him easily. His kissed her . . . soothed her . . . pressed deeper . . . deeper still . . .

She clutched his shoulders against the stinging stretch, pressed her cheek so hard against his jaw that his beard abraded her skin. When he was finally buried, she gave a sob.

He kissed the corners of her eyes, her mouth, caressed her breasts. Only then did he move in a slow, hard thrust . . .

She sobbed and arched.

He began to move in earnest. The muscles in his back and shoulders quivered beneath her palms, and the slow, deep throb inside her built. Nothing existed but the bed, their bodies, a lush, blazing wildness.

Thrust and withdraw. Arch and accept.

The ancient rhythms pushed them into oblivion.

*   *   *

Contentment radiated from her in waves, and that made Mat feel so good he couldn't keep the smile off his face. He rubbed her shoulder. She was soft everywhere. Soft, sweet, and irresistible.

Her hair brushed his chin, and she curled a bare leg over his. If she moved her leg much farther, she'd discover that he was hard again, something he didn't want her to figure out quite yet. She needed some time. Hell, so did he. Not time for his body to adjust, but his mind.

Her breath tickled his chest hair as she spoke. "That was fabulous."

She had no idea.

It shouldn't have been so good. It should have been intimidating, considering who she was. Setting that aside, it should have been what sex generally was to him, a great time with a nice lady. But this particular lady hadn't been all that nice. She'd been snooty and snappy, deliberately provoking, exciting in ways he'd never expected.

And what he couldn't seem to take in . . . this *thing* that he kept trying to push out of his mind only to have it jump right back in . . . it seemed impossible, but everything inside him told him that she'd been new at this. Very new.

He shied away from the idea, only to have it return. She'd been like somebody seeing Paris for the first time, or riding her first roller coaster, or learning how to scuba dive. She hadn't been with anybody. Not even her dead husband, the former President of the United States.

It was knowledge he could never use. He accepted that. But he still wanted to confirm it. Not for a story, but for himself.

She'd started doodling on his chest. "I know I'm too skinny. Thank you for not mentioning it."

He smiled. Women and their bodies. He'd heard every complaint in the book, right down to one sister insisting her thumbs were too fat and another who'd spent three days with her thighs bound in Saran Wrap.

"Women starve themselves to have a body like yours."

"It's too skinny."

That was true, but her thinness was part of her identity. It was as if her enthusiasm for life burned up the food she ate before it could settle anywhere. He put his hand over her stomach. "In case you haven't noticed, your stomach isn't as flat as it was the day we met."

She shoved his hand out of the way and replaced it with her own. "Yes, it is. I can't feel anything."

He hid his smile in her hair. "Sure, it feels flat now because you're lying down, but when you get up, you'll see that you're getting a belly."

"I am not!"

He laughed.

She rolled on top of him to wrestle the laugh away and immediately discovered his secret. Her eyes widened with delight. "Son of a gun."

In an instant, he had her beneath him.

Lucy crept into the house with Button in her arms and Squid lumbering behind. Just once she wished her sister would sleep past six-thirty. She gazed at the baby resentfully. "If you make a single sound, I'm going to be really mad. I mean it. You've got to keep quiet."

"Tak!" She poked her fingers in Lucy's mouth.

Lucy frowned at her and carried her to the stairs. If it weren't for her sister, she could have packed up her stuff this morning, walked out to the highway, and hitchhiked to California or somewhere before Mat could get hold of her. But she was trapped until Button was safe. That didn't mean, though, that she wasn't going to disappear for a while this morning. Mat was always grouchy when he woke up, even when nothing was wrong. Just think how he'd be today.

The baby tucked her face into Lucy's neck. Lucy knew she was going to have slobber all over her, but she didn't mind. It was hard being responsible for Button, but it was nice knowing there was one person in the world who loved her.

By the time they reached the top of the stairs, the baby had gotten heavy and Lucy's arms were hurting. She set her down in the hallway and slipped the key into the lock as quietly as she could. She winced against the clicking sound as she turned it, but she didn't hear any noise coming from the other side of the door.

The baby started crawling after Squid. Lucy hurried after her and picked her up.

"Lal!"

Lucy smeared her hand over her mouth. More slobber. She carried her back to the door and whispered in her ear to be quiet. Then she pulled her hand away and slowly turned the knob.

The door gave a little creak as she pushed it open. As much as she wanted to reassure herself that everything was okay again with Mat and Nell, she didn't look at the bed because she'd be grossed out if she saw anything. Instead, she set Button on the floor inside and closed the door.

The moment the lock clicked, she and Squid fled downstairs and out the front door. There was a Dunkin' Donuts not too far away. The two of them would hang out there until the stores opened, then they'd walk around downtown. She only hoped Mat and Nell had both cooled down by the time she came back.

"Gah!"

Mat peeled his eyes open and squinted against the light. He'd lost count of how many times they'd made love during the night, and he wasn't nearly ready for morning.

Nealy was curled against him, and he shifted his hand

so it covered her breast. It made a soft, warm weight in his palm. His lids drooped. He settled back around her.

Something wet and sharp invaded his ear canal.

He twisted his head and stared into a beaming baby face.

"Daaaaaa . . ."

He groaned. "Aww, man . . ."

She slapped the mattress with her hands, then reached toward him. He glanced toward the closed door, but Lucy had beat a hasty retreat.

"DA . . . DA . . . DA . . . DA!" The baby squealed and beat on the mattress like a bongo.

Nealy stirred next to him. The Demon squealed louder, the familiar mulish look on her face declaring she was a woman to be reckoned with. He reached over, scooped her up, and dumped her on his chest.

She beamed at him and dropped some spit on his chin. "Daaaa . . ."

Nealy turned, her eyes slowly opening.

The Demon gave a delighted shriek and dug her knees into his belly. Seconds later, she plopped on top of Nealy.

Nealy let out an *oof,* then her forehead crumpled in distress. "Oh, Mat!"

The baby crawled up her body as if it were the yellow brick road, sprawled across her face, and reached for the brass headboard.

"Agile little thing, isn't she?"

Nealy shifted the baby's butt enough to free her face. "This is terrible!"

"Could be a lot worse. At least that diaper's not loaded."

"That's not what I mean. We're naked!"

Mat slid his hand around Nealy's thigh. "Son of a gun. You're right."

"Don't you dare try to be funny about this."

"Tell me we're not back to that thing about trauma-tizing her for life."

"We're naked. This bedroom reeks of . . . well, you know what I mean."

He regarded her blankly. "I have no idea what you're talking about."

"Monkey business, that's what!"

"Monkey business? Is that what you call some of the best sex either one of us is ever going to have?"

"Really?" The soft, vulnerable look made him wish he'd kept his big mouth shut, but his brain always woke up a few minutes after his body.

The Demon grabbed a handful of Nealy's hair and beamed down at her. Nealy's expression grew troubled again, but the baby kept smiling. Then she started this soft little babble, talking to Nealy as if she could un-derstand every word. Nealy's face began to glow in a way that made Mat's insides cramp. This whole thing—the baby in their bed, Nealy curled next to him, the memory of last night—it was all too much for him.

He slipped out from under the covers and grabbed his shorts from the floor. Nealy alternated between staring at him and trying to spare the baby the sight of a buck-naked, fully erect man.

The Demon was making more happy sounds, giving Nealy the adoration she normally bestowed on him. Ap-parently the baby believed she had him right where she wanted and was now free to move on to her next con-quest. Not far from the truth.

She dropped her head and pressed her wet mouth to Nealy's chin. For a moment Nealy just lay there, then she cradled the baby's head. At the same time, her mouth set in this stubborn line that told him she wanted to cry, but wouldn't do it.

He forgot about snapping his jeans. "What's wrong?"

"She's just so perfect."

He gazed down at the baby, who had now plopped

her thumb in her mouth and stretched full length on top
of Nealy. He started to make some wiseass remark about
how nobody could call the Demon perfect, but the words
stuck in his throat because they looked so beautiful lying
there together.

Then he started seeing visions of hair bows, Barbies,
tampons, and thirty-six shades of lipstick. This was not
what he wanted! He needed to get out of this room—he
felt claustrophobic—but he couldn't leave with Nealy
working so hard at keeping her eyes dry.

He scooped up the baby and sat on the side of the
bed. "Tell me what's wrong."

For a moment she didn't say anything, and then the
words came in a rush. "I'm afraid I'll hurt her. It's . . .
When I was young . . ." She struggled to hold it back,
but couldn't. "There was a photograph taken of me when
I was sixteen. In Ethiopia, with a baby who was starving . . ."

"I remember."

"The baby died, Mat. Right after the picture was
taken. When I was still holding her."

"Oh, sweetheart . . ."

"And that wasn't the end. There have been so many
since then. Babies in terrible agony, suffering from star-
vation, from unspeakable diseases. AIDS babies. Crack
babies. You can't imagine . . ."

As it all spilled out of her, he understood the price
she'd paid for those photographs of America's immac-
ulately groomed, perfectly poised First Lady holding an
afflicted infant. It was no wonder she believed she was
somehow cursed.

"I couldn't stop. There's so much need. But I . . . I
started thinking of myself as the—" Her voice broke.
"The Angel of Baby Death."

He put the Demon on the floor and drew her against
his chest. "It's all right, sweetheart . . . It's all right . . ."
He stroked her bare, soft back, whispered goofy stuff

into her ear, did everything he could to take away the hurt.

The Demon didn't like being set aside, and it wasn't long before she started to yelp. Nealy got embarrassed and pulled back from him. "This is silly. I shouldn't have—"

"Just shut up," he said gently. "You're entitled to a couple of well-earned neuroses."

She gave a watery smile. "That's what this is, isn't it?"

He nodded. The Demon's screams grew louder. Nealy frowned and he could feel her growing agitated. "She's really upset."

He gently caught her chin and turned her head toward the furious infant. "Look at her, Nealy. Just look at her. She's screaming her lungs out, but there's not a single tear in those eyes. She's just testing her limits."

"Yes, but—"

"All babies aren't suffering. I know you understand that in your head. Just try to feel it in your heart."

He picked up the Demon, and as he set her in Nealy's arms, he knew there was no bromide he could offer that would undo all those years of trauma. Button would have to do the job on her own.

Lucy still hadn't returned by the time he and Nealy had finished eating a breakfast neither of them wanted. Although she'd taken the dog with her, she'd left all her things in the motor home, so he knew she planned on coming back. He tried to figure out how he was going to deal with her when that happened.

He and Nealy hadn't talked much since they'd left the bedroom. She kept making busywork for herself so she could pretend she was tough as nails and hadn't lost her dignity getting teary over the Demon. He wanted to take her back upstairs and start all over again, but the baby was in the way.

Both of their heads came up as they heard a dog bark. Nealy grabbed the Demon and followed him outside.

Lucy was approaching the front porch with Squid on a new leash. She froze as she saw him standing there.

He glowered down at her. "You're so busted."

That small head came up, those little shoulders shot back, her top lip trembled. "Big deal. I don't care."

He shoved his hand toward the garage. "Go in there and find some garden tools. I want every weed pulled from that flower bed in the back. And make it snappy."

She stared at him. "You want me to weed that dinky little flower bed?"

"You got a hearing problem?"

"No. No!" Delighted that she had escaped so easily, she ran to the garage.

Nealy regarded him with amusement. "You're one tough hombre. That's going to take her . . . oh, maybe an hour."

He smiled back at her. "She was responsible for one of the best nights of my life. It's hard to get too mad at her."

She nodded. And then she said the strangest thing. "Thanks."

He was standing there basking in her approval and grinning like a fool when a truck towing a silver Airstream drew up in front of the house.

He stared at it. He'd seen lots of Airstreams recently, but there was something familiar about this one.

The door of the truck opened and two badly dressed senior citizens climbed out.

No. It wasn't *possible*!

"Yoo-hoo! Mat! Nell!"

Nealy gave a delighted squeal as Bertis and Charlie Wayne charged up the sidewalk.

He sagged against the porch post. Just when he

thought it couldn't get worse . . . First it had been the kids . . . then he'd added a wife and a dog. Next had come a house in Iowa . . . then a Ford Explorer.

Now Grandma and Grandpa had shown up.

17

CHARLIE SHOOK HANDS WITH MAT WHILE BERTIS hugged Nealy and tweaked Button's toes. Nealy still couldn't believe they were here. "How did you know where to find us?"

"Didn't Lucy tell you? She gave us the address just before you left. What a dickens that child is."

Just seeing Bertis made Nealy feel better. Last night had turned her world upside down. She'd expected to enjoy making love with Mat, but she hadn't expected that great rush of feeling to last.

It was hard to remind herself this was only a fling. If she was lucky, they would have another one or two nights together, but then it would end. Sometime in the distant future when it wouldn't be so painful, she could see herself taking out the memories to examine while she was standing in a receiving line or listening to an overly long speech. The idea depressed her. Bertis and Charlie had arrived at a perfect time.

"Lucy'll be thrilled to see you." She shifted Button to her hip. "She's working out back right now."

"It's good to keep them busy." Bertis slipped on her reading glasses, peered at Button, and wiped a speck from the baby's chin. "Since we were heading west anyway, we decided to stop by and check on you."

Charlie stretched to ease a kink from his back. "We're going to Yosemite, always wanted to see it. But we aren't in any hurry, and Bertis was worried about Lucy."

Bertis let her reading glasses fall back onto their chain. "We thought it might be hard on her finally having to face her grandmother's death."

Mat's eyes narrowed. "You knew about her grandmother?"

"Oh, she told us all about her." She clucked her tongue in disapproval. "Imagine a fifty-three-year-old woman marrying one of her students. Of course, I didn't say what I was thinking to Lucy."

Mat's jaw was starting to twitch. "You knew about Nico, too?"

"See, Charlie, I told you his name wasn't Nick, but you always argue with me."

Charlie scratched his head. "What kind of name is Nico?"

"That's not the point. The point is that I was right and you were wrong."

"Which is a good thing because if it ever turns out the other way around, I'll probably have that heart attack you're always warning me about."

She gave his hand a fond pat, then turned to study Mat. "You and Nell sure have been busy these last few days."

Mat smiled. "Things happen."

Nealy couldn't figure out why everybody was looking at her. "What?"

Mat regarded her with a combination of amusement and warning. "I think Bertis and Charlie have noticed your recent pregnancy."

Nealy's hand flew to her waist. She'd been so surprised by their appearance that she'd completely forgotten. Two days ago when they'd last seen the Waynes, her stomach had been flat. She regarded them with dismay. "Oh. I . . ."

"Why don't you come inside?" Mat walked up the steps to the porch, not looking all that upset about having them around. "I'll put on a fresh pot of coffee."

"Good idea." Bertis bustled after him. "Charlie, go get those Jiffy blueberry muffins I made this morning." She regarded Nealy conspiratorially. "I fix them from scratch when I'm home, but there's nothing like a Jiffy mix when you're on the road. That's one product they've been smart enough not to tinker with."

Nealy had never heard of Jiffy mixes, and she tried to figure out how she was going to explain the pregnancy padding.

Mat's hand settled warm and comforting against the small of her back. "Blueberry muffins sound great."

As he fixed coffee, Bertis made no reference to Nealy's phony pregnancy. Instead, she chatted about her own grandchildren, then put the muffins Charlie brought on a pottery plate Nell found in the cupboard. They carried everything out to the sunporch, then Bertis called out to Lucy, who was working around the rosebushes.

Her face lit up when she saw them, and she flew inside. "You came! Ohmygod, I can't believe it!" She hugged them fiercely, then backed away and tried to act cool. "I mean, it would have been okay if you'd gone right to Yosemite. How long are you going to stay?" The shadow of anxiety appeared in her eyes. "You're going to stay, aren't you?"

"For a couple of days. There's a real nice campground right outside town. As long as Nell and Mat don't mind having us around, of course."

Lucy turned to Mat, and all her cool faded as a pleading expression came over her. "They can stay, can't they?"

Nealy hid her amusement as Mat struggled to sound enthusiastic. "Sure they can stay. It'll be great having them around."

Lucy's smile spread. Then she reached for a muffin.

"Stop right there, young lady, and go wash those hands."

Lucy grinned at Bertis and shot into the house. Button, who was trying to waddle across the Oriental rug without holding on to anything, fell on her bottom and scowled.

Charlie chuckled. Bertis gazed after Lucy with a smile. "She's really something, isn't she? You can just tell by looking at her that she's special."

A flash of pride shot through Nealy. "Yes, we think she's pretty special, too." *We.* As if Lucy were hers and Mat's.

Charlie carried his coffee mug to the couch. "I guess Bertis and I are worried about her. Worried about both the girls."

"They're fine." Mat sounded more than a little defensive.

"For now." Bertis brushed a speck of muffin from her bright pink shorts. "But what about after the three of you get that paternity test Lucy seems so sure she can prevent? I don't like speaking ill of the dead, but your ex-wife was a very irresponsible woman."

"You're right about that." He carried his mug to the door that led to the back step and leaned against the frame, subtly distancing himself from them.

"Mat thinks we're nibby," Bertis confided to Nealy as if Mat weren't standing right there. "We're naturally curious, but we don't pry. People just tell us things."

"It's mainly Bertis," Charlie said. "People know they can trust her."

"Now, don't you sell yourself short, Charlie. Remember that truck driver yesterday at the rest stop."

Nealy smiled. Bertis and Charlie had the girls' best interests at heart, and she couldn't see any reason to keep them in the dark. Maybe they could come up with a solution.

She reached down and brushed a hand over Button's dandelion fluff. "Mat's taking the girls to Davenport today for blood tests. Then they'll be going back to Pennsylvania." She didn't mention foster care, but Bertis's next words told her she didn't have to.

"Those girls will be split up as sure as anything. Somebody'll adopt Button, but Lucy's too old." She toyed with the chain on her glasses as if it were a string of worry beads.

"I can't keep them," Mat said, and Nealy could feel the guilt trickling from him.

Bertis turned to Nealy. "What about you, Nell? You already act like they're your own. Maybe you could take them."

That tantalizing thought had been tugging at Nealy since yesterday, but every time it appeared, she rejected it. Bringing them into her world would set off a media feeding frenzy that would ruin their lives.

She knew what it was like to grow up without any privacy—having every part of your life reported by the press. Her father had pounded the doctrine of obedience into her at an early age, so she'd managed to cope, but Lucy wasn't like that. The intense pubic scrutiny she'd receive wouldn't give her any room to make mistakes. Although her quick mind and stubborn spirit were her strengths, they would also inevitably get her into trouble. She needed to be able to finish growing up without the world watching.

Nealy shook her head. "I'd love to keep her, but I can't. My life is . . . it's complicated right now."

Mat must have sensed her inability to lie to them because he sat down and began unwinding the story of her imaginary ex-husband and nefarious in-laws. Lucy came back out onto the sunporch while he was talking and attacked the muffin.

Bertis and Charlie listened carefully until Mat was finished, then Charlie regarded Nealy sympathetically. "You know you can count on us."

She felt so guilty for deceiving them that she could barely manage a nod.

*   *   *

Despite his grumbling, Mat seemed to enjoy having
another man around, and he and Charlie were engaged
in a discussion of Chicago sports as they went off to get
the Explorer Mat had rented the day before. As soon as
they returned, Mat took Nealy aside and told her he'd
finished arranging the paperwork for the blood test, and
he wanted to leave for Davenport as soon as possible.
He seemed to take it for granted that Nealy would come
with him, but she refused to have anything to do with
it. He ended up threatening her with the wrath of God—
meaning his own—if she stuck her head out of the house
while he was gone. She knew how concerned he was,
so she gave him her word.

Lucy was a different matter, and Mat locked horns
with her in the backyard. Nealy couldn't hear what either
of them said, but he must have come up with something
because Lucy finally made her way to the Explorer, her
feet dragging. Button needed no convincing. She was
more than willing to go off with her favorite man.

After he'd loaded her into the car seat he'd moved to
the Explorer, he turned to Bertis. "Promise me you'll
keep her inside. Her ex-husband's as crazy as a loon."

"We'll watch out for her, Mat. Now you go on."

He looked at Nealy. "Bertis and Charlie said they'd
keep the girls company tonight so we could go out to
dinner without you worrying about them. How about it?"

She smiled. "Okay."

"Good. It's a date."

Thinking about the evening ahead, along with the lim-
itations of her wardrobe, kept her from obsessing over
the girls. She didn't want to go out on her first date with
Mat wearing shorts, but she'd also said she wouldn't
leave the house, so she consulted Willow Grove's yellow pages and made some phone calls. Before long, she
had a list.

Bertis agreed to pick up everything for her while

Charlie did some maintenance work on the Airstream. By late afternoon, the older woman had bustled back in with the items Nealy had chosen over the phone.

The straps on the high-heeled shoes pinched, but they were sexy and she didn't regret them. And the short tangerine maternity dress had a deeply scooped neckline, so at least it looked good from the bust up. Her favorite item, however, was a delicate black and gold choker with a tiny beaded heart that rested in the hollow of her throat.

She put everything away until later and settled in the kitchen with Bertis. They were drinking glasses of the sun tea she'd made earlier when Lucy charged in, extending her arm to display the bandage.

"It was so gross. You should have been there. The needle was this big, and they took out a ton of blood, and it really hurt, and Mat fainted."

"I didn't faint!" Mat was trying to placate a very fussy baby as he came into the kitchen, but his eyes were on Nealy. He seemed to be reassuring himself that she was still safe.

"Almost," Lucy retorted. "You got real white and your eyes shut."

"I was thinking."

"About fainting."

Button's matted hair and creased cheek indicated she'd just awakened. She had a bandage on the inside of her small arm, just as Mat and Lucy did. On a baby, however, it looked cruel, and Nealy felt an irrational stab of anger at Mat for having forced her to undergo something so painful.

The baby squirmed in his arms. Her whimpers turned into sobs, and Lucy went to her. "Come here, Button." She held out her arms, but the baby batted them away and howled louder.

Mat shifted her to his shoulder. "I swear she screamed

for forty miles. She only fell asleep about ten minutes ago."

"If your arm was as small as hers, you'd be crying, too," Nealy snapped.

Guilt ruined the scowl he tried to give her. He began to walk the baby around the kitchen, but she refused to settle down, so he took her into the living room. Before long, Nealy heard the faint sound of a cow mooing, but the baby's screams continued unabated.

"Bring her here and let me try," Bertis called out. But when he returned, Button only screamed louder and twisted her head until her teary eyes came to rest on Nealy.

Her bottom lip protruded, and she looked so pitiful that Nealy could hardly bear it. She rose and moved toward the miserable infant, although why she thought Button would come to a second-stringer like herself after she'd already rejected her favorite people, she couldn't imagine.

To her astonishment, Button reached out. Nealy took her in her arms, and the baby gripped her as if she'd come home. Shaken, Nealy set her to her shoulder. As she stroked her back, her tiny spine shook beneath her palm. Nealy felt like crying herself. She carried her out to the sunporch where they could be alone and settled the two of them in the big wooden rocker.

The porch was warm from the afternoon heat, but the rocker sat in a corner that was shaded by a maple growing at the side of the house, and the ceiling fan stirred the breeze coming through the screen door. Button curled against her breast as if Nealy were all she had left. Gradually the hiccuping sobs faded as Nealy stroked her, kissed her Band-Aid, and crooned nonsense. She heard the low voices of Lucy and Bertis in the kitchen, but nothing from Mat.

Button finally looked up into Nealy's eyes, her expression full of trust. As Nealy gazed back, she could almost feel her heart expanding until it filled all the dark, cold spaces that had been carved out inside her. This little baby had absolute confidence in her.

Nealy heard a rushing in her ears, the sound of great black wings beating a final retreat, and as she looked down at the beautiful little girl curled in her lap, she finally felt free.

Button gave a triumphant chortle, almost as if she could read Nealy's mind. Nealy laughed and blinked away tears.

Button was finally ready to address what had happened. She settled herself more comfortably in Nealy's lap, grabbed her toes, and began to talk. Multisyllabic words, long sentences, complex paragraphs of baby chatter, detailing the injury, the *insult* of her experience.

Nealy gazed into that small, expressive face and nodded in response. "Yes . . . I know . . . A terrible thing."

Button's chatter grew more adamant.

"He should be hung."

More outrage.

"You think hanging's too good for him?" Nealy stroked her cheek. "Well, all right. How about torture?"

A bloodthirsty squeal.

"All his veins at once? Yes, that sounds about right."

"Enjoying yourself?" Mat wandered onto the sunporch, both hands shoved into the pockets of his shorts.

Button shot him a look of betrayal and turned her face into Nealy's breast. Nealy felt so blissfully happy that she wanted to sing. "You've got some big making up to do. With both of us."

Guilt oozed from him. "Come on, Nealy. She'll recover. And it had to be done."

"Button doesn't think so, do you, sweetheart?"

The baby stuck her fingers in her mouth and glowered at him.

He tried to brazen it out, but he was so obviously

upset that Nealy took pity on him. "She'll forgive you soon."

"Yeah. I guess." He didn't sound convinced.

"How did you manage to get Lucy to go along with you?"

"Bribery. I promised her we'd stay a couple of extra days if she cooperated." He looked uncomfortable. "It probably wasn't smart since I'm just postponing the inevitable, but I did it anyway."

Her emotions shifted from joy at having a few more stolen days to growing dread over the girls' future.

If only . . .

The Willow Grove Inn was an old stagecoach stop that had been recently refurbished with lots of warm wood and chintz. Mat cased the place for terrorists and stray lunatics, then decided she'd be safest outside on the enclosed flagstone patio.

Nealy's frivolous haircut floated in wisps around her face as she walked toward the table, and her dress swirled above her knees, while the little beaded heart tickled the hollow of her throat. Her heels clicked on the flagstones and Armani's newest fragrance drifted from her pulse points. The vaguely stunned look on Mat's face when she'd come downstairs had been her reward.

She wasn't the only one who had taken special pains with her appearance. He looked devastatingly handsome in light gray slacks and a pale blue shirt. The gold watch at his wrist glimmered against his suntanned arms as he seated her, then picked up the wine list to study. Although the decorative wrought-iron chair was too small for his big body, he settled back into it with perfect ease.

The waiter gave Nealy a disapproving look when Mat chose an expensive wine. "Doctor's orders," Mat told him. "She has a hormonal condition that requires alcohol."

Nealy smiled and bent her head to study the menu. She couldn't remember the last time she'd been unobserved in a restaurant. Behind them, a trellis holding deep purple clematis and coral roses bloomed, and the nearest table was just far enough away to give them a delicious sense of privacy.

They chatted about nothing until the waiter returned with the wine, then took their orders. After he left, Mat lifted his glass and touched it to hers. His smile bathed her in sexual promise. "To wonderful food, a hot summer night, and my very beautiful, very sexy First Lady."

She tried not to drink in Mat along with the wine. It was difficult when the knowledge of what would happen between them tonight seemed like a third guest at the table. Suddenly she wanted to rush through this meal she'd been anticipating all day. "You steeltown boys sure are smooth talkers."

He settled back in the too-small chair. Like her, he seemed to realize that they'd combust before dinner arrived if they didn't steer the subject toward cooler waters. "Only a minor-league smooth talker compared to your crowd."

"There's that cynicism I've come to know and adore."

"It's amazing how many ways your pals in Washington manage to avoid ever speaking the truth."

She instinctively responded to the light of challenge gleaming in his eyes. "You're boring me."

"Spoken like a born and bred politician."

When politics had come up that night at the campground with Bertis and Charlie, she hadn't been able to participate, but tonight she could. "Cynicism is easy," she retorted. "Easy and cheap."

"It's also democracy's best friend."

"And its biggest enemy. My father raised me to believe that cynicism is nothing more than an excuse for underachievement."

"Meaning?"

"Meaning that it's easier to criticize others than do your part to fix a tough problem." She leaned forward, relishing the chance to lock horns with him, especially concerning something she felt so passionately about. "Cynicism gives decent people an out. They can assume a posture of moral superiority without ever getting their hands dirty coming up with real solutions."

"It's tough not to be cynical."

"That's laziness talking. Pure laziness."

"Interesting theory." He smiled. "It's hard to figure out how such a confirmed do-gooder has survived in Washington for so long."

"I love Washington. Most of it, anyway."

"What don't you love?"

Old habits of privacy began to close around her, but she was tired of her own caution. "I ran away because I burned out. Being First Lady is the worst job in the country. There's no job description, and everybody has a different idea of what you should be doing. It's a no-win situation."

"You seem to have won. Barbara Bush is the only First Lady with approval ratings as high as yours."

"She got them honestly. I got them by pretending to be something I'm not. But just because I've grown to hate being First Lady doesn't mean I hate politics." Now that she'd started, she didn't want to stop. "I know you may find it hard to believe, but I've always loved the intrinsic honor of a political life."

"Honor and politics aren't words you hear in the same sentence very often."

She met his skepticism head-on. "It's an honor to be given the people's trust. An honor to serve. Every once in a while, I even think about—" Appalled, she broke off.

"Tell me."

"There's nothing more to say."

"Come on. I've seen you naked." He gave her a crooked smile.

"That doesn't mean you're going to see into my head."

He'd always been too perceptive where she was concerned, and a strange alertness came over him. "I'll be damned. Hillary Clinton's not the only one. You're thinking about running for office yourself, aren't you?"

She nearly knocked over her wine goblet. How could a person she'd known for such a short time understand something she hadn't completely articulated even to herself? "No. I'm not thinking about it at all. I've . . . well, I've thought about it, but . . . not really."

"Tell me."

His intensity made her wish she'd never started this. "Chicken."

She was so tired of always being cautious, and she wanted to talk, damn it! Maybe it was time to give these vague ideas a little fresh air. "Well . . . I'm not serious about this, but I've thought about it a little."

"More than a little, I'll bet."

"Just these past few months." She met those penetrating gray eyes. "I've been an inside observer for most of my life—living right at the heart of power, but not having any real power myself. I've had influence, sure, but no real authority to fix things. Still, there are some advantages to being an observer."

"Such as?"

"I've watched the very best and worst we have. I've seen their successes and failures, and I've learned from them."

"What have you learned?"

"That this country is in crisis. That we don't have enough politicians who are either willing or able to make the hard calls."

"But you are?"

She considered it, then nodded. "Yes. Yes, I think I am."

He regarded her thoughtfully. "Where would you start?"

So she told him. Not all of her ideas—that would have taken hours—but some of them. The more she talked, the more excited she got, and the more she believed in what she was saying.

He began to look slightly dazed. "You've got the quirkiest politics of anyone I know. Left wing here, right wing there, then middle of the road. It's a wonder you can walk straight."

"I've never believed in labels. I only believe in looking at what's best for the country. Partisan politics have stolen our legislators' backbones."

"In Washington, real backbone only comes from personal power."

She smiled. "I know."

He shook his head. "You're too much of a featherweight. You lead with your heart. The big boys would chomp you up and spit you out."

She laughed. "For all your talk, you're incredibly naive. The big boys have watched me grow up. I've sat on their knees and played with their children. They've patted me on the head and danced at my wedding. I'm one of their own."

"All that gets you is patronized."

"You forget that I hold trump."

"What do you mean?"

She picked up her wineglass, took a slow sip while she thought it over, then set it down. "I'm a national icon."

For a long time, he simply stared at her. Then he gradually began to soak in what she wasn't quite ready to put into words. He looked slightly dazed as he leaned back in his chair. "You could really pull it off, couldn't you?"

She propped her chin on the back of her hand and gazed dreamily off into the distance. "If I set my mind to it, I imagine I could assemble the biggest power base anyone in Washington has ever seen."

"And like a fairy godmother, use it only for good deeds."

His cynicism was back, but she didn't flinch from it. "Exactly."

"That's not the way the game's played."

"I may be the only person in the country who doesn't need to play the game. I've already won."

"How do you figure?"

"I'm not ego-driven, and when you take the ego out of the politician, what's left is a public servant. I have instant, bone-deep credibility."

"This past week has put a big dent in that."

"Not if I spin it right."

"The spin," he drawled. "I was wondering when we'd get to that."

"There's nothing wrong with spin as long as it's honest. People understand job dissatisfaction. I had to escape a job that was strangling me. That's something everybody can identify with."

"A lot more is involved than escaping an unsatisfactory job. There's the matter of where you've been and what you've been doing. The press won't give up until they have the whole story."

"Believe me, I know more about getting around journalists than you can imagine."

He began studying the tablecloth.

"You have to trust me, Mat. I love the girls. I'd never let any harm come to them."

He nodded, but he didn't look at her.

The waiter arrived with their salads, and she decided it might be best to change the subject. "I've gone on and on about myself, but you've hardly told me anything about your own work."

"There's nothing much to tell. Do you want a roll?" He picked up the green wicker basket the waiter had brought earlier.

"No, thanks. Do you like your job?"

"I guess I'm going through a career crisis right now." He shifted his weight and no longer looked so comfortable in the small chair.

"Maybe I can help."

"I don't think so."

"Candor only works one way, is that it? I tell you all my secrets, but you hold yours back."

"I'm not too proud of some of my secrets."

She'd never seen him look so serious.

He set down his fork and pushed away his salad. "There's something we need to talk about. Something I have to tell you."

Her stomach sank. She knew exactly what he was going to say, and she didn't want to hear it.

18

MAT HAD TO TELL HER THE TRUTH. HE'D KNOWN THAT last night.

"You don't have to worry," she said. "I may be naive about some things, but I understand about last night."

He frowned as he tried to switch mental gears. His big story had just gotten bigger with the revelation that she was thinking about running for public office, but that made no difference. She needed to hear what he did for a living.

Just thinking about the way she was going to react made his tongue clumsy. "Last night? That wasn't what I meant. I need to— Exactly what do you think you understand about last night?"

The waiter chose that moment to appear with their entrees. After they were served, Mat leaned back in his chair. "Go on. I want to hear what you have to say about last night."

"Why don't you go first?"

"You're having second thoughts, aren't you?"

"And third and fourth," she said. "What about you?"

There was a good reason for him to have second thoughts, but it bothered him to know that she was, too. "My only thought is that Lucy and that baby had better be asleep when we get back so we can head right for the bedroom."

"Just get to it, is that it?"

"Yes." He blocked out what he had to tell her. Soon. Before they finished their dinner. "Don't try to pretend you don't want the same thing. Remember that I was there last night. Besides, you've been looking at me all evening as if I'm dessert."

"I have not! Well, maybe I have, but it's only because you've been doing that eye thing."

"What eye thing would that be?"

"You know what eye thing." A haughty little sniff. "Where you trickled them all over me while I'm talking."

"Trickling eyes. Nice image."

"Don't play dumb. You know what I mean."

"As a matter of fact, I do." He smiled and drank in the sight of her. The First Lady of the United States of America had gotten dressed up just for him.

She wore that orange maternity dress as if it were a designer original, and the little beaded necklace thing was the sexiest piece of jewelry he'd ever seen. The tiny heart that dangled from it nestled in the hollow of her throat, one of the many places he'd kissed last night. She was a woman in a class by herself, but, even though he was a writer, he didn't know how to say everything he was feeling out loud, so he got to the main point.

"Have I told you that you look beautiful and that I can't wait to make love with you?"

"Not with words you haven't."

"The trickling eyes?"

"You bet."

His urge to tease faded, and he touched her hand. "I got a little carried away last night. You're all right, aren't you?"

"More than all right. But thanks for asking."

He stroked her palm with his fingertips, urged himself to tell her the truth right now . . . right this minute . . .

Believe me, I know more about getting around journalists than you can imagine.

He visualized those beautiful blue eyes—as blue as the sky on an American flag—clouding over when they heard what he really did for a living.

He reached across the table and touched the very tip of her finger. "Tonight . . . if things start going too fast for you, I want you to say something."

"So you can stop?"

"Are you kidding? I want to hear you beg."

She laughed, then slipped her hand under his and stroked his palm. A rush of heat shot through his bloodstream. He reminded himself that it wasn't as if he'd been keeping this a secret from her for weeks. He'd learned who she was less than forty-eight hours ago.

"I didn't know it could be like this." Her voice held a husky note that no news footage had ever captured. "Lusty and crazy, but still funny."

"It can be whatever we want it to be."

"Sex has always seemed so serious to me." She withdrew her hand. "So . . . difficult."

He didn't want to hear about her relationship with Case, not when he hadn't told her the truth. "You probably shouldn't tell me too many secrets."

She didn't like that. "What are the rules here, Mat? I don't have your depth of experience with casual affairs." Like the skilled politician she was, she'd leaned on the words so he'd feel their sting. "Maybe you'd better spell out what you want to say."

"This doesn't have anything to do with rules. It's . . ." His deception was eating away at him, and he tried to ease into the subject. "What if you were to confide in me about something? Something you don't want the world to know. Like the fact that you're thinking about running for office." *Like the fact that your husband was gay,* but he didn't say that. "How do you know you can trust me to keep your secrets?"

"Because you would. You have the most over-developed sense of responsibility of anyone I know."

She surprised him by smiling. "You charge through life like a bull, butting at people with your horns, intimidating everybody with your size. You paw the ground, and snort at the wind, and roar at everybody who displeases you. But you always do the right thing. And because of that, I trust you."

She was ripping a hole right through him. He had to tell her.

Her patrician nose shot back up in the air. "Are you afraid I'm going to attach more importance to last night than I should? I'm not that naive. I understand that this is only about sex."

She'd finally given him a target to deflect his guilt, and he lowered his voice to a furious whisper. "What kind of talk is that from a woman who's supposed to be this country's moral beacon?"

"It's realistic talk."

He should be grateful that she understood how this kind of relationship worked, but he snapped at her instead. "Well, that just goes to show what you know. Now I suggest you eat the rest of that fish before it gets cold."

He was the one who hadn't touched his dinner, not her, but she didn't call him on it. He forced himself to pick up his knife and cut a bite of steak. Just as determinedly, he turned the conversation in a less personal direction. She went along with him, but he suspected she was just biding her time.

They finished their dinner and declined dessert but not coffee. Just as he was taking his first sip, he felt the toe of her shoe stroke his calf.

"Are you going to take all night to drink that?" Her mouth curled in a smile that managed to be both mischievous and provocative.

He leaned back and let his eyes glide over her breasts just to give her a hard time. "What's the hurry?"

"The hurry, big guy, is that I've decided it's time for you to strut your stuff."

He nearly devoured her on the spot, but somehow they managed to make it as far as the car. Then his hands were all over her, right there in the front seat of the Explorer.

A truck drove into the parking lot, bringing him to his senses. "We've got to get out of here . . ."

"It's only nine," she said breathlessly. "Lucy'll still be up. And Bertis and Charlie may have stayed around to keep her company."

He threw the car into gear. "Then you're about to have another new experience."

He raced out of town, found a narrow road that roughly paralleled the river, then turned down a gravel lane that ended at a small boat ramp. He maneuvered the Explorer past the ramp and into some brush, where he killed his lights, put down the front windows, and turned off the ignition. "I know we're both a little old for this . . ."

"Speak for yourself." Just like that his lap was full of frisky First Lady. Or at least the part of his lap she could get to with the steering wheel in the way.

It wasn't gentlemanly of him, but he went for her panties first, banging his elbow against the door panel as he reached under that billowy orange skirt, then grinding his hip into the armrest as he whipped them down her shapely legs and pitched them out the car window.

Her sweet little tongue slipped from his mouth. "Did you just throw my panties out the window?"

"No."

She laughed and reached for his zipper. "I want yours."

"Oh, you're going to get mine, all right." He tore off the Wal-Mart pillow and slid across the seat, taking her with him. His knee scraped the dash, his head bumped the roof, but he didn't care.

She threw her leg over his thighs to straddle him. This was too sweet. He nuzzled the little beaded heart at her throat, caught her bottom lip between his own. "I see you've done this before."

"Dozens of times. I invented it."

Damned if she didn't have his pants open. And she was giving a whole new meaning to the term *full disclosure.*

He'd decided last night that he wasn't getting within ten feet of her without packing a condom. After he'd found what he needed, he grasped the tab on her zipper and pulled it down so he could slip the dress off her shoulders. Within seconds he was squeezing a small, hard nipple.

"That hurts," she murmured. "Do it again."

He smiled and did as she asked.

Something between a growl and a purr made a gentle vibration inside her mouth. He felt it with his tongue and it drove him crazy.

He pushed his hand under her skirt again and cupped her between those generously splayed thighs. She was wet and slick. He rubbed.

"Don't . . . do . . . that . . ."

He slipped his finger inside her and whispered, "Is this better?"

She moaned and gripped his head between her hands, taking over their kiss, abrading her nipples against his shirt.

He had her cradled in his hand, but he was so wild for her that it wasn't enough. He left that sweet warm place to grasp her hips. He lowered her . . .

She locked her knees. Brushed herself across him. Open. Soft damp feathers. Back and forth.

He groaned. His shirt was sticking to his chest, his muscles clenched. He found her breast. Sucked.

She was a siren, a vixen. Teasing and tormenting.

He drove up . . . pulled her down . . .

She gasped and let him into her body.

She was so new and eager that he tried to slow down, but she wanted to ride him in her own way. He needed to enfold her and protect her and engorge himself upon her all at the same time. She was wicked, magnificent, unbelievably precious.

The interior of the car became their only world, and the night breeze rustling through the riverbank trees their only music. They clung to each other as if no one else existed. And then they catapulted into space.

The next morning Nealy sat on the back step with her knees tucked under her nightgown and gazed into a backyard shining with the dew of a new Iowa morning. As steam rose from the coffee mug next to her, she breathed in the knowledge that had awakened her.

She had fallen in love with Mat.

Without wanting to, she'd fallen in love with his big voice and crooked smile, his booming laughter and agile brain. And last night, his generous, uninhibited love-making. But most of all, she'd fallen in love with the way his basic sense of decency wouldn't let him turn his back on the two little girls he wanted out of his life. And so, in less than a week, she had unwittingly given him her heart. A heart he hadn't asked for.

How could she have let something so damaging happen? And she hadn't even seen it coming. She'd been so intent on chalking up her feelings to lust that she hadn't taken into consideration what she knew about herself—she was a woman who would never give herself to a man she didn't love.

It was hard to conceive of a more hopeless match. She was wise enough in the ways of celebrity to know she could never fit into his world, and she couldn't imagine him fitting into hers. Why couldn't he be an Ivy Leaguer who'd just made partner in a prestigious Washington law firm? Why couldn't she be a schoolteacher, or a social worker, or a bookstore clerk?

As she tortured herself with might-have-beens, she thought of the many ways in which they were a perfect match. She was cool to his hot, quiet to his loud, thoughtful to his impulsive. But none of that made any difference.

She drowned her despair in the shower and, afterward, sneaked into the motor home to get Button before she woke up her sister. Even though Lucy didn't complain about it, she seldom got to sleep in like a normal teenager. When Nealy returned to the kitchen, she flipped on the radio.

"Today marks the eighth day of the disappearance of First Lady Cornelia . . ."

She flipped it back off.

Mat got up just as Nealy was feeding Button her cereal. He gave her a toothpaste kiss, then asked her to stay in the house while he went out for a run. She was dividing her time between pondering yesterday's *Wall Street Journal* report on federal interest rates and keeping an eye on Button when Lucy appeared on the sunporch shortly after ten o'clock.

"Are Bertis and Charlie here? They said me and Button could go swimming at their campground. The pool has a big slide and three diving boards."

"I just talked to Bertis on the phone, and they're going to pick you up around noon. I'll keep Button here."

The baby squawked with displeasure as Squid eluded her by hiding under the couch.

"Where's Mat?"

"He went out for a run. He mentioned something about the two of you going over to that playground across the street to shoot some baskets when he got back."

"Really?" Her face lit up.

"But I told him there was no way you'd do something as silly as shooting baskets."

"You didn't!"

Nealy laughed and got up from the couch. "You're such a dork." She grabbed Lucy and hugged her as hard as she could.

"You're so weird." Lucy curled against her.

"I know. That's why we like each other."

"Who said I liked you?"

"You didn't have to say it." Without thinking, she kissed the top of the teenager's head. For a few seconds, Lucy seemed to go limp in her arms, then she pulled away, as if a simple kiss were too much for her. Or as if she thought Nealy might take it back if she didn't get away first.

Nealy smiled at her. "I've got an idea, but don't make fun of me, okay?"

"Why would I make fun of you?" Lucy sat cross-legged on the floor and grabbed Button for a morning cuddle.

"Because I want us to do something that you're going to think is really dumb."

Lucy grinned. "Like what else is new?"

"I want to do makeovers."

"Get real!"

"No, really. I want to."

"Because you think I wear too much makeup, right?"

"You do wear too much makeup. Come on, Luce, it'll be fun. Get your stuff and I'll get mine."

Lucy regarded her with teenage condescension. "If it'll make you happy."

"I'll be delirious."

After they'd both gotten their cosmetics, Lucy insisted on fixing up Nealy first. While Button toddled after a long-suffering Squid, the teenager applied layers of makeup to Nealy's face, then surveyed the results with a matchmaker's satisfaction. "You look so hot. Wait till Mat sees you."

Nealy studied herself in the mirror they'd propped on the arm of the couch. All she needed was a pimp and a street corner. She was afraid to laugh for fear her face would crack. "It's my turn."

"I'm going to look like such a dweeb."

"But you'll be a cute dweeb."

She set to work, applying only the lightest touch of eye makeup, then running her own pale lip pencil over Lucy's mouth, followed by a layer of colorless Blistex. "This is what Sandra Bullock uses instead of lipstick."

"Like how would you know?"

Like Sandra Bullock had told her. "I read it in a magazine."

Lucy regarded herself a little less critically.

Nealy pulled out three pink butterfly pins she'd hidden in the pocket of her shorts. She'd bought them as a surprise, and now she slipped them into Lucy's bangs.

Lucy stared at her reflection. "Ohmygod, Nell, they're so cool."

"Look at you, Luce. You're completely gorgeous. Promise me you'll only wear that heavy makeup if you're having one of those I-feel-like-a-slut days."

Lucy rolled her eyes.

"You don't need to hide behind a mask," Nealy said softly. "You know exactly who you are."

Lucy began picking at the arm of the chair. Nealy decided to give her a few minutes to think about what she'd said and picked up Button, who was trying to stuff her head in the wastebasket. "Come on, punkin'. It's your turn."

She set the baby on the chair, dabbed the tip of her nose with pink lipstick, then drew on a delicate set of whiskers with Lucy's eyebrow pencil. Lucy giggled.

Button was carrying on a delighted monologue with her reflection when the sultan of the palace walked into his harem. He'd finished his run, and he had a basketball tucked against his sweaty T-shirt. All three of them turned at once.

The sultan was wise in the ways of women, and he knew exactly what to do. "Who's this cute little mouse?" He rubbed Button's downy head, and she gave a round of baby applause.

Then his eyes settled on Lucy.

Nealy saw a whole world of feelings pass across her face: uncertainty, longing, and the protective armor of her sullenness.

"You look beautiful," he said simply.

She took a shaky breath. "You're just saying that."

"I say what I mean."

She began to glow. He squeezed her shoulder, then slowly turned to Nealy, but her appearance seemed to have left him at a loss for words. He studied the heavy foundation, the sooty eyes with their thick coat of black mascara, and her crimson mouth.

"Doesn't Nell look great," Lucy exclaimed. "I mean, if she didn't have that stupid pillow on, she'd look like a model."

"She does have commercial appeal."

He countered Nealy's raised eyebrows with a grin, then turned back to Lucy. "Come on, kid. Get your shoes and let's go shoot some baskets. Nell, stay here, you got it?"

"Got it." She tossed him a salute.

Lucy frowned. "You shouldn't let him boss you around so much."

"She likes it." Mat gave Lucy a gentle push toward the door.

Nealy smiled after them. Watching Lucy these days was like seeing a flower bloom.

She hummed to herself as she put away their mess, then gave Button a snack and changed her. Afterward, she decided to take her across the street to the playground so they could watch the basketball game.

She was just stepping out the front door when a dark blue Taurus pulled up in front of the house. The doors of the sedan opened, and a man and a woman dressed in business suits got out. They had "government agents" written all over them, and she felt the blood rush from her head.

Not yet! She had a house and a dog. She had two little girls and a man with whom she'd fallen in love! Just a little longer.

She wanted to run back inside and lock the door, but she pulled Button closer and forced herself to the edge of the front porch.

Both of them studied her carefully as they came up the sidewalk. "I'm Agent DeLucca with the FBI," the woman said. "This is Agent Williams, Secret Service." They took in her stomach, and she silently blessed Mat for forcing her to wear the padding.

She kept her overly made-up face carefully blank. "Yes?"

"You're Mrs. Case." Williams made it a statement instead of a question, but she thought she detected a thread of doubt in his eyes.

"Mrs. Case? You mean the First Lady?" She attempted Lucy's you're-a-moron look. "Yeah, right. That's me."

"Could we see some identification, ma'am?" the female agent asked.

"You mean like a driver's license?" Her heart was pounding so hard she was afraid they'd hear it.

"That would be fine."

"I don't have one. Someone stole my purse a couple of days ago when I was at a Laundromat." She swallowed. "Is that what this is about? Did you find my purse?"

She saw their hesitation. They thought they had her, but they weren't absolutely certain. A spark of hope flared inside her. If she'd been positively identified, there'd be a battalion of agents here, not just these two.

"We'd like to talk with you privately, ma'am. Could we go inside?"

Once she let them in the house, they could interrogate her for hours. "I'd rather talk here."

Mat came roaring up like the cavalry. His T-shirt clung to his chest and one of his sweat socks had collapsed near his ankle. "What's going on?"

"I—I think they found my purse," she managed.

Mat didn't miss a beat. He immediately turned to confront them. "Do you have her purse?"

Neither agent responded. Instead, the woman asked for his driver's license.

Lucy, looking wide-eyed and nervous, ran up as he handed it over. She had the basketball clutched to her chest as if it were a life jacket. She recognized authority when she saw it, and Nealy realized she thought they were after her. "It's okay, Luce. They want to talk to me."

"Why?"

"Do you have any identification at all, ma'am?" Agent Williams asked her.

"Everything was in my purse."

"She's my wife," Mat said. "Nell Jorik. That's all the identification you need."

The female agent gave him a hard look. "Mr. Jorik, we happen to know you're single."

"I was until a month ago. Nell and I got married in Mexico. And why do you know anything about me at all?"

"Whose children are these, sir?"

"My ex-wife's. She died about six weeks ago."

Lucy crept closer to Nealy.

Williams spoke. "Ma'am, could we step inside so we can talk in private?"

She shook her head. "No, the place is a mess."

She could see that they wanted to press the issue, and she blessed the Fourth Amendment. She decided to take a chance. "Luce, this is Agent DeLucca and Agent Williams. They're looking for Cornelia Case."

"And they think you're her?"

"I guess."

All the tension left Lucy's body. "Nell's not Mrs. Case! This is because she was in that contest, isn't it? That was my idea because I wanted to win a television so my baby sister could watch *Teletubbies*, but all I got was a power drill." She turned to Nealy. "I didn't mean to get you in trouble."

"You didn't get me in trouble." Nealy felt a twist of guilt. Lucy was defending her out of perfect innocence.

The agents exchanged glances. They knew something wasn't right, but Lucy's obvious sincerity had been effective, and they still weren't certain of Nealy's identity.

The female agent gave her a woman-to-woman look designed to inspire camaraderie. "You'd really help us out if we could sit down in the house and talk this through."

"There's nothing to talk about," Mr. Tough Guy said. "You want in the house, you come back with a search warrant."

Williams gazed at Nealy. "It seems to me that someone who doesn't have anything to hide would be more cooperative."

"It seems to me that you should have better things to do than hassle a pregnant woman," Mat countered.

Nealy stepped in before he got himself arrested. "Maybe you'd better go. We can't help you."

Agent DeLucca gave her a long, clear-eyed gaze, then turned to Lucy. "How long have you known . . . Mrs. Jorik?"

"About a week. But she's nice and everything, and she wouldn't do anything wrong."

"So you just met her?"

Lucy nodded slowly.

"You don't have to talk to them, Luce," Mat interrupted. "Go on inside."

Lucy looked confused, but she did as he asked. Button squirmed in Nealy's arms and reached toward Mat. "Da . . ."

He took her.

"Boy or a girl?" Agent DeLucca asked, glancing toward Nealy's stomach.

"Boy," Mat said without hesitation. "For sure."

Nealy pressed her hand to the small of her back and tried to look frail. "He's a big baby, and I've been having a hard time. I'm not really supposed to walk around too much."

Mat slipped his arm around her shoulder. "Why don't you go on in, honey, and lie down?"

"I think I will. Sorry I couldn't help." She gave the agents what she hoped was a wan smile and turned away.

"MA!" Button squealed at the top of her small lungs. Nealy turned back.

Button threw up her arms—So big—then reached out. She took her from Mat and buried her lips in that dandelion hair.

Neither Toni nor Jason spoke as they drove away from the house. Toni took a left when they reached the main drag, then pulled into a KFC parking lot. She found a place off to the side, turned off the ignition, and stared through the windshield at the Burger King across the street.

Jason finally broke the silence. "It's her."

"Did you see a freckle by her eyebrow?"

"She was wearing too much makeup."

"She's pregnant! Barbara Shields didn't say a damn thing about that!"

Toni reached for her cell phone, and a few minutes

later she had Shields on the phone. Their conversation was short and to the point. When she hung up, she looked over at Jason.

"At first she said it wasn't possible. Then she admitted she didn't get a clear look at her stomach because the baby was in the car seat, along with some groceries. And Jorik blocked her view when he stepped in front of her to pay."

"Damn."

"You're right. It is her," Toni said.

"She sure doesn't want to be found."

"Did you see the way she looked at those kids? Like they were her own."

"Maybe she isn't Aurora." He rubbed the bridge of his nose.

"Do you believe that?"

"I don't know what I believe."

They watched two businessmen come out of the restaurant and walk toward a new Camry.

"We can lift some prints from the door of the motor home, but we'll have to wait until dark to do it," Toni said.

Jason gazed straight ahead and asked the question that was on both their minds. "Are we going to contact the boss now or later?"

"Do you want to tell Ken that we talked with her but still aren't sure if we have Aurora?"

"Not particularly."

"Neither do I." She reached for her sunglasses. "Let's give ourselves a couple of hours and see what else we can come up with."

"My thoughts exactly."

Mat walked out onto the sunporch and regarded Nealy grimly. "Looks like the jig's up."

She pressed her lips to the baby's soft cheek, trying to shut everything out except this wiggly little bundle.

"I'm sure Button didn't know what she was saying when she called me *ma*."

"Hard to tell." The expression in his eyes mirrored her own feelings. "Nealy, they've got you."

"Not yet. They don't know for sure. If they did, this place would be swarming with Secret Service."

"The day's still young."

She gave him her best attempt at a cheeky smile. "You were coming on out there like Public Enemy Number One."

"I've always wanted to talk back to cops, and I decided this was the best chance I'd ever get. As long as I'm with you, I figure I've got diplomatic immunity."

"I wouldn't push it." She gazed out into the backyard. "I need to find Lucy."

He gave her a long slow look. "Are you going to tell her?"

"I used her out there. Now I have to make up for it."

"Do you want me to come with you?"

"No. I have to do this by myself."

She searched the house and the motor home before she found Lucy sitting in the hollyhocks that grew behind the garage. Her knees were tucked against her chest, her shoulders bowed.

Nealy eased down next to her. "I've been looking for you."

At first Lucy didn't respond. When she finally glanced over at Nealy, her expression was wary. "Did they come here because of your husband?"

"Sort of." She took a deep breath. "But not the husband I told you about."

"What do you mean?"

Nealy watched a pair of bumblebees explore the skirt of a bright yellow hollyhock blossom. "My husband was President Case, Luce."

"No!"

"I'm sorry."

She jumped to her feet. "You're lying. You're just saying this. You're Nell! You're—" Her voice broke. "Just say you're Nell."

"I can't. I'm Cornelia Case."

Lucy's eyes filled with tears. "You lied to us. You lied to all of us."

"I know. I'm sorry."

"Did you tell Mat?"

"He figured it out a couple of days ago."

"And nobody told me."

"We couldn't."

Lucy was smart, and she already understood exactly what this meant to her. A shudder passed through her. "You won't marry him now, will you?"

Her insides cramped. "There was never a question of the two of us getting married."

"Yes, there was!" Her lips trembled, and she looked as if her entire world had crumbled. "You like him! You liked him a lot! And you cared about me and Button!"

"I still care. This doesn't change the way I feel about the two of you."

"But this means you won't ever marry Mat. Not after you were married to the President. And somebody like you wouldn't ever adopt Button."

"Lucy, let me explain . . ."

But Lucy didn't want to hear any explanations. She was already running toward the house.

19

MAT FOUND NEALY IN THE HOLLYHOCKS A SHORT TIME later. He sat beside her in the same place Lucy had been, except he was crushing part of a plant. He'd taken a quick shower and his damp hair had finger marks where he'd run his hand through it. Drawing up his knees, he propped his forearms on top and gazed over at her. "I'm guessing you've had better days."

Nealy rubbed her eyes. "What's Lucy doing now?"

"Charlie showed up to take her swimming right after she ran into the house. At first she told him she wouldn't go, but he said Bertis was making fudge and her feelings would be hurt, so she grabbed Button and they took off."

"You let her take Button?"

"Lucy protects Button better than the Secret Service protected you." He straightened one leg, gazed out into the backyard of the house behind them. "And the baby needs time away from us."

"What do you mean?"

"She's . . ." He looked uncomfortable. "She's getting pretty attached."

Even though she knew what he meant, a chill crept through her. "Babies are supposed to get attached. That's what being a baby is all about."

"Nealy . . ."

She rose to her feet. "*People* are supposed to get attached."

294

"What are you trying to say?"

"Nothing. Forget it."

She walked away from him and hurried into the house. As soon as she got inside, she went upstairs to put away her clothes, anything to keep from thinking, but she heard his tread on the steps.

The bed was still rumpled, the place where they'd made love last night. Things like making beds had always been done for her, and she kept forgetting she needed to do it for herself.

He stopped inside the door. "I can't keep those kids. That's what you want, isn't it? You want me to keep them."

She grabbed the sheet and pulled it up. "You should have seen Lucy's face when I told her who I was. She's built this fantasy around the two of us. I know we both told her it wasn't realistic, but she refused to believe it. She thought if she clung to her dreams hard enough, she could make them come true."

"That's not our problem."

Her frustration boiled over, and she rounded on him. "What's so great about that manly, solitary life you're trying so hard to get back to? Tell me, Mat. What's so great about a life that doesn't include them?" *And me*, she wanted to cry. *What's so great about a life without me?*

"You're not being fair," he said steadily.

"I don't care! I saw Lucy's face, and fair doesn't do it for me right now."

"I don't have to justify my life to you."

She turned away from him, busied herself with the bed. "No, you don't."

"Listen to me, Nealy. I didn't make this situation. It was forced on me."

"Yes, I believe you've mentioned that before." The sharpness in her voice came from pain. Maybe they'd only been together for a week, but during that time, they'd been a family. While that bond was a burden to him, it meant everything to her.

"Is this about the kids or is it about us?"

He didn't have a high tolerance for subtlety, and she should have known he'd plunge right in.

"There isn't any us," she managed, praying he'd disagree. "We both know that. Not beyond what exists right now."

"Do you want there to be?"

Oh, no. She wouldn't let him do this to her. "How can there be? I'm female, remember? Part of the evil empire. Not to mention a national institution."

"You're really pissing me off."

"And you know what? I don't care."

Everything was out of control—her emotions, her life, her love for this man who didn't love her back. They couldn't even rationally discuss all the reasons that a marriage between them was impossible because his feelings for her didn't run that deep.

She waited for him to stomp away, but he didn't. Instead, he came closer, extended those long arms, and pulled her into them. "You're being a brat," he said gruffly.

That wonderful kindness. She felt his big hands in her hair, and a sob caught in her throat. She swallowed it and pressed her cheek against his chest. "I know."

His lips brushed her hair. "Will it make you feel better if I fight with you?"

"I think so."

"Okay. Take off your clothes."

If only it were that easy. She sighed. "We can't solve this with sex."

"Take 'em off anyway. I need to be serviced."

"Serviced? Is that any way to talk to the First Lady?"

"You're my First Lady, and I'm just getting started." He reached under her top. One of the ties ripped as he pulled off her pillow. "Damn, I hate this thing."

"Of course you do. You hate everything that has to do with children."

"You're not playing fair."

"Sue me."

"I've got a better idea." Her eyes flew open as he told her, in very earthy language, exactly what he had in mind.

Desire, as powerful as her pain, rushed through her. "Are you sure you can keep up with me?"

"I'll try my best."

Their clothes flew off and, within moments, they were in bed. He rolled on top of her and ravished her with his mouth. She opened herself to his hands, his big body, and, inevitably, welcomed the hard, deep thrust.

Their lovemaking was fierce and reckless, with neither of them holding anything back . . . except the love words she couldn't say and he didn't feel.

After it was over, he caressed her as if she were small and delicate. He kissed her forehead, the corners of her eyes, the tip of her nose. Kissed her as if he were memorizing her face.

She dipped her thumb into the hollow beneath his collarbone, pressed her lips to his chest.

He stroked her shoulder, buried his face in her hair. Gradually, she felt him tensing again, and she trailed her fingers over his flat stomach to encourage him.

His voice was the barest whisper. "I have something I need to tell you."

He sounded so grave, and time had become her enemy. She let her fingers move lower. "Later."

His breath caught as she touched him. He closed his palm over her wandering hand. "It has to be now. I've already put it off too long."

"The girls will be back soon. One last time."

He rolled on his side so that he was facing her. His mood was so sober that she felt her first trickle of foreboding.

"I should have told you last night—even before—but I kept chickening out. You're not going to like it."

Her sexual lassitude disappeared. She waited, and when he hesitated, she began to feel sick. "You're married."

"No!" His eyes flared with outrage. "What kind of man do you think I am?"

Limp with relief, she sank back onto the pillow. Nothing he could tell her would be as bad as that.

"Nealy, I don't work in a steel mill."

She turned her head, gazed up at him. He looked so upset. So serious. She wanted to comfort him, tell him that whatever was bothering him didn't matter.

"I'm a journalist."

Her world tilted on its axis.

"I tried to tell you at the restaurant last night, but I was selfish. I wanted another night together."

A long silent scream built inside her.

He began talking. Explaining. ". . . working in L.A. . . . tabloid television . . . hated my job . . ."

She was flying apart.

". . . looking for a big story so I could hold my head up again, but—"

"A big story?" His words finally penetrated.

"I'd sold out, Nealy. And I discovered the hard way that money doesn't mean anything if you don't respect yourself."

Her voice seemed to be coming from a faraway place. "That's what I am? Your big story? Your ticket to *self-respect*?"

"No! Please don't look at me like that."

This was too cruel. Her most private moments hadn't been private at all. She'd been sleeping with the enemy.

"I'm not going to hurt you," he said.

"You won't write about me?"

His hesitation lasted only a few seconds, but it was enough. She sprang from the bed, reached for her clothes. "I'm leaving as soon as I tell Lucy good-bye."

"Wait. Let me explain."

And she did. She waited . . . watched him rise from the bed . . . struggle for words, but the ones he finally came up with weren't nearly good enough. "I didn't mean to hurt you."

She needed to get to the bathroom before she was sick in front of him. She thought of what she'd told him about Dennis and hated herself. Even though she hadn't confirmed it, she'd let him make love with her, and he knew.

"Nealy," he said softly, "I give you my word that I won't betray you."

Her throat felt dry and rusty. "It's too late. You already have." She rushed blindly for the bathroom and closed herself in.

Afterward, Mat came up with a dozen better ways he could have told her. He should have eased up on it instead of just blurting it out. He should have been more gentle, done whatever he needed to so that porcelain skin wouldn't go pale, so those patriot-blue eyes wouldn't look so stricken.

The frail world they'd built together had toppled, and it was his fault. He turned away from the bathroom door and slowly made his way downstairs. There was nothing he could say to make it better, no excuse he could offer.

The dark blue Taurus was parked across the street. They might still not be absolutely certain who she was, but they weren't taking any chances.

Knowing she'd be safe, he grabbed the keys to the Explorer and stalked outside. He had to be by himself for just a little while. Maybe that would clear his head enough so he could figure out what to do next.

Button curled her fingers in a tired bye-bye wave as Charlie drove away from the house. Then she snuggled against Lucy and whimpered. Lucy remembered how

much Button was starting to like snuggling up with Nell
when she was tired.

Not Nell. Mrs. Case. Cornelia Case.

Lucy hadn't told Charlie and Bertis who Nell really
was. She hadn't told them that Nell would be going
away soon, going back to Washington and being the
First Lady.

It was all Lucy's fault. If she hadn't dragged Nell into
that lookalike contest, nobody would have found out and
everything could have gone on like it was, with just the
four of them and Button snuggling in Nell's lap when
she got cranky.

But Lucy knew she was lying to herself. Nell still
wouldn't have married Mat. She was Mrs. Case. If she
ever got married again, she'd marry somebody famous.
And even if she did decide to adopt some kids, they'd
be polite, smart kids, not poor, beat-up kids like her and
Button.

As for Mat . . . he hadn't wanted them from the beginning.

She pulled the baby closer over the hurt in her stomach and tried to tell herself she wasn't scared, but she
was. The whole time she'd been with Bertis and Charlie,
she'd been thinking about what she had to do. She knew
if she didn't act right away, her baby sister would end
up with strangers. And no matter how scared she was,
she couldn't let that happen, so she reached in the pocket
of her shorts and pulled out the key to Mabel that she'd
stuck there before she'd left. No strangers were going to
take her baby sister away from her.

Nealy stared through the window at the Iowa River
curling in the distance. But it wasn't her river. Her river
was a thousand miles away, flowing past Arlington National Cemetery into Chesapeake Bay.

She was dressed again in the clothes she'd worn earlier, and she'd wiped off most of the makeup Lucy had

applied. Mat had driven away in the Explorer ten minutes ago, so she wouldn't have to deal with him. She stepped over the Wal-Mart pillow and began packing her clothes, even though she knew she wouldn't ever wear any of them again. A noise outside distracted her. The sound of Mabel's engine.

She reached the bedroom window in time to see the Winnebago creeping crookedly down the drive, then lurch over the curb and into the street, barely missing the car parked on the other side. Her hand flew to her mouth as she caught a glimpse of Lucy behind the wheel. Then the motor home pulled away.

Panicked, she raced for the stairs and reached the front porch just in time to see Lucy narrowly miss a stop sign as she turned onto the cross street and then disappeared.

Let me drive. I know how to drive this thing.

She was dizzy with fear. Driving the Winnebago was a challenge for someone with experience, let alone a fourteen-year-old without a license. And Lucy wouldn't be alone. She'd never have left Button behind.

Nealy clutched the porch railing and forced herself to think. The Explorer was gone, and she didn't have a car. Maybe a neighbor . . .

Just then she noticed the dark blue Taurus parked across the street. DeLucca, the female agent, was out of the car on the passenger side, staring in the direction the motor home had taken and reaching for her cell phone.

Nealy didn't even hesitate. "Put away the phone!" she cried as she ran toward her.

De Lucca snapped to attention. Williams jumped from behind the wheel, ready to throw himself between her and a bullet.

"She's only fourteen," Nealy said, "and she's taken the baby with her."

Neither of them asked any questions. DeLucca was already climbing back in the car while Williams pulled open the rear door, then slammed it closed after Nealy.

She grabbed the back of the seat. "They can't have gone far. You have to catch up with them."

Williams hit the accelerator. DeLucca turned to gaze at Nealy's now flat stomach, but she didn't ask any questions. What was the point? She already knew the truth.

They were on a wider residential street now, but there was no sign of the Winnebago. Nealy guessed Lucy was heading for the highway.

"Turn right at the intersection."

"Are you sure you don't want the police, Mrs. Case?" Williams asked.

"No. Lucy might panic."

Nealy ignored the glance the agents exchanged. He'd called her by her real name, and she hadn't denied it. Her glorious adventure had ended the moment Mat had told her how he earned his living.

They spotted the Winnebago at the edge of town. Lucy was driving under the speed limit, but she was having a hard time steering the cumbersome vehicle, and she kept creeping toward the center line. The blood in Nealy's veins turned to ice.

"My daughter took my car once when she was fourteen," DeLucca said. "It was about the same time my hair started to turn gray."

Nealy dug her fingernails into her palms. "Right now I feel like I'm eighty."

"Kids'll do that to you. I'm Toni, by the way. Jason's driving."

She acknowledged the introductions with a distracted nod. "Try to pull up so she can see me, but whatever you do, don't scare her by putting on a siren."

The road was fairly straight and traffic blessedly light. Before long, Jason was able to ease into the other lane. As he drew alongside the Winnebago, Nealy saw Lucy. She was staring straight ahead, and she had what looked like a death grip on the steering wheel.

"Oh, God, don't honk!"

"I'll pull in front to slow her down," he said. "Just relax, Mrs. Case. Everything's going to be fine."

She wanted to scream that he had no way of knowing that.

He slipped in front of the Winnebago and slowed. Nealy twisted around to look out the rear window, but Lucy's eyes were fixed straight ahead, and she didn't see her.

Mabel drew closer, then closer still. *Brake! Put on the brakes!*

She gasped as Lucy swerved toward the shoulder. She seemed to be fighting the wheel, but she got Mabel back in the lane. She looked terrified.

Jason tapped the horn, and Lucy finally saw Nealy gesturing through the back window.

She hit the brakes hard.

Nealy gasped as the motor home fishtailed. Lucy jerked the wheel, and it fishtailed again. The tires hit the shoulder and gravel sprayed. Finally, the vehicle shuddered and jerked to a stop.

Nealy remembered how to breathe.

Within seconds, she was out of the car and racing toward the motor home with Toni and Jason following. She lunged for the door handle, but it was locked.

Nealy pounded with her fist. "Open the door right now!"

"Go away!"

"Do what I say. Open up!"

Through the window she could see that Lucy looked furious and determined, even as tears ran down her cheeks.

"Lucy, I mean it! If you don't do what I say, you're going to be in so much trouble."

"I'm already in trouble."

She strained to see if Button was all right. "You could have been killed! Just what do you think you're *doing*?"

"I'm getting a job! And we're going to live in Mabel! And you can't stop me!"

Button began to cry.

Toni pushed past Nealy and gave the door a hard rap. "Open up, Lucy. FBI."

Lucy bit her fingernails and looked straight ahead.

Toni raised her voice. "If you don't open the door, I'm going to instruct Agent Williams to shoot out all the tires, and then shoot you."

Jason stared at her. She lowered her voice to Nealy. "Teenagers see so many government conspiracy movies, they always believe the worst."

But not this teenager. "What kind of moron do you think I am?"

Nealy'd had enough. "Open up, Luce, or I'll shoot you myself! I mean it!"

There was a long silence. Finally Lucy seemed to realize she wasn't going anywhere. She bit her fingernails, looked at Nealy through the window. "Promise you won't tell Mat."

"I'm not promising a thing."

Button's screams grew louder.

Slowly . . . very slowly . . . Lucy dragged herself from behind the wheel and released the door latch.

Nealy rushed in, lifted her hand, and smacked her on the side of the head.

"Hey!"

She pulled her hard against her breast. "You scared the life out of me."

"MA!" Button squawked.

As Nealy clutched Lucy and gazed at the irate baby, she knew she'd reached one more crossroad in her life.

There was no sign of the dark blue Taurus. The space in front of the garage that held the motor home was empty. And Nealy was gone.

Mat had already searched the house for clues, but

what he'd found—Nealy's satchel partially packed with her clothes—didn't tell him anything he didn't already know.

His fear was growing by the minute. Something was very wrong. The girls should have been back by now, the motor home should be here, and Nealy—

He heard a car door slam and raced to the front porch in time to see her emerge from the passenger side of the Taurus. He didn't mean to yell, but he heard himself do it anyway.

"Are you all right? Where have you been?" He rounded on the Secret Service agent who was standing next to her. "What happened? Have you been hassling her?" He didn't wait for the guy to answer, but confronted Nealy again. "Where's the motor home? Where are the girls?"

She turned away from him as if he didn't exist. Just then, the motor home lumbered into the drive with the female agent behind the wheel.

"The girls are inside Mabel," she said so coolly she might have been talking to a stranger. Then she gazed at Williams. "How much time can you give me?"

"Not much, Mrs. Case. We have to report in."

Mat's stomach sank.

"Not until I say so," Nealy replied. "I need at least an hour."

Williams regarded her unhappily. "I don't think that will be possible."

"Unless you want to be known as the agent who lost Cornelia Case for the second time, you'll make it possible."

He seemed to realize the deck was stacked against him and gave a slow nod. "An hour."

DeLucca stepped out of Mabel. Lucy followed, with Button hanging heavily from her arms. Lucy wasn't in any hurry to get closer to him, which pretty much told

Mat everything he needed to know about who was responsible for whatever had happened.

He gazed at her as he took Button away. "Get in the house." The baby curled against his chest as if he were the world's most comfortable pillow. Her eyelids drooped.

Lucy shot Nealy an imploring look. "He's going to kill me."

"We'll all go inside." Nealy walked ahead, not looking at him, her spine straight as a flagpole.

He watched the agents disperse, one toward the front of the house, one toward the rear. Nealy lived like this all the time, he realized, with people watching her, guarding her, hounding her. He'd understood it intellectually, but that was different from watching it happen.

They headed for the sunporch. Lucy was looking for a fingernail she hadn't already bitten to the quick and trying to figure out how to tell him what he'd already figured out. His sister Ann Elizabeth had been fifteen when she'd taken off in the family car, but she hadn't brought a baby with her.

Lucy slouched into the brown wicker armchair, doing her best to bristle with attitude but not pulling it off. Nealy, looking stiff and formal, positioned herself in the opposite chair as if she were getting ready to preside over an unpleasant staff meeting.

He sat on the couch and lay sleepy Button next to him, then shifted his legs so she couldn't roll off. Nealy regarded him as if he'd just crawled out of a piece of spoiled meat.

"Can I assume this is off the record?"

He deserved it, so her snipe shouldn't have made him so mad. "Don't push me."

"A simple yes or no will do it."

She knew he'd never exploit the girls, but he took his medicine and said tightly, "Off the record."

Lucy regarded their exchange with curiosity, but he wasn't offering any more explanations right now.

"Lucy ran away with Button," Nealy said slowly. "She took Mabel."

He'd figured out that much. At the same time, he realized Nealy hadn't hesitated to rush to the two federal agents for help, even though she'd known it would blow her cover forever.

He turned to Lucy, who was trying to make herself smaller by creeping farther down into the chair. "Why?"

She lifted her chin, ready to take him on. "I'm not giving Button to strangers!"

"So you risked her life instead."

"I know how to drive," she said sullenly.

"No, you don't," Nealy countered. "That motor home was all over the road."

His chest grew even tighter. "This is the stupidest thing you've ever done."

She didn't have the courage to take him on, so she turned on Nealy. "This is all your fault! If you hadn't been Mrs. Case, you and Mat could have gotten married!"

"Stop it," he snapped. "You're not going to deflect the blame on this. Not only did you risk your own life, but you risked your sister's as well."

"What do you care? You're giving her away!"

Something tight clutched at his chest. The baby rolled to her side and went for her thumb. He'd already noticed she wasn't much of a thumb-sucker, so she must need some extra comfort. God, she was a great baby. World class. She was smart, bighearted, and gutsy—exactly the qualities that were going to help her get ahead in the world . . . if she could just catch a break.

"There's something else you should know." Nealy's lips tightened. "When I got inside the motor home, I slapped Lucy. Not hard. But I definitely slapped her."

"It's no big deal," Lucy grumbled. "I don't know why you had to tell him."

Mat didn't like the idea of anybody hitting the little

delinquent, not even Nealy, but he understood.

"It *is* a big deal," Nealy insisted. "Nobody deserves to be hit." She turned to Mat. "I need to talk to Lucy alone."

Her starchy manner got his back up. "Whatever you have to say to her, you say in front of me."

"That's pretty much like saying it in front of the whole world, isn't it?"

"I don't deserve that."

"All that and more."

"You're the one who started the secret-keeping business."

"Don't fight," Lucy said in a small voice.

Lucy had heard them argue before, but she seemed to know that something fundamental had changed between them. He realized he had to tell her the truth, too.

"Nealy wasn't the only one holding back on you, Luce."

Lucy stared at him, and then her forehead crumbled. "Shit. You're married."

"No, I'm not married! What is it with you two? And I thought you were going to watch your language."

Button made a low mewing sound, unhappy to have her slumber interrupted by his gruff voice. He rubbed her back. She lifted one heavy eyelid, saw it was him, and, reassured, closed it again. His chest grew even tighter.

"I told Nealy I worked in a steel mill, but it's not true. I'm a journalist."

"Journalist? You write for newspapers?"

"I've been doing some other things, but yes, mainly I write for newspapers."

Lucy, being Lucy, went straight to the point. "Are you going to write about Nell?"

"I have to. That's why she's so mad at me."

Lucy studied Nealy. "Is it bad that Mat's a journalist?"

Nealy wouldn't look at him. "Yes. It's bad."

"Why?"

Nealy gazed down at her hands. "This was a private time for me. And I told him some things that I didn't want anybody else to know."

Lucy's expression brightened. "That's okay, then. He'll change his mind. Won't you, Mat?"

Nealy jumped to her feet and turned away from them, clutching her arms across her chest.

Lucy frowned. "Tell her, Mat. Tell her you won't write about her."

Nealy turned back, her blue eyes icy. "Yes, Mat, tell me."

Lucy's eyes darted between the two of them. "You aren't going to write about her, are you?"

"Of course he is, Lucy. It's too big a story for him to ignore."

Right then, it struck him that it was all coming to an end, and he was going to lose her. Not in the indefinite future, but now, this afternoon.

"Mat?" Lucy's eyes were imploring.

"I won't betray her, Luce. I already told her that, but she's not buying it."

Nealy took a deep breath, then turned to Lucy as if he weren't in the room, and gave her a frozen facsimile of a smile. "Don't worry about it. It has nothing to do with you."

Lucy's apprehension had returned. "Then why did you want to talk to me alone? What about?"

Nealy's chest rose; her arms fell to her sides. "I want to adopt you and Button."

20

NEALY HAD PLANNED TO APPROACH LUCY PRIVATELY about this, but since Mat wouldn't let her, she pretended he didn't exist. Lucy stared at her as if she couldn't believe what she was hearing. Nealy smiled and repeated herself.

"I want to adopt the two of you."

"You . . . you do?" Lucy's voice squeaked on the last word.

"Don't you think we should have talked about this first?" Mat uncoiled from the couch vertebra by vertebra.

Lucy hadn't taken her eyes off her. "You don't mean both of us. Button and . . . *me*."

"Of course I mean both of you."

Mat swept the sleeping baby into his arms. "Nealy, I want to talk to you."

She ignored him. "The thing is, you're going to have to think very hard about this because a lot of bad stuff will happen if you go with me, and I won't be able to do anything about it."

Lucy's eyes were wide. "What do you mean? How could anything bad happen?"

Nealy rose and walked over to the ottoman at the foot of Lucy's chair. "I'm a public figure, and that won't go away, even when I'm no longer First Lady." She sat down and took Lucy's hand, rubbed her slim, cold fingers. "We'll be connected, so lots of people will be waiting for you to do something wrong."

Lucy's throat worked as she swallowed. "I don't care about that."

"You'll care. Believe me. It's a terrible thing to lose your privacy, and that's what you'll be doing. You'll have Secret Service following you everywhere—when you're with your friends, the first time you're on a date, wherever you want to go. You'll never be able to go anywhere by yourself."

"You did."

"This has only been temporary. I knew from the beginning that I'd have to go back to my real life." She rubbed Lucy's knuckles. "And it's not just the big things in your life that will be destroyed; it's the little things, too. Think about how much you love going to the mall. You won't be able to do that without causing all kinds of trouble, and pretty soon you'll realize it's not worth it. You're going to miss things like that a lot."

"I never said I had to go to malls."

Nealy needed to make her understand exactly what she was walking into. "Wait until you screw up, Luce, because that won't be just between the two of us. The whole world will know about it."

Mat took a step closer to the windows, Button limp in his arms, his expression growing more foreboding. He should be her partner in this, not her adversary, and her resentment deepened.

She returned her attention to Lucy. "If you curse in public, or talk too loud, or decide to go back to that awful purple hair, it's going to end up in the newspapers, and then everybody will starting criticizing you. One day you'll turn on the television, and some psychologist will be analyzing your personality for all of America."

"That blows."

Her words had finally penetrated. "It really does. And it'll happen, I promise you."

"Did people say a lot of bad things about you in the newspaper while you were growing up?"

"Not too much."

"Then why do you think they'll say them about me?"

She gave Lucy a sympathetic smile. "Don't take this the wrong way, but I was an angel compared to you. My father wouldn't have had it any other way. And that's another big problem. My father."

"Is he mean?"

"Not mean, but he can be very difficult. He's a big part of my life, though, so you'll be stuck with him, too. And even if I tell him not to, he'll give you lectures about how you have to set an example. When you do something wrong, he has this way of looking at you that makes you feel bad about yourself. He'll always be comparing the way you are to the way I was, and he'll make sure you come up short. You're not going to like him very much, but you'll still have to put up with him."

Lucy's chest quivered as she took a breath. "You really mean it, don't you? You'd adopt us like . . . forever?"

"Oh, sweetheart, I know this is what you think you want more than anything, but it's not going to be easy. And here's the thing . . . you have to make this decision for two people, not just for yourself."

"For Button, too."

Nealy nodded. "At least you'll remember what it was like to live as a normal person, but public life will be the only life she'll know. And I promise you, the day will come when she'll blame you for that."

Lucy studied her for a long time. "You're really serious?"

"I'm serious. Unfortunately, you don't have much time to think it over, even though this is probably the biggest decision you'll ever make."

"My mind's already made up." She jumped up. "We're coming with you!"

Nealy wasn't surprised, and she almost wanted Mat to object, but when she glanced at him, his expression was stony.

"Go get your things together," she said quietly. "We have to leave soon."

Lucy rushed toward the door, only to stop. "There's something you should know. Button's name. It's really . . ." She grimaced. "It's . . . Beatrice."

Nealy managed a smile. "Thanks for telling me."

For a moment Lucy simply stood there, and then those abused fingernails shot to her mouth. "I know why you want to adopt Button—because she's so cute and everything. But . . ." She withdrew her fingers, picked at her thumb. Her voice became small and defenseless. "Why do you want to adopt me?"

Nealy rose from the ottoman. "Because I love you, Luce."

"That's so bogus." Despite her words, she looked puzzled instead of belligerent. "How could you love me after what I just did?"

"Because you're you. I guess you're the kid I always wanted to be."

"What do you mean?"

"You're brave, and you stand up for yourself. You know what you want out of life, and you're willing to put yourself on the line to get it."

For once, Lucy was speechless. It didn't last, however, and her expression grew fierce. "I love you, too, Nell. And I promise I won't ever let anybody give you any shit!"

"That's what I'm afraid of."

The teenager gave her a blazing smile and raced from the sunporch.

Lucy had been so excited that she hadn't even looked at Mat, let alone consulted him. He came toward Nealy.

"I wish you'd talked to me about this first."

"Why? I'm the answer to your prayers, Mat. In less

than an hour, you're going to have everything you want. No females and the story of your life."

"That's not . . ." He seemed to be struggling for his words. "I'm not sure this is the best thing for them."

"I know it's not. Do you have something better in mind?"

He started to sit, then seemed to change his mind. He began to come closer, stopped. For the first time since she'd known him, he looked ungainly, as if those long legs and strong arms didn't belong to him.

"I think . . . it's . . ." He shifted Button from one side to the other. "Yeah, you're right. I don't have anything better in mind. I'll give you the name of the attorney who's been handling this. I'm sure your friends in Washington can straighten everything out with the Pennsylvania Child Services people."

"I'll get it taken care of."

"Yoo-hoo!"

Nothing could have told Nealy more clearly that her adventure was over than the sight of Bertis and Charlie standing in the backyard, with Toni detaining them on one side, Jason on the other.

"These people won't let us in!" Bertis exclaimed, waving wildly.

Nealy felt her shoulders sag. This was the world she was thrusting those children into.

"I'm sorry, Nealy."

Startled, she looked up to see Mat regarding her with something that looked like compassion. She didn't want his sympathy, hated him so much at that moment for giving it to her that she could barely manage a shrug. "Life goes on."

"Yeah, it sure does."

In the end, he was the one who rescued the Waynes and brought them inside. They'd already figured out Nealy's identity, but when she tried to explain why she'd left Washington, she couldn't manage it, and he took

over. He also told them what was happening with the
girls. When he was done, Nealy waited for them to
change into different people, but Bertis merely shook her
head and extended the plate she'd been carrying.

"Have some fudge, you poor thing. It'll make you feel
better."

As Nealy packed the last of Button's clothes, Lucy
flew from one spot in the motor home to another, talking
a mile a minute and getting in the way. ". . . do the
dishes every night, and take care of Button, and clean
my room. I'll clean the whole house—I'll even clean the
White House—and I'll—"

The door opened and Mat wedged himself inside.
"Luce, Bertis and Charlie are on the sunporch watching
Button. Why don't you say your good-byes?"

"I'll invite them to come visit us!" The door banged
behind her as she ran outside.

Mat's betrayal clung to Nealy like bitter dust. She
turned her attention to packing up the last of Button's
rompers.

"The vultures are already descending," he said. "A
patrol car just showed up."

She placed the stack of clothes inside the suitcase and
pretended it didn't matter. Mat moved closer, filling up
what was left of the floor space. She thought about Dennis and the truth she hadn't quite revealed, but which
Mat had, nonetheless, guessed. Before she left, she had
to confront him about it.

"What do I have to do to keep you from telling my
secrets?"

He regarded her with watchful eyes. "I guess you're
going to have to trust me."

"Why? Never trust the press—one of the first rules I
learned."

"I'm not just the press," he said tightly. "I'm your
friend."

Her *friend*. Not her lover. Not her beloved. It shouldn't hurt so much.

She forced herself to remember that she had a legacy to protect and there were larger issues at stake than a broken heart. Maybe she'd mistaken his intention and judged him too harshly. "Does that mean you're not going to write about any of this?"

"I have to," he said quietly.

She shouldn't have been so devastated, but she was.

"Listen to me, Nealy. The press is going to be in a feeding frenzy. I'm the best protection you've got."

"Aren't I lucky," she shot back.

"I could give you a dozen reasons why I have to write this story, but you're not going to listen to any of them, are you? I've been tried and convicted."

She clenched her fists. "Don't you dare try and take the moral high road! I've seen some slimy journalistic tactics over the years, but you get the prize. Do you always sleep with your big stories?"

"Stop it," he said tightly.

She fumbled with the zipper on the suitcase. "Get out. I don't have anything more to say to you."

"Nealy, use your head. Somebody's going to have to set the record straight about where you've been or you'll never have any peace."

"So you're doing this as a favor?"

"I don't want us to part as enemies."

"You want us to part friends?" She yanked hard on the zipper. "You'd love that, wouldn't you? As your *friend*, I'd feel obligated to toss some juicy insider stories your way."

"Is that what you think of me?"

She was glad that she'd finally provoked his anger because it made everything easier. "You don't want to know what I think of you."

She grabbed the suitcase and tried to push past him,

but he shoved it aside and crushed her to his chest. "Damn it, Nealy!"

His mouth descended on hers. The kiss was painful, a travesty of what they'd shared just that morning. He seemed to realize it, too, and he stopped, rested his forehead against hers. "Don't do this, Nealy. Don't let it end like this."

She pulled away, needing to hurt him as badly as he'd hurt her. "You were a diversion, Mat. Now it's over."

The motor home burst open, and Lucy rushed in, too caught up in her own excitement to notice anything was wrong. "Ohmygod, Nell! There are two police cars out there now, and these television guys just showed up! And Toni said they've got a helicopter coming in to a field not too far away. Are we going to ride in it? Ohmygod, I've never been in a helicopter! Do you think Button will get scared? You're going to have to hold her, Mat. Maybe she won't be scared if—"

Right then, it hit her.

She stared at Mat, her mouth still partially open, and even as she asked the question, she seemed to know the answer because she was shaking her head. "You're coming with us, aren't you?"

"No. No, I'm not."

All the light went out of her eyes. "You have to! Tell him, Nell. Tell him he has to!"

"Lucy, you know Mat can't come with us. He has a job. Another life."

"But . . . I guess you can't live with us, but you'll come visit us all the time, won't you? You'll come see us next week or something."

He took a ragged breath. "Sorry, Luce. I'm afraid not."

"What do you mean? You have to! Not to see me, but Button . . . you know how she is. She doesn't understand things, and . . ." She drew a jagged breath. "She thinks you're her dad."

His voice sounded hoarse. "She'll forget about me."

Lucy spun toward Nealy. "Tell him he can't do this, Nell. I know you're mad at him, but tell him he can't just go away like this."

Nealy wouldn't let her own bitterness spoil Lucy's memories of Mat. "He has things he needs to do, Lucy. He's busy, and he has to get back to his real life."

"But—" Her eyes returned to him. "But you two guys love each other. I know you've been fighting a lot lately, but everybody fights. It doesn't mean anything. You're gonna want to see each other again."

Nealy barely managed to keep her voice steady. "We don't love each other. I know it's hard for you to understand, but we're very different people. We just happened to have been thrown together by peculiar circumstances."

"I'll write you letters," Mat said. "I'll write you a lot."

"I don't want your dumb letters!" Her face contorted. "Don't even bother sending them! If you don't want to come see us, then I won't ever talk to you again!"

Eyes brimming with tears, she ran from the motor home.

Even though Nealy wanted him to hurt, she didn't want it to be like this. "I'm sure she'll change her mind."

His expression was stony. "It's better this way."

While Nealy made her final preparations, Mat stood in the yard engaged in an angry conversation with Jason Williams about the circus that was gathering. She hadn't spoken to him since he'd stormed out of the motor home half an hour earlier. There was nothing left to say.

Through the living room window, she saw curious neighbors crowding their front yards trying to see why the street had been blocked off. Even though only one television news crew had been lucky enough to be close by, she knew it wouldn't be long before the small town was invaded by media representatives from all over the world.

Their shabby suitcases had been loaded into one of the patrol cars, along with several plastic grocery sacks filled with Lucy's Walkman, Button's toys, and other precious objects that couldn't be left behind. Unfortunately, that included Squid.

Nealy walked toward Lucy, who was holding Button, while Bertis and Charlie hovered nearby. Her conscience urged her to make one last attempt. "Take a look out the window, Luce. This is what you're getting yourself into."

"I already looked, and I don't care." Despite her brave words, she was obviously shaken, and she drew Button closer.

"You still have time to change your mind. I'll do everything I can to make certain both of you are placed with a good family."

Lucy gazed up, her expression imploring. "Please, Nell. Don't give us back."

Nealy surrendered. "I won't, kiddo. From now on, both of you are mine. For better or for worse."

"Now, Lucy, don't you forget to write," Bertis said. "And you need to start eating more vegetables. I should have made you my green bean casserole."

Nealy tried not to think about the man she'd fallen in love with as she gave them a hug. "Thank you for everything. I'll call. Are you ready, Luce?"

Lucy swallowed hard and nodded.

"We can do this one of two ways. We can make a run for the car, so we don't have to face anybody right now, or we can hold up our heads, smile at the cameras, and show the world that we don't have anything to hide."

"Da!"

Mat came in the front door. Nealy wasn't going to be spared.

His eyes found hers—the same gray eyes she'd gazed into this morning as his body moved inside her own. She wanted to cry until she couldn't cry anymore, to scream at him because she loved him and he didn't love her back. Instead, she arranged her features in a blank, polite mask.

He flinched, then went to Lucy and Button. Brushing his thumb over the baby's cheek, he said, "You give 'em hell, Demon."

He gazed down at Lucy, but her expression was a heartbreak happening and he didn't try to touch her. Nealy swallowed and looked away.

"You watch out for yourself, ace. And try to behave."

Lucy bit down on her lip and looked away.

Finally he moved toward Nealy, but everyone was watching them, and there was nothing left to say. His eyes clouded, and his voice had a rasp. "Have a good life, Nealy."

She managed a stiff nod, turned to Lucy, and took the baby. Then she stepped back into the world she knew too well.

Cornelia Case had come in from the cold.

21

"Hollings has been in the Senate for twelve years, Cornelia! I forbid you to go any farther with this nonsense."

Nealy rubbed her eyes wearily, then looked up from her satinwood desk at James Litchfield. Her office was located in a sunny room at the rear of the Georgian home that had once belonged to Dennis, but now belonged to her. The estate sat on twenty wooded acres in Middleburg, the heart of Virginia hunt country. She'd always loved the place more than Dennis, who'd preferred Washington, and now she'd made it her permanent home.

The office was one of her favorite rooms—creamy walls with chalk-white trim, a mishmash of good antiques, and a cozy fireplace. Soft floral draperies hung at long, rectangular windows that looked out over a lush stretch of trees just beginning to wear fall colors.

She set down her pen. "Hollings is an idiot, and the people of Virginia deserve better. What did you put in your mouth, you little dickens?"

Button had been playing on the English needlepoint rug. Its delicate moss and rose pattern was strewn with a collection of her toys, along with a cardboard toilet paper roll, an empty oatmeal box, and kitchen measuring cups. Her eyes were innocent as she returned Nealy's gaze, but her cheeks bulged with contraband, probably part of the dinner roll she'd been carrying around the day before.

"Take that away from her, Dad."

Litchfield regarded the baby severely. "Give it to me, Beatrice."

"Nah!"

Fortunately, Button's exclamation discharged the chunk of roll. In a motion as elegant as the sweep of a polo mallet, Litchfield whipped a snowy handkerchief from the pocket of his slacks, picked up the gummy dough, and deposited it in the wastebasket that sat on top of Nealy's credenza, away from toddler temptation.

"Hollings may not be the best senator we have, but he's always been loyal to the party, and he's extremely upset."

She and her father had been arguing over her decision to run for the Senate ever since she'd made up her mind last month. Now she leaned back in her chair and propped one of her stockinged feet on Squid, who was curled beneath her desk. "Then find some other way to reward him because I'm going after his seat in the primary."

"Not without my support, you won't!"

"Dad," she said, as gently as she could, "I don't need your support."

The office door banged open and Lucy rushed in— teenage cavalry to the rescue. "I'm home."

"So I see." Nealy smiled at her very protective new daughter-to-be.

She looked like most of the other fourteen-year-olds in the private school the two of them had chosen for its excellent academics and democratic atmosphere: drawstring pants, skimpy dark brown sweater, ugly thicksoled shoes, and too many ear-pierces. But Lucy's fresh young beauty shone through.

She wore her shiny brown hair in a funky little cut with a pair of small oval barrettes holding back her bangs. The complexion problems that tormented so many girls her age had passed Lucy by, and her sweet, smooth skin was mercifully free of the thick cosmetics she'd once hidden behind. Her fingernails were no longer bitten to the quick, and she held herself with new assurance. Nealy's heart swelled with pride.

Lucy studiously ignored James Litchfield as she marched over to stand next to her. "So . . . do you want to come listen to my new CD?"

Nealy had already listened to Lucy's new CD, and she wasn't fooled. "Later, honey. Dad and I are discussing my political future." And then, just to stir things up . . . "He's still fighting me about going after Hollings's seat."

"Really, Cornelia, Lucille's much too young to understand this. I hardly think she's interested."

"I'm *very* interested," Lucille shot back. "I even get to work on the campaign."

He gave a dismissive sniff. "You know nothing at all about campaigning."

"I know that some of the seniors at my school are eighteen, which means they can vote. And all the kids my age have parents who vote. Me and Mom are working on a brochure just for teenagers so they'll understand what their senator does."

Nealy still wasn't used to having Lucy call her Mom instead of Nell. It had only started a few weeks ago, and Lucy had never talked to her about it or asked permission, she'd just started doing it. Button, on the other hand, had been calling her *ma*—usually shrieked at the top of her lungs—since that day three months ago when they'd all walked out of the house in Iowa.

Not all of them, she reminded herself. One member of their makeshift, not-quite-a-family had stayed behind.

But Nealy had learned not to think about Mat unless she was alone, and she forced her attention back to the battle of wits going on between Lucy and her father.

". . . so I asked Lardbutt—"

"Lucy . . ." Nealy's voiced sounded a warning note.

"I asked *Mrs. Fegan* if Mom could come in and talk at a school assembly, not about her campaign—that'd be so obvious even a moron could see through it—but about the contributions of First Ladies. Mom's got lots of good stories, like how Abigail Adams was a women's libber, and Nellie Taft got the cherry blossoms planted in Washington, and Edith Wilson ran the country when Woodrow was sick."

"That wasn't exactly a contribution," Nealy reminded her. "Edith Wilson nearly drove the country into a constitutional crisis."

"I still think it was cool."

"You would."

Lucy folded into her favorite place, the easy chair across from Nealy's desk, and spoke with all the aplomb of a seasoned campaign manager. "We're going to whip Hollings's a—butt in the primary."

James Litchfield narrowed his eyes, but he was too cagey to openly reprimand Lucy. At the very beginning, Nealy had made it clear that was her job, and he'd quickly discovered that she meant what she said. The fastest way out of her life was to show open hostility toward either of her girls.

Her poor father. She'd actually begun to feel sorry for him. The girls had been a bitter pill for him to swallow, but swallow it he had. At the same time, he'd also been forced to deal with the unrelenting publicity her disappearance had caused.

For the past three months, Nealy had been subjected to the type of tabloid scrutiny usually reserved for drugged-out movie stars. Everyone she'd come into contact with during her seven days on the road had been interviewed. Bertis and Charlie had done her proud, and Nico hadn't been the disaster she'd feared. Even the Celebrity Lookalike Contest organizers had received their fifteen minutes of fame. Everyone had been interviewed except Mat, who'd told the story in his own way and, to this day, refused to appear on camera.

Nealy had gone public only twice—in an obligatory Barbara Walters television interview and in a *Woman's Day* feature that had been accompanied by informal photographs of her with the girls. Exposing them had been a difficult decision, but she knew they'd be hounded by paparazzi if she didn't, and *Woman's Day* was the perfect forum. Besides, Lucy thought it was cool.

Through it all, her father had stood relentlessly behind her. His teeth had been clenched, his jaw rigid, but he'd been there for her, even six weeks ago when she'd finally stepped aside as Lester Vandervort's First Lady.

Taking her place were the three women she'd handpicked for the job. Two of them were longtime congressional wives wise to the ways of Washington. The third was Lester's feisty twenty-two-year-old niece, an outspoken Ivy League graduate who provided a perfect contrast to the older women and the stuffy president. Although Nealy continued to advise the triumvirate, they were growing more confident in their job, which gave Nealy time to concentrate on her own future.

The girls were her first priority. She knew she had to have help with Button if she was to run for the Senate, but it wasn't easy finding what she was looking for. She and Lucy had interviewed dozens of candidates before they'd found Tamarah, a nineteen-year-old single mother with a nose ring, a ready laugh, and a determination to finish her education.

Tamarah and her six-month-old baby Andre now lived in a small apartment over the kitchen. Nealy and Lucy had been a little jealous of how quickly Button, Tamarah, and Andre had taken to each other. But even with child care, Nealy tried to make the majority of her phone calls during her toddler's naptime, then do her planning and paperwork late at night. It left her bone-tired, hum-ble, and even more committed to helping single mothers who didn't have her financial resources.

"I still can't believe you're serious about this," her father said.

"She's . . . like . . . *so* serious."

"I'm not addressing you."

"Like, I have opinions, y'know."

"Far more opinions than a *child* needs."

Lucy was too shrewd to make the insolent response that would force Nealy to send her to her room. Instead, she gave him a wily smile. "In four years, I'll be a voting citizen. And so will all my friends."

"Doubtless the republic will survive."

"And the Democrats, too."

Oh, this was too rich. Nealy had grown to enjoy watching the two of them go at it.

In the beginning, she'd counted on Button's baby charm to win over her father, but he'd been far more interested in Lucy. Her father loved a worthy opponent, and the fact that Lucy had declared herself his mortal enemy before they'd ever met had whetted his competitive instincts.

Nealy had recently begun to wonder if they didn't look forward to their sparring matches. They had the oddest similarities. Each was stubborn, crafty, manipulative, and absolutely loyal to her.

Squid stirred beneath her feet. "I'm going to make a formal announcement in ten days. Terry's setting up the press conference now."

As soon as she'd confided her plans to Terry, he'd asked to be appointed her press secretary. She'd been touched and delighted.

"Dad, I understand this puts you in an impossible position, and I know you have to stay out of it, so I'm not planning to—"

"Stay out of it?" He assumed his Prince Philip posture and gazed at her from beneath his noble brow. "My daughter, the former First Lady of the United States, is running for the Senate, and you expect me to stay out of it? I hardly think so. I'll have Jim Millington contact you tomorrow. Ackerman's good, but he'll need help."

She couldn't believe her father, after all his posturing, had finally backed down. Jim Millington was the best campaign manager in the business.

Lucy needed to make sure she could relax her guard. "So you're not going to give her any more crap about this, right?"

"Lucille, this is not your concern. I've done my best to dissuade her, but since she's refused to listen, I have no choice but to support the campaign."

Lucy grinned at him. "Awesome!"

Nealy smiled and rose. "Why don't you stay for dinner, Dad? It's pizza night."

Something that almost looked like disappointment passed over his stern features. "Some other time. Your stepmother and I are meeting the Ambersons for cocktails. Don't forget that she expects all of you for Sunday brunch."

"She expects Button, you mean," Lucy muttered.

Nealy's stepmother was horrified by Lucy, but she adored Button, who was currently wearing one of the outrageously expensive outfits she'd bought her.

"That's because Beatrice has never cursed at her dinner table."

"It was an accident. And this time could you ask her to, like, please buy some Dunkin' Donuts or something?"

Her father scowled at Lucy as if she were an unbearable nuisance. "If she forgets, I suppose you and I will have to go out and purchase some ourselves."

"You mean it?"

"Unlike some people, I'm not in the habit of rattling away just to hear myself talk."

Lucy grinned. "Cool."

Somehow they all survived the Sunday brunch. That evening, Nealy rocked Button to sleep, then helped Lucy with her history project. At eleven o'clock, when the house was finally quiet, she made her way to her bedroom, undressed, and slipped into a robe.

During the day, she did her best not to think about Mat, but nights were harder, and Sunday nights the hardest of all, maybe because they marked the beginning of a new week without him. At first she'd tried to talk herself out of it, but that just seemed to make her sadness spill over into Monday. Finally, she'd learned to give in to her Sunday night blues.

NIGHTS OF PASSION WITH
AMERICA'S FIRST LADY
by Mat Jorik

The first time I spoke with Cornelia Case, she was hot to trot, and no wonder, since her husband, the former president of the United States, was—are you ready for this?—GAY! Her lust slid over me like cheap lingerie . . .

It was the story Nealy had imagined, but not the one Mat had written. She sat in the window seat, remembering how she'd felt when she'd held the *Chicago Standard* in her hand and seen his exclusive.

The first time I spoke with Cornelia Case, she was rescuing a baby at a truck stop outside McConnellsburg, Pennsylvania. Rescuing babies is something she's good at, since she's been trying to do it most of her life. When she fails, as she often does, she takes it more personally than she should, but more about that later.

I didn't know she was Cornelia Case then. She was wearing navy shorts, cheap white sneakers, and a yellow maternity top with some ducks marching across it. Her hair was cut short, and she had what looked like an eight-month pregnancy sticking out in front of her.

None of the stories written about her ever mention that the lady has a temper, but, believe me, she does. For all her polish, Nealy Case can go after you when she gets upset. And she was definitely upset with me . . .

The *Chicago Standard* had published Mat's story in six parts that had been quoted and analyzed in every media outlet in the world. In the articles, he'd detailed both the girls' plight and how Nealy had come into their lives. He'd described the incident at the covered bridge, dinner at Grannie Peg's, and the Celebrity Lookalike Contest. He'd written about meeting Bertis and Charlie, and the night he'd confronted Nealy about her identity. Mabel and Squid had come alive as his story unfolded, along with Nico and the house in Iowa.

In every article, he'd made his own decisions about what should be on or off the record. On the record were the details of her escape, her frustrations with being First Lady, her enthusiasm for picnics, Frisbees, convenience stores, and two motherless little girls. At first she'd been stunned that he'd revealed so much about the girls, but by appeasing the public's curiosity so quickly, he'd called off the bloodhounds and done more to protect their privacy than an army of security guards.

Also on the record were her political ambitions as well as her aversion to being around healthy babies, although, as Mat wrote about it, her neurosis no longer seemed like such a weakness.

Off the record was her sexual relationship with him and everything about Dennis Case. He'd asked for her trust, but she hadn't been able to give it. Now she admitted she should have remembered his rock-solid sense of responsibility and not passed judgment so swiftly.

Although he'd exposed far more of her private world than any other journalist, he'd also transformed her from a national icon into a living, breathing woman. He'd described the way she cared about people and her delight in the ordinary, her deep sense of patriotism and her love of politics—although she didn't appreciate being labeled a "dewy-eyed optimist." He made her seem more vulnerable than she thought she was, but she appreciated the way he stressed her deep knowledge of national and international affairs.

Only as he described his own relationship with her did he become vague, which left her to do the clean-up work. Barbara Walters hadn't made it easy.

BW: *Mrs. Case, in Mat Jorik's series of articles in the* Chicago Standard, *he describes your feelings about the girls at some length, but he doesn't say much about your relationship with each other. Would you care to comment?*

CC: *Mat is a fine journalist, and he wrote about what happened in more detail than I ever could. I don't think he left much out.*

BW: *But how would you describe your relationship?*

CC: *Two hard-headed adults trying to figure out what was best for the girls. Emphasis on the hard-headed.*

BW: *Mat does mention your quarrels.*

CC: *[laughs] Which would never have happened if he hadn't been wrong so often.*

That laughter hurt. Pretending it had meant nothing.

BW: *And are you still friends?*

CC: *How could we not be friends after going through an adventure like that? You've heard about soldiers during wartime. Even though they never see each other again, there will always be a special bond between them.*

Special and oh, so painful.

BW: *Have you and Mat spoken since then?*

CC: *At this point, he's still the girls' legal guardian, and we have the adoption to sort out, so of course there's been communication.*

No need to say that it had all been through their attorneys.

BW: *Just to set the record straight, there was no romantic relationship between the two of you.*

CC: *Romantic? We were only together for a week. And don't forget that we had two very active chaperones. It would have been a difficult trick to pull off.*

Very difficult ... but not impossible.

Tightening the sash on her ice-blue silk robe, she walked across her bedroom carpet to the cherry armoire that held her stereo equipment and flicked on her CD player. She pushed a few buttons, then turned down the volume so only she could hear.

The lush sounds of Whitney Houston signing her anthem for broken hearts washed over her, and Nealy's first burning, self-indulgent, oh-so-necessary tears began to fall.

Because she would always love him ...

Squeezing her arms tightly over her chest, she'd listen to Whitney sing it as it was.

Bittersweet memories ...

She pulled the box from the bottom of her closet and carried it to her bed where she sat cross-legged, the silk robe falling open over her knees. Inside the box were her own bittersweet memories: a matchbook cover from Grannie Peg's, a smooth river stone she'd picked up by the covered bridge, her little beaded choker, and the pink rose he'd plucked for her the night they'd explored the old farmhouse. It grew more brittle every time she handled it.

She drew it to her face, but the fragrance had faded.

He was the second man she'd loved. The second man who hadn't loved her back.

The song began to play again.

Her self-indulgence was so melodramatic that she always wanted to laugh at herself. But somehow she never managed it.

Bittersweet memories . . .

Just once a week to relive those old memories. Was that so terrible? Once a week, so she could make it through the rest of the days and nights of her life.

I will always love you.

Mat had everything he'd ever wanted. Money. Respect. A job he loved. And privacy.

If he reached for his flannel shirt when he came home from work, it was exactly where he'd left it. When he opened his bathroom cabinets, he found shaving cream, deodorant, Ace bandages, and foot powder. Nobody got into his root beer, left her Walkman where he could step on it, or threw up on the carpet of the townhouse he was renting in Chicago's Lincoln Park.

He was only responsible for himself. He could change his plans on a moment's notice, watch the Bears lose without anybody interrupting him, and call his buddies to shoot some baskets whenever he felt like it. His life was perfect.

So why did he feel as if he'd somehow been cheated?

He set aside the newspaper he hadn't read. Most Saturday mornings he drove to Fullerton Beach and ran along the lake, but today he didn't feel like it. He didn't feel like doing much of anything. Maybe he'd try to get a start on next week's columns.

He gazed across his living room, which was furnished with big chairs and an extra-long couch, and wondered what they'd be doing today. Was Lucy getting along with the other girls at that ritzy private school Nealy had stuck her into? Had Button learned any new words? Did they miss him? Did they even think about him?

And Nealy . . . it looked like she was getting ready to make a run for Jack Hollings's seat in the Senate. He was happy for her—really happy—so he didn't know why he felt as if something were tearing open inside him every time he saw a photograph of her decked out in one of her designer suits.

He was tired of being alone with his own misery, so he started upstairs to change into his running shorts only to be stopped by the doorbell.

The last thing he wanted was Saturday morning company. He stalked over to the door and jerked it open. "What d'you—"

"Surprise!"

"Surprise! Surprise!"

"Surprise!"

Seven of them. Seven *surprises*. His sisters burst inside and hurled themselves into his arms.

Mary Margaret Jorik Dubrovski . . . Deborah Jorik . . . Denise Jorik . . . Catherine Jorik Mathews . . . Sharon Jorik Jenkins Gros . . . Jacqueline Jorik-Eames . . . and Sister Ann Elizabeth Jorik.

Chubby and skinny; pretty and plain; college students, stay-at-home moms, professional women; single, married, divorced, bride of Christ—they exploded into his space.

"You've sounded depressed when we've talked to you . . ."

". . . so we got together and decided to visit."

"To cheer you up!"

"Out of the way. I have to pee!"

". . . hope you have decaf."

"Oh, God, my hair! Why didn't you tell me it looked like . . ."

"... use the phone so I can call the sitter."

"... all the publicity these past few months has been so hard on you."

"Shit! I snagged my new ..."

"... what are sisters for?"

"... anybody have a Midol?"

They were barely in the door before, one by one, they started drawing him aside.

"... worried about Cathy. She might be doing her bulimia thing again, and ..."

"... ran up my Visa ..."

"... need to talk to you about Don. I know you never liked him, but ..."

"... obvious that the prof hates me ..."

"... if I should change jobs or ..."

"... all two-year-olds are temperamental, but ..."

"... give communion, and the fact that Father Francis can consecrate the host, but I can't ..."

In little more than an hour, they got lipstick on his T-shirt, moved his favorite chair, snooped through his private organizer, borrowed fifty bucks, and broke the carafe on his Krups coffeemaker.

God, he was glad to see them.

Two of his sisters spent the night at the Drake, two more stayed with Mary Margaret at her place in Oak Park, and two stayed with him. Since he was sleeping like crap anyway, he gave them his king-sized bed and took the guest room.

As usual, he woke up a couple of hours after he'd fallen asleep and wandered downstairs. He ended up in the living room, where he gazed out at the dead leaves and branches scattered across his small patio. He envisioned Nealy, the way she looked after they'd made love, her hair tousled, skin flushed ...

"We're awful, aren't we?"

He turned and saw Ann coming downstairs. She wore a god-awful gray robe that looked like the same one she'd taken off to the convent. Her springy hair stood out in mischievous curls from her round, chubby face.

"Pretty awful," he agreed.

"I know I shouldn't complain to you about church politics, but the other nuns are so conservative, and—" She gave him a rueful smile. "We always do this to you, don't we? The Jorik girls are strong, independent women until we're around our big brother, and then we fall back into our old patterns."

"I don't mind."

"Yes, you do. And I don't blame you."

He smiled and hugged her. What a hellion she'd been as a kid. So much like Lucy . . . Pain shot through him.

"What's wrong, Mat?"

"Why do you think anything's wrong?"

"Because you should be on top of the world, and you're not. You were part of the biggest human-interest story of the year. Everybody in the country knows who you are. You've got your job back, and you've had offers from the best papers and newsmagazines in the country. Everything you've wanted has happened. But you don't seem happy."

"I'm happy. Really. Now tell me about Father Francis. What did he do to piss you off?"

She took the bait, which spared him from trying to tell her what he didn't want to explain—that he'd finally gotten exactly what he wanted out of life, and he hated every minute of it.

Instead of playing ice hockey, he wanted to go on a picnic. Instead of heading for the United Center, he wanted to put a baby girl in a sandbox and throw a Frisbee with her big sister. Instead of dating any of the women who kept coming on to him, he wanted to wrap his arms around a sweet, stubborn First Lady with eyes as blue as an American sky.

A sweet, stubborn First Lady who'd *run off with his damn family*!

Ann finally stopped talking. "Okay, buddy, I've given you some breathing room. Now it's time to 'fess up. What's going on?"

The cork he'd shoved so tightly into his self-awareness finally popped. "I've screwed up, that's what." He started to glower at his sister, but all the fight had run out of him. "I'm in love with Nealy Case."

22

HE WAS IN LOVE! MAT FELT AS IF HE'D TAKEN A hockey puck right to the head. Of all the jerk-off, lame-brained, self-defeating things he'd ever done, taking this long to figure out he loved Nealy was the worst.

If he had to fall in love, why couldn't it be with someone ordinary? But, no. Not him. Not Mr. Lunkhead. Because that would be too frigging *easy*! Instead, he had to fall in love with the most famous woman in America!

For the rest of the morning, Ann hovered around him, a pitying look in her eyes. Every once in a while he saw her lips move and knew she was praying over him, which made him want to tell her to keep her damn prayers to herself, except he'd never needed them more, so he pretended not to notice.

He took his sisters to lunch at one of the city's trendy Clark Street bistros, then fought the urge to ask them not to leave as they headed for their cars or the airport. They kissed him and hugged him and smeared their makeup on another one of his shirts.

That night, his house seemed even lonelier than usual. No sisters ambushing him with their problems. No diapers to change or smart-mouthed teenager to keep an eye on. Even worse, there were no patriot-blue eyes smiling at him.

How could he have been so blind? From the moment they'd met, he'd been drawn to her like hot fudge to ice cream. He'd never enjoyed a woman's company more, never been so aroused by one. And not just physically, but intellectually and emotionally. If some evil genie came up to him right this minute and said he could have Nealy forever, but they could never make love again, he'd still take her. And what kind of thing was *that*?

He had it bad.

He couldn't stand being cooped up inside, so he grabbed his jacket, headed outside, and climbed in the Ford Explorer he'd bought to replace his sports convertible. The car was badly suited to downtown Chicago's crowded parking, but he'd justified buying it because it handled well on the expressways, and it was almost big enough to fit him. The truth was, he liked the memories it brought back.

As he drove aimlessly through the narrow streets of Lincoln Park, he tried to figure out what he was supposed to do. He had no idea how deeply Nealy's feelings ran toward him. She'd enjoyed his company, and she sure as hell liked his lovemaking, but he'd also argued with her, deceived her, and manhandled her, so he could hardly expect her to run into his arms. He could hardly expect her to . . .

Marry him.

He nearly rear-ended a white Subaru. Did he really expect America's uncrowned queen to bind herself for life to an overgrown Slovak roughneck?

You're damned right he did.

The next morning he packed up his laptop and his cell phone, threw some clothes in a suitcase, and tossed everything into the Explorer. He called his editor from the road to give him some mumbo-jumbo about a follow-up piece, promised not to blow his deadline for Wednesday's column, and set the cruise control. He and America's former First Lady had some serious talking to do.

Nealy's attorney refused to give him her address, so he used his connections in the Washington press corps, and by the next day he was in Middleburg, Virginia. The house wasn't visible from the road, but the eight-foot fence that surrounded it was plain to see, along with an elaborate set of electronic gates. He pulled the Explorer into the drive. Her press conference was tomorrow; he prayed she was home getting ready for it.

Above his head, a set of video cameras zeroed in on him. He hoped the fence was electrified, too, and a pack of Dobermans ran loose behind it. He had nightmares about her safety.

"Can I help you?" A man's voice came from a panel set in the brick.

"Mat Jorik. I'm here to see Mrs. Case."

"Is she expecting you?"

"Yes," he lied.

There was a brief pause. "You don't seem to be on the list."

"I wasn't sure when I'd get here. If you ask her, she'll tell you it's all right."

"Hold on."

He hoped he looked more confident than he felt. Seeing these gates and the spacious grounds that stretched behind them made the gap between him and Nealy real instead of theoretical. He drummed his hands on the steering wheel. Why was it taking so long?

"Mr. Jorik?"

"Yes."

"I'm sorry, sir, but Mrs. Case won't be able to see you."

Mat gripped the wheel. "I'll come back later today."

"No, sir."

He waited, and the longer he waited, the more uneasy he felt. "How about tomorrow morning?"

"No. Mrs. Case won't see you at all."

* * *

Nealy's stomach was in a knot, and her hands were freezing. Mat was here. Right outside her gate. She wanted to race from the house and down the drive, fling herself in his arms . . . only to be pushed away again.

It hadn't taken her long to figure out why he was here. Even though he'd been kept informed about the girls, he'd wanted to see for himself. Mr. Responsible.

Her hand trembled as she reached for the telephone in the family room to call her attorney. Mat couldn't simply breeze in and out of the girls' lives at his whim. It wasn't good for them, and it would be devastating for her. She had a campaign to concentrate on. A new life to build.

"Ma!" Button had already decided she didn't like having Nealy on the telephone. She banged her plastic truck against the carpet and gazed at her with a mulish expression that looked so much like Mat's it made Nealy want to weep.

She set down the phone, pushed aside the briefing book she'd been studying, and went over to sit cross-legged on the floor. Button immediately climbed into her lap, bringing along her truck and one of Andre's tiny blue sneakers.

"Gah bleg flel ma."

Nealy hugged her close to comfort herself. "Me, too." She kissed her cheek and toyed with a lock of her hair, which was longer now and beginning to curl. "How can Mat do this?"

"Da?"

It was the first time Button had said the word since they'd left Iowa. The baby frowned and said it again. "Da?" Filled those lungs. "DA!"

Nealy couldn't let him in. She was barely getting through the nights as it was, and she couldn't make herself start the whole grieving process all over again. Especially when she had the most important press conference of her life tomorrow.

Nealy kissed her hand. "Sorry, sweetheart. It's not going to happen."

Button stuck out her lower lip, and her eyes formed big blue circles. She rested her cheek against Nealy's breast.

Nealy stroked her hair and wished the four of them were back on the road again.

Mat parked on the street outside the gates with a half-baked plan to intercept Lucy when she came home from school, but a snub-nosed Secret Service agent had other ideas.

Mat started to point out that this was a public street, then decided not to give the guy a hard time. He was only doing his job, and his job was to keep Mat's family safe. The family Mat had walked away from.

As he headed to his hotel, he tried to think. But every insulting thing he'd said to Nealy, every order he'd tossed out, every complaint he'd made about being surrounded by women came back to haunt him. Nobody could ever accuse him of showing her his best side.

He was so caught up in misery that he drove past the hotel. What kind of jerk threw away something so precious? What kind of jerk threw away his family?

As he turned around, he decided he could spend the rest of his life beating himself up, or he could try to fix what he'd done his best to ruin. And to do that, he needed a plan.

Nealy exploded. "What do you mean, he's going on CNN?" She gripped her cell phone tighter and sank back into the leather interior of her Lincoln Town Car.

Steve Cruzak, the Secret Service agent who was driving tonight, glanced at her in the rearview mirror, then looked over at his partner, sitting in the passenger seat. Beyond the tinted windows, the rolling hills of northern Virginia gleamed in the morning sun as they headed east toward the Arlington hotel where Nealy would make her announcement.

"He didn't offer any explanations," her attorney replied.

The heavy Chanel earring she'd tugged off to answer her phone bit into her palm. Normally her assistant would have been in the car with her, but she had the flu. Jim Millington, her new campaign manager, along with Terry and her key staffers, were already at the hotel mingling with the press as they awaited her arrival.

For three months Mat had refused to give any television interviews, but the day of the most important press conference in her career, he suddenly changed his mind. He was blackmailing her.

"Maybe you should talk to him," her lawyer said.

"No."

"Nealy, I'm not a political advisor, but the eyes of the entire country are going to be on your campaign. This guy's a loose cannon. Who knows what he has in mind? It wouldn't do any harm to sound him out."

More harm than he could imagine. "It's out of the question."

"I'll try to talk to him."

She returned her phone to the brown leather tote she carried instead of a purse, then clipped her gold earring back on. For her press conference, she was wearing a soft butterscotch wool Armani sheath with a silk scarf knotted at her throat. The untidy haircut she'd worn on the road had been reshaped by her longtime hairdresser so that it looked sophisticated, but still contemporary. She'd decided to keep it short, just as she'd decided to keep her color natural. They were small changes, but to her they were significant. Each change was a sign that she had finally taken control of her life, which was why she couldn't let Mat force her into a meeting that would only cause her grief.

She pulled out her leather portfolio and studied the

notes she'd been compiling for the past three months. They no longer made sense. Since Mat was so determined to speak with her, why hadn't he used the most obvious means at his disposal? Why hadn't he threatened to call a halt to the adoption if she refused to meet with him?

Because something that ugly would never have occurred to him.

"We're here, Mrs. Case."

She realized they'd arrived at the hotel. The butterflies in her stomach began to tango as she put her notes away, then let the agent open the door for her.

A cluster of photographers waited, along with Jim Millington, a crusty Georgia-born political handler with a Deep South accent. "We've got ourselves a full house," he whispered, as he took her tote from her. "Reporters from all over the country. You ready to rumble?"

"As ready as I'll ever be."

Jim led her into the ballroom, which was filled with far more reporters than anyone else's primary campaign could attract. Nobody went through free food faster than the press, and the food tables looked as though they'd been attacked.

Terry approached her just as the speakers began playing Van Halen's "Right Now." A fist squeezed her heart. It had been Dennis's campaign song and now it was hers. She and Terry had debated using it, but in the end they knew it would be both a tribute and a symbol of transition.

Terry took her arm. "Steady, babe."

"Hearing that song . . ."

"I know. God, he'd love watching you do this."

She smiled at her chubby, rumpled friend. He looked better than he had at any time since Dennis's death. This campaign was good for him.

With Terry and Jim just behind her, she smiled, waved, and worked her way through the crowd to the platform at the front of the room. Her father was already there, along with other party leaders. One of them, a popular local congressman, stepped to the microphone and introduced her.

The reporters applauded politely, and her campaign workers cheered. She moved to the microphone and began her thank-yous. Then she launched into the heart of her speech.

"Most of you know why I called this press conference. Usually political candidates say they've thought long and hard before they decide to run for office. I didn't have to do that. This is something I've wanted for a long time, although I didn't realize how much until recently." She made a few brief references to the proud history of Virginia and the need for strong leadership in a new millennium. Then she declared her intention of challenging Jack Hollings in the June primary.

". . . and so today I am officially stepping into the ring and asking the wonderful people of the Commonwealth of Virginia to honor me with their trust and elect me as their next United States Senator."

The cameras flashed and television reporters spoke into their microphones over the applause. When the room finally quieted, she began outlining the major issues she'd be campaigning on, then cocked her head to take questions. Up until now, she'd been scripted. It was time to think on her feet.

"Callie Burns, *Richmond Times-Dispatch*. Mrs. Case, how does your decision to run for office relate to your disappearance?"

It was a question she'd expected. Reporters knew their readers were more interested right now in her personal life than her political views. "Getting away from the White House gave me a chance to put my life in perspective . . ." Her preparation had paid off, and she had no trouble answering.

"Harry Jenkins, *Roanoke Times*. You've made no se-

cret of your dissatisfaction with political life. Why work
so hard to get back into it?"

"As First Lady, I had no real power to effect
change . . ."

One question followed another. Although she'd been
expecting it, she was still disappointed that so few dealt
with the issues.

Suddenly a deep voice rang out above the others.
"Mat Jorik, *Chicago Standard.*"

She stiffened. The ballroom instantly quieted as
everyone tried to locate the source of that voice.

Mat stepped out from behind one of the square pillars
at the back of the ballroom. He'd tucked one hand into
the pocket of his slacks, and a well-worn brown leather
bomber jacket hung open over his shirt. Even from a
distance, he seemed to fill up the room—all big body,
commanding voice, and rough edges.

A thousand images flashed through her mind. Her fingers tightened on the corner of the podium as she tried
to push them away and stay focused. She heard herself
speak in a voice that was almost steady. "Hello, Mat."

The crowd buzzed. Cameras flashed. His presence
was a story all its own.

He nodded. Curt. Down to business. "You said you
were going to focus your campaign on economic issues.
Could you be more specific?"

She somehow managed her public smile. "Thank you
for giving me the opportunity to talk about a topic of
vital importance to the people of Virginia . . ."

Even with Mat staring her down, she somehow managed to launch into the remarks she'd prepared, but
she'd barely finished before he came at her with a
follow-up question. When she'd finished responding, another reporter jumped in with a question about the
Balkans.

Mat kept silent after that, but he stayed where he
was—arms crossed, one shoulder resting against the pil-

lar behind him, never taking his eyes off her.

Terry finally stepped in to end the questions and thank everyone for attending. Her father closed in on one side, Jim Millington on the other, Terry behind. She looked around for Mat, but he'd disappeared.

Her father rode with her to their next stop. "I suppose I shouldn't have been so surprised to see that Jorik fellow. He'll probably make a career out of writing about you."

She shuddered at the idea.

Her next speech, an hour and a half later, was in the meeting room of a banquet hall. She'd barely begun before she spotted Mat standing in the back watching her. He asked no more questions, but she didn't mistake his intentions. Until she arranged a meeting, he wasn't going away.

By nine-thirty that evening, as she finished her last speech at a Chamber of Commerce dinner, she'd made up her mind. If he thought she was going to let him play cat and mouse with her, he was gravely mistaken.

She broke away from shaking hands with the members of the Falls Church Chamber of Commerce and made her way toward him before he could slip away. The photographers who were still following her surged forward to get the first pictures of the two of them together.

She regarded Mat levelly. "I want to see you at my house at ten tomorrow morning."

He smiled. "Yes, ma'am."

She barely slept that night, something she could ill afford with a full afternoon of meetings ahead of her. As soon as Tamarah put Andre down for his morning nap, she sent her into town with Button on a series of errands that would keep the baby out of the house until Mat was gone. Then she watched the clock crawl toward ten o'clock.

Squid perked up his ears as the sound of a whimper came over the baby intercom. Andre usually took a long morning nap, but today he'd apparently decided to wake early. Her housekeeper wouldn't be arriving until noon, so Nealy hurried to get him, the dog following.

The baby lay on his back in the crib. He wore a bright blue Winnie the Pooh sleeper, and his brown eyes were filled with tears that stopped falling as soon as he spotted her. For a few moments Nealy forgot her own troubles as she gazed down at him, so sweet and full of personality.

"What's the matter, little guy? Have a bad dream?" She scooped her hands beneath his warm body and lifted him to her shoulder. He was a beautiful baby with milk chocolate skin and a studious air, as if he hadn't yet decided what to make of the world.

The intercom from the front gate buzzed twice, announcing that she had company on the way, and Nealy said one of Button Jorik's favorite words. "Sit!"

She tucked the baby in the crook of her arm and made her way to the front of the house. "Okay, buddy, it's just you, me, and the dog."

The bell rang. She counted to ten, then reached for the knob.

23

MAT GAZED AT THE WOMAN IN THE DOORWAY AND felt everything inside him melt. He'd been able to hold it together yesterday when there'd been cameras around, but now there were none, and she was only a step away.

Unfortunately, the woman standing before him wasn't the Nealy he'd left in Iowa. This Nealy was elegant. Aristocratic. Pure WASP from the top of her patrician head to the toes of her Cole Haan loafers. She was wearing a strand of pearls that had probably come over on the Mayflower, a simple sweater that could only be cashmere, and perfectly tailored gray flannel slacks. Only the mangy dog who'd come out on the porch to jump on him and the cute brown-skinned baby nestled in her arms didn't fit the image.

God, it was good to see her again. He itched to sweep her up and carry her to the bedroom where he could strip away all the signs of her wealth and position, but he figured that might not go over too well—either with her or with the Secret Service agent watching from the edge of the drive.

His heart swelled in his chest, but he couldn't think of anything to say except *I love you*, which seemed a little premature, so he greeted the dog. "Hey, Squid."

The baby blinked at Mat's voice, then gave him a gummy smile.

The Queen of America stepped back from her door to

let him in. His stomach sank. She was looking at him as if he were a distant memory of someone she'd once seen in steerage.

He followed her down a hallway that should have been in the Smithsonian and into a formal living room with lots of cherry, wing chairs, and old oil paintings. He'd grown up in a house full of mismatched furniture, Formica tabletops, and wooden crucifixes with dried-out palm fronds stuck behind them.

She gestured toward a spindly-legged love seat with a camel back. He carefully lowered his weight, half expecting the sucker to buckle underneath him.

She regarded him with all the confidence of a woman who finally knew exactly who she was. "I'd offer you something to drink, but we're fresh out of root beer."

Right now he'd settle for scotch, straight from the bottle. He noticed she was holding the baby so tight the kid was starting to squirm. "A new addition?"

"Andre belongs to Tamarah, the woman who watches Button."

"I thought you were watching Button!" He winced at the accusing note in his voice.

She gave him a steely glare and didn't bother to respond.

"Sorry." His palms had started to sweat.

She chose a wing chair near a fireplace that the Founding Fathers had probably gathered around to discuss exactly how far they wanted to go with this Constitution thing.

The baby was still fidgeting. He waited for her to shift him to a more comfortable position, but she didn't do it. She almost seemed to have forgotten she was holding him. He hoped that meant she was nervous.

She didn't look nervous.

The love seat creaked ominously as he settled back into it and extended his legs. If he didn't say something soon, he'd look like a complete fool. "How are they? The girls?"

"You know how they are. I've been sending regular reports."

The baby wriggled. He wondered where she'd stashed Button. He'd give anything to see that little baby girl again—change one of those stinky diapers, have her drop some drool on him, receive one of her I-love-you-more-than-anybody smiles. "A report isn't the same as seeing for myself. I've missed them."

"I'm sure you have, but that doesn't mean you can bounce in and out of their lives when you want. We have an agreement."

This wasn't going the way he'd hoped. The baby whimpered. "I understand that, but . . ." Although she was still thin, that gaunt look she'd had when they'd first met was gone. He was relieved . . . and disappointed. Some part of him wanted her wasting away for him.

As if Nealy Case would waste away over a man.

There was only one thing to do, and it flew in the face of every ounce of testosterone in his body. He drew a deep breath. "I've missed you, too."

She didn't look impressed.

He retrenched. "I've missed you and the girls."

Another whimper came from the blue sleeper. The baby kept trying to get his arms free, but she had too tight a grip. Mat couldn't stand it anymore, and he leaped up. "Give me the kid before you strangle him to death!"

"What—"

He whipped up the little guy and put him to his shoulder. The kid relaxed right away. He smelled good. Like a boy.

She narrowed her eyes, then tapped her fingers on the arm of the chair. "What happened with the results of the

DNA tests? My attorney's asked for a copy several times, but he still hasn't received one."

Oh, man . . . Busted. He'd torn up the envelope he'd received from the lab in Davenport without ever opening it. "Me either. I guess the lab misplaced it."

"Misplaced it?"

"It happens."

She tilted her head, studied him closely. "I know how important this is to you. Maybe the tests should be done again."

"Are you crazy? Do you want to put Button through something like that again? I guess it's easy for you to say because you weren't there. You didn't see the way they held her down!"

She gazed at him as if he'd lost his mind, which was so close to the truth that he had to turn his back on her and head for the fireplace.

"What are you doing here, Mat?"

The baby's head settled against his jaw. He glared at her. "Okay, here's the way it is. I screwed up, all right? I admit it, so let's put it behind both of us and move on."

"Move on?" Cold as a flock of Presbyterians in an unheated church.

"Because, the thing is, it's the future that counts." Was it hot in here, or was it just him? "We need to look ahead and not behind us."

Everything about the stare she leveled at him reeked of aristocratic disdain. He suddenly felt as if he were wearing a red satin bowling shirt and gulping down a kielbasa. It was time to cut to the chase.

"I need to know how you feel about me."

"That's what you wanted to talk to me about?"

Mat nodded. The baby tucked his head against his neck, and he would have given anything right then to go play with him instead of facing how bleak his own future was going to be if the ice queen living inside Nealy's body kicked him out.

"Well . . . I'm very appreciative that you didn't betray me in the articles you wrote."

"Appreciative?"

"And I'm grateful that you're trusting me with the girls."

"You're grateful?" This was a nightmare. He sank back down on the ancestral couch.

"Immensely."

The grandfather clock ticked away in the corner. She didn't seem to mind the silence that was stretching longer and longer.

"Anything else?" he asked.

"No, I don't believe so."

That ticked him off. She damn well had to have felt something more than that or she'd never have let him near all those hot, moist places he'd made his own.

He set his jaw. Shifted the baby to his other shoulder. "Think harder."

She arched an eyebrow. Touched the pearls with her fingertips. "Nothing else springs to mind."

He leaped up from the chair. "Well, something else springs to my mind! I love you, damn it! And if you don't like it, that's too damn bad."

The baby gave a mew of displeasure. Nealy's eyes shot open. "You love me?"

He waited for her lips to bloom in a smile, her eyes to soften. Instead, she looked as if she'd been hit by the first round of musket fire at Lexington.

Lunkhead! He slipped the baby under his arm and moved forward. "I'm sorry. That didn't come out right. I just— Is it hot in here? Maybe your furnace isn't working right. I could look at it."

What was wrong with him? He'd lived around women for years. He understood their habits. Why was he falling apart when he most needed to keep himself together?

A thousand emotions flickered across her face, but for the life of him he couldn't identify any of them. She leaned back in the chair, crossed those slim legs, and made a little Protestant church steeple with her fingers. "When did you have this startling—and obviously unwelcome—revelation?"

"Sunday."

Her nostrils flared. "This *past* Sunday?" Not a question but an accusation.

"Yes! And it wasn't unwelcome." The baby's whimpers grew louder. He jiggled him.

"You only discovered this *two days ago*?"

"That doesn't mean I haven't felt it all along." As a line of defense, it seemed weak even to him. His voice cracked. "I've loved you for a long time."

"Ahh . . . I see." She rose and walked over to him, not to fall into his lap as he hoped, but to take the baby back.

The pint-sized Benedict Arnold seemed more than happy to resettle on her shoulder. "You don't look very happy about it," she said. The baby wrapped a fist around the Mayflower pearls and shoved them in his mouth.

"I'm happy! I'm delirious!"

There went that eyebrow again.

Damn it! He made his living with words. Why had they deserted him now? It went against his grain, but he knew the time had come to throw himself on the mercy of the court. "Nealy, I love you. I'm sorry it took me so long to figure it out, but that doesn't make it any less true. What we have together is too good to throw away just because I screwed up."

She didn't seem impressed. "Your idea of showing your tender feelings is to go on CNN and talk about me to the world. Is that right?"

"I was bluffing. You wouldn't take my phone calls, remember? I needed to get your attention."

"My mistake. And what do you propose to do about these newfound feelings of yours?"

"I propose to marry you, what do you think?"

"Ah."

The baby gummed happily away at her pearls. Mat would have liked to do a little gumming of his own—on her bottom lip, her earlobe . . . a breast. He nearly groaned. Now was definitely not the time to be thinking about breasts, or any other enticing body parts. "Well?"

"Well, what?"

"Are you going to marry me?"

She gave him a frigid look that told him he needed a really good argument. Something logical instead of emotional. "I know you probably think of it as marrying down, since I'm not an aristocrat like you. But it might be time to refresh the Litchfield family genetic pool. Add a little Eastern European peasant blood to the mixture."

"Then make a run for the Triple Crown?"

He narrowed his eyes. Exactly what was going on here?

Nealy watched him tilt that big, handsome head and study her as if she were a specimen under a microscope. She hurt so badly she could barely maintain her composure. Had he really thought she'd believe this begrudging declaration of love and accept that pitiful excuse for a marriage proposal?

Now she recognized her mistake in trying to cut the girls out of his life. Even though he hadn't been able to express it, she should have known how much he loved them. But she would never have suspected he'd go this far to have them back in his life. She would never have imagined he'd be desperate enough to suggest marriage.

It still didn't seem to have occurred to him that he could simply take the girls away from her. He was their legal guardian, and the adoption wasn't final. All he had to do was say that he'd changed his mind. But his sense of honor would never allow that.

Her knees turned to water. Would his sense of honor permit him to ask a woman he didn't love to marry him just so he could get his children back?

Her head had begun to throb. What if it were true? What if he really did love her? Could this just be another example of Mat's predictable clumsiness around the mysterious minefield of his own deeper emotions? Or were his feelings for the girls so strong that he was willing to marry someone he liked, but didn't love, just so he could keep them in his life?

Only one thing was certain . . . despite the months she'd spent hugging his stupid T-shirt and whimpering over Whitney Houston, she was no longer the emotionally needy woman who'd wed Dennis Case. In the past year, she'd learned that she deserved better, and nothing was going to make her question another man's love. If Mat Jorik burned for her, he'd have to find a better way than this to make her feel the flames.

"Nealy, I know I've done this badly, but . . ."

"Badly doesn't begin to describe it." She glanced at her watch, rose from the chair, and strode toward the hallway. "Sorry, but I'm out of time."

Mat had no choice but to follow her. "How about if I ride along with you today? Some insider press coverage wouldn't hurt."

She didn't need any more coverage, and they both knew it. She opened the door and stepped outside, making him follow. "I'm afraid that's not possible."

"Let me have your phone number. We need to talk again."

"I'm sure if you try hard enough, you can find a way to get it."

She slipped back inside before he could stop her and closed the door. Then she drew the baby closer and tried to decide whether she wanted to cry or scream.

*   *   *

Mat knew he'd blown it. He'd spent so many years erecting a privacy barrier between himself and his sisters that he hadn't been able to pull it down when he most needed to. He sat behind the wheel of the car without turning on the ignition and stared blindly through the windshield. If only he'd had the guts to take her in his arms the moment he'd seen her and tell her everything that was in his heart. Instead, he'd bumbled around like an idiot.

Now he had nothing. No date to see her again. No phone number. Nothing.

He was so angry with himself that he nearly missed the flash of yellow jutting out from behind the garage as he began to pull away. He looked more closely and realized it was the rear end of a battered Winnebago.

He couldn't believe it. Just before he'd left Iowa he'd sold Mabel to a dealer and sent the check to Nealy's attorney for the girls. Why had she gone to all the trouble of buying it herself? He felt a faint spark of hope. Not much to hold on to, but it was all he had.

He pulled up the name of Lucy's new school from his memory bank and phoned for directions. After he arrived, he established his credentials with the principal and was shown into an empty office. Just before the walls finished closing in on him, the door opened and Lucy was standing there.

A smile took possession of his face. He felt only a momentary pang of nostalgia for the hooker makeup and purple hair. She looked wonderful—all scrubbed up, shiny, and pretty. Had Nealy smoothed away her rough edges or did Lucy not need them anymore?

He itched to wrap his arms around her, but the conflicting emotions he saw on her face made him hesitate. He'd hurt her badly when he'd let her walk away, and she wasn't going to forgive him easily.

"What d'you want?"

He hesitated, then decided he couldn't afford any more fumbles. "I want my family back."

"Your family?" She hadn't lost her street smarts, and she bristled with suspicion. "What do you mean?"

"You and Button and Nealy."

She gave him her familiar bullheaded look. "We're not your family."

"Who says?" He took a step closer, only to watch her withdraw. "You're still mad at me, aren't you?"

She shrugged, then, true to her nature, looked him right in the eye. "Why are you here?"

He thought that one over. How much could he tell her and still be fair to Nealy?

To hell with fairness. "I'm here because I found out I couldn't stand not having all of you in my life."

She leaned against the corner of the desk, her posture awkward and unsure. "So?"

"So, I'm back."

"Big deal."

The hurt she was trying so hard to hide cut into his heart. "It is for me. I've been pretty lonely. Plus I've been kicking myself for taking so long to figure out what's important to me."

She looked down at her thumbnail, brought it to her mouth, then seemed to realize what she was doing and pulled it away. "Yeah, I guess you missed Button a lot."

Her insecurities were still so close to the surface they made him ache. "How's the little rug rat doing these days?"

"Pretty good. She says lots more words now. She calls Squid Skid." She shot him a glare filled with reproach. "But she never says *Da* anymore. Not ever."

"I miss her a lot." He paused, then moved closer again. "But I miss you even more."

"You do?"

He nodded. "I love Button, but she's still a baby. You know how that is. I can't really talk to her about anything interesting or play basketball with her. And don't look so surprised. You and I have understood each other from the beginning." He paused. "Did you ever hear of a soul mate?"

She nodded warily

"I think the two of us might be soul mates."

"You do?"

"Don't you?"

"Yeah, but I didn't think you—"

"You're such a jerk." He smiled at her. "When are you going to figure out what a great kid you are?"

She stared at him and then her face crumpled. "I didn't think you ever wanted to see us again."

He no longer cared whether she wanted to be hugged or not. He grabbed her and pulled her tight against his chest. "I'm a lot bigger jerk than you. I missed you, Luce. I missed you so much."

One hand crept tentatively around his waist. He rubbed her back and blinked. How could he ever have walked away from these females? "I love you, Lucy." It should have been hard to say, but it wasn't. In fact, it was so easy that he said it again. "I love you so much."

She buried her face in his shirt. Although her words were muffled, he didn't have any trouble hearing them. "Loveyousomuchtoo."

They stood that way for a while, both of them embarrassed, but neither of them willing to let the other go. When they finally parted, she looked vulnerable and scared. "You're not going to try to take us away from her, are you?"

"I'd never do anything like that! Thanks a lot."

Her shoulders sagged in relief. "I had to make sure."

"No, you didn't. The fact is, I need some help, and you're the only one who can give it to me."

She instantly responded. "What do you want?"

Now he was the one who had to look away. "I saw

Nealy this morning, but I got nervous and screwed everything up."

"For only the millionth time."

"You don't need to rub it in. Anyway, she's even madder at me now than she was before. Sooner or later, she might talk to me again, but I can't stand to wait. That's why I need help."

He explained what he wanted, and when he was done, a cagey smile curled her mouth. He congratulated himself on his strategy. There was nothing a good woman liked more than meddling in other people's business, and this daughter of his heart was definitely a good woman.

Some of Nealy's tension eased as she sat on the floor cuddling Button and listening to Lucy chatter about her day. The scents of roasted chicken and garlic coming from the kitchen reminded her that she hadn't eaten since breakfast.

It had been an awful day. Instead of concentrating on her meetings, she'd kept thinking about Mat and wondering what was going on in his head.

Her housekeeper stepped into the family room. "If your hands aren't clean, wash up. Dinner'll be on the table in five minutes."

"Thanks, Tina."

The doorbell rang and Lucy leaped up. "I'll get it! I told Cliff it was okay."

Cliff was on duty monitoring the gate, which explained why the intercom hadn't buzzed.

Lucy raced for the hallway. "I invited a friend for dinner. Tina said I could."

Nealy regarded her curiously. It wasn't the first time Lucy had invited someone over, but she'd always let Nealy know in advance. Still, Nealy was so grateful she was making new friends that she didn't object.

She straightened the cuff on Button's lavender jeans.

"Okay, messy bessy, let's pick up some of these toys before we eat."

"Hi, sweetheart."

Nealy froze as Mat's voice boomed from the entrance hall.

Button's eyes widened, and she dropped the plastic turtle she'd been carrying around. *"DA!"* Moving as fast as her chubby legs would carry her, she scurried toward the sound of that familiar voice.

In the hallway Mat was giving Lucy her second hug of the day when he heard Button's high-pitched squeal followed by the thud of tiny sneakers. He looked up just as his pint-sized beauty queen came waddling around the corner.

"Daaaaa!"

At her shriek of joy, he dashed forward, swept her up into his arms, and started planting kisses on those rosy little cheeks. She was already taller, he noticed. Her hair was longer and didn't look as much like dandelion fuzz. Someone had tied a piece of ribbon around a lock on top and it stuck straight up in a little fountain. She was wearing purple sneakers, lavender jeans, and a bright red T-shirt that said HOT STUFF.

The fact that she hadn't forgotten him made his eyes sting for the third time that day. She wriggled and caught him in the stomach with one of her sneakers, but he didn't care. She smelled of baby shampoo, orange juice, and Nealy.

"Da!" Button drew back her head, puckered her lips, and gave him her familiar mulish look. It was a new trick, but he caught on right away and planted a kiss on the exact middle of that rosebud mouth. "Hey, stinker."

"Tink! *Tink!*"

"That's right." With one arm around the baby and his other around Lucy, he prayed he was two-thirds of the way home.

The final third appeared at the back of the hallway,

and the accusation in her beautiful eyes told him he wasn't even close.

"What are you doing here?"

"I invited him," Lucy piped up. "I knew you wouldn't mind."

Nealy turned on him. "When did you see her?"

Lucy didn't give him a chance to answer. "He came to my school today."

That legendary self-control couldn't hide how much she wanted to take him apart for approaching Lucy without her permission, but she wouldn't attack in front of the girls.

Her restraint made him even more aware of the perilous ground he was treading. Although he was prepared to fight to his last breath convincing Nealy he loved her, he'd live the rest of his life alone before he'd hurt the girls.

"I told the principal who I was. She let me talk to Lucy for a few minutes."

"I see." Icicles dripped from her words.

"I have presents for everybody out in the car," he said quickly, "but the Service wanted to go through them before I brought them in." He gazed at Nealy. "I didn't know what color roses you liked, so I brought you an assortment." An assortment of six dozen roses, in shades ranging from vermilion to a peach-tipped white. He'd hoped to use them as a distraction when he'd walked in the door, but the Secret Service had spoiled that.

Her lips barely moved. "How thoughtful."

A ginger-haired woman in her forties poked her head around the corner. "Dinner's on." She regarded Mat curiously.

"This is the friend I told you I invited to eat with us tonight," Lucy told her.

The woman smiled. "You high school kids get bigger every day."

He smiled back. "Hope I didn't disrupt anything."

She flushed. "No . . . no, of course not. Come on, everybody, before the chicken gets cold."

Lucy grabbed his arm and steered him past Nealy toward the kitchen. "Wait till you taste Tina's chicken. She cooks it with all this garlic."

"I love garlic."

"Me, too."

"Did you ever eat jalapeños?"

"Plain?"

"Yeah, plain. What are you, some kind of a wimp?"

Nealy listened to their chatter as Mat disappeared through the family room with an arm around each of her daughters. Both of them were looking at him as if he'd hung the moon and stars just to entertain them. She realized she was shaking and drew a deep breath before she headed for the kitchen.

He was lowering Button into her high chair as she came in. He looked completely at home in the cozy kitchen with its cherry cabinets, shiny copper, and collection of bright orange pumpkins on the counter. The round table sat in a bay overlooking the garden at the side of the house. It was set with pottery plates, chunky green goblets, and Button's special Alice in Wonderland dishes.

"Sit here, Mat!" Lucy indicated her own chair, directly to Nealy's right. "Usually Andre and Tamarah eat with us, but Andre got his shots this afternoon, so he's cranky, and Tamarah's trying to study for a math test."

"I've got a hockey stick for Andre out in the car," he said. "And some skates."

Nealy stared at him. He'd bought a six-month-old baby hockey equipment?

"Cool." Lucy sat on the other side of Button's high chair, safely out of spill range. "Since Button's so messy, we don't eat in the dining room unless we have important company." She pulled a face. "Like you-know-who."

"No, I don't."

Lucy rolled her eyes. "Graaaandfather Liiiitchfield. He calls me Lucille. Doesn't that blow? And he calls Button Beatrice, even though she hates it. She threw up on him once. It was hysterical, wasn't it, Mom?"

Nealy watched Mat's expression change as he heard Lucy call her *Mom*, but she couldn't identify exactly what she saw there. "It was definitely one of Button's finer moments," she managed.

Mat leaned back in his chair and gazed at her. Had he noticed how much they looked like a family?

"How did your meetings go today? Did you jiggle any change loose from those corporate high rollers?"

"A little." She couldn't carry on casual conversation with him, so she turned to Button. "Do you like your potatoes?"

The baby pulled a food-smeared fist from her mouth and pointed at her sister. "Woos!"

Lucy giggled. "That's what she calls me. Woos. She just started it a couple weeks ago."

"Ma!"

Nealy smiled. "You've got that one down pat, don't you, cupcake?"

"Da!"

Mat looked at Nealy instead of the baby. "She's got that right, too."

Nealy wouldn't let him do this. He couldn't worm his way into their lives because he'd finally decided he missed the girls. She might have to come to terms with letting him see them, but that didn't mean she had to accept those leftover, lukewarm feelings he was tossing at her and pretend they were something more.

She folded her napkin, set it next to her plate, and stood. "I'm not feeling well. If you'll excuse me . . . Tina, would you bring Button upstairs when she's done eating?"

"Sure."

He rose. "Nealy . . ."

"Good-bye, Mat. I'm sure Lucy will keep you entertained." She turned her back on all of them and left the
kitchen.

24

NEALY SEALED HERSELF AWAY IN HER BEDROOM WITH her briefing book and a laptop computer, stopping work only long enough to read Button a bedtime story and tuck her in when Tina brought her upstairs. As she returned to her room, she heard Mat talking to Lucy downstairs. The low intensity of his voice made her want to strain to listen. Instead, she hurried into her room, put on some Chopin, and turned up the volume.

Lucy came in an hour later. Her eyes were bright with excitement, but she must have known Nealy wouldn't appreciate hearing how happy she was to see Mat again, so she gave her a fierce good-night hug and disappeared.

Now that Mat had left, Nealy felt even more depressed. She changed into her favorite baby blue flannel pajamas. They were printed with fluffy white clouds and smelled like fabric softener. She tried to return to work, but hunger pangs distracted her. It was nearly eleven o'clock, and she'd barely eaten all day. She set aside her laptop and padded downstairs barefoot.

Tina had turned on the stove light before she'd left, and Tamarah and Andre were settled in for the night. Nealy went into the pantry and leaned down to pull a box of cereal from the shelf. As she straightened, a hand clamped over her mouth.

Her eyes flew open. Her heart hammered.

A muscular arm wrapped around her waist and pulled

her against a very hard, very familiar chest. "Just pretend
I'm an enemy of the state," he whispered, "and consider
yourself kidnapped."

Only as she felt herself being dragged toward the back
door did she realize Mat wasn't just messing around.

He didn't even grunt when her bare heel caught him
in the shin. Why hadn't she put on shoes before she
came downstairs?

Somehow he managed to maneuver the back door
open. She felt his breath, warm against her cheek. "The
only way I can talk to you is to get you away from this
house, so that's where we're going. You can try to
scream if you like, but if you get away with it, your
friends in the Secret Service are going to come running,
and they won't ask a single question before they shoot.
Now, how bad do you want me dead?"

He had no idea!

She tried to bite his palm, but she couldn't sink her
teeth in.

"That's right, sweetheart. Fight all you want. Just,
please, don't make too much noise while you're doing
it because those buddies of yours play for keeps."

One of her feet made a furrow in the fallen leaves as
he half carried, half dragged her across the terrace and
through the grass without loosening his grip on her
mouth. He was strong as an ox, and she was beside
herself with frustration. She could probably manage to
make some kind of noise, but she didn't dare try. Although she definitely wanted him to die a brutal and
bloody death, she intended to do the job herself. She
was even afraid to kick him again for fear one of her
barefoot blows would inflict enough damage to make
him cry out. Oh, this was impossible! What an infuri-
ating, miserable, depraved man!

She twisted against him, fighting as hard as she could
without making a sound. Then she saw a familiar yellow
shape ahead. Mabel! He was taking her to Mabel! That

was good. That was wonderful! He couldn't get inside because she'd locked up the motor home herself and left the key—

He unlocked the door.

Lucy! That vile little matchmaking monster! She knew exactly where Nealy kept the key, and she'd given it to him.

He hauled her into the musty interior, dragged her toward the back, opened the bathroom door, and pushed her inside.

She opened her mouth to blast him. *"I'm going to—"*

"Later." He shut the door in her face.

She lunged for the knob, but he wedged something against the door, and she couldn't open it. Moments later, she heard the engine grind away, then turn over.

She almost laughed. He wasn't nearly as smart as he thought he was. Did he think he could simply drive through those electronic gates? Apparently he didn't know that only a guard could open them without one of the special remotes—

She sagged against the shower door. Of course he had one of the remotes. The teenage traitor was in his corner, and Lucy wanted a family more than anything. It would have been child's play for her to swipe the remote from the Town Car and give it to him.

Mat was going to do it, she realized. He was going to kidnap the former First Lady of the United States, and there wasn't a thing she could do about it.

She dutifully banged on the siding as the motor home rolled forward, even though she knew it was hopeless. In addition to the video surveillance at the gates, there was a microphone, but it would never pick up her thumps over the rough noise of Mabel's engine. Still, she thumped away, just so Mat would know she wasn't going peacefully.

The motor home came to a brief stop, and she could

imagine Mat giving the surveillance camera an innocent
wave, knew exactly what Lucy would have told them.
*Mom is letting Mat borrow the Winnebago for a couple
of days.*

She thumped louder, then gave it up as they pulled
away from the gates. She slumped down on the toilet
seat. Her feet were cold, the cuffs of her pajamas damp.
Why couldn't she have fallen in love with an ordinary
man? Some nice Ivy Leaguer who courted women with
moonlight dinners instead of a moonlight kidnapping.
Some nice Ivy Leaguer who'd love her for herself and
not just for everything attached to her. She concentrated
on her anger so she'd be ready for him when he opened
the door.

Middleburg was a rural area, dotted with celebrity
horse farms and large estates. Mat wouldn't have any
trouble finding a deserted spot for their confrontation,
and she wasn't surprised when he turned off a paved
road onto gravel. Gradually the road grew rougher. She
grabbed the edge of the sink as Mabel lurched along
before finally shuddering to a stop.

She set her lips in a grim line, straightened her shoulders, and waited for the door to open. It didn't take long.

She vaulted to her feet. "If you think—"

He scooped her up by the shoulders, planted a hard
kiss on her mouth, then pulled her out of the bathroom.
"Before you say any more, I'm sorry for a lot of things,
but I'm not sorry for this. How am I supposed to talk
to you when you can snap your fingers and have your
palace guard throw me out?"

"You could have—"

He thrust her down on the couch, then knelt in front
of her. "I'd like a more romantic setting, but we started
out in Mabel, so I guess this is where we'll settle it."
He picked up her cold feet and cradled them in his
hands. "I've got things to say to you, and I want you to
listen. Okay?"

She realized he looked more upset than triumphant. The warmth from his hands began to sink in. "I don't have much choice, do I?"

"No, you don't." His thumbs massaged her instep. "I love you, Nealy Case. I love you from the very bottom of my soul." He drew a deep breath. "Not just from my heart, you understand. I love you from my soul."

Her toes curled into his palm.

"I've been getting an awful feeling that you don't love me back, but that doesn't change what I feel about you or make it any less real. Even if you throw me out of your life forever, I want you to know that you'll always be the best part of me."

His voice turned into a whisper so full of feeling she felt as if she could touch it. "You're the air I breathe, the food I eat, the water I drink. You're my shelter and my refuge; you're my energy and my inspiration; my ambition, my enthusiasm. You're my resting place."

She felt boneless as he bathed her in poetry. He smiled. "Just looking at you shines sunlight on every moment I live. Before I knew you, I wasn't even alive. I thought I knew what I wanted, but I didn't have any idea. You barged into my life and changed it forever. I love you, I admire you, I lust after you, I adore you . . ."

His words enfolded her—sonnets of love, a rhapsody of devotion. This brusque man who'd tried so hard to separate himself from the feminine was every woman's dream.

"You make me see the world in new ways. You're the first thing my heart greets when I wake up in the morning. You're the last thing I see in my mind before I fall asleep."

He let go of her feet and took one of her hands in both of his. "Sometimes I daydream about this, just holding your hand. That's all. Just holding it. And I get a picture of the two of us going through life like that. Hand in hand. I even sometimes think about us having this colossal argument—hand in hand. Or just sitting on a couch together. Or—" Now a trace of aggression emerged as he reasserted himself.

"I know this is corny, but I don't care—those rocking chairs people talk about." He narrowed his eyes, just to let her know he wasn't a complete wimp. "I see that. I see this big front porch and these two rockers side by side, and you and me all old and wrinkled." His voice softened again. "The kids gone, grown up, only us, and I want to kiss every one of those wrinkles on your face and just sit there and rock with you."

Her head swirled. Her heart sang. He circled her palm with his thumb.

"I can't even talk about how much I love making love with you. Do you know that you make the most amazing sounds? And you hold me like I'm all you have, and that makes me feel like I'm some kind of god."

He brushed her cheek, locked his gaze with hers. "I love being inside you, and touching your face, and opening my eyes so I know it's really you."

She shivered.

"And after we're finished, I go into a fever thinking about a day when I can leave myself inside you. When I'll steal the soap and turn off the water so I stay there . . . inside you . . . part of you."

Her skin burned. He rubbed his thumb across her bottom lip, and his voice was a husky seduction. "I think about you walking around that way, talking to people, going about your business, and you and I are the only ones who know that I'm there inside you."

She burst into flames.

"And I finally understand the whole unbelievable beauty of two people being one because that's the way I want it to be, the two of us one."

His eyes had begun to glisten with tears. Her own spilled over her bottom lids and trickled down her cheeks.

His voice grew fierce and raw. "You'll never ever find a man who'll love you as much as I do, who'll protect you better than you've ever been protected—even from yourself—and who'll be right at your side while you become the best person you can be. Because I know that's what you're making me, the best man I can be."

A hiccup rattled her chest.

"And I don't give a damn about living with all the red, white, and blue star-spangled baggage you're carrying around. In fact, I love it because it's made you what you are—the best woman I've ever known, and the only woman I'll ever love."

He finally stopped and simply gazed at her. It was as if all the words had run out of him, leaving raw emotion in their place.

She touched his face with the tips of her fingers, traced the moist tracks down the hard, handsome planes of his cheekbones, and absorbed the absolute rightness of everything he'd said. Yes. This was what she'd dreamed of but never believed she'd have.

When she managed to speak, she could think of only one thing to say. "Could you please repeat all that?"

He let out a ragged bellow of a laugh, pulled her into his arms, and made love with her just the way he'd imagined.

Epilogue

NEALY HAD NEVER LOOKED MORE BEAUTIFUL TO MAT than she did that January day as she stood in front of the United States Capitol with the sun glinting in her hair. One end of the red, white, and blue scarf draped around the collar of her wool coat caught the wind and fluttered behind her, giving the cameras another great shot.

All of their family was gathered with them. Button had one little sister on each side of her. At nine, she was just as strong-willed as she'd been as a baby and she only permitted the family to call her Button behind closed doors. To the rest of the world, she was Tracy, her own way of dealing with the name Beatrice. Her long blond hair whipped in the breeze as she kept a careful eye on Holly, since the four-year-old tended to be unpredictable at public gatherings. Six-year-old Charlotte stood on her other side. Although she was on her dignity at the moment, Mat knew it wouldn't last. Both girls had his dark hair and their mother's blue eyes.

Lucy, the big sister all three girls idolized, stood just behind them with Bertis and Charlie, most of his own sisters, and her pompous old goat of a grandfather, who'd slipped his hand in hers. At twenty-two, his oldest daughter had a fresh new college degree in social work and a thirst to change the world. Although she scoffed when he brought it up, he suspected it was only a matter of time before she followed her mother into political life. He was more proud of all of them than he could ever express.

Nealy's eyes met his, and he could almost hear her thoughts. *Another new adventure, my love. Are you ready?*

He could hardly wait. They'd already had so many adventures together. He thought of the past eight years—the joy and laughter, the hard work, long hours, heated discussions, and even more heated lovemaking. So much happiness.

Not that there hadn't been hard times, too. The worst had come when they'd lost their beloved nanny Tamarah to a virulent case of pneumonia, but even that had eventually led to joy. His chest filled with pride as he gazed at his only son, eight-year-old Andre.

Most families were made when sperm met egg, but his had been put together less conventionally with blood that was red, blue, and black. If families had pedigrees, his could only be classified as American mutt.

He realized it was time to play his part, and he proudly lifted the tattered Jorik family Bible. Nealy's hand was steady as it rested on top. Steady at the helm of the Ship of State.

The occasion was a solemn one, but he couldn't keep the smile off his face when she began to speak.

"*I, Cornelia Litchfield Case Jorik . . .*"

After all these years, he still couldn't quite believe that she'd taken his name.

"*. . . do solemnly swear . . .*"

He held his breath.

"*. . . that I will faithfully execute . . .*"

Damn right she would.

"*. . . the office of President of the United States . . .*"

The President of the United States. His wife was finally claiming the job she'd been born to hold.

The country was lucky to have her. In addition to intelligence, she possessed vision, experience, integrity, and a stunning lack of personal ego. Just as important, her time in Congress had demonstrated her rare ability to bring people together, even longtime political enemies. Somehow she managed to get the most out of everyone, maybe because no one had the courage to disappoint her. She'd also aquired a bone-deep serenity that came from learning how to live a public life and still be true to herself.

"... *and will to the best of my ability* ..."

He'd given a lot of thought to his new position as the republic's first First Husband, and he intended to do a kick-ass job. He was the man who'd set the precedent for all the others who followed, and he understood his priorities.

Along with Nealy's welfare came the well-being of his five children. In a series of columns he'd written since the election, he'd made it clear to the American public that he and the new President were the parents of kids who were sometimes angels, sometimes brats, and frequently everything in between. The President was answerable to the American people, but her children weren't, and anybody who had a problem with that could just vote for someone else next election, then take the consequences.

"... *preserve, protect, and defend the Constitution of the United States.*"

He was awed to think of his wife as the defender of that most precious document. And if she ever forgot, even for a moment, what a responsibility that was, he'd be right there to remind her. It was about time a topflight journalist had an inside seat on history, and Citizen Mathias Jorik had decided there was no more noble role for the First Husband than that of the people's watchdog.

The next few hours flew by until it was finally time for the Inaugural Parade. He and Nealy had decided to walk the route, and they started off hand in hand with the kids following. Before long, however, Andre and Charlotte got into a spat and had to be separated. Holly was too young to walk for long, and she wanted to be carried. Then Charlotte wanted up, too, so he passed Holly off to Lucy.

Andre was definitely captivating the crowd, but Mat wondered if he and Nealy had made him too aware of his place in history as the first African-American child of a United States President. They exchanged amused glances as their eight-year-old son once more raised his small brown fist to the crowd.

Lucy's arms wore out, and Mat put Holly into the limousine that was following them, with Jason Williams and Toni DeLucca doing honorary guard duty. Then Charlotte wanted in, too. Andre stuck it out nearly to the end before deciding his raised fist would look even more imposing coming from the open window of the presidential limousine. Within minutes, his sisters commandeered the opposite window so they, too, could demonstrate their solidarity with the African-American community.

Finally it was just the four of them, the way it had been eight years ago. Nealy walked slightly ahead, having the time of her life as she waved to the crowd. Lucy came up on one side of him, Button on the other. He wrapped an arm around each of them, then smiled to himself as he remembered how desperately he'd fought having a family. Now he was the most visible family man in the free world.

His beautiful oldest daughter gave him a hug. "It's been a long strange journey, hasn't it, Dad?"

"I wouldn't trade it for the world."

"Me either." Button momentarily rested her head against his chest, and he said a little prayer of thanksgiving that his worse nightmare, having a family, had come true. Then he let his daughters go so he could take his place next to his wife.

The new Commander in Chief's eyes sparkled as she gazed up at him. "And to think I once risked everything to get out of the White House."

"It was the second best decision you ever made, after marrying me."

She smiled. "Have I told you that I love you?"

"You sure have." And then, right in the middle of Pennsylvania Avenue, with the whole world looking on, he planted a long, lingering kiss on the lips of the President of the United States.